"Williams's language is lyrical and elegant…. The dialogue has a patina of Britishness about it that adds to the feeling of other that permeates the book. The first in a series, *Snake Agent* set the pace for what will no doubt be an exciting and worthwhile series. I am looking forward to the next Inspector Chen novel."
— Beth Dugan, *Bookslut*

"What we have here is the beginning of what appears to be one of the most intriguing series I have seen in a long time…. fifteen minutes into the future and dial up the supernatural elements and you've got a pretty close bead on what you can expect from Liz Williams' *Snake Agent*."
— Rick Kleffel, *The Agony Column*

"…alongside China Miéville and Jeff VanderMeer, [Liz Williams is] someone whose imagination is so twisted that it would need the 10-or-so dimensions of String Theory to fully describe it. Highly recommended."
— Cheryl Morgan, *Emerald City*

"Liz Williams really can write… She doesn't balk at throwing in some proper science fiction, nor does she neglect to tell a grand mythic fantasy story"
— *infinity plus*

"Williams has an astonishing ability to create strange worlds and complex characters with only a few words. She finds new tangents with standard myths… and uses non-Western concepts (a bu to great effect."
— *Publishers Weekly*

"Williams joins A.A. Attanasio and China Miéville as one of the best contemporary practitioners of a kind of imaginative literature that fuses the intellect of SF with the heart of fantasy."
— Paul Di Filippo, *Scifi.com*

"Like all of Williams' work, this is a smooth, sharp read. Her wit and erudition are on ready display, as is her knack for portraying scenes and setting utterly alien to the Western reader with an easy familiarity that can pass unnoticed."
— Jay Lake, author of *Rocket Science*, and *Trial of Flowers*

蛇警探

SNAKE AGENT

Other books by Liz Williams include:

The Ghost Sister
Empire of Bones
The Poison Master
Nine Layers of Sky
Banner of Souls
The Banquet of the Lords of Night
Darkland
The Demon and the City: A Detective Inspector Chen Novel
Precious Dragon: A Detective Inspector Chen Novel (Forthcoming)

蛇警探

SNAKE AGENT

A Detective Inspector Chen Novel

Liz Williams

NIGHT SHADE BOOKS
SAN FRANCISCO & PORTLAND

First Edition
Printed in Canada
ISBN-10: 1-59780-043-0
ISBN-13: 978-1-59780-043-3

Night Shade Books
Please visit us on the web at
http://www.nightshadebooks.com

PROLOGUE
Hell

Hanging by his heels and twisting slowly in the draught that slipped beneath the crimson door, Detective Inspector Chen tried desperately to attract the demon's attention. Yet despite his whispered pleas, the demon's eyes remained tightly shut, and his wet, black lips moved faintly, as if in prayer. Hearing the alchemist's heels retreating down the passage, Chen tried again. "Tso! Listen to me!"

The demon's only response was to squeeze his eyes even more firmly closed. Chen sighed. Tso had never liked to confront uncomfortable realities, and had gone to some lengths to avoid them, but now he, too, was dangling by his heels from a hook in the ceiling and—thought Chen, bitterly—the truth of what the demon had done must finally be faced.

"Tso, I know you've probably had a bang on the head, but I'm quite well aware you're still conscious. We have to find a way of getting down," Chen insisted.

"No use," the demon whined, without opening his eyes. "There's no way out of here."

"Nonsense," Chen said, more firmly than he felt. The blood was rushing to his head and making him dizzy: the metal walls of the chamber seemed to tilt and spin. Reflected within them, his face was no more than a blurred, unhappy moon. He tried not to think about Inari, but it was hard to keep anxiety at bay. *Stop fretting about your wife,* he told himself. *The badger will look after Inari; all you have to do is worry about getting down and getting out of here.* To the demon he said, "The alchemist will be back in a little while, and then we'll really have problems. Now, listen. My rosary's on the table to your right—can you see it? I want you to try and reach it."

The demon's eyes opened at last, dazzling and sudden. Chen stared, blinking, into the hot-coal heart of the demon's gaze.

1

"Reach your rosary?" Tso said, nonplussed. "How? My hands are tied."

"You'll have to swing over and see if you can grab it with your tongue."

"But my tongue will get burned!"

"When that nightmare of an alchemist comes back you'll have a damned sight more to worry about than a sore tongue," Chen said with barely re-strained patience. The demon's mouth opened and Tso emitted a long, hissing breath that stank of offal. Chen was unable to repress a shudder.

"Oh, very well!" the demon complained. "I'll try."

He began to swing, dangling like some monstrous piece of bait from the hook in the ceiling. Chen watched, holding his breath, as the demon came within a couple of feet of the table. The long, black tongue shot out and flickered over the surface, missing the rosary. Tso tried again, anchoring himself to the table-leg with his tongue. The barbed, sensitive tip probed over the surface of the table, flicked the rosary, and recoiled.

"*Hurts!*" the demon said, indistinctly.

"I'm truly sorry. But if we don't get out of here..."

Tso tried again, and this time flicked the rosary off the table with all the neatness of a toad catching flies.

"Well done!" Chen enthused. The demon hissed with pain as the rosary seared the end of his tongue, but the barbs held it securely. Swinging back, Tso flicked the rosary in the direction of Chen, who lunged for it with his teeth and missed. The rosary, detaching itself from Tso's tongue, wrapped around an ornately carved pineapple that decorated the edge of the alchemist's desk, where it hung, dangling tantalizingly out of reach just as the alchemist stepped back through the lacquered door, ceremonial machete in hand.

PART ONE

ONE
Singapore Three, Earth
One Week Earlier

Detective Inspector Chen brushed aside the chaos on his desk and carefully lit a single stick of scarlet incense. Smoke spiraled up into the air, contributing to the brown smear that marked the ceiling like a bloodstain immediately above Chen's desk and adding to the heat of the city outside. The air conditioning had failed again, a lamentably regular occurrence in the steamy South China summer. Chen bent his head in a brief prayer, then picked up the photograph and held it over the stream of smoke. The girl's face appeared by degrees, manifesting out of a dark background. She was standing in the doorway of a go-down, gazing fearfully over her shoulder. Her hair was still scraped back into its funeral braids, and her white face gleamed out of the shadows like the ghost she was. Studying the photo, and the expression on the girl's face, Chen was aware of the sudden hot glow of rage in his heart. How many more young women might have gone the same way after their deaths, unnoticed and unmourned? But whoever was behind all this had made a mistake this time, choosing the daughter of Singapore Three's premier industrialist rather than some nameless prostitute. Chen held the photograph out to the woman sitting on the other side of the desk and said gently, "Let's begin at the beginning, Mrs Tang. Are you sure that this is your daughter?"

Mrs Tang's grip tightened around the handle of her Miucci handbag as she studied the photograph. In a little whispery voice she said, "Yes. Yes, that's Pearl."

"Now, you say someone sent this to you?"

"Yesterday. I didn't go out of the house, and I'm sure no one came in—it was the servants' afternoon off. But when I walked into the living room, the photo was sitting on the bureau. In a red envelope. I didn't know what it was at first. There was a note, telling me what to do." She gestured towards the spiraling incense. "You can see her face for a little while, but then it fades

5

again."

"And did you notice anything—strange? Apart from the envelope?"

Mrs Tang moistened dry lips. "There was some ash. Like dust. At first I thought the maid hadn't been cleaning properly, but it was white and soft. Like incense ash."

"I see. Mrs Tang, I know how hard this is for you, but at least we have a lead. You must try and be hopeful."

Mrs Tang's face began to crumple.

"You will find her, won't you?"

Reaching across, Chen patted her hand. "Don't worry. We'll find your daughter, and we'll make absolutely sure that this time she completes her journey to the afterlife." He did his best to sound reassuring.

"Thank you," Mrs Tang murmured. She pushed her expensive sunglasses to the top of her head and rubbed her eyes; they were rimmed with redness. "I'd better go. I couldn't tell my husband I was coming here; he'd be furious if he knew I'd gone to the police. I told him I was going shopping."

Chen sighed. This was an added complication, but hardly an unfamiliar one. "Is there anything you can do to change your husband's mind?"

"I don't think so. H'suen's a hard man to talk to sometimes. I've tried discussing it with him, but he won't listen." Mrs Tang gave a brittle, bitter smile. "He says it doesn't make any difference; Pearl's dead and that's that. You see, he adored Pearl. At first, anyway. She was such a sweet little girl, but then she started growing up. I mean, she was always a—well, she was a lovely, *lovely* girl, but she could be a little bit difficult. Willful. She was fourteen, and I used to say to him: 'What do you expect these days?' They all go out with boys, and Pearl was very popular. He used to get so angry...And then he found out that she'd been charging money for what she did and of course he was *furious*, we both were, but I said Pearl needed help, not scolding...And I think her eating problems started around then..."

She seemed to have forgotten that she had been on the point of leaving. Patiently, Chen listened as she talked, building up a picture of the dead girl. Disobedience, anorexia, promiscuity and what amounted to prostitution did not make a pretty picture, but Chen said nothing. Years of police work had taught him that sympathy won more confidences than judgment, and anyway, it came more naturally. Chen didn't feel that he was in any position to judge anyone else, certainly not these days. He sat gazing at Mrs Tang, making sympathetic noises while she rambled on about her daughter, and occasionally handing her a tissue to dry her eyes. Yet despite the tears, Chen was increasingly beginning to feel that there was something not quite right about this exhibition of maternal consideration. It was a little too artless, a little too staged. He could smell a lie, somewhere, like the stink of rotting meat beneath spice, but he did not yet know where it lay. Perhaps it related to nothing more than guilt over the peculiar combination of self-indulgence and neglect that the rich habitually displayed towards their offspring, perhaps to something darker. What had driven the fourteen-year-old daughter of one of the city's most privileged households not only to provide sexual services, but to seek payment for them? Chen mentally ran through possibilities with the hard-won objectivity of a man who has seen much to revolt him. At last Mrs Tang wiped her eyes and said, "You've been very kind, Detective Inspector. I know you'll do your best in finding Pearl." She looked momentarily embarrassed, as though she'd said too much. She leaned forwards, peering curiously at the framed photograph that sat on Chen's desk. "Oh, she's pretty. Is she your wife?"

"That's right." Once again, Chen cursed the impulse that had led him to place Inari's photo on the desk. Everyone noticed it and this was a problem, but it made his job easier, somehow, if he could glance at her face occasionally. He should just keep a picture in his wallet – but that made him feel as though he was shaming her somehow.

"What's her name? She looks Japanese."

"She's called Inari." Chen shifted impatiently in his chair. He got the impression that Mrs Tang was delaying her return home, but then again, it didn't sound as though she had a lot to look forward to.

Mrs Tang said, "She's lovely, even behind those big sunglasses. Is she a model? You know, my sister runs an agency and she's always looking for people. If you like, I could take your wife's number."

Chen said hastily, "I think maybe not. It's very flattering, but actually Inari doesn't really like going out all that much and—anyway, thank you."

"What a pity. She really is beautiful."

Chen allowed himself a small, smug smile, then stifled it. It didn't do to dwell too much on his marital luck.

"I'm very fortunate," he murmured. Mrs Tang sighed, no doubt thinking of her own lack of fortune in that department.

"I really should go now," she said reluctantly, and rose from her chair.

Chen saw her to the door of the precinct, then made his way slowly to the vending machine. Sergeant Ma was bending over it, thumping the side with an immense fist.

"Damn machine's not working again. I—oh." He stood hastily back as he saw who it was.

"Take your time," Chen said politely.

"No no no no no. It's quite all right. It's all yours," Ma muttered, and made a rapid, waddling exit in the direction of the canteen. With a resigned sigh, Chen managed to extract a paper cup of green tea from the machine, and carried it back to his desk. As he turned the corner, he saw that Sergeant Ma had come back and was surreptitiously waving a blessing paper over the vending machine. Chen was used to being a pariah, but some days his colleagues' aversion to him got him down. He sipped his scalding, tasteless tea and contemplated the girl's photograph for a few moments longer, then collected his jacket from the back of his chair and left the precinct.

It was only the beginning of summer, but already the heat had built to oppressive levels. Despite the heat of the precinct, stepping out onto Jiang Mi Road was like diving into a warm bath. Chen glanced at the pollution meter on a nearby wall, but the results were too depressing to take seriously. He walked slowly down towards the harbor, lost in thought. By the time he reached the edge of the typhoon shelter, the weather had grown a little cooler. There was a storm building out over the South China Sea, and the air tasted of lightning and rain. Chen smiled, picturing Inari resting her elbows on the windowsill of the houseboat, waiting for the thunder to break. His wife loved storms; she had once told him that they reminded her of her home. *The only good thing about the place,* she had added bitterly. The ferry terminal lay a short distance along the quay, and Chen sat down on the bench to wait. Someone had left a newspaper, and he picked it up, beginning idly to read. Singapore was opening yet another franchise city, this time along the Myanmar coast. Chen could remember a time when Singapore Three was the last in the franchise line; this new development would be the sixth city. Chen read on, learning that this version of Singapore would be developed along the same lines as all the others, and he smiled again, fancifully imagining another Detective Chen sitting on an identical ferry terminal bench, several thousand miles to the south.

A distant humming interrupted his thoughts and he looked up to see the wallowing shape of the ferry as it approached the terminal. Fifteen minutes later Chen stepped off at the opposite dock and into the labyrinth of streets that constituted Zhen Shu Island.

This was a rough area, and Chen walked warily, but no one bothered him. He supposed that he was anonymous enough: a middle-aged man wearing unfashionable indigo clothes. But occasionally he would see someone start and shy away, and realize that he, or at least the aura of his profession, had been recognized. No one liked policemen, and cops who were in league with Hell were doubly unwelcome. So Chen walked unmolested through the narrow streets of Zhen Shu until he found himself standing in front of Su Lo Ling's Funeral Parlor.

Unlike the neighboring shops, the funeral parlor was a magnificent building. A black faux-marble facade boasted gilded columns on either side of the door, and red lanterns hung from the gable in a gaudy, tasteless display. This was hardly inappropriate, Chen reflected, given the number of citizens who met their end in a similar manner. A narrow alleyway ran along one side, leading further into the maze of Zhen Shu. The sign on the door proclaimed that the funeral parlor was closed. Undeterred, Chen kept his finger on the bell until blinds twitched from the shops on either side. Over the insistent jangling of the doorbell, he could hear footsteps hastening down the hall. The door was flung open to reveal a short, stout gentleman in a long, red robe.

"What do you want? This is a place of rest, not some kind of—oh." His eyes widened. Chen never knew how people could tell; it must be something behind his eyes, some inner darkness that revealed his close association with the worlds beyond the world. When younger he had spent hours peering into the mirror, trying to detect what it was that made people so afraid, but even to himself his round, ordinary face seemed as bland and inexpressive as the moon. Perhaps this very impassiveness was what unnerved others.

"I'm sorry," the stout man said in more conciliatory tones. "I didn't realize."

Chen displayed his badge. "Franchise Police Department. Precinct Thirteen. Detective Inspector Chen. Do you mind if I come in? I'd like to ask you a few questions."

With many protestations of the honor done to the establishment, the stout man ushered Chen inside. The interior of the funeral parlor was as ostentatious as the facade. Chen was shown into a long, mirrored room with a scarlet rug. Carp floated in a wall-length tank at the far end of the room, their reflections drifting to infinity in the multiple mirrors. The stout man clapped his hands, twice, summoning a small, wan maid.

"Tea?" whispered the maid.

"Thanks. What sort do you have?"

The maid closed her eyes for a moment and recited:

"Jade Dragon Oolong; Peach and Ginseng; Gunpowder Black..." She rattled through a list of some fifteen teas before Chen could stop her. Evidently the funeral parlor was not short of funds.

"I'll have any of the oolongs. Thank you."

"Now, Detective Inspector." The stout owner of the funeral parlor settled himself into a nearby armchair. "I am Su Lo Ling, the proprietor of this establishment. What can we do to help?"

"I understand you handled the funeral arrangements for a ceremony a week ago, for a girl named Pearl Tang. The daughter of someone who needs no introduction from me."

"Indeed, indeed. So very sad. Such a young woman. Anorexia is a most tragic condition. It just goes to show," and here Mr Ling shook his head philosophically, "that not even the materially blessed among us may attain true happiness."

"How very wise. Forgive me for asking such a delicate question, but were there any—irregularities—with the funeral?"

"None whatsoever. You must understand, Detective Inspector, that we are a very old firm. The Lings have been in the funeral business since the seventeenth century, in what was then Peking, before I moved the business here. Our connections with the relevant authorities are ancient. There have never been any difficulties with the paperwork." A small pause. "Might I ask why you pose such a question?"

"Your establishment does indeed possess a most honorable reputation," Chen said. "However, I fear that an irregularity—doubtless nothing to do with the manner in which Pearl's funeral was handled—has nonetheless occurred."

"Oh?" There was the faintest flicker of unease in Ling's face, which Chen noted.

"You see, it appears that the young lady in question did not in fact reach the Celestial Shores. A ghost-photograph of her has been taken, revealing her current whereabouts to be somewhere in the port area of Hell."

Ling's mouth sagged open in shock.

"In *Hell?* But the payments were made, the sacrifices impeccably ordered... I don't understand."

"Neither does her mother."

"The poor woman must be distraught."

"She is naturally concerned that the spirit of her only child is not now reclining among the peach orchards of Heaven, but currently appears to be wandering around a region best described as dodgy," Chen said.

"I'll show you the paperwork. I'll go and get it now."

Together, Ling and Chen pored over the documents. To Chen's experienced eyes, everything seemed to be in order: the immigration visa with the Celestial authorities, the docking fees of the ghost-boat, the license of passage across the Sea of Night. He felt sure that the explanation for Pearl's manifestation in the infernal realms could be traced back to Ling, but the parlor owner's round face was a paradigm of bland concern.

"Well," Chen said at last. "This is indeed a tragedy, but I can see nothing here that is at all irregular. I realize that you operate a policy of strict confidentiality, but if you should happen to hear anything—"

"Your august ears will be the first to know," Ling assured him, and with innumerable expressions of mutual gratitude, Chen departed.

He returned to the precinct, intending to make some additions to his report, but on arrival he was summoned to the office of the precinct captain. Sung eyed him warily as he stepped through the door. Captain Su Sung looked more like one of Genghis Khan's descendants than ever, Chen reflected. Sung's family was Uighur, from the far west of China, and he was known to be proud of the fact. A subtle man, Chen reflected, a man who looked like everyone's notion of a barbarian and capitalized upon it to hide a quick intelligence.

"Afternoon, Detective Inspector," Sung said now, with civility.

"Good afternoon, sir," Chen said with equal politeness.

"H'suen Tang's wife has been to see you." It was a statement rather than a question.

"That's right. This morning. Her daughter's gone missing."

"And her daughter's already dead, right?"

"That's correct, sir."

Captain Sung sighed. "All right, Detective. I leave all this supernatural business to you, as you know, and I'd prefer to keep it that way. But I've had an e-mail from the governor's office this afternoon. The governor's a friend of the Tangs, it seems, and apparently Mrs Tang hasn't been—well, quite right in the head since her daughter died. In fact, she's evidently been behaving strangely for months, and Tang's naturally concerned. The last thing he wants is a scandal."

Su Sung sat back in his chair and contemplated his subordinate through half-closed lids. The air conditioning was still down, and the captain's office was as hot as an oven. A thin thread of sweat trickled down the back of Chen's neck.

"Scandal?" Chen said with careful neutrality. "Perhaps you might elaborate?"

"Do enough work to keep Mrs Tang happy, but don't start shit-stirring. The last thing anyone wants is for the press to get hold of the fact that H'suen Tang's fourteen-year-old daughter was working as a cut-price whore."

"I'll be discreet," Chen said. Unexpectedly, Sung smiled, which transformed his heavy features into something resembling menace.

"Make sure you are," the captain said.

Chen went back to his desk, pretending not to notice that his colleagues hastily drew coats and papers aside as he passed by. He sat down, reached for the little phial containing the flatscreen, then poured its contents carefully over the desk panel. The thin nanofilm of the flatscreen oozed across the panel like watery slime, and Chen wondered again whether he'd done the right thing in choosing this particular color scheme. When the new technology had been introduced, most of Chen's colleagues had selected lucky red as their flatscreen color, but Chen had chosen green, feeling in the back of his mind that the less resemblance the thing bore to blood, the better. Now, he watched suspiciously as the flatscreen settled into its panel and its programs started to run. He did not trust all this new biotech, no matter how much the media raved about it. What was wrong with good, old-fashioned electronics, and a nice colored box like a large, boiled sweet that you could turn on and off with your finger? As for the technology that lay behind it—using actual human beings as interface nexi for this new equipment, let alone subjecting them to supposedly benign viruses—it all sounded deeply unnatural to Chen. Then again, the nexi volunteered, and they were certainly rumored to be well paid. Well, that was progress for you. Chen heaved a sigh of relief as the data scrolled across the screen; at least he'd done it properly this time and the screen hadn't ended up oozing onto the floor.

Moving the pen with care across the surface of the screen, Chen called up a list of the city's death records over the course of the last month. Pearl Tang's name was among them, and so were the names of a number of young girls. Chen frowned, and scrolled through the records of the spring, summoning up coroners' reports and trying to discern patterns. Anorexia was reported in a number of cases, but then, this was hardly unusual. If he really wanted a lead (which given the captain's warnings, Chen was not sure that he did), it would make sense to call up the Celestial records as well.

Sighing, Chen scribbled a note on a piece of red paper and took out his cigarette lighter. At least this was technology that he could understand. He folded the note into an intricate octagon, muttered a brief prayer, and set the note alight. Then he waited as it crumbled into fragrant ash and dispersed into whatever airs existed between Heaven and the world of Earth. Time for another cup of tea, Chen decided, and made his way as unobtrusively as possible to the vending machine.

When he returned, the requested data was already scrolling down the screen: some conscientious Celestial clerk in the Immigration Office, Chen supposed. He was rather hazy about the *modus operandi* of communications between the other realms and the world of the living; once upon a time, the mandates of the gods would have been made known through signs in the heavens or from the lips of prophets, but now that the People's Republic of China was a modern twenty-first-century state, who knew how deities and demons alike managed the interfaces? One thing was certain, however: this new method of bio-communication was a lot faster than the old system. In the old days—that is, up until a year ago—he would have had to wait over an hour before the required data was transmitted. Now, it had come through in minutes.

Sipping his tea, Chen began cross-referencing the names of the girls who had died against the names of those spirits who had actually arrived in Heaven. The Celestial Immigration Department was a body of legendary pedantry and thoroughness, and Chen was sure that no one would have slipped through the net. Yet at least five of the names on the deceased list were not matched by corresponding records in Immigration. This might mean, of course, only that the spirits had been destined for Hell, not Heaven; getting hold of Hell's records would take longer, and would also mean calling in several favors. Chen glanced at the clock. It was already close to seven, long after the end of his shift. If he could get hold of his contacts this evening, he thought, pressure might be brought to bear... He was about to pick up his jacket and leave the precinct house when the large and tremulous face of Sergeant Ma manifested like an apparition over the partition of the cubicle.

"Detective Inspector?"

"Yes?"

"There's a phone call for you. From H'suen Tang. He says it's urgent."

Chen was suddenly aware of a cold constriction in his chest, as though his lungs had begun to crystallize. He said, "Okay. Thanks for telling me. Put him through."

At the other end of the line, H'suen Tang's voice sounded tinny and distant, as though he were speaking from the bottom of a well. The industrialist said without preamble, "Chen, isn't it? My wife came to see you this morning. Your name and number were written in her diary." He paused, expectantly, but Chen said nothing, deeming it better to await developments. Besides, he resented the industrialist's preemptory tone, and he'd long since ceased to be impressed by the power wielded by other human beings. In terms of the larger metaphysical picture, Tang was a very small fish indeed. But Tang's next words surprised him. The industrialist said, "Look, I need your help. I think something's happened to my wife."

"What do you mean?"

"I think you'd better come over and see for yourself." Tang sounded both afraid and irritable, as if annoyed by the unfamiliar phenomenon of his own fear. Calmly, Chen took the details of the address and hung up. He considered calling a taxi, but the traffic situation in Singapore Three was so dire at rush hour that it was quicker to go by tram. Chen left the precinct house at a brisk trot and headed for the nearest stop, where he found a disconsolate queue of people waiting for the next available tram. It was, if such a thing were possible, even more humid than the afternoon. Chen mopped his brow with a tissue, but was instantly moist once more. He thought with longing of his home: the houseboat swaying gently in the currents of the harbor, and the breezes from the South China Sea like the breath of water dragons, spice-laden and cool. He closed his eyes and pictured Inari as she pottered about the houseboat: watering plants; humming to herself beneath her breath as she selected ingredients for the hot dishes she loved to make, as close an approximation as she could to the meals of her native home. Chen hoped he wouldn't be home too late, and wondered with unease precisely what Tang had meant by "something."

A rattling roar from around the corner and the singing of the rails in the heat signaled the approach of the tram. Two elderly ladies elbowed Chen out of the way and sat down in the only free seats like a pair of collapsed puppets, smiling in triumph. Chen didn't begrudge the seats, but he wished that the tram was not quite so steamy and crowded, and did not smell so pungently of garlic. Hanging grimly to a strap, he closed his eyes once more as the tram lurched towards downtown. After what seemed like several hours, but could only have been fifteen minutes or so, the tram swayed to a stop outside the Pellucid Island Opera House and Chen fought his way to the door, eventually being expelled like a firecracker onto the sweltering street.

It was now past seven, and the light was beginning to die over the port: apricot deepening to rose where a sliver of sky was revealed between the skyscrapers. The Tang family lived behind the Opera House, in the Garden District. Chen made his way around the imposing wedding-cake bulk of the Opera House, automatically noting the program. If the weekend didn't turn out to be occupied with corpses and visitations, perhaps he would take Inari to a show. Reaching the edge of the Garden District, Chen stopped and looked back. The length of Shaopeng Street ran like an arrow towards the port, golden with the gleam of neon, but around the Opera House the lamps were coming on, hazy in the growing twilight. Cicadas rattled in the branches of the oleander, and the air smelled of pollution and food. Checking the address that Tang had given him, Chen made his way through suddenly quiet streets, each garden seemingly merging into the rest and heavy with hibiscus and magnolia. Chen knew, however, that if he stepped incautiously onto the edge of one of those velvet lawns, alarms would sound and tripwires would be activated. The thought of a brace of sharkhounds racing towards him was not appealing, either; Chen took good care to keep to the pavement.

Once he reached the Tang's mansion, he paused for a moment and stood considering it. The mansion was built in the worse excesses of *fin de siècle* taste: turrets and balconies sprouted here and there, and two anomalous Greek naiads, both facing the same way, flanked the portico. Chen thought of his modest houseboat with increased longing. No lights appeared to be on, and Chen regarded this as ominous. He stepped up to the entry post and activated the scanner. There was a whirr as the defenses were dismissed, and a voice said, "Enter."

Chen walked up the driveway to find that the front door was open and an emaciated man in late middle age was standing in the doorway.

"H'suen Tang?" Chen asked in some surprise, since it seemed hardly likely that the industrialist would be answering his own front door, but the man said in a voice like an ancient bird, "Yes, indeed. And you are Detective Inspector Chen? Come in, come in."

Chen had seen Tang's face plastered beneath a hundred headlines in the financial press, but his impression had been of a jowly individual with an arrogant, impassive stare. This man was thin and reedy; a Mandarin scholar rather than a key player in the nation's industrial base. When Chen studied him more closely, he saw that traces of the jowls remained; Tang's face sagged, like wax that had been held too close to a flame.

"And Mrs Tang?" Chen murmured.

The industrialist's face grew blank, as though he did not want to listen to his own words. He said, "Through here."

Chen followed him into an ornate room, evidently some kind of parlor. The room was furnished with little acknowledgement to taste: Chen's initial impression was of a stuffy, overwhelming opulence, a banquet of crimson velvet and gilded wood. It was the kind of room that someone with too much money and a passing acquaintance with Versailles might have attempted to reproduce, unhindered by concepts relating to vulgarity. Chen was immediately reminded of the funeral parlor. On a red, stuffed chair harnessed by flying cherubs sat Mrs Tang. Her face was perfectly blank. She smiled slightly, and her hands were clasped about the Miucci purse that rested in her silken lap. At first, Chen thought she was wearing gloves, but then he saw that the skin of her hands was blood-red.

"I found her like that an hour ago," Tang said mournfully. "She hasn't moved."

Chen approached the motionless woman and crouched on his heels in front of her. Her eyes were wide open, and behind them he could see a curious gilded film. He glanced over his shoulder to find out where the light was coming from, only to find that the door was shut and the only illumination came from one of the chandeliers at the other end of the room, behind Mrs Tang. He reached out and touched a tentative finger to the pulse in the woman's throat, where he detected a faint, irregular beat.

"Have you called a doctor?" Chen asked.

The industrialist nodded. "My personal physician has been to see her. He's upstairs now, on the phone."

"And his diagnosis?"

Tang shuffled his feet, ashamed. "Possession."

"Yes, I'm inclined to agree. Something's apparently got to her... Well, we'd better arrange for an exorcism."

"Detective Inspector," said Tang, clawing at Chen's arm. "You do realize that I am anxious to avoid a scandal?"

"Don't worry," Chen said. "We'll be very discreet." He glanced at a nearby ormolu clock and sighed. It was already close to eight. "Do you mind if I make a quick phone call?"

"Certainly."

Chen stepped out into the hall, reluctant to let whatever might be occupying Mrs Tang, to overhear his conversation. He dialed the home number of the departmental exorcist, and after a moment, Lao's familiar, irritable voice answered.

"Chen, is that you? What is it this time?"

Chen explained, and Lao gave a martyred sigh. "Can't it wait till tomorrow? My wife's just put dinner on the table."

"Sorry, but no," Chen said firmly.

"If you put the victim to bed and keep their feet warm it sometimes goes away of its own accord. Green tea helps, too."

"Lao, this is urgent."

"Oh, very well," the exorcist grumbled. "Where is it?"

Chen told him.

"Not on the other side of town, then, as it usually is... Give me a moment to find my shoes."

Chen closed the connection, then rang Inari. "Darling, it's me. Look, I'm sorry, but it looks as though I'm going to be late tonight. Something's come up that I have to deal with myself, and—"

"It doesn't matter," Inari's voice was resigned. "I'll make some dinner and leave it on the stove. It's not a problem."

"Thanks," Chen said. He added, "How's your day been?"

"Fine," Inari said brightly. "I've been shopping. To the market."

"On your own?" Chen blinked. His wife's adventurousness was commendable but worrying. He could hear music in the background: something quick and foreign. Inari laughed.

"No, of course not. I took the teakettle with me. Don't *worry*, Wei."

"Well," Chen said. "I'll be home as soon as I can. Look after yourself."

"You, too," Inari said, and rang off. Chen stepped back through the door of the parlor. There was a rustle behind the door as something grabbed him by the throat and tipped him neatly onto the carpet. Chen found himself staring up into the furnace gaze of Mrs Tang: her eyes as hot and yellow as the sun. Her tongue flicked out, stinging his cheek like a razor. Frantically, Chen rolled away, glimpsing the crumpled body of the industrialist as he did so. Mrs Tang hissed with fury and leaped high in the air, coming down astride Chen's body. Chen snatched at his pocket, seeking his rosary, but Mrs Tang flung his hand aside. Her jaw dropped in dislocation and Chen watched with fascinated horror as her teeth began to grow, twisting into sharp points like the tendrils of vines breaking from the earth. Her clawed hand clamped around Chen's throat. The world grew red as blood.

TWO

"See?" Inari said to the teakettle. She held up the radish, carved into a delicate lace of petals. "Isn't that pretty?" She placed the radish in the middle of the table and studied it with her head to one side. Even though she had followed the instructions in the magazine so diligently, it was the first time she had managed to finish a whole one without the edges breaking off. She gave the teakettle a look of mock disapproval.

"I hope you're not sulking because we went out without telling Chen Wei. Or perhaps you're just tired. We walked a long way today, didn't we?" She grimaced suddenly, and sat down on the couch to examine her feet. Even though she had put on the thick cotton tabis, the soles of her feet still felt a little raw, but at least they had not burned as badly as they had on her first excursion. And this was now the third time she had ventured from the safe confines of the houseboat. Inari felt encouraged. "Not so bad today," she said hopefully, to the teakettle.

She thought back to the market: a marvelous place, filled with lights. When evening began to draw closer, the lamps that hung from the high beams of the market came on, sending shadows across the green mounds of pak choi and cabbage; gleaming from the glistening sides of carp and mullet. Clutching the bag containing the teakettle, Inari had walked in a trance through the coolness of the fish stalls; sensing the flickering, newly released spirits all around her as they snapped their tails and swam towards a different sea. The meat section had, in turn, been filled with the vast, bewildered shades of cattle: stepping delicately across the blood-wet floor to where the shadowy avatar of Wei Lo, lord of the herds, waited with infinite, enduring patience. Their presence, and their acceptance of their fate, had saddened Inari and she moved on, among the stalls where the vegetables were stacked in rows and the air was redolent of earth and greenness and growing, sunlight and storms. Inari bent over the leafy bales of kale, and tasted rain.

The rest of the market was filled with things: clothes and trinkets and electronic equipment, none of which Inari understood. They were dead, and always had been; she passed them by. But she spent a long time in the remedy section of the market, studying the powders and roots, the acupuncture diagrams and the posters depicting the shiatsu meridians. Bamboo and dandelion; lotus and plantain... The spirits of the plants surrounded Inari, murmuring of healing, and she stopped to listen. A basket filled to the brim with pale, dried snakes rustled into life as she passed, hissing sibilant warnings into the air, and Inari looked up to find the stall holder staring at her with manifest suspicion. The teakettle stirred uneasily in its bag. Inari gave the stall holder an apologetic smile, and walked hastily on. Her favorite stalls of all contained spices and money. She lingered over cinnamon and star anise, scenting the incense meals of her childhood: her mother stepping barefoot about the kitchen, trailing odors of cardamom and ginger and fire in her wake. She studied the hell money with a grin, noting how little it cost, and she fingered the paper stoves and chairs and teacups—flimsy shreds suitable only for a dollhouse. Inari sighed, knowing that these days she could afford to replace all the furniture in her mother's home for less than the price of lunch in the local noodle bar, but she did not yet dare. The authorities were watching; the *wu'ei* constant in their vindictive vigilance, and the last thing Inari wanted was to bring more trouble on her family, whatever they had done to her. Reluctantly, she had left the market and stepped out into the rose-gold light of evening.

Now, back on the houseboat, Inari emerged from her memories to see that something was happening to the teakettle. It had begun to rock back and forth on the stove, as if in agitation. Its shiny iron sides seemed to twitch. Then the metal sides of the kettle sprouted into a thick pelt of striped fur. The handle disconnected itself at one end and flattened into a short tail. The spout of the kettle snaked through the air, as if seeking a shape, and then shortened. Two cold black eyes appeared above the spout. Teakettle had become badger.

"Whatever is it?" Inari asked in alarm.

The badger sat up on powerful hind legs and spoke in a dark, earthy voice. "Danger!" it said.

THREE

The chanting seemed to have been going on for years. Chen could not remember a time when it had not been ringing in his ears: a surging, insistent
note, threaded through with discord. He blinked, trying to clear his head.
A red and gold ceiling swam above him; lights sparkled by. By degrees, he
realized that he was still lying flat on his back on H'suen Tang's carpet. The
chandelier that hung at the far end of the room was spinning like some gigantic crystalline top. The harsh voice chanted on, and there was now something
distinctly familiar about it. Chen raised his head. Lao Li, the police exorcist,
was standing in the centre of the room, his feet braced apart beneath his
robes. The long, scarlet tail of a charm fluttered behind him as he recited,
vanishing into sparks as he called forth the words. Under the chandelier, Mrs
Tang was spinning, too. She whirled too fast for Chen to see her properly,
and she was emitting a wail like a steam kettle. A painful heat pricked across
Chen's chest and for a dazed moment he wondered whether he was having a
heart attack. Then he realized that the stinging sensation was coming from
his own rosary, tucked into the inner pocket of his jacket. Chen seized the
rosary and struggled to his feet to assist the exorcist. Whatever had possessed
Mrs Tang was close to emerging. Chen could smell the betraying reek of Hell:
spice and metal and blood. Mrs Tang's revolving form began to slow, and
her head snapped from side to side. Something long and thin crept from her
gaping mouth, congealing into a greasy stain upon the air. Teeth snapped
from a blind, narrow head; it reminded Chen of one of the phallic clams that
occasionally crept from buckets along the harbor wall. The thing bunched
itself into a mass of wrinkles, aiming at the chandelier, but at that point Chen
threw the rosary. The string of beads, each one a hot, glowing coal, snaked
through the air and wrapped around the creature's bunched body. There was
the sudden pungent smell of seared flesh and the two halves of the entity fell

writhing onto the floor. Chen glimpsed a thick honeycomb of cells within, and then the demon was nothing more than a little heap of ash. Mrs Tang lay quite still, her head twisted at a distressingly unnatural angle. Chen crouched by her side and checked her pulse, though he knew it was useless. He raised his head to meet the angry eyes of the police exorcist.

"Shit," Lao said, brushing ash from his hands. "Couldn't hold it. I fucking *hate* losing them."

"You did what you could," Chen said in resignation. "You probably saved my life, anyway." From the look on Lao's face, this accounted for remarkably little.

"But not Mrs Tang's," the exorcist added bitterly. Chen straightened up. "Where's her husband gone?"

"What husband? Was Tang here?"

"She jumped me when I came through the door. I saw him lying on the rug."

Lao passed a distracted hand through what remained of his hair. "When I came in—the front door was wide open, by the way—there was just you and the woman. She was on the point of finishing you off, so I skipped the formal introductions."

They stared at one another for a moment, and then Chen said with quiet anger, "Then where the hell's Tang?"

Together, Chen and Lao conducted a hasty search of the mansion, but there was no one to be seen. Tang had mentioned the presence of his personal physician, but Chen could find no trace of anyone. The servants' quarters were tidy and empty and quiet.

"All right," Chen said wearily, as they came back down the stairs. "One corpse, and one missing person. At least. I'd better call the specialists."

It was some time before the forensic unit arrived. Chen and Lao spent the time cautiously searching garden and house. Chen lingered in the bedroom that had evidently belonged to Pearl: a sad shrine, with cosmetics and stuffed toys lining the large, white dressing table like objects upon an altar. Methodically, Chen searched all the obvious secret places, found nothing except a box of novelty condoms, and turned his attention to the undersides of drawers and the backs of photographs. This yielded a single item of interest: a snapshot of an ornamental facade, a dragon lantern washed by rain and a girl's face staring from a window. The face was not that of Pearl Tang. This girl was equally as young, and in the sharp, digitized image of the photograph her face seemed filled with a kind of repressed excitement, the mouth pursed as though she was trying not to laugh. Her hair was arranged into an over-elaborate style that looked curiously antiquated. Chen tucked the photo carefully into his wallet and resumed his search. He found nothing more.

Downstairs, the forensic unit was arriving. They were not, as Chen had specifically requested, the special team that dealt principally with supernatural cases. Chen sighed. Yet more evidence of prejudice on the part of the department, or, more likely, sheer penny-pinching. Beside him, Lao echoed the sigh.

"Just what we need. A bunch of skeptical arseholes trampling over everything and ignoring the obvious. Are you going to deal with them, or shall I?"

"Best if I do it," Chen said hastily. Lao had a tendency to become patronizing, and subsequently argumentative, when dealing with non-specialists.

The scientist in charge of the team was someone that Chen had never seen before: a small neat woman of Vietnamese extraction. Chen took her aside and explained the situation as best he could. To his relieved surprise, however, Dr Nguyen volunteered none of the usual inane remarks to which Chen had become resigned over the years, saying only, "I see. Well, we'll take the body back to the lab and I'll make sure that your team gets a look in at the autopsy. Tell me what tests to run and I'll make sure they're completed."

Chen gave her a brief itinerary, then went back into the hallway where Lao was pulling on his coat.

"Can I go back to my dinner now? You won't be needing me any longer," the exorcist said. In the half-light, his long face looked even more mournful than usual, and his rat's tail moustache quivered. "Or so I fervently hope."

"I hope so, too," Chen said, and meant it.

Two hours later, the forensic team completed their work and left. Chen checked back with the station to see how the search for Tang was progressing, and decided that enough was enough. He took a taxi back to the harbor, then walked along the wharf. It was now close to midnight, an hour that Chen preferred not to spend alone. Dark water lapped against the sides of the wharf, and the neon lights of Shaopeng obscured the stars. In the little window of the houseboat, a single candle was burning, welcoming him home.

FOUR

"We were worried," Inari said. She got up from the couch and padded across to the stove, where the teakettle was once more sitting, peacefully inanimate. "It changed, you see, and told me you were in danger. We tried to phone you, but there was no reply. So we phoned the station and they wouldn't tell me where you were. So I cursed them."

"Oh, *Inari*—" As if he didn't have enough to worry about, Chen thought.

His wife said defensively, "It was only a little curse. And it won't last beyond dawn."

"The thing is, love, *your* ideas of what's little and other *people*'s tend to be a bit at odds. Remember that poor man's beard?" A startling sequence of possibilities was flashing before Chen's mind's eye: the precinct house transformed, scorpions in the lavatory, filing cabinets changed to the semblance of decaying flesh. "And remember that I'm the one who has to do penance. Not to mention apologize to my colleagues."

Inari's face fell, and she looked down at the floor. "I'm sorry," she whispered. "I've made problems for you. Again."

Chen reached out and took her hand. It was no use blaming Inari; she was what she was, after all. "Oh, look. No, I'm sure you haven't. It'll be all right. Don't worry." He spoke as swiftly and as reassuringly as he could. It was nearly one in the morning, he had a case starting that had all the hallmarks of the murder from Hell, and the last thing he wanted was to make Inari feel guilty over what she couldn't help. They were back to the same old problem again: the pivotal difficulty on which their marriage spun, and at this hour of the night Chen simply couldn't face it. He turned and looked at his wife. In the dim light of the houseboat, her pupils had expanded until they lay like great dark wells among the elegant planes of her face. Only a thin rim

22

of crimson delineated each iris. In this light, Chen thought with a rush of affection, she might almost be human.

"Let's go to bed," he said, and rising, blew the single candle out. Beyond, there was only darkness, and the soft sound of water under the night wind.

When Chen awoke next morning, the sun was flooding through the shutters and Inari was already up. The bitter fragrance of green tea was spreading throughout the houseboat. Chen wrapped himself in a silk dressing gown and went out onto the deck. Something soft and furry brushed his ankles as he stepped through the door; looking down, he saw nothing, but the teakettle was no longer sitting on the stove. The neighbors were already up, and going about their business. Old Mr Wu was doing his t'ai ch'i on the dock, and empty spaces among the houseboats revealed that the fisher families had long since departed for the morning's catch. The skyscrapers of Shaopeng were towers of shadow against the strong morning sunlight, which lay in a dazzling arc out across the bay. A single gull wheeled up from the water and was lost in the sun's glare. Chen moved briskly through his *ch'i kung* exercises, then went downstairs to get dressed. It was still not eight o'clock. Inari was humming under her breath: a quick, complicated tune, very different from the discordant songs that she had sung when Chen had first met her. Like himself, she was not one for conversation first thing in the morning, communicating via eyebrows and gestures. They drank tea in companionable silence.

"Weather forecast says there might be more storms this afternoon," Chen said at last.

"That'll be nice."

"Going to the market today?" Chen asked, with careful indifference.

"Maybe," Inari said in a small voice.

"Well, look after yourself," Chen said, and was rewarded with her startled smile. "Time's getting on. I'd better go."

As usual, he caught the tram to the temple of Kuan Yin, which lay a few blocks from the precinct house. At this hour of the day, the temple was always busy, filled with office workers from the banking district and, lately, the lab technicians of the new *gherao* dormitories of the bioweb, the latter clad in their distinctive white overalls. There were the regulars, too: the madwoman who ate chrysanthemums petal by petal, the young boy with an anxious face who seemed always to be looking for someone, a pale girl in a black dress. Chen exchanged small nods of mutual recognition and purchased his customary gift: a thick stick of crimson incense, which he placed carefully in the sand below the brazier, and lit. Then he bowed his head in prayer, and said the words that he had, a year ago, so painstakingly written: *Kuan Yin, forgive me for my betrayal. Hear my penance, and my regret for causing you, the Compassionate and the Merciful, such sorrow. Hear my prayer, and my plea...*

As always, he was obliged to force away the ungrateful thought that he was not regretful at all. If he had to do the same thing all over again, he would; he could not do otherwise. It was ironic, he reflected, that it was effectively the goddess' own instructions which had led to his sin, but then all gods were like that: the knife behind the smile, the drop of poison in the honey jar. They like to bind you to them, make you dance on razorblades. Now, Kuan Yin's voice echoed inside his mind, the words she had spoken at his dedication so long ago: *All you have to do to merit my eternal protection, Wei Chen, is to be immaculate in your dealings. All you have to do...* From the way she'd said it, with all the calmness and serenity of the changeless celestial present, anyone might think it was easy. To his eighteen-year-old self, indeed, it *had* sounded easy and perhaps it even would have been, too, if Chen had been a poet or a gardener, but it was hard to behave in a manner worthy of a Taoist sage when you were a functioning member of the Chinese police force, with corpses and informers and double-dealing colleagues at every turn. But then, Chen had to admit, it had been his own choice to compound his problems a thousandfold, and marry a demon.

He was getting off the subject again. He repeated the prayer, trying to infuse it with a greater degree of conviction, and opened his eyes. The incense was smoldering, sending a thin thread of mixed emotions into the ether on Chen's behalf. Uneasily, he turned to bow to the statue of the goddess that stood, book in one hand, peach in the other, at the far end of the courtyard. Her flawless jade face looked even more austere than usual; Chen felt like the boy at the back of the class, caught with comics or catapult. It was an uncomfortable feeling at the age of forty-three. Chen had to restrain himself from shuffling his feet.

Leaving the temple, he walked quickly to the precinct, lured by the possibility of repaired air conditioning, but as soon as he sat down at his desk he found a summons to the captain's office waiting for him. Chen sat and stared at it, hoping it would go away. The last thing he wanted right now was another political lecture. At last he crumpled the note between his fingers and went across to the captain's office. Sung swiveled around in his chair, impatiently drumming his thick fingers on the desk.

"Good, you're here. They think they've found Tang," the police chief said. "But they're not sure. A man corresponding to his description was picked up on the security camera at the Zhen Shu ferry terminal."

"Ling's Funeral Parlor," Chen said. A piece of the puzzle seemed to click into place in his mind. "That's in Zhen Shu." Sung's eyes narrowed; his face became even more of a mask.

"You think that's where he's gone? Why?"

"I've no idea why, unless he planned to speak to the owner about his daughter's death. But two related elements of the case are now connected with the Zhen Shu district. I'm inclined to think they fit together."

"Would he have gone to the funeral parlor for protection? The owner's known to have connections with the—" Sung glanced uneasily at his subordinate "—the underworld. In both senses of the word. Perhaps he thought Ling could protect him against whatever possessed his wife."

"Or perhaps he wanted to warn Ling that whatever game they're playing was about to be up."

"Explain."

"I think Mrs Tang was sincere in her desire to find out what had happened to her daughter. But I also think she suspected her husband of having something to do with it. She was adamant that he shouldn't know she'd gone to the police. It's at least a working hypothesis that he was suspicious when she came home after a prolonged absence, searched through her bag, and found my name and number. Then, I think he arranged for an associate to take care of Mrs Tang and tried to avert suspicion from himself. He saw the exorcist coming—a person who could reasonably be expected to tackle a demon and win—and fled."

"All right," the police chief murmured. "As you say, it's a working hypothesis. I've sent a man down to Zhen Shu, to watch the funeral parlor. I suggest you go down there and join him."

"Who have you sent?"

"Tzu Ma."

"Sergeant Ma? With respect, Chief, is that a wise choice?"

Sung's eyebrows rose slowly up his broad forehead.

"And why wouldn't it be?"

"It's just that me and my—connections—seem to make Sergeant Ma particularly nervous."

"Well, he'll just have to get over it, won't he. He's a big lad, after all," said Sung, dismissing the matter. With a distinct sense of déjà vu, Chen went down to the ferry terminal and caught a boat across to the island.

In the bright morning sunlight, the zone seemed especially dark: a little fragment of night scored across the glittering expanse of the harbor. He found Sergeant Ma sitting disconsolately in a teahouse across the street from the funeral parlor. Ma blanched visibly when he saw who had arrived.

"Nothing's happened yet," Ma said defensively. Chen sighed. Ma was clad in a fawn jacket and huge boots: evidently his idea of civilian garb. Chen had never seen anyone who looked more like a policeman.

"I hope someone's watching the back," Chen said, with a faint note of query. Ma nodded.

"A patrolman. Don't worry, he's well-hidden."

"Frankly, I'll be surprised if we get a glimpse of anything," Chen told him. "Even if he's in there, Tang needn't leave the house in order to make his escape."

"Why not?"

"Places like funeral parlors and temples are nexus points—junctions between the worlds. Since it's licensed, that parlor will have access to both Hell and the Celestial regions. A temple will have an actual correlate in both; so there's a version of Kuan Yin's temple in the part of Hell that relates to our district, for instance."

Ma furrowed his brow in painful concentration as he grappled with this concept.

"Sergeant," Chen said, trying not to sound too sarcastic. "Can I ask how familiar you actually are with the precepts of your own religion?"

Ma looked up unhappily.

"It *isn't* my religion, though. I was brought up by my grandparents—grandma was a Christian and grandfather only believed in money. He wouldn't let my grandma take me to church, but she told me a lot about Hell."

"You come from Da Lo Province, isn't that right?" Chen said. Gloomily, Ma nodded. Chen began to see where the pattern had begun: an impressionable child from a rural backwater, fed with half-digested facts about the nature of the afterlife from someone who almost certainly had no idea what she was talking about. He decided that a few clarifying details might be in order.

"I don't know what your grandma told you about Hell," he said, "but it isn't a fiery sort of place where the dead suffer eternal torment. When you die, you either go to Heaven or Hell, but first you have to pass through a kind of process. You see, you've got two souls, not one as the Christians tell people. One is called the *hun*, and the other is called the *p'o*. When you die, the *hun* goes out into the universe and tries to find its way to Heaven—usually it just wanders about until it gets reincarnated—but the *p'o* is different. It used to remain with the corpse for about three years, but that was before the other worlds speeded up the process to bring their bureaucracies more in line with modern times. Now, when a person dies, the *p'o* goes to the afterlife—either Heaven, or Hell—the Yellow Springs."

"Why is Hell called the Yellow Springs?" Ma asked, frowning. Chen shrugged.

"It's a bit like somewhere being called 'Big Hill.' I suppose there are yellow springs somewhere in Hell. It's also known as 'Di Yu,' the 'Prisons of the Earth'—that's probably a bit more accurate. Each soul who ends up in Hell has earned their place, and they get a fitting punishment, but it isn't eternal. Eventually you get to come back to this world when you reincarnate. Demons live in Hell, too, but they're just a different kind of entity to ourselves."

"I hope I never see Hell," Ma remarked fervently. Chen smiled.

"You probably already have. Anyway, Heaven's not all that wonderful, either—it's enchantingly pretty, granted, but Imperial Court etiquette is still positively medieval and it's just as much bound by bureaucracy as Hell itself."

"So what actually happens when you—when you die?" Ma whispered.

"Usually, if you die in a normal manner, an officer comes to you with a warrant, and takes you to the Night Harbor, which is where the boat leaves for the other worlds. In other places in China, it's different—you might find yourself going down into a cave, for example—but here, because we're a coastal city, we're closely bound in with the *feng shui* of the sea and so souls have to cross the Sea of Night in order to enter one of the other realms. When a soul actually gets to the Night Harbor, it has to pass through a number of stages—it has to pay the Gate demons, then it has to get itself weighed, then it has to get through Bad Dog village, where demonic beasts torment the evil passers-by. Then it meets a mirror which tells it what it's likely to be reincarnated as, and then it gets taken to an observation post where it can look back on its earthly home and family for the last time and ruefully admit that it's completely screwed up and deserves everything that's coming to it. Finally it has to cross a chasm to the dock, and then it gets on the boat. When the soul's time in Heaven or Hell is up, the warrant officers take it back before the Wheel of the Law and it gets hurled out again into its next incarnation, having first been given a special drink to make sure it doesn't remember anything." Chen smiled encouragingly at Ma. "It's a bit like a package tour, really. If it's Tuesday, this must be Bad Dog village."

Ma did not smile in return. He said, "You've been to Hell, haven't you? When you were still alive, I mean."

Chen refrained from pointing out that he was still alive now. "Yes," he said quietly. "Yes, I've been to Hell. I have a dispensation, I don't need to go through all the various stages, though I do have to find my way through the Night Harbor. But it takes its toll, Ma." He sighed. "And I'm not the only one. If Tang's serious about being on the run, and he has the right contacts, it's feasible that he could hide out in Hell—I very much doubt they'd let him into Heaven, though you never know."

A tremor seemed to pass over Ma's face: like a ripple of water over the moon's reflection.

"Hell? You mean we might have to go to *Hell* to get him back?"

"Sergeant, please keep your voice down. No, that is not strictly accurate. *You* will not have to go to Hell to retrieve our suspect. But *I* might."

This effectively silenced Ma. He sat in thunderous contemplation, hunched over his little bowl of tea, while Chen took his turn at peering through the grubby lace curtains of the teahouse. The funeral parlor was literally as silent as the grave. Chen turned back to speak to Ma, and caught movement from the corner of his eye. The door of the funeral parlor was opening. The portly figure of Su Lo Ling stepped out onto the street, glanced hastily around him, and set off at a brisk trot along the road.

"Stay here," Chen said, rising quickly from his chair. "Don't take your eyes off that house, and keep in touch with the patrolman."

It was a risk that by going after the funeral parlor owner, he might lose the suspect—assuming Tang was even on the premises. Chen thought it worth the risk. Stepping cautiously out onto the pavement, he could see Ling disappearing down the street. Chen followed. The street grew suddenly darker, as a cloud engulfed the sun. Not a good omen, Chen thought.

He was halfway down the street when the rain began, a torrent of water that hammered the dusty pavements and plastered Chen's hair flat against his head in the first minute of its descent. Cursing, Chen squinted through the rain and saw Ling's figure whisk into a doorway. Chen hurried up the street and dodged beneath an awning. The building into which Ling had gone seemed to be some kind of go-down; it might even be derelict. The windows were securely boarded up and the cracks taped over. The door through which Ling had gone was tightly closed. Chen put his ear to the door and heard nothing. After the events of the previous evening, he was reluctant to step into another trap without sufficient support. He was not, however, to be given a choice.

The door of the go-down was flung open, startling Chen. A long, ebony spine whipped out and wrapped itself tightly around his ankle. Chen was thrown flat on his back and dragged through the doorway. Something tall and dark loomed over him; the hem of a stiff silk coat brushed his face like a gigantic moth. He groped frantically in his inner pocket for his rosary; finding it, he struck out with it like a flail. It connected with a bony carapace, producing a trail of sparks and the odor of scorched silk. There was a hissing curse and his ankle was abruptly released. Struggling to his feet, Chen began to say the rosary, speaking the Fourteen Unnamable Pronouncements in a swift, urgent voice. His assailant sprang to the far end of the room, and Chen saw a string of rubies glowing in the shadows as the demon produced a rosary of its own. Chen had a head start, but the demon spoke in several voices at once, Pronouncements clicking and snapping from its flexible throat. Chen speeded up and beat the demon by a single syllable. There was a blast of furnace-light as a crack opened up and the demon was catapulted back to Hell, leaving a noxious wisp of smoke behind it.

Wheezing, Chen stepped clear and the smoke crystallized into dust motes and fell to the floor, where it turned into a swarm of tiny, red locusts that raced between the cracks in the floorboards. Chen leaned back against the wall. The rosary was red hot, but he didn't dare let go. Gritting his teeth against the pain, he limped back through the door of the go-down and out into the street, where the rosary hissed cold in the pelting rain. His ankle was swelling to alarming proportions. Chen, limping along, fished in his pocket for the mobile and called for reinforcements. Sergeant Ma was still waiting in the teahouse, gaze glued to the window.

"Come on," Chen said. "We're going in."

Ma's mouth fell open.

"What happened to you?"

"I was attacked. By a *something*."

As an incentive to decisive action, this perhaps left a little to be desired. Ma's eyes grew round with horror. "What *kind* of something?"

"I'm not sure. Come *on*."

"I'm not going near that place if there are demons," Ma said with finality.

"If you're thinking of disobeying a direct order, Sergeant, you'll have to face something worse than demons," Chen said, feeling mean. "You'll have to face *me*."

Hastily, he and Ma ran down the alleyway and found themselves at the back of the funeral parlor. A high wall, topped with razor wire, separated the alley from what was apparently a courtyard. At their feet lay the cover of a drain. Chen looked at Ma and sighed.

"All right, then. Give me a hand."

Ten distasteful minutes later, they were standing in the courtyard at the back of the building. The rear end of the funeral parlor was considerably less imposing than its facade. A narrow window faced the courtyard. Gritting his teeth against the pain in his ankle, Chen held up his palm.

"It's guarded. Never mind—" Gritting his teeth, he took a sheathed scalpel from his pocket. Before Sergeant Ma's horrified gaze, he slashed a character across his palm, then held his bleeding hand up towards the window. The guarding spell hissed into black steam and nothingness. Sergeant Ma's eyes were as round as tea bowls. Hoisting himself through the window, Chen landed in a narrow hallway. Checking to see that Ma was still behind him, he hobbled down the corridor until they reached the door of a room that Chen estimated to be the main parlor. Muffled voices came from within.

"Wait here," Chen said. He went swiftly up the stairs and found himself before a row of doors. Each of them flickered with a quiet light and Chen felt the rosary begin to grow hot in his pocket. His skin flushed cold, as if in response. Each of those doorways was an entrance into Hell. The left-hand side of his jacket seemed to be growing heavier: pulling downward with grotesque force. Bemused, Chen put his hand in his pocket and encountered something flat and icy. When he pulled it out, he found that it was the photograph of the unknown girl that he had taken from Pearl Tang's bedroom. Chen took a moment to reconsider the snapshot. The dragon lantern to the left of the picture looked very similar to the ones that hung outside the funeral parlor.

Chen blew on the photo, then glazed it with a thin smear of his own blood. Balancing the photo on the palm of his hand, he placed his little *feng shui* compass on top of it. The needle swung wildly for a moment, before settling in the direction of one of the doors. It seemed the girl's spirit was here.

Cautiously, Chen held out his palm to display the still-bleeding wound and released his second spell of the day. Soundlessly, the door swung open. With the rosary wrapped tightly around his knuckles, Chen stepped forward. Even with the protection afforded by the rosary, his skin began to prickle and burn: a sure sign that the room was no longer entirely in the realm of the living. Across the room, a girl lay upon a divan. Her eyes were closed, and she was curled around herself like a cat. Her skin was as white as ash. She did not stir. Chen crossed swiftly to the divan, but as he reached it, a demon leaped through a second door on the other side of the room. It was one of the more humanoid of its kind: Chen glimpsed a pale, mantis face and slick black hair. It was wearing a long silk coat which was, Chen noticed, marred with an ugly burn. They had met before: this was the thing that had so recently attacked him. The demon's taloned fingers grasped a bloody katana. It came forward in a sudden rush; the sword raised above its head. Chen dropped, hitting the floor beneath the arc of the katana. Kicking out, he swept the demon's feet from under it and whipped the rosary across the demon's wrist, making it howl. Its curiously jointed fingers flew open, releasing the katana. Seizing the sword, Chen drew back for the final blow. But as he did so, a shadow fell across his shoulder.

"Look out!" Ma's panicky voice came from the doorway. Chen turned in time to see the ghost of the girl, a skinning knife in her hand, crouched to spring. Tang H'suen was close behind her, spitting imprecations. The ghost's gaze was locked on Chen's throat. He brought the demon's katana down upon her, splitting the spirit from head to crotch and spilling her essence out across the floor in flakes of fragrant ash, while Ma leaped for Tang H'suen.

Chen turned in the direction of the demon as Ma wrestled Tang to the floor. The demon was sitting on the ground, nursing its wounded wrist, but as Chen stepped in for the kill it hastily snatched something from an inner pocket of its silk coat. It held up a black badge. The demon said mildly, "Seneschal Zhu Irzh. Vice Division, Fourth District, Hell. Can I have my sword back? When you're ready, of course."

FIVE

"Cigarette?" asked the demon languidly.

"No, thank you. I don't smoke." Chen was methodically winding a bandage around his injured hand. The azure lights of the police car outside spun in endless refraction from the mirrored parlor.

"Too bad. Helps you relax, you know. How about you?" Courteously, the demon offered the packet of thin, red cigarettes to H'suen Tang, who still sat, head bowed in fury or shame. "No? I'm assuming you're not smoking at the moment, either," he said to the second prisoner, split in two, who favored him with a furious glare from an eye somewhere around the level of her waist. Zhu Irzh lit the cigarette with a touch of his taloned thumb and the sweet, faint scent of opium drifted through the air.

"So," said Chen mildly. "Mind telling me what your interest is in this?"

"Sure. But outside."

Chen accompanied the demon to the door and they stepped out under the thunderous sky. A great anvil head of cloud was building up in the direction of the port. Chen could smell rain on the wind.

"Look," Zhu Irzh said. "I told you, I'm with Vice."

"I know your bureaucracy doesn't work in quite the same way as ours," Chen said. "But I'm not sure I see quite why the Vice Division is interested in missing souls."

"Vice is interested in all sorts of things—in the promotion of prostitution, for example, throughout both Hell and your world. As such, we tend to take a dim view of efforts to curb the trade, but we're also law abiding. You know how bureaucratic Hell is... We have a strict policy of enforcement of taxation, and we're compelled to go after individuals who try to get round those restrictions." Zhu Irzh took a final drag on his cigarette, which flared into a thin column of ash. The demon tossed it into the gutter, where it lay, hissing.

31

"So you encourage the trade as long as it pays?" Chen said.

"As long as the profits go directly into the Imperial coffers, we're happy. But you know, Detective Inspector, that Hell is hardly a united place. And there's always someone who thinks they can beat the system—that's the nature of Hell, after all."

"Tang being one of them?" Chen was fishing for answers.

"The human is a very small part of a very large puzzle," the demon said. "It seems the enterprising Mr Tang has been supplying the souls of the virtuous to Hell."

"Kidnapping? You mean the ghost-trade?"

"Effectively, yes. In fact, there's evidence that he's been helping them along with a judiciously administered poison, one that mimics the effects of anorexia. It must be something pretty subtle, or your coroners would probably have detected it. And once they've died, the spirits of a number of nicely brought up young ladies—" here the demon gave a sidelong, ambivalent smile "—rather than stepping out onto the insipidly pastel shores of their Heavenly abode, have been turning up in Hell's more select establishments of pleasure. I'm sure you know the type I mean."

Chen grimaced. "I've been in a demon lounge before. Purely in a professional capacity, of course."

"Of course. In that case, I'm sure you can imagine the popularity of such rarefied spirits among the rather more, ah, *jaded* members of the cognoscenti. Normally, this would be amusing—however, the girls aren't licensed; the Imperial Civil Service has to pay a hefty fine if Heaven gets wind of the matter, and the owners of these emporiums aren't paying tax. So it's got to stop."

"There," said Chen, "we are in agreement, though I imagine for entirely different reasons. So who's the girl?" He nodded in the direction of the funeral parlor.

"Her name's Rainy Jhun. She's apparently one of the virtuous souls we've just been discussing, though it seems her virtue lay in the fact that she was never properly allowed to exercise her talent for corruption until liberated by death. She's Tang's accomplice in Hell. The girls' bodies were brought here, to a supposedly high-class and respectable funeral parlor, where Su Lo Ling falsified the visa documents so that virtuous girls bound for the Celestial Shores would end up—elsewhere. Mainly working as ghosts in Miu's brothel, of which the parlor is a counterpart. Human customers would come here to visit the ghost-girls under the guise of enquiring at the funeral parlor; people from Hell would come directly."

"So who sent the ghost-photograph of Pearl to her mother?"

"That's an interesting question. I don't know. Some rival operative, maybe. As I said, Hell's a jealous place." The demon yawned, displaying sharp, gilded teeth. "Sorry about assaulting you, by the way. I mistook you for one of

Ling's clients; I was hoping for information. My department's billing yours for the damage to my coat."

"Don't worry about it," Chen said absently.

The demon's golden eyes evinced a spark of curiosity. "That's quite some rosary you've got there. Mind my asking where you got it?"

Chen smiled. "No one you've ever met."

Zhu Irzh appeared mildly hurt. "I suppose you think I'm not good enough to associate with the Immortals? Well, I've met quite a few in my time, and not all of them have been unimpressed." He added mournfully, "No one understands how difficult it is to be a denizen of Hell. Yin and yang, you know. Darkness and light. Without us, nothing else could exist, and we still get all the flak."

"Don't think me unsympathetic," Chen said. "But shouldn't you be getting back there?"

"I suppose I should," Zhu Irzh said, gazing up at the stormy heavens. "It's interesting, to visit your world." His shoulders rippled like a cat's. "But I don't like rain, I must admit. Not your sort of rain. I don't like getting wet."

Chen looked at him. The golden eyes were wide and candid, filled with an almost innocent evil. Suddenly, Zhu Irzh reminded Chen of Inari, and it wasn't a comparison he wanted to entertain.

"Your prisoner's waiting," he told the demon. "And so is mine."

Returning to the funeral parlor, he accompanied Ma and Tang to the patrol car.

"I'm saying nothing," Tang muttered, handcuffed to the sergeant, whose expression was betraying the view that he would as soon be attached to a cobra. "I want my lawyer."

"So do I," Chen said grimly. "You can call him as soon as we get back to the station."

They drove to the ferry in silence, until Ma said, with the air of one who does not really want to know the answer to his question, "Where did that—that *person* go?"

"Seneschal Zhu Irzh? Back to Hell, I hope. I suggested we liaise over the prosecution details. Told him to e-mail me."

"Will he come back?" Ma asked.

"I doubt it," Chen said. "Once he's taken his prisoner home, there's little reason to return. Humans deal with humans, but Hell takes care of its own... There have been very few cross-prosecutions. Of course, once our Mr Tang departs this life, he might find that he has a few remaining repercussions to deal with." Chen gave a wintry smile. The prisoner scowled.

"I've never seen a demon before," Ma said tentatively, as though even the mere mention of the subject might conjure something up.

"Haven't you?" Chen said absently.

"I thought—I thought they'd be really horrible," Ma mused. "I didn't expect them to look so human."

"They vary. And it depends where they are—spending time in another world can change you. Some are quite inhuman; some of them look almost like us. Looks aren't everything, Ma. The most innocent facade can conceal evil, and vice versa."

"Evil," Ma echoed, and shuddered. "I don't know how you can associate with such vile creatures."

"Not all demons want to cause suffering and pain," Chen said, trying to keep his annoyance at Ma's prejudice out of his voice. "They have the same needs and desires, the same capacity to love—" Aware that he was on the verge of saying too much, he broke off abruptly and stared out of the window in the direction of the port. *Where was Inari now?* he wondered anxiously. Sitting in the houseboat with her elbows on the windowsill, watching the storm in safety? Or out on the rain-washed streets risking discovery from every person she passed? He didn't want to keep her cooped up inside, and yet... He remembered the stories that his grandmother used to tell when he was still a boy, tales of her own mother in Hunan Province.

His great-grandmother had been the concubine of a wealthy man; her feet bound so that she could only totter a few steps without pain. For the rest of the time she lay in an upstairs room, gazing out over the garden as the seasons passed: snow drifting down from the eaves, turning into cherry blossoms as spring came round again, the petals bearing fruit like drops of blood among the dark branches, then the light deepening as the year turned and the leaves reddened and fell... Chen, that concubine's great-grandson, did not want such a life for his own wife, for Inari. Foot binding was a thing of the past, except perhaps among the fetish fashionistas of Beijing where it enjoyed occasional limited revivals, but there were other restrictions upon Inari that might prove equally as constraining. But Chen had risked a great deal to save Inari from the wishes of other people and he wanted her to become whatever she most desired; he wanted her to be free. It was still a matter of miracle that Inari had chosen to stay with him rather than seek her fortunes in the world; the safety that he could provide for her was limited at best, Chen thought, and there were others who could offer her a far greater degree of protection than he could. Yet despite the difficulties that his marriage had brought, both for himself and for Inari, Chen could not find it in his heart to regret it. He blinked, overcome with sudden emotion, and chided himself: What would Ma think, to see his sinister superior gulping like a frog?

The ferry wallowed into shore and the patrol car drove off, heading for the station. Tang was placed in custody and his lawyer summoned, but the interrogation proved brief. Tang refused to say a word: sitting mute and contemptuous while Chen alternatively cajoled, threatened, and applied the iron bar of logic. Recognizing intransigence when he saw it, Chen gave up and allowed the lawyer to set bail.

"Thinks his money can get him out of it," he said to Captain Sung, outside the interrogation room.

"He might be right," Sung said gloomily. "He's an influential man. I've already had the governor shouting down the phone at me. We might have to let this one go."

Chen felt outrage building in his chest like unruly *ch'i*, and forced it down. "We may be talking about several counts of murder," he said, as mildly as he could. "And this is with regard to the living, remember—it isn't a case that involves the dead alone."

"I know, I know. I'll do my best, Chen. But you're as much of a realist as I am. Don't get your hopes up."

"I never do," said Chen.

It was late afternoon. The air conditioning had failed again, after a few erratic attempts at functioning, and the station house was becoming oppressively hot. Chen excused himself from duty and walked the few blocks to the temple of Kuan Yin. Being in his patron goddess' bad books had lessened the feeling of serenity and security that he had always associated with the temple, but the events of the last year had not entirely dissipated it. He stepped through the iron doors of the temple into the quiet courtyard, and took a deep breath of fragrant air.

The rest of the temple's regulars were presumably either at work or asleep in the heat of the day. Chen walked across to the small shrine and opened the door. Inside, it was dark and quiet. The goddess stood at the end of the room: a tall column of jade, so flawlessly green that she might have been carved from a wave of the sea. As Chen approached her, the statue rippled and moved.

"Wei Chen," the goddess said, in a voice that was as cool and remote as ocean.

"You're still speaking to me then?" Chen said diffidently.

Kuan Yin's face flowed with a lambent reproach. "It is you who have ceased to speak to me," she said. "You think I am not listening, when it is really you who refuse to hear."

"When I—" Chen paused for a moment, choosing his words carefully. "When I rescued Inari from Hell, and took responsibility for her, you told me that I had committed a grave sin in bringing a demon into this world. And you told me, too, that I would have to do penance for seven years, and that I could no longer count on your support, even though I am your sworn follower and servant."

"That is true. But do you think that I do not know how hard it is? Human-kind calls me the compassionate and the merciful because I hear each and every cry of suffering in this world. Do you think I do not hear you, too, or Inari as she prays every night for me to release you from your penance, so that you may no longer walk unprotected and in danger?"

"I didn't know she did that," Chen whispered.

"The act of such prayer means that you both reflect upon what you have done, and the consequences of your actions. It is not a punishment. It is a reminder. I have not sentenced you to anything, Chen. You have sentenced yourself."

Chen bowed his head for a moment. "I know."

"Did you come here to ask for my help?"

Chen smiled ruefully. "Would I get it?"

"Heaven is good at listening, Wei Chen, but not so good when it comes to acting. That is why we need people like you to do our work in the world. Any help I could give you is already to be found in your own soul." The goddess' features seemed to swim in the lamplight; her eyes were as golden as the evening sun, or a demon's own. He had not expected any answers, but at least she had condescended to notice him. Chen bowed again, and walked out into the heat of the day.

INTERLUDE
Hell

Even for Hell, the day was uncomfortably hot, and the mansion of Tsin Tsi—the First Lord of Banking of the Ministry of Wealth—was stuffy. Seneschal Zhu Irzh was relieved when the First Lord suggested that they discuss matters in the gardens. Having requested permission to do so, he took off his long coat and tucked it over one arm. He was pleased to see that the coat's burn mark was almost invisible: Ren Ji might be a terrible shrew, but she could certainly sew. He followed Tsin Tsi out into the garden and down to the shade of the willow trees, which trailed their long, black fronds in the oily waters of the pond.

"Fish," the First Lord said, with gloomy enthusiasm. "Do you like fish, Seneschal Zhu?"

"As food? Or decoration?"

"Either. My carp are purely ornamental, of course. The souls of rich American businessmen, transmuted. It's a painful process, I understand, but they could do worse than end up in my carp pond, given the lives that some of them have led." The First Lord of Banking rearranged his heavy, brocaded robes with a flick of his tail.

"I imagine such rarities must be expensive," Zhu said.

"Horribly so. But I like them and my first wife likes them, and I like to indulge her. Are you married, Seneschal?"

"Not yet."

"A young man like you? You can't be more than a few hundred years old, surely... I'm surprised. But perhaps you haven't met the right girl yet."

"I'm still thinking about it," Zhu Irzh said, trying not to wince. His mother had been particularly acerbic on the subject during his last visit to the parental home, but he wasn't going to marry Xu Yu Li and that was that, however influential her father was in the Ministry of Epidemics. There were plenty

37

of other possibilities, but none seemed satisfactory somehow. Faces swam smiling through his mind. Ren Ji would drive him mad in no time, whereas Sha Xei, despite being marvelous in bed, didn't have a thought in either of her beautiful heads. His family expected him to marry for money; his friends expected him to play around as heartlessly as they, but Zhu Irzh harbored unsettling ideas about love. He sometimes awoke in a chilly sweat, wondering whether he was cursed with morals. Imperial Majesty alone knew where such principles had come from; few of demonkind seemed so afflicted. He might even have to take a cure, but he wasn't sure if his health insurance would cover it... Zhu Irzh gave a martyred sigh.

"Seneschal? I asked you a question." The First Lord of Banking was staring at him with a gaze the color of old blood.

"What? Forgive me, Lord. Just wanted to give a considered reply," Zhu Irzh said hastily, adding: "Your decision on the matter would be most wise." He wondered frantically what the question had been, but Tsin Tsi appeared pleased with his reply.

The First Lord of Banking leaned on the ornamental bridge that crossed the pond, and fed the carp, forming pellets of flesh between his claws and dropping them into the green water. The carp rose slowly upwards: the empty bags of their mouths opened and closed, engulfing the tidbits and rippling the waters of the pond. Zhu Irzh found it too warm, despite the cool breath of air which rose from the carp pond.

The First Lord said, "I'm sure you're wondering why I contacted your department today, and asked for you. You see, I've called you here on a matter of some delicacy."

"My Lord?"

"This case you've been investigating. The brothel."

"Oh, that."

"There is a small matter relating to it which requires—a certain degree of *style*, shall we say, an element of personal attention which I am reluctant to entrust to anyone less experienced."

"I'm flattered by your confidence in me, My Lord," Zhu Irzh said cautiously. "Might I be trusted to know what the matter entails?"

Tsin Tsi absently gnawed a long and ornamental fingernail, stopping himself with an effort. "I need you to find a young lady. One of the souls snatched from her rightful place on the voyage to Heaven. I have had word from her."

Zhu Irzh frowned. "A human soul had the temerity to contact *you*, Lord?"

"Indeed." The First Lord of Banking permitted himself a thin smile. "A very enterprising young lady, is Miss Pearl Tang."

Forgetting himself, Zhu Irzh stared at him. "*Pearl Tang* contacted you?"

"I can see that I will have to explain myself," the First Lord said, rather acidly. "You were brought into this case by your superiors, Zhu Irzh, purely on the basis of the brothel's unpaid taxes on a spot of ghost-trading. You thought, no doubt, that this was all that this case involved. However, this recent episode of commerce in the souls of the virtuous is not a simple matter of profit. There is more to it than meets the eye. You will recall that Pearl's father was a formidable financier. How do you think that came about?"

"You are the Lord of the Ministry of Wealth," Zhu Irzh said. "I would therefore imagine that you had something to do with it."

"Precisely. I set Tang up, Seneschal. I made him the man he is today. In return, he promised me certain services—never mind what those might be—and until recently, he performed to the most exacting standards. However, it is always tempting for those of us who enjoy the delights of power to overstretch personnel. In retrospect, I may have asked rather too much of Tang. I've noticed a decline in his services over the last year or so, and a corresponding decrease in his willingness to do as I ask. That suggests to me that Mr Tang has gone forth and found himself another patron, and his dabbling in the ghost-trade seems to be related to that, though I don't yet know how. When she found herself here, Pearl Tang's spirit contacted me, secretly and at considerable risk to herself. In her message, she wrote that the ghost-trading was part of a plot of her father's, against me"—here Zhu Irzh looked suitably shocked, and the First Lord continued—"and she also told me to 'beware the Ministry.' "

"Which Ministry?"

"Well, quite. Which indeed? Most of my esteemed colleagues have it in for me, Zhu Irzh, just as I have devoted so much of my life to making their own a misery. But whether it's the Ministry of War, or Flesh, or Earthquakes, or Epidemics who are aiming for my downfall with the unreliable Mr Tang's connivance, one can only speculate."

"And you would like me to retrieve Pearl Tang from Miu's brothel and interrogate her?"

"If she was still in the brothel," the First Lord said with some asperity, "I could delegate the matter to a lesser official. However, it seems she has gone missing."

"Missing?"

"Please stop echoing everything I say in that vacuous manner. Until last Darkday her services were engaged as an active participant of the brothel. Then, she apparently found a way to escape and ran away."

"I find it difficult to believe that a new and relatively innocent soul would be able to get very far in its flight through Hell," Zhu Irzh said reflectively.

"So do I. I think the owner of that particular establishment is either lying to me, and has secreted her away for his own nefarious purposes, or she has had help. Neither scenario is encouraging. I want you to find this tiresome little ghost, Zhu Irzh. Find her and bring her back."

PART TWO

SIX
Singapore Three, Earth

Chen spent his walk back to the station thinking about the angles he might use to induce Tang to speak. He was, therefore, irate to discover that the industrialist had already been released on bail. Chen went straight to the captain's office to complain.

"Chen, I told you it might happen. I did what I could," Sung said. His heavy face looked gray and rumpled, the sign of a difficult afternoon. "I've had the governor on my back and lawyers coming through the windows... We'll get it to trial if we can, but don't count on it."

"So Tang can be responsible for the deaths of several young girls, including, it seems, his own daughter—not to mention his wife—and simply walk free?" Chen asked in disgust. "Oh, I suppose I should know better by now, but it still makes me furious."

Captain Sung gave a shrug of sympathy. "You know how the world works as well as I do. We're not young men, Detective Inspector."

"So I'd noticed," Chen said dryly. He already felt about a hundred and ten. He returned to his desk and began studying his notes for a minor case of fraudulent exorcism, and the revised proposal for the *feng shui* practitioners' licensing rules. Neither document managed to hold his attention. He rang Inari. There was no reply. The thought of Tang's freedom chafed at him like a yak-hair shirt. Checking through his pockets, Chen made sure that his rosary, scalpel, compass and other pieces of equipment were safe. He hunted through his desk drawers for two small octagonal mirrors and a tube of superglue, which he wrapped carefully in a tissue and placed in his pocket. Then, as he had done on the previous evening, he walked out into the humid city and caught the next tram to the Garden District.

Tang's private car was parked in front of the mansion, half-hidden in the shadows cast by the magnolia trees. Chen sidled along the street, making sure that he was well outside the security perimeter and that no one could see him from the mansion, then took one of the mirrors from his pocket. Murmuring a few words, he glued the mirror to the underside of the Mercedes' fender. He was taking a risk that the car might be monitored, but he was fairly sure that any security arrangements would be set to detect electronic equipment or explosives, not a cheap plastic mirror. Then he set off back down the street. He kept his hand on the second mirror in his pocket, but it remained cold.

Once he had reached the Opera House, however, the mirror flushed warm against the palm of his hand. Swiftly, Chen found a nearby teahouse, ordered a pot of dragon oolong tea, and sat down with the mirror in his lap.

Reflected in the surface of the mirror, as minute and precise as a digitized film, he could see the Mercedes pulling out from the curb. Tang himself was at the wheel, and as far as Chen could see, there was no one else in the car. He followed the image of the Mercedes as it turned north at the end of the street, heading into the suburbs. Circumscribed by the edges of the mirror, Chen caught glimpses of tower blocks and concrete ruins overgrown with creeper; perhaps bomb damage from the winter's terrorist attacks, perhaps simply areas of land where building had been planned but the money had run out. He glimpsed the flashy new facade of the temple of Woi Tsin: supposedly part of the urban regeneration project, and wondered what defenses the Mercedes enjoyed, that Tang risked driving through such poor and edgy ghettos. Leaving the zones behind, Tang drove up into richer country. Mansions appeared once more, flanked behind acres of ground, and Chen enjoyed the sight of the road to Shunan, stretching in a dizzying curve around the mountainside with the sweep of the sea beyond. The sun had fallen, and the sky was a pale, aquatic green. Chen took a sip of black tea and watched as Tang turned off the road. The Mercedes bumped down a dirt track, leaving the vista of the coast behind, and slowed to a halt in front of a shack. Tang got out and went inside. Chen finished his bowl of tea and poured another, then signaled to the waitress and ordered an egg bun. After the bun, he called for another pot of tea, which he drank slowly. Tang still had not emerged from the shack. Chen visited the gents, surreptitiously keeping an eye on the mirror as he did so and feeling more than a little self-conscious. On his return from the lavatory, he found that the café owner had switched on the seven o'clock news. Chen listened as he continued to stare fixedly into the mirror. A deal had been struck over the Texan secession. The Turkistan Alliance had come to an accord with the Chinese government over the Uighur border, and the Dagestani Liberation Front had agreed to a cease-fire. Peace appeared to be breaking out all over the place. For once, the news failed to depress Chen quite as much as usual.

The headlines were followed by a local report on the new *gherao* dormitory being built out in Jhu Ku. It seemed that the media's fascination with the bioweb and its effects had still not drawn to a close. Perhaps there was something about the bioweb nexi themselves that piqued interest: after all, most were women, and most were young. Chen recalled vaguely that bioweb technology had started in Malaysia, where girls signed up for a two-year stint as nexi in order to pay their own dowries... Momentarily distracted from the non-events in the mirror, Chen glanced up at the rows of motionless forms depicted on the television screen, each nexus floating serenely in her shallow bath of nutrient fluid, wrapped in the embrace of synaptic wiring as they silently and invisibly passed information to and fro. If he half-closed his eyes, he could imagine the girls lying at the edge of the sea, lapped by waves, cocooned in weed. The images were organic and disturbing. Chen had grown up in a world where technology was hard-edged: plastic and metal and steel, not soft and mortal flesh. The televised pictures of the *gherao* interfaces made him queasy; he began to regret the egg bun. He looked down at the mirror in his lap just in time to see Tang's reflection walking from the shack, holding something small and evidently fragile. Chen squinted into the mirror, trying to see. The thing looked like a jar. Tang placed it carefully in the back of the car, got in and drove off. Rising from his seat, and grateful that he didn't have to sit through yet another pot of tea, Chen headed swiftly back to the Garden District through the gathering dusk.

SEVEN

Seneschal Zhu Irzh knocked on the door of the demon lounge and waited. The towering clouds of Hell raced high above his head, shrouding the metal towers. Lightning snapped on the wind. Zhu Irzh shivered pleasurably. After a few moments, the door was opened by a young woman. She bestowed a long and appraising look upon Zhu Irzh, who gave her his most charming smile. The girl grinned back, revealing lacquered black teeth, each one ending in a delicate point. Her eyes were as dark and pellucid as oil and her skin was dusted with lotus powder. Beneath his silk coat, the tip of Zhu Irzh's tail twitched once, in appreciation.

"Can I help you?" the girl said in a little, breathy voice.

Zhu Irzh stared demurely down at his feet and murmured, "I was hoping for an evening's entertainment. I don't know if you might be able to provide something diverting?"

The girl's opaque gaze took in Zhu Irzh's expensive silk coat, his black brocade waistcoat and gilded teeth, as well as the ruby that dangled from one earlobe.

"This is a poor establishment, hardly worthy of your attention. Nevertheless..."

"I knew you would," Zhu Irzh said, and stepped smartly through the door.

Inside, he found himself in a hallway decorated with metal panels and thick with the musky scent of incense. The girl swayed closer, enchanting him with her perfume. Zhu Irzh smelled amber and blood. He murmured into her ear:

"You're very lovely, and if I didn't have very *particular* tastes, I'd ask you to be my companion, but..."

With a faint hiss, the girl withdrew. "What is it that you want, Lord?" she

46

said, winter beneath her words.

"Something closer to life than you or I, alas. Something *fresh*."

"Something to share?" the girl said, drawing closer once more. Zhu Irzh laughed.

"Later, perhaps. There are certain desires I'd like to satisfy first."

The girl stood on tiptoe and he felt the sting of her teeth in his ear. His senses swam. His hands closed around the girl's waist: she was cool and hard and flexible. He thought with distaste of soft flesh and warm blood; eyes that saw so little. Some people might get off on ghosts and humans, but he wasn't one of them. The thought of sleeping with someone only recently mortal was less than appealing; at least he wouldn't actually have to go through with it and then, perhaps, he could return to this young lady... The visage of the First Lord of Banking swam, unwelcomed, before his mind's eye. Zhu Irzh reminded himself sternly that he had a job to do.

"Do you have such creatures?" he whispered. "Human ghosts?"

The girl gave a sniff of contempt. "Upstairs," she said, and taking him by the hand, led him up a narrow, turning staircase. Zhu Irzh could see his own face reflected in the metal panels along the walls: his features blurred to nothing more than a bright-eyed shadow. Something seemed to rustle and whisper, just beneath the edge of hearing. Zhu Irzh smiled. The girl stopped outside an iron door.

"In there." She tossed her elaborate, lacquered head. "Have fun."

Zhu Irzh stepped through the door and found himself in a narrow room lined with stifling velvet drapes. In the middle of the room stood a divan. The room was empty. Puzzled, Zhu Irzh looked about him. From the corner of his eye, he could see an unnatural shiver of the air. Zhu Irzh strolled across the room, as if heading for the divan, then turned and struck out. His taloned hand closed on a frail wrist. Something shrieked and squirmed.

"Hold still," Zhu Irzh said, irritated. "I'm not going to hurt you."

The ghost wailed aloud. Zhu Irzh could not see her very clearly; she seemed to merge with the shadows and the drifting dust.

"Stay *still*." Zhu Irzh hissed. The ghost became quiet and limp in his hands, and solidified a little further. Zhu Irzh saw a small, thin child, with wide eyes. He was not good at guessing the ages of humans; to him, they seemed to have such brief, dragonfly lives, but she was certainly very young.

"Listen, I'm not going to hurt you, I promise," Zhu Irzh repeated. "I just want to talk."

"Talk?" the ghost faltered. "What about?" The words were strangely accented; she spoke Gweilin falteringly, marking her as one who had only recently come from life. It always took a while before the language of the otherworld took root in what remained of their brains. Looking at her more closely, Zhu Irzh could tell that she retained a degree of her *hun*, her personality, but her *p'o*, her animating spirit, had entirely gone. He frowned. He wasn't entirely clear about human spiritual anatomy, but that didn't seem quite right.

"Come and sit down. There. That's right. Sit by me and we'll talk. Now, when you died, you were supposed to go to the Celestial Realms, is that right?" Mutely, the ghost nodded. "But something went wrong and you ended up here." Another nod. "Do you know why?"

The ghost burst into suddenly impassioned speech.

"No! No, I don't know why. I always tried to be good; I really did. I don't know why I'm in Hell..." Her face crumpled. Zhu Irzh almost felt sorry for her. This pale little thing ought to be skipping among the fragile peach blossoms of Heaven, not servicing demons in some netherworld seraglio. Some people certainly had weird tastes. Any sexual favors from this one would be subtle to the point of vapidity; one might as well not bother.

"Are you going to take me away?" The ghost faltered. Zhu Irzh looked at her. He could almost see straight through her. That uncomfortable, nagging sensation was back. He'd suffered from this on and off since childhood, like the prick of a pin inside his mind, and had even gone so far as to visit a remedy maker. What had the old man called it? Conscience, or some such—a human disease, anyway, and there was apparently nothing that could be done about it. It irritated Zhu Irzh. To make it go away, he said, "I'll see what I can do."

The ghost clutched at his arm like a moth. Zhu Irzh brushed her away.

"What's your name?"

"Xi Fu."

"Xi, have you ever met a young girl named Pearl Tang?"

"Yes," the ghost said, surprised. "We were in the same class at school; I used to go to her house. In fact—" her spectral brow furrowed with the effort of fading memory. "I think I might have *died* in her house...And I think she was here, but I don't know when..."

"Do you have any idea where she is now?"

"I thought she was still here. There were others, too, but they took them away. I saw them. Pearl wasn't one of them."

"*They?*"

"Some—some people. Like you, your kind. They came from the Ministry, someone said."

At this, Zhu Irzh frowned. The message that Pearl Tang had smuggled out to the First Lord of Banking had mentioned a Ministry. The ghost went on: "I overheard them in the hall. They came and looked at me, and made me open my mouth so they could inspect me, and then one of them said something like: I'd do for the next batch but they wanted the stronger ones first."

"And you say they came from the 'Ministry.' Did anyone say which one?"

"No. But they had badges on their coats."

"What sort of badges?"

"I don't know," the ghost said.

"What would any of the Ministries want with the ghosts of the virtuous?" Zhu Irzh wondered aloud. The girl stared at him vacantly.

"I don't know."

"No," said Zhu Irzh with a sigh. "No, I don't suppose you do. All right. Thank you."

"Are you going now?" the ghost asked, with unflattering eagerness.

"Yes." Zhu Irzh turned and took her fragile chin in his hand. "Now, stay still." He could see the memories of life chasing around in her translucent skull like tiny sparks. It would be doing her a favor, really, if they were no longer there to torment her. He reached through and snuffed them out between the claws of finger and thumb. The ghost's face grew utterly blank. "Goodbye," Zhu Irzh murmured, and left the room, leaving the ghost sitting numbly on the divan.

Once outside in the corridor, Zhu Irzh looked about him. There was no one in sight. He sidled up to a neighboring door and opened it, cautiously. The room was similar to the one he had just left. Quietly, Zhu Irzh closed the door and tried another. This one was occupied. He could see the elegant curve of a scaly shoulder and the long arch of spine, tapering down to a coiling tail. As he stared, the girl mumbled something in her sleep and rolled over to reveal a pretty, Pekinese face and small breasts. One hand plucked fretfully at the fallen cover with claws that were long and spiraled like a mandarin's nails. Zhu Irzh backed quietly out of the doorway and at the sudden movement the girl awoke. She uncurled sinuously up from the couch and gave him an inviting smile. Her small mouth parted and the tip of a dark tongue protruded for a moment. Then, before Zhu Irzh could move, the tongue uncoiled, flicked out and licked him wetly in the ear. Zhu Irzh leaped back and slammed the door shut. From inside the room, someone gave a silvery laugh. Exasperated, he hastened to the top of the stairs and stopped. In the hallway stood a short, squat woman, overbalanced by a towering coil of hair. Zhu Irzh could not see her face, but her rigid back was eloquent of disapproval. Before her stood the black-toothed receptionist.

"—seems to have come looking for one of the little ones, the fresh spirits..." the squat person was saying, in a voice like the sound of a wasp buzzing in the rafters.

"He asked for one of the new ghosts," the receptionist replied, in evident bewilderment. "They've been very popular, and—"

"What has happened to the ghost of Pearl Tang? Is she safely returned to Earth?"

"Her father came for her this evening."

"To the counterpart of this establishment?"

"No, it was done through the ministrations of the *gwei s'sa*. Tang's father did not deem it wise to return to the funeral parlor; there was trouble, he said. He planned to take her back to Earth and hide her there. He was angry about her collusion with that client, the one who was carrying messages from her. He said if we couldn't guard her properly then he wouldn't have bothered sending her here in the first place."

"Trouble? From humans? Or Hell-kind?"

"From both."

"It is not good news," the squat woman said, "when humans and Hell-kind begin working together. It betokens a lack of harmony in the universe. Now. Where is the young gentleman who showed such interest in fresh ghosts?"

"Upstairs," the receptionist said. "Room three—I'll show you." Hoisting the heavy skirts of her robe, the squat woman turned to the stairs, accompanied by the receptionist. Zhu Irzh melted back among the draperies until he was no more than a shadow against black velvet. He listened to the wheezing breath and heavy tread of the squat woman; peering out, he saw that she had a wide, flat face, as though something large had sat on it, and eyes like small black seeds. Someone from a lower level of Hell than himself, Zhu Irzh thought. That was not encouraging. He waited until they had passed his hiding place. He could hear them knocking on the metal door of the ghost's room, a harsh, tinny sound, and then the soft click as the door opened. Zhu Irzh slipped from behind the draperies and slunk down the stairs. He recalled the little ghost upstairs, with her missing *p'o*, and bit his lip, wondering what it might mean. If he had not exactly found the missing spirit of Pearl Tang, at least he knew where she might be. Her father had taken her back to Earth, it seemed, and it would be a simple enough matter to locate the father's house. He hoped the First Lord of Banking would be sufficiently pleased to grant him authorization for an exit visa. He had taken rather a fancy to the world above. And it would be most interesting to see what it looked like at night.

EIGHT

Chen was just in time. As he reached Tang's mansion, the Mercedes turned the corner of the street. Concealing himself in the neighboring bushes, Chen waited until the car swung into the driveway. The house defenses hummed down and Chen hopped across the now-deactivated tripwire running into the flowerbeds. Through a gap in the oleander, he could see Tang reaching into the back seat of the car. From it, Tang removed a large jar. Under the house lights, Chen could see that it was filled with some cloudy substance, which seemed to swirl like smoke within the glass walls of the jar. Tang carried it carefully inside and shut the door behind him. Chen crept around the corner of the house, keeping to the shadows. The mansion was dark and silent. Even if he was fortunate enough to find an open window, the defenses would be up and the house might be armed: he would have to resort to other methods. He reached in his pocket for the scalpel.

The action that had so appalled Sergeant Ma had long been a routine matter to Chen, but it still hurt. Gritting his teeth, he rolled up his sleeve and swiftly carved the spell sign on his palm. These days, the palms of his hands were so callused by scar tissue that it was difficult to find sufficiently thin skin to cut; he reminded himself of a junkie, probing for a vein. It was not a reassuring comparison. There was only a faint smear of blood, but it would be enough to satisfy the goddess. He could hear Kuan Yin's voice in his mind, saying the words that she had used so many years before. *Every time you use magic, Chen, there is a price to pay.* Her gentleness and her implacability had impressed him deeply then, and perhaps still did, but he found himself growing increasingly weary of this razor line between the worlds. Still, he reflected, it had brought him Inari, and that was worth a little pain now and again. Holding his bleeding palm before him, he watched as part of the wall vanished into smoke. There was no one on the other side. Chen stepped through. The wall returned to opacity behind him.

He was standing in a study. A roll-top desk was lined with an expensive battery of computer equipment; Chen could see the fluid gleam of a biolife flatscreen spread out across the desk. It gleamed gold: a later and more expensive model than his own. Books lined the walls, but when Chen, unable to resist the habit of a lifetime, went over to investigate he realized that all but a few were fakes: welded together into a single indigestible mass of artificial leather and plastic. He wondered fleetingly what possible satisfaction could be gleaned from such fraudulent erudition. Voices were coming from the hall and Chen stepped quickly back behind the door. He could hear the slurred, roller-coaster speech of Beijing. Chen put an eye to the crack of the door and glimpsed two retreating backs clad in short, black uniforms: servants. He waited until they had turned the corner, then slipped from the study and into the hall. There was no way of getting a fix on Tang; he would just have to search the mansion until he found him. Uttering a heartfelt, but not particularly hopeful, prayer to the goddess, Chen began a methodical, surreptitious investigation.

Apart from the maids, and a young man in a waistcoat who was reading a pornographic comic in the kitchen, the mansion seemed to be deserted. Chen made his way through the dark and silent upper floor, then went back down to ground level, expecting discovery at any moment. When he got to the main hallway, he saw that there was a second small door beyond the one that led to the parlor. This one was ajar. Chen slipped down the hall and peered through the door. It was black as pitch. Chen thought for a moment, then stepped around the door. He found himself standing on a small landing. As his eyes adjusted to the darkness, he saw that a staircase led down towards a dim source of light. Feeling his way forwards, Chen made his way downstairs. He held the scalpel in front of him; the goddess had forbidden him to carry weapons, but the scalpel was an essential piece of spell-casting equipment (Chen held the thought firmly in the front of his mind, just in case). Someone was muttering. Remaining perfectly still, Chen traced the sound to the dimness ahead. He thought he recognized the voice of H'suen Tang, but he wasn't sure. He had come to the bottom of the staircase. He took a single step forwards, just as a smooth hand clamped itself around his mouth. Chen was lifted, with apparent ease, by means of an arm around his waist. Talons grazed his cheek. Chen kicked swiftly backwards and encountered only air. He was carried, rapidly and in silence, to what appeared to be an alcove in the cellar wall, where he was deposited unceremoniously upon the floor. The hand remained across his mouth, clasped as tightly as an iron band. His arms were pinned to his body. Chen rolled a frantic eye and encountered a slanted, golden gaze, lit by amusement.

"Detective Inspector Chen," the demon's voice murmured like silk in his ear. "What an unanticipated delight it is to see you again."

Chen was abruptly released. He could feel Zhu Irzh's hard, cool body behind him, so reminiscent of that of Inari, and in consequence disturbingly and suddenly erotic.

"What—" he sighed, and to his extreme distaste a reproving tongue flickered over his cheek.

"Sshh," Zhu Irzh said. "Wait here." Inhuman limbs uncoiled and the demon stepped over Chen and disappeared in the direction of the dim light. Chen, in a rare moment of ruffled pride, decided that he preferred not to lose face by complying with the instructions of a denizen of Hell. He clambered to his feet and followed Zhu Irzh.

The demon was standing at the entrance to a small chamber, peering through the curtains. He held out a warning hand as Chen approached. Chen stood on tiptoe to look over Zhu Irzh's angular shoulder and saw Tang. The industrialist was crouching in the middle of a circle, outlined by a harsh and constant light. Before him rested the jar, and as Chen and the demon stared, Tang opened the lid. A smoky substance, lit with sparks, began to pour forth and Tang smiled. Picking up the jar, he stepped out of the circle. The dazzling light began to contract, sending spirals into the circle. The smoke was beginning to congeal, taking rudimentary human form. Chen could see stumpy limbs, and a round, vague patch that might have been a head. As he watched, the limbs lengthened and the head put forth a face. As it sharpened into focus, Chen recognized it from the photograph that he had been given only yesterday. The thing before him was the ghost of Pearl Tang.

The ghost's mouth opened into a gaping hole. The back of her head was missing, like a scooped melon rind. Her hands fluttered, the fingers contracting and extending as they sought to settle into their natural length. The spiral of light was climbing about her limbs like some parasitic creeper, tightening as it grew. Chen saw myriad tiny legs, groping for purchase. A tendril, ending in a puckered fleshy hole, curled about the ghost's throat and lay there like a noose. The ghost lost her balance and fell soundlessly to the floor. Her mouth still gaped; her eyes were white, and wide with horror.

"Let's see you continue to betray me now," her father hissed. "It seems that not even Hell can control such a child as you. Go behind my back to my enemies, would you? Seek trouble for your own father? Well, then, I'll see to you myself."

Zhu Irzh stepped swiftly back, pinning Chen behind him so that the policeman could feel the bony vertebrae of the demon's spine pressing uncomfortably into his rib cage. A moment later, H'suen Tang strode past in a rustle of silk Armani. The door at the top of the stairs clicked shut and Chen heard the familiar whine of a security lock being activated. He was shut in Tang's cellar, with a demon and a missing ghost.

NINE

Inari knew, perhaps better than anyone else, how closely her husband worked with Hell, but usually she could maintain the pretence that it did not impinge too closely upon their lives. Much of Chen's work was essentially bureaucratic, after all, with the occasional murder thrown in, and though Inari knew that he conversed with spirits and demons on a daily basis, this was generally done by e-mail or over the phone. This latest case, however, was preoccupying her. Chen had told her of the demon, the Seneschal, and Inari did not like the sound of that at all. Hell had a long memory, and no forgiveness. Suppose this demon's visit was nothing more than a pretext to get close to Chen, and therefore to Inari? Chen had given the houseboat some defenses, it was true—wards and guardian spells—but nothing was foolproof.

Inari sat cross-legged on the deck, watching the storm clouds build out over the dark line of the horizon, and her thoughts grew black and bleak. She would not return to Hell. She would sooner die, not the brief flicker of passage between one world and the next, or the many and different levels of Hell, but true death, the death that can only come to someone who has never truly been alive: the extinction of the soul. Better that, than return to what had once been home.

The first drops of rain hit the deck and Inari raised her face to the storm. Her spirits lifted with the taste of salt on the wind, a wild, fresh smell that drove the incense stench of Hell from her mind. Thunder cracked high overhead and Inari blinked beneath a wave of rain and spray. Her hair streamed down her back in rats' tails and the skin of her hands glistened as if lit from within. Inari reached out a palm and snapped lightning down from the storm: seizing a handful of energy. She tossed it up in a shower of sparks and it cascaded over her, pricking her skin like a thousand needles and sizzling in the rain on the deck. Along the harbor wall, the lamps were blurred by the rain. The houseboat tossed, churning in the squall, but Inari rose like a dancer and stepped to the far end of the prow, where she stood with her hair whipping in the wind and lightning playing around her.

The storm was soon gone, taking the heat with it. The sky cleared to a twilit green in the west and the harbor lamps shone out with undiminished clarity, reflected in the settling water. Inari sighed. Her skin tingled. She turned to go back into the boat, but then she froze. Someone was standing on the dock, watching her across the jumble of ropes and nets. Inari could see the figure clearly: a tall man in a leather coat. She could see the hilt of a sword slung over his shoulder. His hands rested in his pockets. His eyes met hers and though he did not seem to see her, she felt the shock of sudden challenge.

"Who are you?" she called, but her voice was snatched away by the wind. The man turned to walk swiftly back along the harbor wall. Inari shivered. The energy lent by the lightning was ebbing away; she heard her own hot footsteps hiss on the wet deck as she went slowly back inside.

TEN

"Well," Zhu Irzh said, his sharp features creased with smugness. "It seems Fate is kind, if not the gods." He bent his head and flame flared briefly from a talon as he lit a cigarette.

"How so?" Chen said, more to hear what the demon might say than anything else. He had his own ideas as to the nature of the opportunity presented to them.

"My prisoner has been delivered to me. Little Pearl Tang, trussed like a sacrificial chicken and ready for her plucking in Hell."

"Forgive me," Chen said with utmost politeness. "But I consider that to be a touch optimistic."

The demon turned to face him, frowning.

"I thought we were in accord, Detective Inspector. Two hearts beating as one? At least, if I *had* a heart..." he added as an afterthought. "What's the problem? I'll return the young lady to her rightful domain, and you can arrest your human suspect on the usual charges. Unlicensed trafficking with the netherworld, or whatever the offense may be. I'll even give you a hand."

"Hell is not that ghost's rightful domain, as you know very well. If it hadn't been for the machinations of her own parent, she'd be strolling through the orchards of Heaven at this very moment. In fact, she'd probably be alive. I'm sorry, Seneschal. I don't know what you want with that ghost, but you're certainly not entitled to her."

"You're questioning my authority?" Zhu Irzh said. There was a dangerous glint in the long, golden eyes.

"I'm afraid that I most certainly am," Chen said, equally mild. He met the demon's gaze. He could feel compulsion growing: a weakness spreading throughout his stomach. The smell of the demon's opium cigarette was suddenly overpowering. His heart fluttered. Chen took a deep breath, marshaled *ch'i,* and silently uttered a warding mantra. The weakness dispelled. The demon's eyes widened with honest respect.

"Look," Zhu Irzh said, placatingly. "I've no wish to argue. Let's rescue our distressed damsel first, shall we? And then we can talk about what we're going to do with her." He stepped through the door.

Chen, following, knelt by the ghost's side. "I know this is frightening," he whispered, "but please try to keep calm. Nod if you can hear me." The ghost managed a tight little gesture. The bond tightened around her throat. "Can you speak?"

The ghost whispered something, but her voice was as dry and faint as a breath of air. The noose slid tighter. Zhu Irzh reached out and touched the bonds: there was a sizzling sound, like meat placed on a griddle, and the demon snatched his hand back.

"That *hurt,*" Zhu Irzh said, surprised.

"We're going to have a problem moving her, in any case," Chen said. "If we could release the bonds, she could go back in the jar."

The demon's eyes narrowed in thought.

"I don't know what this is," he said, indicating the fleshy thing that was tightly wound around the ghost's form. "It looks like something from one of the lower levels, but I've never seen anything like it before."

"Neither have I." Chen stood and looked around him. The chamber was dusty and smelled of mould. There was nothing to suggest that magic was practiced there regularly: the place was devoid of the usual accoutrements. Perhaps Tang pursued his dark arts elsewhere, or maybe he did not practice much at all but simply engaged the services of other people's skills. At the far side of the chamber, one of the floorboards had come loose. Chen went across to investigate. He could see a shadowy hole underneath the loose board. Something glinted. Curious, Chen tugged at the board, snagging his hand in the process. Rusty nails gave way and the board broke in a shower of rotten wood. The source of the gleam was revealed: nothing more than a Shenzen dollar. Chen plucked it out from its resting place and noted the date of minting: 2017. In irritation, he tossed the coin to Zhu Irzh. The demon caught it so swiftly that Chen did not even see him move.

"You're bleeding," the demon said softly. The tip of his black tongue flicked across his lower lip.

"Don't get any ideas," Chen said, dabbing at his hand with a tissue.

"Sorry," Zhu Irzh murmured. He appeared momentarily, but genuinely, embarrassed. "Bit of a delicacy, you know, where I come from, and—"

"I know," Chen said sourly. "My—that is, an acquaintance of mine used to work in an emporium in your neck of the woods. Rhu Shu Street. He sold human blood."

"Tso's?" the demon said, clearly delighted. "But I know that place! It's been going for *years*. And you know the proprietor?"

"Certainly. Although rumor has it he's not in charge anymore."

"Small worlds," Zhu Irzh said, then hissed in surprise.

The end of the bond that secured the ghost had begun to move. It quested out across the air, like a vine seeking light. A bolt of energy shot along its length, causing the ghost to wince. Chen could see the row of spiny feet on the underside of the tendril. He was reminded of lampreys, of centipedes. A round mouth opened with a sound like a suck.

"I think it's alive," the demon said. "It seems to like you."

Chen forced himself to stay still as the probing mouth wove in front of his face. But to reach him, it would have to uncoil further; realizing this, Chen moved warily back. The tendril followed, until only its tail remained, hooked in the noose around the ghost's throat. Its legs waved gently, like a rag worm in the tide. The ghost watched, wide-eyed.

"It's after the blood," said Zhu Irzh. Chen flicked an experimental drop onto the floorboards, and the blind, narrow head moved after it. The mouth opened wider and the blood was gone. "Never seen anything like that," the demon echoed. "*Must* be something from the lower levels."

Chen's uninjured hand crept towards the pocket in which he kept the scalpel. Moving backwards, he held out his bloodstained thumb to the creature, which pulsed and flashed with energy. The tail slithered free of the ghost's throat and the creature slid forwards in a rush. Chen struck down with the scalpel, cutting the creature neatly in half. A bolt of energy shot up the metal blade, numbing Chen's arm and throwing him backwards. He felt as though he had plugged his hand into the mains; his hair stood fleetingly on end. Zhu Irzh gave a quick, astonished hiss of laughter.

"Some help would be appreciated," Chen said, through rattling teeth. The two halves of the creature thrashed about in front of him, but the light that ran along its side was beginning to flicker and die. Gradually, it became still and gray, like dead neon. Zhu Irzh reached across and hauled Chen to his feet.

"There," the demon said with mock solicitousness, dusting Chen down. "Well done. I like a man who can think quickly—and where do you think *you're* going?" Striding across the chamber, he seized the little ghost by the wrist and dragged her back into the room. The ghost squeaked.

"Careful!" Chen barked.

"Oh, really," the demon said, irritated. "She can't feel anything. Not like that, anyway."

"Nevertheless, Zhu Irzh...Let her go."

The ghost ran to Chen and hid behind him. She seemed to be growing smaller. "Honestly," the demon said. "Anyone would think I'd done something *barbarous*."

"We'd better leave," Chen murmured, deeming it best not to reply to this remark. "Tell me, Seneschal, how did you get here?"

"I entered your world through one of the temples. But I got into the house through the sewers."

Chen looked at Zhu Irzh. The demon's long, silk coat was immaculate; his boots shone and his hair was sleek. He smelled faintly of opium and the incense of Hell, but nothing more unpleasant.

"Vice Division, you see," Zhu Irzh said, by way of explanation. "They do say that shit doesn't stick."

Chen sighed. "Not to you, perhaps. Ah well. I suppose it's the most unobtrusive route out."

"Aren't you going after Tang?"

"No, not now. Not yet, anyway. My principal concern is his daughter's safety." He lowered his voice, hoping that the ghost could not hear. "And I want to find out exactly why he killed her, dispatched her to Hell, then brought her back again. I want to know why her father wants to keep so close an eye on her."

The demon nodded reflectively. "I'd like to know that, too."

Swooping suddenly at the little ghost, he turned her face to the light. She ducked out of his grip and dodged away again, but not before Zhu Irzh had given a hiss of irritation.

"What are you doing?" Chen demanded.

"Looking to see if she's still got her *p'o*."

Chen glanced down. The glow of the ghost's soul was still faintly visible, a miasma behind the wreck of her skull.

"You can see that she still has her soul. Why?"

The demon's eyes narrowed. He seemed to be debating something with himself, but after a moment he said, "I saw the ghost of another of Tang's victims. Her *p'o* was missing."

"Odd," Chen said. "Usually, the *p'o* only goes when they've gone the legitimate route to the otherworlds. But Tang's victims were illegally processed."

"I know. Which suggests that something else removed her soul once she reached Hell."

"Soul trafficking," Chen said. "That's really serious, even more so than the ghost-trade."

"And indicates that our Mr Tang is involved in something very dark indeed."

"Any idea what that might be?"

A shadow crossed the demon's face. He shook his head. Chen was certain that Zhu Irzh was holding something back, but it would have to wait.

"Talking of Tang," he said, "we can't stay here... But I want to get a watch on him. I want to see what he does, where he goes. I am beginning to think that he's more useful to me if he's walking around as a free man."

"Up to you," the demon said with a shrug. "He's your suspect, after all."

The emphasis he placed on the words carried the subtle implication that the ghost was the demon's own. Chen glanced down and saw that Pearl's fragile hand was clasped firmly around his arm; he felt nothing.

"You'd best show us the way," Chen said. Inside his pocket, the rosary was still wrapped around his hand. The only way that he was going to bid farewell to the little ghost would be to wave good-bye as she left on a boat for Heaven. He considered the demon's retreating back. Zhu Irzh moved with a sinuous litheness that suggested powerful *ch'i,* and Chen had already noted his strength. If it came to a fight, he thought uneasily, it may very well be that Zhu Irzh would be more than a match for him. But then again, he had beaten Zhu Irzh once already, and any fight would take place on Chen's own earthly territory, which evened the odds. Chen preferred realism to pessimism; he would see, he thought, but he was determined not to let the ghost of poor Pearl Tang go back to Hell without a struggle.

The demon stopped, and pointed. Chen saw a round iron hatch set level with the floor. "Sewers?"

The demon nodded.

"Indeed. Very well, Detective Inspector. Down we go." Bending, he hooked a clawed finger around the hatch and hauled it from its resting place. Chen took a step back at the resulting smell, and even Zhu Irzh's aristocratic nose wrinkled. Only the ghost remained unmoved, staring numbly ahead of her.

"All right," Chen said. "You first."

The demon smiled. Teeth glittered in the darkness. "But I insist. After *you.*"

They glared at each other over polite, rictus smiles. Chen was hardly obsessive over the matter of *face,* regarding it as at best a necessary courtesy and at worst a neurosis, but dealing with Hell was all about power games and he had decided to concede as little ground as possible to Zhu Irzh. After a moment's standoff, however, the ghost seemed to make a decision. With a sudden touch of hauteur, she stepped onto the empty air above the hatch and descended as smoothly as someone stepping into an elevator.

"Oh," Zhu Irzh said, somewhat discomposed. Chen's smile widened, in mimicry of the demon's own. He sat down and lowered himself through the hatch. The shaft was shallow. Chen landed in a foot of unpleasant water. The smell was overwhelming. Chen clapped a hand over his mouth and gave vent to a prolonged fit of retching. The hatch clanged shut overhead.

"Do you think you might try to be a little quieter?" the demon's voice said, inches from his ear. Zhu Irzh's eyes resembled an eclipse of the sun: the pupils expanding until only a thin, bright corona remained.

"Sorry," Chen muttered through the sleeve of his coat. After a few moments he adjusted to breathing through his mouth, but the smell was still noxious.

"Can you see me?" Zhu Irzh said.

"No. Not unless you turn your head and I can see your eyes."

In his dark clothes, Zhu Irzh was lost in the gloom. It was easier to see the ghost, a faint dim gleam. Something thin and hard wrapped itself around Chen's wrist with a hiss like a whip; he could not restrain a cry. A moment later, he realized what it was: the demon's tail.

"My uncle has an excellent apothecary," Zhu Irzh remarked, irrelevantly. "He sells remedies for all manner of ills. I can procure you something, if you like."

"For what?" Chen replied nasally.

"If you don't mind my saying so, you seem to suffer a trifle from nerves... I've got a cousin like that; always starting at every little sound."

The demon stepped delicately forwards into the darkness, pulling Chen with him in a rustle of silk. Ahead, the ghost emitted a faint phosphorescence, like radiation.

ELEVEN

"Tell me again what he looked like, this man upon the harbor wall?" the badger-teakettle said in its inhuman voice. To Inari, the badger sounded as earth would if it could talk: deep and thick and slow. The badger was sitting on the bed beside Inari, its paws folded and its long claws meshed. Its eyes appeared to be closed, but she could see a black gleam beneath the wrinkled lids.

"Tall. Not young. I think his hair was gray, but I sometimes find it difficult to judge, in this light of Earth. A hard face, like something found on the side of a tomb, with eyebrows like a bar. A long coat, such as demons wear. A sword."

The badger ducked its head and said, "I do not know such a person." The reproof was plain.

"I did not imagine him," Inari snapped. "He was real and he was there, watching me."

"Perhaps your husband has assigned a guardian."

"He didn't look like a policeman."

The badger's eyes opened wide, catching the candlelight so that the dark irises contained a tiny, perfect flame.

"Hell, then. Kindred."

"He did not feel like kin to me. He smelled human, even at such a distance. And why would my family use a human to spy upon me?"

"I don't know," the badger admitted. There was a short, contemplative pause. "And if it is your kin, what will you do?"

"I won't go back."

"I know you will not go back, Inari. I asked you what you would do." The badger's eyes were like polished iron and there was no pity in them. *Animals do not feel pity, and neither do spirits,* thought Inari, *it is a failing of humankind, and sometimes of my own.*

"Well," she said reluctantly. "I won't put Chen Wei in danger."

"He is already in danger, and was so from the day you first set eyes upon one another. If you left him, and vanished to the furthest depths of the storm-breeding ocean, or to the highest winter peak of the Zhai Fu Lo, it would make no difference. If they chose to do so, the *wu'ei* could still hunt him down."

"I know," Inari whispered. She had always known that this day would come: the day on which she had to face the truth. She wanted to pretend that the man she had seen on the harbor wall was no one of importance, and perhaps it was true, but it still didn't matter. The consequences of her actions were inescapable. "I could not have done otherwise," she said. "You know what I am. Demons cannot help but *use*, however greatly they may love. And I could not face marriage to—to that person."

"Yes, Dao Yi, your betrothed," the badger said. "We have heard nothing from him since the day you left Hell."

"My family paid him the dowry," Inari said, and even to her own ears her voice sounded hollow and unconvincing. "That was what Dao Yi wanted, after all: not me."

"You know better than that," the badger said.

Inari rose and paced to the window. It was now quite dark. She could see her own image reflected in the candlelight on the glass: a pale, pointed face, and eyes like wells of blood. She turned this way and that, trying to imagine herself human, as if she wished hard enough, transformation would come. Change flickered in the reflection beyond her shoulder: the badger, a teakettle once more, in silent rejection of all that she was trying to pretend.

TWELVE

Chen, Zhu Irzh and the ghost surfaced in a street that Chen did not immediately recognize. He stood taking deep breaths of comparatively fresh air and glanced around him. His trouser legs were sodden, and clung unpleasantly to his shins. He did not dare look down at his shoes. The street was narrow: the usual welter of machine shops and cafés, all silent under the moon, their facades hidden behind steel shutters. Turning, Chen glimpsed a peaked roof and realized where they were. They were standing at the back of Kuan Yin's second temple, in Xiangfan below the Garden District.

"Well," the demon said softly.

"You came here? Through the temple?" Chen asked, nonplussed. The sudden sensation of betrayal rose in his throat, though he knew perfectly well that the temples were gates between the worlds. The demon gave a fluid shrug.

"It's as good a place as any other. Besides, it's not far from where I live, in my world. What's it to you?"

"Kuan Yin is my patron."

"Mmm." Zhu Irzh murmured in surprise. A flicker of unease crossed his face. *Surely,* Chen thought, *surely the goddess will not let him steal Pearl's soul back to Hell from her own precincts?* The same thought had evidently crossed the demon's mind, too. He adjusted the cuffs of his silk coat with some semblance of embarrassment. Thunder cracked in the distance and heavy drops of rain began to drum on the corrugated iron roofs around them. Zhu Irzh's head snapped back.

"Rain," he said, dismayed. A single droplet fell from the heavens and streaked Zhu Irzh's cheek like a tear. The demon hissed in pain and clapped a hand to his face.

"I suggest we get out of the wet," Chen said, silently thanking the goddess that Zhu Irzh was clearly not of the same storm-loving lineage as Inari. He took the demon's arm and drew him aside. "You want to talk to Pearl, don't you? Well, so do I. And she'll feel safer in the temple."

Ducking beneath an awning, Zhu Irzh said, "Detective Inspector, you know that if it were up to me, I'd be perfectly content for you to put Pearl Tang on the next Celestial boat and that would be that. But I have my orders."

"Who's your superior?"

"Supreme Seneschal Yhu."

"Perhaps if I spoke to him, explained the situation—"

"No!" the demon said hastily. "That is, there are political complications."

"There usually are. Look. It's going to pour in a minute. Let's at least get out of the rain and have a chat with this unfortunate spirit."

Zhu Irzh bolted towards the temple with his coat held over his head. The rain was driving hard now, but at least it had the advantage of cleaning Chen's trousers. The thought of turning up at his goddess' temple reeking of the city sewers had not been an appealing one. As always, the doors were open, symbolizing Kuan Yin's permanent openness to those who suffered. No one was about, save for a large and melancholy frog sitting in the middle of the courtyard. Chen led the ghost to the main temple and opened the door.

Inside, the temple was silent. Two guardian spirits, represented in stone, stood by the entrance. Chen lit a taper and their faces flared into sudden nightmare prominence. The ghost gave a small, muffled cry. Chen found three kneeling-mats and sat down on one of them.

"Now," he said, as gently as he could, to the ghost. "Do you understand what I'm saying?" The ghost stared at him in silent incomprehension. "Can you understand me? Can you speak?"

"It might be a language problem," Zhu Irzh suggested. "Sometimes they lose the language of life after they've crossed over. You speak Gweilin, don't you, Chen?"

"It's a possibility she might have lost her Cantonese. That's usually a result of death caused from head injury, isn't it? Well, we'll try."

He repeated his questions in Gweilin and a spark of understanding appeared in the ghost's white eyes.

"Can you tell me anything at all?" Chen said.

The demon leaned across and said in fluent, rasping Gweilin, "Listen, Pearl. You're dead, okay? Either your dad had you murdered or did it himself. Then he arranged for you to be sent to Hell, but brought you back again. Why?"

The ghost gaped at him. Chen snapped, "Don't you think she's suffered enough?"

Zhu Irzh spread his hands. "She'll have to face facts sooner or later."

In a high, wondering voice the ghost said, "He killed me because I found out about the others. He had them killed, too, because the *Xi Guan* told him to."

Chen frowned. "What's the *Xi Guan?*"

"I don't know."

"No use looking at me," Zhu Irzh said, in response to Chen's questioning glance. "It's just a title. It means 'The Pre-Eminent.'"

"Where did you hear the word?" Chen asked the ghost.

"My dad." She twisted her hands. "I knew a lot about what my dad was doing. I used to go through his stuff in the study when he was out and no one was around. I knew he signed a bargain with the Ministry of Wealth, long ago, and that's why we were rich. But lately, over the last year or so, he started to get angry. His investments weren't doing so well—he hadn't put any money into bioweb technology because he thought it was a fad, but then it got really popular and he kept saying the Ministry of Wealth had cheated him, they should have told him, and he was going to look for someone else to help him. Then one night, very late, a man came to the house. I—I'd gone out, by myself, to see someone—I was coming back through my bedroom window when I saw the man. I couldn't see him very clearly, he was wearing a hood, but he stank. He smelled like something that had gone rotten, and he moved in a funny way. I didn't stick around, I went back into my bedroom. After that, things got a bit better and dad seemed to calm down. But then—then all my friends started dying, we all had problems—they said it was anorexia. And I just got depressed. And one night I got so hungry I couldn't stand it. I went downstairs to the kitchen. Dad was in his study, on the phone. He sounded tense, like he did when he was pretending not to be angry. He said, 'I've done everything the *Xi Guan* asked me to do. Do you realize the danger I've put myself in over these deaths? Seven virgin souls for your experiments—that's what the *Xi Guan* wanted and that's what you got. I've kept my part of the bargain. Now it's your turn.'

"He hung up and he was coming out of the room, so I turned to run, but I—I hadn't eaten anything that day, and I caught my foot on the rug and fell. He grabbed me just as I was getting up. 'What did you hear?' he shouted. 'What did you hear?' I told him I hadn't heard anything, but he knew I was lying. He pulled me up by my nightdress and took me into the study. He took something out of the desk—I don't know what it was. It moved. It was like a lump of flesh, a big shrimp. And he forced it into my mouth—" the ghost's voice wavered "—so that I couldn't speak or breathe properly, and then he made me go back upstairs. He made me lie down on the bed and then he just—he just sat there, looking at me. Watching me choke. And he kept saying something—a name, I don't remember, and something came through the wall and stood by the bed. The back of my head hurt and it got worse and then... And then the person by the bed leaned over me, and I heard my father say, 'Why is this so important?' and the person was saying something, and all at once I knew why my father was doing these things, but it was too late."

Chen was watching her closely. He said, "And why was it so important, Pearl? What was he doing?"

Pearl's spectral face creased in concentration, but then she said, "It's no use. It's gone. I can't remember. I'm sorry."

"All right. What happened then?"

"It was at the funeral, I think—I could see my mother. I tried to talk to her, to tell them what he'd done, but no one could see me. It was as though they were all behind glass. And then it all went blank and the next thing I remember is someone putting me on a boat. Next thing I knew, I was in Hell. They put me in the brothel with the other girls, we saw clients... and one of them worked for the Ministry of Wealth. I thought, if the First Lord knew that my dad had betrayed him, he might help me, so I got the client to take a message to him." Her shadowy face showed sudden determination, and for the first time, Chen realized how this dead girl had managed to overcome at least some of the sorry circumstances of her life and death. He leaned across and patted the air above the ghost's knee.

"Pearl, I can't give you back your life. But I can make sure that you go where you belong. We'll see if we can get you on the next ship to Heaven."

"Hang on a minute," Zhu Irzh said.

Chen glared at him. "I fail to see what possible use she'll be to you, Seneschal. She was sent to Hell in the first place to keep her quiet. And Heaven won't let sleeping spirits lie. She'll have to go to the right place sooner or later."

"I have my instructions," the demon said stubbornly. "I was told to find her, and bring her back." He lowered his voice. "She has information, Chen. You heard her—she knows something about whatever's going on. My employer wants to see her. I was told to bring her back."

"You don't really want to do this, Zhu Irzh."

"Are you accusing me of having *principles*?" the demon said, outraged. Chen did not see the demon move, but the unwavering tip of the katana was suddenly at Chen's throat. Zhu Irzh took a gliding step forward; Chen backed away until he was up against the wall. He stared along the black blade, to meet the demon's golden eyes.

"This is a gateway," Zhu Irzh said. "As you very well know. I can return to my own world from here. I have license to be here. Besides, your goddess may not be happy with you bringing stray spirits to her door like lost dogs. She might prefer you to sort out your problems by yourself."

This was uncomfortably close to the bone. Chen risked a glance at the little statue of the goddess that stood upon the altar, and saw a cold and motionless piece of stone.

"So," the demon purred, following his gaze. "That's the trouble with Heaven: the only thing it ever rewards is impeccability, and so few of us are capable of *that*, aren't we?"

"You're not taking Pearl Tang back to Hell," Chen said.

"Try and stop me," the demon replied. He raised a hand. The door blew open. Around them, the room began to blur. Red, gritty dust whirled into the room. The two guardian statues turned. Zhu Irzh, momentarily distracted, let the blade waver. Chen snatched the rosary from his pocket and began to chant the Water Sutra: calling on the powers of rain and storm and wind. The guardians creaked back into place and the door slammed shut. The demon shrugged, and once more raised a hand.

"Before you do anything further," Chen said, "and we start shuttling between the worlds like a yoyo, I think I should point something out."

"Oh? What?"

"Look around you," Chen said. Warily, with the katana still at Chen's throat, the demon glanced quickly over his shoulder. The ghost was nowhere to be seen. An expression of baffled dismay crossed Zhu Irzh's face. He performed a swift search of the room, while Chen simply stood and watched.

"Where is she?" Zhu Irzh asked at last, dangerously quiet.

"I've no idea."

"You're lying."

"No, I don't lie. Not often, anyway. It gets me into too much trouble with my goddess. It seems the resourceful Pearl Tang has decided to take responsibility for her own future. When you were pinning me like a moth against the wall, she glided out through the door. I didn't get a chance to stop her," he added, disingenuously. The demon swore.

"Then I'll have to find her," he snapped.

"No, *we'll* have to find her. Before her father does."

Leaving the disconsolate demon standing in the temple, Chen made a quick and thorough search of the courtyard, softly calling the ghost's name. But the gates of the temple rattled in the rising wind, and there was no trace of her in the rain-lashed streets beyond. The storm was rising, filling the air with driving rain. The ghost could have gone anywhere. Soaked and weary, Chen eventually gave up and returned to the temple, and there behind the door he found a single trace of the ghost: a spectral fragment of scarf. It lay in cobweb fragility across his fingers; he tucked it into his damp pocket with utmost care. Zhu Irzh sat in a corner, silently sulking and indistinguishable from one of the surrounding statues. Chen sat down and removed his sopping coat, then stared fixedly into the shadows above the altar. With the demon's immobile presence only a few yards away, the last thing Chen intended to do was go to sleep.

THIRTEEN

A miserable Zhu Irzh stood on the porch of the temple and waited for the rain to stop. Above the roofs, a faint gray light shimmered; it would soon be dawn. The demon shivered, then prowled back into the temple. Detective Inspector Chen lay peacefully upon his back on the carpet, head resting on a ceremonial cushion, his mouth open. He snored slightly. The demon gazed down at his adversary and ally. Chen had promised to help him find the ghost, and Zhu Irzh believed him. But although he understood some of the constraints that the goddess must have placed upon her follower, and although he therefore considered it unlikely that Chen would lie to him, it seemed that the policeman had developed a convenient habit of omitting crucial parts of the truth. Zhu Irzh admired this, and even conceded to himself that it made things more interesting, but it was also an additional problem. And there was always the possibility that Chen might try to trap him here; pull some slick trick. The policeman might work closely with Hell at times, but there was no doubt that it was still his enemy. Chen was uncorrupted, and, more importantly, incorruptible: Zhu Irzh knew this as firmly as he knew that Chen was Chinese. The demon sighed in frustration. He could not return to Hell without the ghost of Pearl Tang: failure would not make his life worth living. The First Lord of Banking did not enjoy being thwarted. Yet Chen had the capacity to make things difficult for him here. Once the ghost was located, Zhu Irzh decided, it might be best to dispatch the policeman, to prevent further tangles. A pity. He liked Detective Inspector Chen, but there you were.

His meditations were interrupted by a sound; a quivering of the air like a distant bell. Zhu Irzh glanced up to see a pair of lambent eyes gazing at him from the statue on the altar. As he realized what was happening, the goddess assumed her human form and size, mantling herself in folds of diaphanous air. She stepped from the altar and walked down the aisle towards the demon. He could not look away. Her face was a mask of glacial perfection; her gaze as cold as the bloom on a plum. The look she bestowed upon Zhu Irzh was all the more quelling for being so devoid of expression; the goddess simply stared, as though he was something quite without significance. Her pale robe glittered, as if with frost. With difficulty, Zhu Irzh found his voice, "Ma'am?"

"I caught," the goddess said icily, "a thought of murder."

Zhu Irzh hastened to reassure her. "A hypothesis briefly entertained, nothing more."

"Even so, there was enough intent in your hypothesis to attract my attention. And your kind needs little enough excuse to kill."

"I'm a pragmatist," Zhu Irzh said warily. "Unlike some of my kin, I don't kill without reason."

"Be very careful, demon. I may not always interfere—Heaven runs by its own rules—but I am always watching."

"I'll be mindful of that," the demon said, trying vainly to match her hauteur. Kuan Yin reached out and tapped him lightly and contemptuously on the cheek with her stone-cold hand. Zhu Irzh's head rang like a gong. The world turned around into a nightmare negative. When the hollow pounding inside his head finally stopped, he found that he was on his knees. The goddess had vanished. Chen had raised himself up on his elbows and was staring quizzically at the demon.

"Good morning. What happened to you?"

"Bad dream," the demon said indistinctly. He hauled himself to his feet and leaned against the wall, breathing hard.

"Well," said Chen, eyeing him curiously. "We'd best get started." Zhu Irzh rubbed his eyes, which felt as though someone had sandblasted them.

"Where do you suggest we begin?"

"I need to call the precinct, and I also need to talk to a spirit-sensor, see how we might track down Pearl. Lao's a good choice—he's the police exorcist."

"I know," Zhu Irzh said, grimacing. "I've run into him a couple of times."

"He's good at his job," Chen said with a smile.

"I know that, too. Is it still raining?"

Chen opened the door of the temple and peered out. "No, it's stopped. Looks as though it's going to be a nice day. Not too many people around, either."

"That won't matter. I've taken precautions," Zhu Irzh said, thinking of the mantle of spells that he had invoked to prevent his presence here being too obvious.

Even at this early hour, there were a few people going about their business in the temple courtyard. They glanced up uneasily as Zhu Irzh and Chen walked past; it seemed that no one was a seer, but they could still sense the presence of evil. Zhu Irzh wondered for an idle moment how they saw him:

a dark, glittering vision crossing the corner of the eye. He rather liked that idea; it seemed glamorous.

"Don't worry, you're not very noticeable," Chen said. Zhu Irzh gave him a hurt look, but the policeman ignored it. "Now," Chen said. "I suggest we go first to Lao."

The demon had never taken a taxi before, and found the experience a novel one. The windscreen was hung with all manner of gaudy charms: plastic rosaries, gods and bells and flowers. There was even a little figure on a cheap gilt cross; the dead God of the Christians. None of it was enough to trouble a being of Zhu Irzh's standing, but his skin prickled in fleeting reaction, and then he sneezed. Eyes watering, he watched with interest as they sped through Xiangfan and skirted the Garden District, then turned down into Shaopeng. Morning light glinted from the myriad mirrors that bedecked the facade of the First National Bank. The driver ducked his head and swore, blinded by stray shafts of reflected light. Zhu Irzh was overcome by momentary dizziness. He shook his head from side to side, trying to clear it.

"What's wrong?" Chen said with some concern.

"*Ch'i*. From the *feng shui* mirrors. I do not like these configurations," the demon snapped. His head hummed like a hive.

"Close your eyes," Chen told him. "Put your head between your knees."

In the rearview mirror, Zhu Irzh glimpsed the startled face of the driver, who had just realized that his passenger appeared to be talking to himself. Zhu Irzh leaned forward, intrigued to see that his own face appeared as no more than a fleeting apparition in the mirror, the glitter of an unnatural eye. The taxi swerved towards the curb, sending the charms into a frantic dance.

"What the hell—?" the driver said. Chen reached into his pocket and took out a wallet, which he displayed to the driver.

"Don't let it worry you," Chen said. The driver's face assumed the professionally stony expression of someone who does not want to risk further involvement. He nipped sharply around the back of a tram and accelerated into the Shaopeng traffic.

"What's that?" Zhu Irzh asked, pointing to the object in Chen's hand.

"My badge."

"May I see?"

Chen handed him the wallet. Inside was inscribed the policeman's precinct and rank, the visa stamp which proclaimed his license to enter Hell, and a truly dreadful photograph which made Chen look as though he had recently escaped from a lunatic asylum. The demon suppressed a smile.

"Looks nothing like you," Zhu Irzh said encouragingly. There was a faint, dark miasma around Chen's head, as though the photo had been smudged: the characteristic taint of those who associated too closely with Hell. The taxi veered past the improbable dome of the Pellucid Island Opera House and cut through a maze of back streets, passing go-downs and cyber-shops and market stalls. Zhu Irzh smelled *ghambang* and chowder; caught the tail-end of other people's dreams. A spirit stepped from beneath an awning and yawned, unscrolling a long, pale tongue, then drifted up into the branches of a tree. The taxi turned down a road which no one had bothered to pave; water pooled in the overflowing gutters from last night's storm. Clad in a skimpy kimono, a prostitute sat with her feet balanced on a deck chair, reading a cheap movie magazine. Zhu Irzh could smell sex and fever threading through the air like old musk. He trailed a hand out of the open window of the taxi, enjoying the sudden humid heat. Chen tapped the driver on the shoulder.

"You can drop us off anywhere here."

The demon stepped out onto packed, peaty earth. His boots were soled with iron, but he could still feel the warmth of the world. He turned to Chen. "A protected place?"

Chen nodded. "Lao's. He takes precautions."

They were standing in front of a low house; its windows shuttered. *Bagua* mirrors hung from the eaves, deflecting ill magic and dark *ch'i*. Turning, the demon saw that a hazy azure strip of sea was visible, far away down the hillside. The house faced it; any negativity would be directed down the slope to be swallowed by the cleansing immensity of the South China Sea. Lao's house lay on the edge of the city; behind, Zhu Irzh could see the steep slope of the back territories, shadowy with trees. The hill seemed suddenly to darken. Light struck the distant surface of the water and Zhu Irzh stepped back with the force of being observed. Something was watching from the hillside, something old and implacable and indifferent to humanity's concerns, and even to those of Hell. He thought of dragon energy, coiling under the land. It made him shiver. The door of the house was opening.

"Well, well," said a very chilly voice. "You've outdone yourself this time, Wei Chen."

Five minutes later, Chen and the demon were sitting in Lao's parlor. The exorcist shuffled about, complaining of his bad back and the weather, and made tea.

"My wife's gone shopping, otherwise she'd do it. What do you want?" he asked the demon, summarily. "Green? Black?"

"Do you have any gunpowder oolong?"

"Somewhere," Lao said. He gave Zhu Irzh a look of deep distrust and pottered off in the direction of the kitchen. "Now," he said, when he returned. "You've lost a ghost, is that right?"

"Yes. Pearl Tang."

"The daughter of the woman I saw the other night? That's tricky. Do you know where the mother is now?"

"Her body's still in the departmental morgue. Apparently her spirit's waiting for an exit visa."

"Where's she bound for? Heaven or Hell?"

"I don't know yet."

"Will they let you into the Night Harbor to talk to her?"

"I've applied for temporary entry. I want to speak to Mrs Tang before she leaves the shores of Earth."

"Ask her to stick around," the exorcist said, with a stony glance in the direction of Zhu Irzh. "She can take her daughter with her. When we find her."

"Tell me," the demon said placatingly, in an effort to establish some rapport with this suspicious character, "how easy do you think it will be to find the ghost of the girl?"

"About as easy as finding a needle in a bloody haystack. You must know what this city's like. If we were in Beijing or Shanghai—somewhere ancient, where people understood about the maintenance of proper boundaries between this world and others, it wouldn't be so bad. But the planners had to go and throw this city up any old how, and of course they didn't consult the *feng shui* practitioners. It sometimes seems to me that any *gwei li jin* who pleases can just wander up from Hell and start making a nuisance of itself." He scowled at Zhu Irzh.

"Well, sorry," the demon said. "I know it must be difficult. But not impossible, surely? This ghost is a new ghost; it does not know how to protect itself, it does not know where to hide."

"That does make our task a little easier," the exorcist admitted, grudgingly. "Ghosts are drawn to temples and to séances, for example. We can make a start by ringing round the temples and seeing if any strays have come in overnight."

"You mentioned séances. Can't we simply summon her up?"

"We can try. I imagine that's what her dad will be doing right now."

"Not if I can help it," Chen said. "I phoned from the temple. Sergeant Ma's gone round with a long list of spurious enquiries, which should keep both of them busy."

"Do you have any personal items that she might have used?"

"Indeed," Zhu Irzh said, anxious to help. "We have this."

From the pocket of his coat, Chen took the wisp of scarf that the ghost had left behind at the temple. Now, fading fast in the morning light, it was no more than a shadow across his fingers. Lao sniffed disparagingly.

"I suppose it will have to do."

"If it doesn't, will you help us track her down?"

"With my back in the state it is? You must be joking. I can't walk to the bottom of the garden at the moment without seizing up, let alone traipse all over the city looking for stray spirits."

"I understand that," Chen said. "But I don't really have the nose for ghosts, and neither, it seems, does Zhu Irzh. We'll try a séance."

"We?" Lao asked, with a frosty glance at Zhu Irzh.

"You and I, then."

"Believe me," Zhu Irzh said hastily, "I have great experience with this kind of thing. You stand a far better chance of a successful séance with my help."

"That is as may be," Lao remarked. "However, I also stand a far better chance of losing my soul. I've no intention of undergoing supernatural procedures in your presence."

Zhu Irzh shrugged. "Fair enough." If Lao didn't trust him, he thought, mildly and irrationally hurt, then Lao would just have to do without his assistance. Leaning back in his chair, he closed his eyes and felt himself become as still as stone.

FOURTEEN

After Chen's phone call informing her that he would not be back that night, Inari went back into the bedroom of the houseboat and sat flatly down on the bed. Such dependency on her husband was both foolish and unfair, but it was a hard habit to break. She knew very well that because he had saved her once, it did not mean that he could do so again. She thought back to the sinister figure she had seen on the dock, and to the anxious days of her betrothal in Hell.

She had been affianced to Dao Yi for seventy years, ever since they were children. Although she had never met her fiancé, in keeping with polite custom, she had grown up in the expectation of the marriage, like any typical scion of the underworld bourgeoisie. Her father was wealthy; her mother was beautiful, with only the vestiges of old scandal hanging about her head to sour the marriage. Inari had never known what this scandal was, only that her parents never spoke about it. She learned of it from overhearing fragments of sentences in half-whispers from older cousins:

"It's lucky that Dao Yi doesn't know...if he did, he'd never take her..."

"Explains a lot about her, don't you think? Not really quite the thing..."

"Always been a bit of a peculiar family..."

So from an early age, Inari had grown up with the ominous expectation that some day, something terrible would happen: she and her family would be disgraced, her father summarily dispatched from his solid job in the Ministry of Wealth and sent with his children scurrying at his heels to some lower echelon of Hell. Inari had heard stories about such places: the worlds of ice, the iron lands where souls do not possess bodies but run shrieking from torment to torment. But scandal did not break, and her family was not sent into exile, and at last the day came when Inari was presented to the fiancé to whom she had been engaged for so long.

And it had been the worst moment of her life. From the days of her child-hood she had been hearing stories about Dao Yi: his subtlety; his intelligence; the cruelty which Inari, as demonkind, had been brought up to admire and yet somehow never could. Dao Yi would be different, she told herself, lying to herself with such conviction as only the young can muster; his cruelty was just a front, hiding a heart as gentle as her own. He had a good job, too: he was a well-respected official in the Ministry of Epidemics. Inari had been in love with this illusion for years; she longed to meet him. And when at last that meeting came, she learned what no one had bothered to mention: that her fiancé was a walking hive of disease, his flesh liquid with gangrene and mottled with hemorrhage. She still remembered that moment of revelation: like black lightning through her veins. After a single look, Inari had gathered the skirts of her robe and fled from the room.

Her revulsion was, moreover, all her own fault. Her family was astounded that she found her fiancé so repulsive. Where could she have inherited such fastidiousness from? they asked with mocking irony, darting cold, reptilian glances towards Inari's mother, who sat with her head bowed in the corner of the room. Any demon worthy of a place in Hell would surely have been thrilled rather than revolted. Inari's response was almost as weak and spine-less as a lesser being's would have been...a human, perhaps. And at this Inari's mother let fall a single tear, that lay in her lap like a bright coral coal, and Inari had learned the truth. Her mother's father had not been a demon at all, but a human. A courtier in the house of the Han Emperor, who had one day seen a spirit walking along the shores of an ornamental lake, and been seduced.

"The family's blood is tainted," Inari's mother said, twitching her tail in anguished mortification. "Who knows what weaknesses we have inherited? Your father was good enough to ignore it, but of course we kept it as quiet as we could, for your sake. Dao Yi's mother would never have agreed to the marriage if she'd known."

"Pity she didn't," Inari had replied, weeping hot tears of her own.

Pity indeed. Dao had not taken his rejection lightly. He promptly sued for false engagement, citing Inari's human blood. The judge, an old family friend of the Yi's, was sympathetic. Inari's father lost much of his wealth paying off the promised dowry, her mother lost her looks, and it had only been with the help of her brother Tso that Inari had been able to run away, stumbling through the streets of Hell until she blundered through a door and found herself in the courtyard of the temple of Kuan Yin. And there, she had found someone waiting: Chen Wei.

Now, just over a year later, the sea slapped against the sides of the houseboat, and a single footstep echoed across the deck like a gunshot. Jolted from her humiliating reverie, Inari started, then rose swiftly from the bed and crept to the window, standing a little back, so that she could not easily be seen.

She could hear someone moving across the deck of the boat. The footsteps were stealthy; the person was walking slowly, and with an irregular rhythm. It was this last thing that unnerved Inari: those who knew demons walked thus, because an enemy may be recognized by the pattern of their tread. Inari held her breath. Behind her, under the stove, the teakettle bristled into animal life. There was a tiny movement at the door of the houseboat and Inari's skin prickled. Someone had placed a charm across the lintel. She glided backwards, toward the opposite window, but the stalker was coming around the deck. That left the stairs that led onto the roof. Silently, step by step, Inari climbed the steps to the hatch, and paused. The visitor was still below, moving around the deck, perhaps peering in. As quietly as she could, Inari lifted the hatch and slid out onto the roof. Edging to the side of the roof, she glanced down.

The man was standing with his back to her. She could see the long coat, and the iron-gray hair caught back in a thin ponytail. And then he turned and sprang, all in one quick, rushing movement. He landed beside her. The sword trailed fire as it came down; Inari heard it hiss through the air, but she was no longer there. She was running swiftly backwards, to the far end of the roof. The assassin leaped again, springing the length of the deck. Inari somersaulted backwards and landed lightly on the lower deck.

"Run," the badger whistled behind her. "Inari, *run*—" but she did not. This man was human. She could smell him, and that made her suddenly angry. She might have fled from Hell, she might have spent the past year licking her wounds on the houseboat and relying on Chen to provide for her, but despite her human blood she was still demon enough for instinct to take over under threat. The sword was a blur in the darkness but she twisted beneath it and struck out. Her long claws raked the assassin's shin. He gave a hiss of pain and sprang backwards, out of her reach. Inari rushed forwards in a scuttling crouch, avoiding the lashing blade. The assassin cut down; she leaped up and over the sword, kicking out wildly. The hard sole of her foot connected with the assassin's cheek, and he staggered against the railing. Inari rolled out of reach. She glimpsed a shadow of black and white fur, moving fast. The badger wove between the assassin's ankles and she saw the glint of teeth. The assassin cried out and flailed backwards against the rail. The badger's eyes were red sparks in the darkness, and Inari could trace the passage of both protector and assailant as they went over the rail and down. There was a distant, muffled splash.

Inari ran to the side of the deck and looked over. There was no sign of anything: the water had swallowed them both. Then, far across the harbor, she saw a narrow wake, heading for shore. It was too small for a human being; it swam too swiftly. Inari leaped down from the houseboat, landing on one of the pontoons. Hopping from deck to deck, she made her way to shore. It was only when she got there that she realized that she was bleeding from a shallow cut in her forearm. Her blood hissed and spat as it reached the salt sand. She was, Inari also realized, still wearing her dressing gown. The badger staggered onto the sand and shook itself like a dog. Inari ran across and dropped to her knees to take it in her arms.

"Are you all right? Are you hurt?"

"No," the badger said, sneezing seawater. A paw clawed the side of its nose. "Must go. Must hide."

The urgency in its voice lit Inari's panic like a flame to kindling. She picked up the badger, which sagged in a heavy, wet bundle in her arms, and ran, sprinting down the harbor wall as the rain once more began. She did not dare look back.

FIFTEEN

Forty minutes after the séance had begun, a frustrated Chen was prepared to admit defeat. Lao had prepared the séance with his customary meticulousness. The protective circle had been drawn seven times with a stick of crimson incense, the guardians of the cardinal directions had been summoned, and the room was now thick with the bitter smoke of nineteen herbs, but the dim, dark circle that formed the channel between the worlds was notable principally for the absence of Pearl Tang. This was not to say that it was entirely silent. Other things kept trying to break through: the shadowy, contorted faces of spirits lost in the depths of the city, but Pearl was not among them. Chen glanced uneasily towards the door, wondering whether involving the demon might not have been worth the risk, after all. At least Zhu Irzh was fixed in one spot, always assuming he had not managed to break free of the subtle restraints that Lao had covertly imposed upon him immediately prior to the séance.

"After all," Lao's sardonic voice echoed in Chen's head. *"We don't want him roaming around all over the place, do we?"* The more control they had over Zhu Irzh, Chen reflected, the better he would feel.

"It's too obvious," Lao murmured, energetically wafting the smoke from the brazier. Chen stifled a cough.

"What is?"

"Pearl. Talk about being conspicuous by your absence. It's almost pointed."

"So what does that mean?"

"It means that someone's blocking us. Even if Pearl's spirit is trying to reach us, it can't get through. See that?" He indicated a patch of shadow in the midst of the circle. "See how solid that is? That's a deliberate block, and I can't even tell where it's coming from. But I can guess."

"Pearl's father?"

Lao nodded. "If he's trying to reach her himself, or—worst case scenario—he's done so already, then one of his paramount concerns will be to make sure that no one else succeeds in doing so."

"All right. Then we should abandon this now and go back to Tang's."

Lao rose stiffly and wearily to his feet. "I think you're right. Well, we've failed with the séance, but that doesn't mean there aren't other things we can try... Give me a moment while I close this down."

Chen waited patiently as Lao went through the closing ceremony and the smoke gradually cleared. He held his breath as they stepped through the door into the living room, but Zhu Irzh was exactly where they had left him; sitting as still and silent as an elegant statue. A molten eye opened as Chen appeared.

"No luck?" the demon asked sarcastically. Chen was too relieved to find him still sitting there to resent the tone.

"Nothing. Lao thinks Tang is blocking us."

"I did try to convince you that my simple presence would probably have been an invaluable addition to your efforts," Zhu Irzh said, with gentle reproof. "But you wouldn't have it... So what do we do now?"

"We're going back into Tang's house. There's always the chance that he might have succeeded where we failed."

"Remember that Tang is Pearl's murderer," Zhu Irzh said. "And although even the feeblest ghost will take pains towards revenge if the opportunity presents itself, Pearl's even more terrified of her father now, after what happened last night."

"I'm counting on that to keep her away from him," Chen murmured. "But he might be too powerful for her, especially if he has help... I was hoping Ma might be able to distract him, but it doesn't seem to have worked. I don't suppose your contacts back in your own realm have any idea who Tang might be working with?"

"I've asked around," the demon said evasively, avoiding Chen's eye. "Haven't come up with anything yet, but you never know."

"All right," Chen said. There was no use in pushing Zhu Irzh. "Now, I need to call the precinct."

The voice on the other end of the telephone was crackling and distorted, and it was a moment before Chen realized that it belonged to Sergeant Ma.

"Detective Inspector? Is that you? You're very faint. I've been trying to get through to you. I hung on as long as I could at Tang's, but then his lawyers showed up."

Chen said, "I'm at Exorcist Lao's. I can barely hear you. There's probably too much interference. What is it?"

"Well, there are two things," Ma said, then hesitated.

"Go ahead."

"The first is Tang. He hasn't left his house. I've left a van on watch with infrared; they'll let me know as soon as Tang does anything."

"Good. What's the second thing?"

"I think there may be a problem at your home," Ma said. Chen felt as though the floor had suddenly opened up to reveal the gaping void beneath his feet. He stopped dead.

"What sort of problem?" His voice sounded very distant, as though it spoke from the bottom of a well.

"I think something may have got into your houseboat," Ma said. He lowered his voice, making it doubly difficult for Chen to hear him through the crackling static. "A *you know what*. A demon."

"How do you know that?" Chen said, still in that voice that was not his own.

"The captain thought things might be getting too much for one person to handle on their own," Ma said. "So, yesterday, he called in reinforcements. Someone's come from Beijing. A demon-hunter."

"A *demon-hunter*? Why wasn't I told?"

"The captain says he tried to get hold of you, but he thinks your mobile was switched off." Chen thought back to the previous day, moving through Tang's house with the mobile silenced in his pocket.

"Why didn't he leave me a message on my voicemail? Or send text?"

"He did, but he said it bounced back—there seem to be problems with the whatsit, the bioweb, at the moment. Anyway," Ma continued, "the demon-hunter arrived yesterday evening. We still couldn't reach you, so he went to your houseboat. And apparently he found—someone."

"Oh, goddess," said Chen involuntarily. "Inari."

"Mrs Chen didn't seem to be there," Ma said. "Probably she was out shopping or something." He sounded none too convinced. "There was no sign of her, anyway—just the creature, and some kind of animal."

"What happened?" Chen asked.

"He engaged the—the thing in combat but it threw him in the harbor," Ma said. Chen's eyebrows rose. Inari was demonkind, true, but hardly a warrior.

"Where is this man now?"

"Back here, in the captain's office. I think he'd like a word with you."

Chen sighed. "All right. Put him through."

The voice that greeted him was one of the coldest Chen had ever heard. A single syllable could have iced the South China Sea. "Comrade Chen?"

"Yes. Good morning."

"Good morning, comrade. My name is Citizen No Ro Shi. You must have heard of me. I've rid the capital of over two hundred hostiles over the last twenty years."

"Yes," said Chen with a sinking heart. "Yes, I know who you are."

"You haven't done so badly yourself," No Ro Shi said magnanimously. "I'm looking forward to working with you. But I'm afraid I have black news. You had a visitor last night. It's fortunate that you weren't at home. Ma told you what happened?"

"Yes."

"It's rare for me to be defeated," No Ro Shi said, without a trace of self-satisfaction "But the hostile caught me unawares. It was a female."

"So I gather," Chen said tightly.

"I'm afraid there's no sign of your wife, not yet."

"That's okay. She's at her mother's," Chen said, lying furiously. He'd pay for it later, when the small disruption in the path of Truth reached Kuan Yin, but for now, it was worth it.

"Reassuring news," No Ro Shi said, with apparently genuine relief. "What a fortunate thing, that she should have been absent from home. She would almost certainly have been slain."

"I'll tell her to stay where she is for now," Chen said hastily. "Just in case the thing comes back. Do you have any idea where it went?" As he spoke an unwelcome vision of Inari's photograph, which customarily sat on Chen's desk, floated into mind. In the picture, Inari was almost unrecognizable behind hat and sunglasses, but No Ro Shi was a suspicious and competent professional. Chen would just have to hope for the best.

"I knew you'd want to get straight on the case," No Ro Shi was saying. "I haven't been able to trace the hostile, but I'm making it a priority."

"Look," Chen said. "I'm right in the middle of an investigation at the moment, so I can't come back to the precinct just now. Can we meet up later?"

"No problem. Anything I can help with?"

"No, I'll explain when I see you."

"I'll get on with finding the intruder then," No Ro Shi said. "See you later, comrade."

"Listen," Chen said, thinking quickly. "Don't worry about me. If Hell's sent someone after me, I must be on the right track. Right now, my main concern is Tang. I want someone close to that house, keeping an eye on him. He's a dangerous man, and a prime suspect."

There was a short, considering silence on the other end of the phone, then No Ro Shi said, "I commend your professionalism. It's rare to find someone these days who puts their duty to the State above their personal feelings. I'll get over there. Where will you be?"

"I'll get over to Tang's as soon as I can. Right now, I need to try and track down a ghost. I'll meet you later." He waited for No Ro Shi's assent, then slammed the phone back in his pocket and swore. Zhu Irzh uncoiled himself from the sofa and strolled across.

"Problems?"

"Yes." Chen said curtly. He felt as though the force of the Tao was pulling him in opposite directions. If he didn't find Pearl Tang's ghost soon, then he was fairly sure that her father would: this was presumably why Tang had not left the premises. Chen imagined the industrialist, still wearing his Armani suit, hunched over his occult preparations in the cellar. But on the other side from duty lay Inari, hunted and afraid, somewhere out in a city where the very ground burned her feet as she ran. Chen studied Zhu Irzh's enquiring face and wondered just how far he could trust the demon. The answer was almost certainly not at all. If he abandoned duty and went after Inari, the goddess' wrath would know no bounds, but if anything happened to his illicit demon love, he'd never be able to live with himself. Apprehension of what Kuan Yin might do formed only a small part of the equation, however: he would not live in fear of the gods, however threatening they may be. Inari could at least look after herself to some degree (here, he thought of his wife precipitating Beijing's foremost demon-hunter into the oily waters of the harbor and gave an involuntary smile), whereas the ghost could not. Pearl would have to come first. Lao was watching him closely.

"Is everything all right?"

"Not entirely. Can I have a word with you?" Pulling Lao into the hallway, he shut the door. "There's no way you can keep Zhu Irzh here, can you?"

"Certainly not. I don't want your hellish friend lounging about in my house."

"Look," Chen said, trying not to sound too impatient. "I've just found out that a man named No Ro Shi is here, from Beijing. The demon-hunter."

"*No Ro Shi* is here? Why?"

"He was drafted to help me, ironically enough."

"What about Zhu Irzh? What about your wife?" Lao said, aghast.

"Precisely. It's a bit of a problem. I have to try and work round the demon-hunter; that's why I need your help."

"Gods know I've got enough grudges against Hell, and usually I'm grateful for any support we can get, but No Ro Shi's a nutter," Lao said. "He's somewhere to the left of Chairman Mao. He's got an ideological axe to grind against any manifestation of the supernatural."

"Thanks for the reassurance," Chen said. "What about Zhu Irzh?"

"There's nothing I can do, not long term. I can keep him here for a couple of hours, like we did this morning, but eventually the restraints will wear off and he'll be free. And I don't honestly know how long I could hold him if he really put his mind to breaking out. He's hanging around because he needs our help, not because we're making him."

"This is getting complicated," Chen lamented. "I obviously don't trust Zhu Irzh, and now I've got a demon-hunter to keep off my back. Zhu Irzh and I just happen to have ended up together—this isn't some kind of formal inter-departmental arrangement. It's entirely fortuitous, and as such, it's likely to be frowned upon. I don't want to risk taking him to Tang's while No Ro Shi is there, and I don't want to leave him on his own in case he succeeds in finding the ghost and snatches her back to Hell. And I can hardly take him home, because No Ro Shi's sniffing around and I can't reach Inari."

"See if you can track down the ghost. It's likely she won't be that far from Tang's; after a while in the world, they're drawn back to the vicinity of their death, unless someone gets hold of them through séance. My advice is to head for Tang's anyway and tell Zhu Irzh to keep his head down. Anyway," Lao added, with a glance at the closed door, "does it really matter if the demon-hunter does us all a favor and takes out the Seneschal?"

Chen sighed. "I don't like being a party to murder. That's what No Ro Shi does, you know. He can kill a demon's presiding spirit—what passes for its soul. He doesn't just dispatch them back to Hell—he can fling them off the Wheel itself. I'm not sure I want that to happen even to Zhu Irzh."

"He's the *enemy*, Chen."

"Nevertheless," Chen said firmly, and went back into the living room.

"Is everything all right?" the demon asked.

"Fine," Chen said abruptly. He did not want to embark on lengthy explanations in front of the demon, although it was worth any money that Zhu Irzh already knew about Inari. "Lao—can we borrow your *tian h'ei?*"

"I suppose so," Lao sighed. "As long as you bring it back in one piece. It'll need something that belonged to the dead girl."

"The only thing I've got is a spectral scarf," Chen said, as Lao shuffled from the room. "It'll have to do."

"You're borrowing his *what?*" the demon asked.

"Surely you've come across them? It's a creature. A ghost-tracker."

"Oh, a *rhu xhur*, in Gweilin. Yes, of course I know what they are; they're as common as rats."

He glanced up as Lao came back into the room, the ghost-tracker in his arms. Zhu Irzh regarded the small, squat, lobster-like thing with some distaste, which appeared to be mutual. The ghost-tracker hunched its bony carapace and rotated its antennae.

"I'll put him on his lead," Lao said. He placed the unappealing beast on the floor and carefully attached a long leather strap to its collar. Claws rattled and snapped.

"You can take charge of it," Zhu Irzh said fastidiously to Chen. Lao seemed surprised.

"Don't you like them?"

"I don't like vermin."

"Vermin!" the exorcist said, outraged. "You're a fine one to talk!"

"What did you say?"

"Gentlemen, please," Chen said, and there was something in his tone which made Zhu Irzh, as well as Lao, fall silent. "We're not here to trade insults."

"I have been a model of exemplary politeness," Zhu Irzh retorted.

The exorcist gave a snort of contempt. "White words; black heart."

The demon gave an icy bow in the direction of the exorcist, turned on his heel and stalked from the room. Behind him, claws rustled on the parquet floor of the parlor as Chen and the ghost-tracker followed.

Down in Shaopeng, Zhu Irzh hurried alongside Chen, occasionally peering with interest into shop windows and smiling with invisibly voracious benevolence at small children. Chen made a foray into the traffic to flag down a taxi, but even though he displayed his badge, three shot past without stopping. The ghost-tracker scuttled along, casting about itself with its long whiskers. Its claws clicked on the pavement. Passers-by took one look at Detective Inspector Chen hastening down the road with a lobster on a string, like one of the more eccentric French surrealists, and gave him a very wide berth. Of course, thought Chen, mortified, it had to be the main street of the entire city; it couldn't have been somewhere unobtrusive and quiet. His bitter musings were interrupted by the sudden warble of his mobile. Chen fished it out of his pocket, almost dropping it in his haste.

"Yes?"

"Is that American Express? I'd like to report a stolen credit card."

"No, I'm afraid it isn't. This is a private cell phone."

"Are you sure? This is the third time I've got the wrong number," the person on the other end of the line complained. "I don't know what's wrong with the system today, I thought all this new technology was supposed to make things better, but if you ask me—"

Shrugging in irritation, Chen cut the caller off. He'd hoped it was Inari who still had not responded to any of the calls that he had made over the course of the morning. All he had got was his own voice on the answer phone. The ghost-tracker was tugging at the leash. A man in an expensive, cowl-collared jacket gave it a horrified glance and crossed the road. Cursing, Chen dodged once more into the mass of cars and this time a taxi swerved towards the curb. Bundling Zhu Irzh and the ghost-tracker inside, Chen said, "The Garden District. And quickly."

SIXTEEN

Tsin Tsi, First Lord of Banking, lifted the skirts of his heavy robe to climb the verandah steps; no wonder he was hot, he thought. He sank onto the verandah seat with a sigh and, taking up a bone fan, beat the steaming air energetically. This produced a minimal effect, but then the phone rang and the First Lord of Banking put down the fan and picked up the receiver.

"Good afternoon."

"This is Taigun. You asked me to report when I had concrete information."

The First Lord of Banking leaned forward, fixing his rapacious gaze on the photograph that lay upon his desk.

"You have something?"

"I believe so. I've been making enquiries port-side. There are rumors, My Lord. Of the ghost-trade. And also of a new and remarkable drug, which is still in the alchemical stages of its making."

The First Lord of Banking frowned. "What sort of drug?"

"A drug that gives dreams."

With a snort, the First Lord of Banking said, "They all do that."

"Not dreams of Heaven, My Lord. Not dreams of everything that is forbidden to us, from which we are eternally barred. Not dreams that are *real*. This drug—or so the rumors say—can take a person to Paradise."

The First Lord of Banking drummed his lacquered talons idly on the polished bone of the table and said, "How much faith do you place in such rumors, Taigun?"

"I have met one who claims to have experienced it."

Softly, the First Lord of Banking said, "And what if he lies?"

"I do not think he does. I can be very persuasive, Lord. That is why you hired me."

"True. Very well. This needs reflection. I have been handed a broken puzzle, Taigun, and I need to work out how to mend it... Who is producing this drug? Do you know?"

"I do not. But rumor also says that it is someone who is very highly placed, who can command immense resources and take much to which we are not entitled. Including the souls of the virtuous."

"Innocent souls? To make a drug? An ambitious plan, and one that would require alchemy of the highest order. We are talking about metaphysical transformation, Taigun. And that requires the mandate of the Imperial Court."

There was a short, tense silence before Taigun said, "Is there any news from the world of the living?"

"None yet." The First Lord of Banking frowned again. "I have had no word from Seneschal Zhu, yet he has now been gone for some time. Zhu Irzh is young, and easily distracted. I think a reminder of his responsibilities might be in order."

"Shall I see to it?"

"No. I'll handle it myself."

Something was causing the back of his neck to prickle and itch. Turning, the First Lord of Banking saw his First Wife glaring at him with a gaze like molten brass. Guiltily, he remembered promising her that he'd go to the opera with her that night. He gave her what he hoped was a reassuring smile. The frown intensified. With a sinking heart, the First Lord of Banking realized that First Wife was already dressed to go out. She was wearing a loud red paneled gown, embroidered with opium poppies, and her hair was arranged on a lattice of gilded wire. Her doe eyes, angry now, were artfully outlined with kohl. Silently, she mouthed, "Hurry up!"

The First Lord of Banking covered the mouth of the receiver for a moment. "I'll be quick," he said placatingly.

"The performance starts in an hour!"

"Call me when you have more to tell me," the First Lord of Banking said hastily into the receiver, and hung up. "There!" he remarked in triumph to the glowering Lady Tsi.

"About time," First Wife replied, sour as a pickled plum.

The First Lord of Banking was not looking forward to the opera, a lot of wailing and hooting if you asked his opinion, but he supposed it was important to attend, show support for the arts and all that. He let his wife lead him to the dressing room and fuss about his clothes, keeping up a running commentary as she did so:

"....can't see why you *insist* on wearing that dreadful old hat..."

"Only around the house!" the First Lord of Banking protested. He clapped one hand to the ancient, beloved skullcap. First Wife muttered something dark that he did not hear, and he submitted to her ministrations. At last, clad in a dignified brocade robe, he made his way downstairs to be transported to the opera. Outside the comparative coolness of the house, a wall of warmth hit them. First Wife smiled. She liked the heat. The First Lord of Banking sighed.

Hell's version of the Pellucid Island Opera House was crowded. The First Lord of Banking and his wife made their way slowly through the throng, greeting other eminent citizens of the underworld. A person clad in a long, formal robe of human skin, the tiny veins like delicate traces of embroidery, turned to greet the First Lord.

"Lord..." He managed to make Tsin Tsi's title sound like the last word in irony. The First Lord of Banking looked into the round, puffed face, like a soft mass of dough, and smiled in return.

"Minister. *What* a surprise."

The Minister's eyes were like drops of blood in the surrounding flesh, and quite without expression. The First Lord of Banking continued, "So how are things in Epidemics these days? I hear great things about this new form of bird flu. But I see they've found a remedy for that autoimmune disease of yours. Bad luck, eh? Still, you had a good run for your money with that one."

"It is the way of things," the Minister of Epidemics said, in a voice that sounded like oil bubbling up in his throat. "Each illness has its season." He reached up to brush a few flakes of skin fastidiously from the collar of his robe, which was lined with fine, blonde fur. The First Lord of Banking wondered enviously where the Minister had managed to obtain the skin of a European, but doubtless he could afford such expensive fashions. Tsin Tsi remembered his American carp and rose a little in his own estimation.

"You seem to be producing more and more diseases. I'm surprised Heaven does not act."

The Minister of Epidemics gave a soft snort. "It's in Heaven's interest not to interfere. Otherwise the world would be wholly overrun. Humans breed, you know. Like vermin." He shuddered, and his fleshy mouth pursed in disapproval. "Our services are valuable ones. Although the Ministry of War doesn't do so badly, I suppose. Yet I like to think we're more reliable on a long-term basis."

"And I suppose your activities do provide the Celestials with a multitude of innocent souls," the First Lord of Banking mused. The Minister of Epidemics stared at him, unblinkingly, for a moment, and to his eternal shame the First Lord found his own unnatural flesh crawling beneath the demon lord's regard. The Minister of Epidemics said softly, "You'd do well not to challenge me, Tsin Tsi. I know you have your own area of influence, but I do not think you want to discover the true length of my arm." He spoke indifferently, as though commenting on nothing more important than the weather, and then he turned his back on the First Lord of Banking and strode away.

"What was all that about?" First Wife asked, bewildered, and the First Lord replied, equally baffled, "I have no idea."

SEVENTEEN

"Detective?" It was the hesitant voice of Sergeant Ma. "At last! I've been trying to reach you, but the communications system—"

"—is not working properly. I noticed." Chen closed the taxi window to shut out the roar of the traffic as they shot along Shaopeng.

"Detective, something's happening at Tang's place."

With a distinct sense of déjà vu, Chen said, "What?"

"We don't really know." Ma sounded both bemused and afraid. "No Ro Shi says he's never seen anything like it."

"All right," Chen informed him wearily. "I'm on my way."

He hung up, saying to the demon, "Something's happening at Tang's. We might have a problem, by the way—I didn't mention it before. A demon-hunter from Beijing's appeared on the scene. Name of No Ro Shi."

"*No Ro Shi?*" Zhu Irzh's head whipped round. "No Ro Shi's here?"

"Apparently so."

"What an unexpected pleasure," the demon said. The tip of his dark tongue snaked out, flickering momentarily over his lower lip. "I haven't seen *him* for a while."

"You had a run-in with him?" Chen asked. The demon shot him an oblique glance.

"You could say that."

Chen rubbed a distracted hand across his forehead. "That might complicate matters. He's a heavy character."

"I'm not afraid of No Ro Shi," the demon said, bridling.

"I didn't suggest that you were. We need to decide how to handle him, though."

The demon gave a fluid shrug. "My task is still the same: to find Pearl and take her back to Hell. If No Ro Shi gets in my way, too bad for him."

"Look," Chen said firmly. "Let me make one thing clear. No Ro Shi's off limits. If you do anything to him, we'll have every authority in Beijing on our backs and it'll be far more trouble than it's worth—for you, not me. People will be prepared to pull strings in Hell on No Ro Shi's behalf."

"He has protection," the demon said in disgust. "So I've heard. But if some accident should befall him…"

"Make sure it doesn't," Chen said. He tapped on the glass screen that separated them from the driver and motioned to the stream of traffic ahead. "The Garden District. And quickly."

EIGHTEEN

A young couple was strolling across the sand. Their heads were close together, and the girl began to laugh, helplessly. Breaking away, she ran down the beach until she was lost in the glare at the edge of the sea. Inari, watching them from her perch high in the rafters of the pier, sighed enviously. She had never been so free from care, not even in the more recent days of her marriage when she had at last made a tentative attempt to find her own freedoms. Humans seemed to think that her kind were so powerful, that they could do whatever they chose and take whatever they wanted, but when you were locked into the rigid and ritual hierarchies of Hell, you realized that this simply wasn't so. Inari leaned back against the dank, weed-strewn struts of the pier. The badger-teakettle, which had remained vigilantly in its animal form, lay fast asleep in a damp bundle in her lap. For the thousandth time, Inari tried to decide what to do. She knew that her husband would be worried about her, but she could not go home in case the assassin was still there, and she did not want to get Chen into further trouble. Moreover, the *feng shui* tides of the city made her feel small and threatened, and the ground would burn her feet if she spent too long walking around. The day seemed too huge and too bright, but the sun was already past its height and beginning to sink through the haze. She would wait until twilight, a more comfortable time for her, and then perhaps she would venture out and try to find money to call Chen, or maybe even steal a phone. In her flight from the houseboat, she had taken nothing with her, and now she cursed her own panic. Even under the circumstances, she should have tried to think ahead. The badger stirred in her lap. The young couple was out of sight along the sand. Inari gazed like an owl into the distance, waiting for night.

NINETEEN

The taxi slowed to a halt at the end of the road where Tang's mansion stood, and Chen leaped out, throwing a handful of change at the driver. With a growing sense of unease he saw that the street had been cordoned off. Two of the department's new anti-riot vehicles were parked at the entrance to the road and a mesh of nanowire had been erected to form an impenetrable barrier. As Chen drew near, a white-faced SWAT officer leaped down from one of the vehicles and began motioning him frantically back.

"Go back, go back! The road's closed!"

Chen flashed his badge and saw the officer's eyes widen in comprehension.

"Sorry, sir, I didn't realize—go on through."

Pausing to check that the flickering form of the demon was still at his shoulder, Chen went down the street at a run. As he drew closer to the mansion he saw that the bulky figure of Sergeant Ma was standing in full view out in the road. Ma was surrounded by uniformed police, a fire engine, and the surveillance van, and as Chen watched, a tall figure strode out into the light. Chen could see the hilt of a ritual sword hanging from the man's back: this, then, must be No Ro Shi, the demon-hunter.

"What's all the fuss?" Zhu Irzh's puzzled voice said in his ear.

"I've no idea." But clasped in Chen's arms, the ghost-tracker gave a rattle of alarm and struggled to be free. Chen dropped it, none too gently, upon the pavement, and it tore the lead out of his hand and disappeared into the bushes. Chen swore.

"Never mind," Zhu Irzh said. "We're better off without it, if you ask me."

There was a cry of recognition as Sergeant Ma spotted Chen. Panting, the sergeant hastened up and began a long, garbled explanation that made no sense whatsoever.

"Sergeant, calm down. I can't understand a word you're saying."

Taking a deep breath, Ma managed to utter a single intelligible word. "Look."

Chen glanced towards the mansion and with an increasing sense of incredulity saw that it was no longer there. Where Tang's pompous, nouveau riche house had stood was nothing more than a whirling cloud of darkness, shot with neon. Chen's stomach churned; Ma's unusual pallor was suddenly explained.

"Ma, what the hell?"

Before Ma could open his mouth, Chen found his hand grasped in an iron grip and a voice barked, "Comrade Chen!"

Chen looked up into a storm-dark gaze. He had never met demon-hunter No Ro Shi before now, but he had seen him plenty of times on documentaries and the news, and No Ro Shi's austere features were frequently plastered over the pages of the Beijing press. Chen's horror at the demon-hunter's presence was slightly softened by admiration: No Ro Shi refused to give way to the cult of celebrity (recognizing, perhaps, that this was in itself a secure pathway to Hell) and apparently eschewed a personal life. His job was all-consuming, from what Chen had heard, and doubtless he would be assured of a prominent position in the hereafter, always assuming that he didn't slip up first. A position of which Chen himself might have been assured, before his marriage; there had been plenty of subsequent nights on which he had lain awake, wondering precisely what the gods had in store after his death. As long as he stayed with Inari, he told himself over and over again, he did not greatly care. He risked a second glance at the phenomenon that had been Tang's house.

"Remarkable," he said as calmly as he could. "Perhaps you'd like to bring me up to speed on what's been going on, Mr—that is to say, Comrade—Shi."

"There's been a surveillance team at the residence since early this morning, as you're aware. I've been watching Tang myself through the infrared; there was relatively little movement until an hour or so ago. He stayed in his study; we've been logging his e-mails. At 1:25 P.M. the scanners showed evidence of hostile activity: increased s/r levels and biomorphic patterning systematic of an incursion from another realm. Tang appeared agitated, seemed to be attempting communication with something unseen. We're analyzing the voice-vibrations now. At 1:48 levels rose and there appeared to be some kind of implosion within the house, centering on Tang's study. The house began to fragment. As you can see, it is still doing so."

"We think Tang was trying to recapture his daughter's spirit," Chen said. "Perhaps he over-reached himself."

"It's a possibility. However, it is also a possibility that one of his associates has decided that the price of failure is termination."

"You're suggesting that Tang's been assassinated? That's quite probable."

No Ro Shi's moustache bristled with satisfaction. "Hostiles rarely tolerate failure. Tang was becoming a liability. He bungled his daughter's illicit passage to Hell and attracted the attention of both the police and the Celestial authorities. You say he was trying to recapture his daughter's spirit? I wasn't aware that it was missing."

Chen gave a brief account of recent events, omitting for now any mention of the demon. He gave an idle glance around him as he spoke, but there was no sign of Zhu Irzh. Chen did not know whether to be relieved that Zhu Irzh had managed to avoid No Ro Shi's attention or alarmed that the demon was no longer in view. His narrative was interrupted by a sudden, soundless explosion in the direction of the house, and a violent shove in the small of his back as someone knocked him to the ground. The shockwave flattened him against the tarmac and a great blast of heat passed overhead. The air itself changed: he was spread-eagled fleetingly in the midst of a spinning cloud of darkness, and then it passed. Spitting dust, Chen raised his head.

Nothing remained of Tang's mansion; not even a smoldering hole in the ground. Instead, a garden was blooming. Roses with soft, ebony petals and thorns as curled as a mandarin's fingernails entwined themselves around the shadowy branches of vines, hung with grapes the color of night. The crimson tongue of a great dark orchid flickered out to catch an unwary cockchafer, humming over black grass. There was a heavy, soporific odor of incense and opium and old honey. It was, Chen silently admitted to himself, something of an improvement upon Tang's vulgar mansion. A hand grasped him by the wrist and hauled him to his feet. No Ro Shi spoke into a voice recorder.

"Termination of direct hostile activity; placement of incursion, 2:33 P.M." His voice echoed through a silence that seemed to fill the whole of the world.

TWENTY

Seneschal Zhu Irzh, after a wild glance around him, realized to his alarm and annoyance that he was back in Hell. He was standing in some kind of parlor; elegantly decorated with lacquer and ivory to give a subtle impression of human flesh. Two spindly chairs were covered with delicate, creamy skin and a massive desk bore the striations of bone. A great deal of money and influence had gone into decorating this room; it was designed to impress, but Zhu Irzh merely felt his irritation growing. He glared at the red lacquered walls and the ornate furnishings, wondering exactly where he might be, but the answer to that question came almost immediately, as the door opened and the First Lord of Banking stepped imperiously through. Angry though he was, Zhu Irzh managed to deliver an appropriately low bow.

"Seneschal? Forgive the interruption of your duties." The First Lord of Banking spoke indifferently, with nothing more than a nod to politesse. "I thought it expedient to bring you back while there was an opening between the worlds."

"Of course, Lord. May I know why I have been summoned?"

"The situation has changed somewhat since our earlier conversation. I told you to find the ghost of Pearl Tang. Clearly, you have failed."

"Lord, I succeeded in finding her, but then events took a rather different turn—I—"

Tsin Tsi dismissed his complaints with a wave of a taloned hand. "No matter. Something is going on, Zhu Irzh. Something to which the Ministry of Wealth is not privy. I need you here. I am telling you this in honesty, no matter that it causes me to lose face. I do not know what this issue might be, only that it involves a Ministry. And I believe now that this Ministry is that of Epidemics."

"Epidemics?" Zhu Irzh said, frowning. When had he last had a conversation

96

about Ministries? Then he remembered. "The girl," he said.

"What about her?" Tsin Tsi's crimson eyes were as bright as fire.

"When I went to the brothel, Pearl was not to be found, but another—a ghost—told me that certain people had come from one of the Ministries, looking for human ghosts."

"Epidemics," mused the First Lord of Banking. "And the souls of virtuous humans. Rumors of a new drug..." He sat down in the heavy bone chair that stood behind his desk and picked up a little round box made of ivory and wood. Zhu Irzh recognized it as a child's toy, a puzzle for infants. "I can't make the pieces fit," the First Lord murmured, turning the box in his hands. "An illegal trade in the ghosts of the virtuous, the Ministry of Epidemics, and now the kidnapping of a human ghost-trader..." He glanced up and gave a raw smile. "That's why I had you brought back, you see. Someone's taken it upon themselves to remove Tang H'suen to more congenial climes before he could be interrogated. Such as Hell."

"Tang's here?"

"So I believe. You saw what they did to his house?"

"Yes, I was there. The police think he's been killed."

"I don't think so. One of my employees has been watching the house. If Tang had died, his soul would have been compelled to travel by the usual means through the Night Harbor, where you or the police might have been able to track him down, but Taigun—my employee—is a soul-smeller and he detected no sign of death. No, Tang has been taken to Hell alive."

"But by whom?"

"That is an interesting question, and I am counting on you to provide an answer to it. By someone very powerful, who will stop at nothing. To snatch Tang's house, with him inside it—that takes power, Zhu Irzh. The kind of power enjoyed by the Minister of Epidemics, among others. It is also a reckless, visible thing to do that suggests someone is playing for high stakes."

"What about the girl? Tang's daughter?"

"It is highly improbable that she knows more than her father," the First Lord said. "From now on, he must be our priority."

"The policeman," Zhu Irzh said. "Detective Chen. He's also interested in hunting down the girl."

"How useful. What is that Western expression? Killing two birds with one stone? If he finds Pearl, then we can catch up with him later, and in any case it may serve to distract him from Tang's disappearance."

"I doubt it. He's quite tenacious."

"Then we'll just have to find Tang first, won't we? I don't approve of human intervention in Hell's affairs; the living can get above themselves on occasion."

"So what do you want me to do now?" asked Zhu Irzh. The First Lord of

Banking spread his hands flat on the table top and smiled.

"Go to the Ministry of Epidemics. I suspect they are the folks who have taken Tang. See what you can find. But be very discreet. You don't want to come down with something nasty, after all."

TWENTY-ONE

The sinister garden that now stood in the place of Tang's house had been sealed off, and a team of exorcists, under the grumbling supervision of Lao, had been moved in to secure the area. Chen made a hasty, covert search for the demon but found nothing. Evidently Zhu Irzh had taken the disturbance as an opportunity to go off on his own pursuits. Nor was there any sign of the ghost-tracker. Chen was about to return to the houseboat when Ma appeared, still pale, and bearing orders from Captain Sung that Chen was to report back immediately. Chafing with annoyance, and certain that any chance he might have had of locating Pearl Tang had been blown, Chen went back to the precinct with Ma and the demon-hunter.

The covert glances darting in his direction in the back of the SWAT vehicle uncomfortably reminded Chen that he had not changed his clothes since the previous day, and there had been the intervening sojourn in the sewers... Using this as his excuse, Chen made a brief detour to the men's locker room and phoned home, but there was still no answer. Frustrated, Chen took a hasty but thorough shower and fished out a spare pair of trousers and a sweatshirt. These were crumpled but clean; at least he would be able to face No Ro Shi and the captain with some semblance of decency. He'd get this interview over, then see what he could do about finding Inari, Chen thought, stifling a now-familiar rush of dismay. There was nothing he could do about Zhu Irzh now, but if he could only get No Ro Shi off his back... As he was folding the rest of his noxious clothes into a plastic bag, the door of the locker room sprang open and Sergeant Ma walked in.

"Oh! Sir, I thought you'd finished in here. I just wanted to freshen up before we speak to the captain, and—"

"Don't worry, Sergeant," Chen said. "I'm sure this locker room's big enough for both of us. Anyway, I'm on my way out." He slapped Ma on the shoulder as he left the room. He had to reach up to do so, but nonetheless he had an uncharacteristically sadistic pleasure in seeing Ma flinch.

When he got upstairs, he could see the demon-hunter's unyielding back standing to attention behind the glass wall of the commander's office.

"No Ro Shi's brought you up to speed on what happened last night, I understand," Captain Sung said as Chen came in.

"On the phone this morning," Chen replied. Deeming it best to make the first move, he added: "I understand I've had a home visit. Must have rattled someone's cage, then. I'm inclined to think it's a promising sign."

No Ro Shi gave a small, tight grimace, which after a moment Chen recognized as a smile of approval. "My thoughts exactly. Whoever's behind all this must be someone of reasonable importance, otherwise they'd never have the authority to send a hostile after you. Tang clearly hasn't been working alone. Now. We need to make sure that your home's secure, or find you alternative accommodations."

"I'd rather go home, if you don't mind," Chen said hastily. "Most of my working implements are there. I'm quite capable of securing things myself—I'm a licensed *feng shui* practitioner, after all. I'll ask Lao to give me a hand."

"What sort of wards did you set originally?" No Ro Shi asked, frowning. "Whatever was occupying your houseboat last night clearly didn't have any problems breaking through."

"The place was heavily warded, as a matter of fact," Chen explained. "But certain spells grow a little stale over time. I've been meaning to upgrade, but things have been pretty busy recently and I just didn't get around to it. My mistake."

"Well, we'll leave all that up to you," Captain Sung said, clearly keen to move on, and to Chen's relief, No Ro Shi simply nodded.

The ensuing conversation was brief and pragmatic. Once Chen had expressed his wish to be relieved of duty for a few hours in order to go home and sort things out, it was decided that No Ro Shi should resume the search for Pearl Tang. Chen informed him of the day's progress, or rather lack of it, and handed over the fading scrap that was Pearl's scarf. He was compelled to discuss Zhu Irzh's involvement in the case; predictably, No Ro Shi was horrified.

"This is most unorthodox! To knowingly involve a hostile in the course of an investigation displays a degree of ideological unsoundness that I can only condemn."

"Well, I didn't have a great deal of choice," Chen said. "And he helped me out at Tang's mansion last night. If it wasn't for Zhu Irzh, I might not have been able to free Pearl."

"Only to lose her again as a direct result of the demon's interference."

"True. But if he hadn't interfered in the first place, Pearl might have disappeared with her father when the mansion imploded. At least now we have a faint chance of finding her."

"Perhaps the mansion was destroyed because Tang let his daughter slip," Ma suggested. Chen had to admit that the sergeant had a point, but it wasn't what he wanted to hear.

"Look," the captain said wearily. "How sure are we that Tang's dead?"

"There was no trace of a body, but frankly, that doesn't mean a whole lot."

"So if Tang *is* dead, then presumably he'll have to pass through this place you say we all go through when we die, isn't that right? The Night Harbor?" Sung's heavy face betrayed his unease; Chen couldn't really blame him.

"Possibly. It depends how powerful his associates in Hell are. It's feasible that they took him straight there."

Puzzled, Ma said, "Can't you just go to the Night Harbor and look?"

"Sergeant, you have to understand that the authorities aren't very keen on me trooping in and out of the Night Harbor as though it were my own living room. If it wasn't so tricky to gain access, then I could solve most of the city's murders on my own—all we'd need to do would be to go down there once or twice a day and ask the victims who killed them. Unfortunately, as we've discussed, it isn't that easy. Celestial protocols are often more stringent than Hell's, oddly enough. I've had to call in quite a few favors to try to see Mrs Tang."

"See what you can do," Sung told him. "Then go home and sort things out there. Is your wife still at her mother's?"

"Yes," said Chen, lying once more. He did not dare think about the reparation he'd have to make to the goddess later; all this was costing him a karmic fortune in terms of his relationship with his patron deity. "I spoke to her this morning."

"It might be best if she stayed there for a while."

"I entirely agree," Chen concurred hastily. Leaving No Ro Shi with the captain, he returned to his neglected desk and sat down at the flatscreen, where he waited patiently for the bioweb connection to establish itself. Nothing happened. The flatscreen was as blank as the silvery light over the sea. Frowning, Chen pressed the force-quit keys, and when this strategy accomplished nothing, he rebooted the machine, only to get a scrolling sequence of incomprehensible error messages. Giving it up as a bad job, Chen took out his cell phone and tried to access the web that way, with an equally negligible result.

"System's down again," Ma said mournfully, looming over the partition.

"What, not the whole bioweb, surely?"

Ma nodded with the gloomy satisfaction of one who has never believed in technology. "Went down earlier this afternoon, the news said, then they booted it up again and now it's crashed."

"What's causing that?" Chen wondered aloud. "Solar flares, maybe?"

"The news on the radio says it's due to a problem with the—the biolinks. What they call the nexi."

"The nexi are human beings, Ma." Chen said with a frown. He thought of the *gherao* dormitories he had seen on the television, each with its silent rows of motionless forms: people earning their annual salaries by dreaming the networks of the bioweb…What could go wrong with so many? It was a sinister thought, but at least the web crash gave him the excuse to leave the office and return home. He could contact the Night Harbor authorities later, by phone if necessary.

Retrieving the noxious bag of laundry from his locker, Chen went back out into the chancy sunlight. It was just past six, and the sun was already sinking down over the port in a smear of fire. Chen boarded the first available tram, and stood in the midst of a packed crowd of commuters, noting the exhaustion that seemed to hang like a miasma over each figure. No wonder people seemed to have so little time these days to devote themselves to considerations of the afterlife, Chen reflected, and no wonder Hell was getting out of hand. Even twenty years ago it was still common to see the small shrines outside each door, and for the old people to speak of the gods as real, living presences. Now, paradoxically, the other worlds were closer than they had been since ancient times; with new technology to speed up all manner of communication, yet people seemed to take less and less interest in spiritual matters. Perhaps it was simply too much to bear, Chen thought; perhaps it was too much to ask of people to concern themselves with something other than the daily grind. Whatever the reason, it did not make his work any easier.

The tram came to a halt and Chen got off. He walked the rest of the way to the harbor, hurrying through the gathering twilight. If he had not been so worried about Inari, it would have been a pleasant walk: the air mild and filled with the soft slap of water against the harbor wall. The houseboat was dark and quiet. Chen made his way across the decks to his own boat, but as he had expected, no one was home. There was a rusty smear at the entrance to the main door: blood, hopefully No Ro Shi's. Turning on the lamp, Chen checked the voicemail. Someone had clearly been trying to leave messages, but there was only static. Chen thought through his options. This was one of the safest times of day for Inari to be out and about; her kind were best suited to the liminal times and places—dawn and twilight, shores, the heights of the mountains, caves. The shoreline seemed to be the obvious choice, since it was closest. The harbor shore itself was no more than a strip of shingle, but if one walked a short distance along the harbor road, one came to a widening bay, once the site of a peaceful string of fishing villages, but now just another of the city's suburbs. Changing hastily into a dark jacket and his soft karate slippers, and checking the wards on the doors and windows, Chen returned to the harbor road and started walking.

TWENTY-TWO

High in the rafters of the derelict pier, Inari perched shivering in her ragged silk robe like a seabird blown in from the storm. She found herself constantly fighting the urge to return home, but what if the assassin was waiting for her? She looked down to see cold eyes in the shadows, and a haze of fur.

"You cannot," the badger-teakettle said, in reproof.

"But I don't know what else to do."

"Ask the coins."

"The *I Ching?* I haven't *got* any coins—in case you haven't noticed, I'm still in my dressing gown."

"Make them, then," the badger said in its thick, impatient voice. Feeling foolish, Inari touched the tip of a talon to her wrist and drew three drops of blood. As she did so, she muttered a word: *change*. The red drops hissed as they touched the cold salt metal of the pier, and Inari reached down to snatch up three old worn coins.

"Now throw," the badger said, as though Inari were a child who needed instruction on the simplest thing. She threw the coins carefully into her silken lap, again and again, and studied the configuration that they made. She called the hexagram to mind: Twenty-nine. *K'an. The Abyss.*

Inari sat back and looked mournfully at the coins in her lap. Abyss upon abyss: grave danger. But no indication of what she should do—go back to the houseboat, or yield to her fears and stay here. It was very difficult. The *I Ching* was like the polished surface of a bowl, revealing nothing of the contents within the Tao and reflecting only a transformed image. Sighing, Inari gathered up the coins in her lap, but as she did so, her hand closed convulsively over them. There was a soft, stealthy footstep from under the pier, a sucking sound like an eel vanishing beneath the sand. The badger's whiskers bristled. Inari shrank back against the rafters and then, very cautiously, peered over the edge. Twenty feet below she could see something moving in the shadows under the pier. It was hunched as if old, it moved slowly, but thin dark tendrils shot from it in all directions, questing across the sand. The badger pressed against Inari's side and she could feel it quivering. She watched in unwilling fascination as a tendril coiled around one of the struts of the pier and began to climb upwards like the fast-forwarded image of a growing vine. On the sand below, the figure was utterly still.

"What is it?" she murmured to the badger.

"I do not know. We must go, Inari. Now."

"But where?" Inari whispered. The tendril had reached the rafters and was snaking blindly towards her, its tip rising from time to time as though it scented the air. From where they were sitting, her only option would be to leap across to one of the neighboring rafters, then down. She clutched the protesting badger to her breast and stood up. The tendril shot forwards like a whip, but Inari was already in midair. Yet the tendril was quicker still. She heard it crack with released tension as it shot through the air, then something like a burning wire wrapped itself around her ankle. Inari, still clasping the badger, fell some fifteen feet towards the sand, only to be brought up short five feet from the ground. Her hip was jolted painfully as the tendril broke her fall, and she dropped the badger. She saw it bolt in a zigzagging blur over the sand. Spinning dizzily, she could see the tendril stretched taut across the rafter, and her inverted gaze met a pair of black dead eyes, as opaque as oil. The thing's face was partly concealed beneath a hood, but what Inari could see was ominous. She caught a glimpse of pale, pasty flesh, peeling like the cracked glaze on an old jar. It held out a puffy, bluish hand. From above, a single red tear fell like rain, then another, and then another. Inari's oracular coins had turned to blood once more. Raising its hand to its mouth, the being licked its palm with a thick, discolored tongue. A red stain welled out across the wet sand beneath its feet which, Inari noticed through a sudden wave of nausea, were turned back to front upon its ankles. The stain paused briefly as it reached the waves, but then the whole of the twilit sea before her turned red and the sky spun crimson above her. The whip-crack grip on her ankle was abruptly released and then Inari was falling, but much further than the short distance to the incarnadined sand, much further than even the bloody smear of the waning moon above her head, all the way down past the ends of the Earth to Hell.

PART THREE

TWENTY-THREE
Hell

Lightning cracked the skies above Rhu Shu Street, briefly illuminating the signs of the demon lounges and apothecaries and bringing with it the smell of hot metal, like a blade through the humid air. Former Bloodmaster Tso walked slowly, bowed down with the wallowing weight of the blood-filled sack. He counted each step: *three hundred and fifty-one, three hundred and fifty-two...* only another two hundred to go. It was a long way from the loading dock to the end of Rhu Shu Street and the square where the Blood Emporium lay, and Tso's feet hurt. They'd never been the same since O Ji had reversed them, so that the toes now pointed to the front—nothing more than a fit of malice, in Tso's opinion, and an action which had had very little to do with his unfortunate family's scandal—but it had caused endless hardship for Tso. He'd always been proud of his feet. Great-grandfather Tso's feet had also faced backwards, and Tso himself had apparently inherited this prestigious gene; a legacy from some unimaginably distant ancestor of the Imperial Court. No one else in the family had backwards feet; not his brother Ghu, not his sister Inari... At this thought, Tso's mind cringed from its own memories. If it hadn't been for Inari, he'd still have his old feet, and come to that, he'd still have his old job: working behind the counter of the Ru Shu Blood Emporium, the respected proprietor instead of the lowliest delivery boy. But it was too late to worry about that now. Now, he was working for the epicene O Ji, whose august magnanimity had bought the Emporium from Tso to pay off his sister's promised dowry, and who had re-employed him at a somewhat lower level... Tso's thoughts spun in their familiar and depressing groove. *Four hundred and ninety-two...* He was nearly at the door of the Emporium, for the seventeenth time that day. With the utmost care, he levered the sack from his back and cradled it as he stepped across the threshold. The slightest drop of lost blood would, he knew from bitter experience, cost him a corresponding deduction in wages; O Ji might look like a languid fop, but he had eyes like those of the *wu'ei* themselves and he didn't miss a trick. Tso waltzed the sack of blood into the back regions of the Emporium, where two gagged servants slaved above the steaming jars. Taking the sack from Tso, and nodding their thanks, they emptied the fresh consignment of blood into the sealed trough. Tso watched resentfully as it gurgled through the pipes to the filling mechanism. In his day, when he was proprietor, there had been no need to gag the staff. He had trusted the servants not to abuse their privileges, and if a stealthy tongue had snapped out to sample a taste of the delicacy on which the Emporium depended, it only made for a happier workforce. This was the trouble with aristocrats, Tso thought: they did not understand the basic principles of industry. Sighing, he turned and was about to make his painful way back to the loading dock when the door to the Emporium jangled open and O Ji stepped through.

Tso immediately bowed low, teetering a little as he did so. The reversed feet made balance difficult, and he was forced to steady himself against the counter.

"You may rise," O Ji said, reeking of smugness. Tso did so, and saw with disgust that O Ji had treated himself to a new suit. He was resplendent in ivory silk, with collar and cuffs of some kind of thick, pale fur, which provided a rough match to his own carefully blond mane. A tracery of scarlet veins formed a labyrinth across his waistcoat. Tso suppressed a frown. O Ji was rich, it was true, and a slave to fashion, but Tso had never seen him looking quite so—well, *expensive*. O Ji's smile grew as Tso covertly eyed the suit.

"My latest acquisition. You like it?"

"Magnificent," Tso said, even more sourly because it was the truth.

"It's by way of a little celebration, I suppose. I have wonderful news, Tso. Would you like to hear it?" He spoke patiently, as to a child, and Tso inwardly seethed.

"Sir?"

"Today I signed a new contract for the Blood Emporium, Tso. One that will add to my already extensive coffers, and make us the envy of the district." He paused, as if for dramatic effect, then continued: "We're going to be the primary suppliers of blood to the Ministry of Epidemics. Isn't that great news? On a regular basis, for a new project they're developing. Science, my dear Tso, is truly a marvelous thing—but Art must take precedence. Our first order is for a consignment of delicacies—blood sorbets, candies, liqueurs, all the usual kind of thing—for the wedding." O Ji floated around the reception area, flicking idle fingers in the direction of the display cabinets.

"The wedding?" Tso echoed.

"That's right, the wedding. Between Lord Dao Yi of the Ministry of Epidemics and your sister."

Tso gaped at him. O Ji said kindly, "It seems your sister's come home at last, Tso. And Dao Yi's decided to forgive her. In a manner of speaking. Of course, it won't be as though she'll be First Wife this time, but still, you can't have everything. What a pity you're no longer manager here. I should think your family will be needing all the help it can get, what with the revised dowry and the penalty fees, after all. Perhaps," O Ji said with a languid, glittering smile as Tso stood motionless in the middle of the room, "we should think about giving you a pay rise." The smile widened. "Or then again, maybe not."

TWENTY-FOUR

Three hours after he had set out from the houseboat, Chen sat wearily on the side of the dock, dangling his aching feet in the cool, oily waters of the harbor. The moon had long since set, but any stars there might have been were blurred by the neon glow of the city. He had found no sign of Inari—not a note, not a sign, not a scrap of cloth or a drop of blood—and he had run out of ideas. He felt almost too tired to move, but at last he rose from the dock and made his way back towards the houseboat. It was dark and silent. Chen paused for a moment, letting his *ch'i* senses run ahead of him. He could feel nothing. His own *ch'i* perceptions were hardly infallible, but combined with the personalized *feng shui* wards which guarded the houseboat, they were good enough to give him some warning if anything menacing—say, a Maoist demon-hunter or a vice squad operative from Hell—happened to be lurking behind the door. Chen stepped unscathed onto the deck of the houseboat and into the kitchen. Something rattled. Eyes glowed red in the faint gleam of sudden transformation, and Chen's heart leaped once, like a bird.

"*Badger?*" He fumbled for the kitchen light and switched it on. The badger was a mess. Sand and salt matted its fur into short, untidy dreadlocks and its nose looked cracked and dry. Chen hastened across the kitchen and reached out a hand.

"Do not!" the badger said irritably. "I will not be touched."

"Sorry. But where's Inari?"

The badger peered miserably up at him, and seemed to deflate. "It is I who should be sorry. I could not save her."

Chen felt as though the floor had fallen in. "Oh, goddess, is she—well, she can't be dead, since she's not really alive in the first place, unless that bloody demon-hunter has —oh, never mind. Tell me what happened."

"We were hiding. From the man with the sword. We did not come back in case he also had returned. We could not find you; we did not know where you might be and Inari did not have the speaking device. We left the boat too swiftly. It was my fault. I did not do enough to distract the hunter."

"It's all right," Chen said. "Don't reproach yourself. You can't think of everything, do everything."

"It is still my fault," the badger said. Chen studied it as it sat on the kitchen counter. Bedraggled as it was, it still retained that semblance of otherness; the darkness of a creature that walked between worlds. Its eyes, black once more now that its transformation was complete, were frosted with an icy haze, yet Chen could see the light of a different day within their depths. He said quietly, "You came from Hell with Inari when no one else would even look at her—not her mother, not her brothers, no one. And you have done your best for her this last year, in a place that is not your own and that has changed so greatly from the China you knew long ago that it might as well be another planet. It is *not* your fault. Now. What happened?"

"Something came. Something from Hell. It snatched her like a bird in a snare and took her with it. I ran from it, but I turned back and I saw it go. It turned the world to blood and then the air opened up. I saw Hell once more—its storms, its iron towers. And my mistress was gone."

Chen sank down onto the nearest chair and rubbed his palms across gritty eyes. "I was right, badger. It isn't your fault. It's mine. If Inari had stayed on the houseboat, Hell might not have been able to touch her. If I hadn't drawn attention to the Tang case, No Ro Shi wouldn't have come here..." He could not seem to think straight; thoughts whirled and would not settle.

"She could not have stayed caged like a cricket forever," the badger murmured in its dark voice. "You could not have done other than you did. I heard what you said about Tang."

"What we have to do now is figure out who's taken her, and why. The obvious candidates are her family, and whoever's been running Tang. And one other party."

"The *wu'ei*."

"I've been trying not to think about the *wu'ei*," Chen said, wincing from the thought.

"They will not give up. They are patient, relentless, eternal."

"They are also vindictive."

"What else could they be? They are the instruments of the Lords of Hell, its iron fist. You know as well as I that Hell is a matter of strict hierarchies. Violation of those hierarchies, that structure, results in the payment of a price. Inari violated that order when she came here, and so did I. The *wu'ei* answer only to the Imperial Court, and that Court is inflexible in its dictates—however long it may take to implement them."

"I'd noticed," Chen said. He felt hollow inside, like a reed with the pith sucked out. He had encountered the *wu'ei* only once before, and never wished to do so again. The *wu'ei*: more than demons, less than deities, but with all the infernal powers of the Imperial Court. It was their task to track down the wrongdoers of Hell, those who had violated the laws of the worlds beyond the world. The thought of Inari being back in Hell was bad enough, but contemplating her in the hands of the vast inimical presences of these underlords was little short of appalling. Rubbing his hands across his face, Chen tried to force his racing brain into considering his options. First thing tomorrow, he would go to the Night Harbor as planned, to see if he could find Pearl Tang, but he would not be coming out again. Instead, he would be traveling on to Hell... Beside him, the badger bristled.

"What—?"

"Be quiet," the badger murmured. "Something is coming."

Chen thrust thoughts of Inari from his mind with an effort and rose from the chair. Moving stealthily to the kitchen door, he peered through the crack. The badger dropped from the kitchen counter and whisked silently around the legs of the chair.

At first, Chen could see nothing except the deck of the houseboat and the ripple of the harbor lights on the water. Then, he noticed that something was coming across the surface of the water itself: a dark wake, bringing something behind it. The thing was no more than a faint glow, a miasma of shadow upon the heave of the sea. It disappeared beneath the houseboat, only to swarm up over the deck and pause, uncertainly. It was the missing, lobster-like ghost-tracker, and with it was the figure of a girl, dressed in the remnants of a funeral robe. The back of her head was missing. It was Pearl Tang.

Motioning the badger to stay in the kitchen, Chen stepped out onto the deck and held out his hand.

"Pearl?" he said, gently. The ghost-tracker scuttled forwards, its antennae swiveling. The ghost turned and he saw her face crumple with relief, only to smooth out moments later into a blank mask as the emotion drained away. Yet he could see fear in the lines of her insubstantial form: a quivering like heat that distorted her as he watched.

"Detective Chen?" Pearl's voice was no more than a shiver in the air.

"Come inside," Chen said. "Quickly, now. I don't know who might be watching."

Fearfully, the ghost glanced once over her shoulder, then brushed past him into the kitchen. Once inside, she was almost swallowed by the light: Chen had to look hard in order to see her at all. The ghost-tracker, finally relieved of its task, crawled beneath the warmth of the stove. The ghost whispered, "That—that person. He's gone, isn't he? The one who wanted to take me back?"

"Zhu Irzh? Yes, he's gone. I'm not quite sure where though." The possibility of Zhu Irzh and Inari both being in Hell produced a curious reaction in Chen: a lifting of the spirits, combined with a pang of sheer anxiety. He was not entirely certain how to account for either emotion.

"It's hard to remember," she said. "You were arguing, and the demon was going to take me, so I ran away. I don't know where I've been. I just drifted through places—I went to the pavilion in the park, but it didn't look like the place I knew anymore, it was full of strange people in the trees, like birds, and their eyes were bright, so I didn't stay. I went through the market, I think—I remember someone standing at the entrance with a sword, and he was all bloody, but he wasn't alive... I don't remember. It was evening, and I think I was going home, but before I could get there, this creature found me."

"Pearl, remember what you told us about your father, and the Ministry, and the person who stood by your bed and talked with your father about why he was doing these things? Do you remember anything else? Anything at all?"

The ghost looked utterly blank. She shook what remained of her head.

"You're quite sure?"

"I told you! I don't remember."

"All right," Chen said wearily. "Then we need to get you out of here and into Heaven where you belong."

"How can we do that?" Pearl asked, puzzled, and Chen replied, "Don't worry. I know someone who might be able to help."

TWENTY-FIVE

Seneschal Zhu Irzh's second cousin twice removed was a terrible hypochondriac. Usually, this was not a characteristic that Zhu Irzh found endearing and, moreover, the cousin was a meager little person, with lank, gray hair and a permanent sniff, completely lacking in anything resembling feminine charm. She was, however, on first name terms with practically every apothecary and remedy-maker in Hell, and Zhu Irzh was confident that someone, somewhere, would have contacts in the Ministry of Epidemics. Such contacts were needed. Hell's health-care system being what it was, the waiting list for appointments at the Ministry reached practically to infinity and Zhu Irzh needed to get through its iron doors that day. As soon as he could, therefore, he collected a bunch of herbs (morning glory, purging croton and blackberry lily) and a box of blood candies, and went to pay a visit to his neglected relative.

He found his cousin sitting in an armchair, gazing beadily out at the events in the street beyond. As he stepped through the door, however, she collapsed into a huddle beneath a blanket, and emitted a faint, but convincing, moan.

"I thought you might be a touch poorly, so I've brought you these," Zhu Irzh said, trying to sound sympathetic.

His cousin opened a small, red eye and inspected the presents. She poked the candies suspiciously. "These look musty. Where did you get them? Tso's?"

"No, I purchased them in another fine emporium," Zhu Irzh said loudly, as the cousin was genuinely somewhat deaf. "Near the Opera House."

"The where?"

"*The Opera House!*" Zhu Irzh shouted into her ear. The cousin sniffed, and her small bony hands tightened around the bundle of herbs.

"And these are all wilted. What did you do, sit on them?"

"They were fine when I bought them," Zhu Irzh said, bridling. "It's not my fault if it's a trifle warm outside. I'll put them in a vase for you. Anyway, how are you feeling?" He tried not to sound too apprehensive as he spoke these last words. He had a feeling he was about to be told.

Half an hour later, his cousin finally came to the end of a long list of ailments, some of them involving rather more personal information than Zhu Irzh wished to hear. The litany did, however, seem to mollify his cousin to some degree, and she even ventured a wintry smile. Beaming back, Zhu Irzh embarked upon a careful round of questions and arrived at a list of some eight medical practitioners who enjoyed a close working relationship with the Ministry of Epidemics. Armed with this list, he accepted a small and nasty cup of herbal tea and then departed, with protestations that he would come again soon. He got the impression that he left his cousin happier than when he had arrived, a consequence that disturbed him. Zhu Irzh was suspicious of good deeds.

The first two practitioners on the list were out. The third was in, but a queue of scowling, suffering citizens extended through the door and Zhu Irzh had no desire to spend another hour like the previous one, treated to a recitation of suffering. He thus proceeded to the fourth practitioner, a handsome establishment in the Shadow District, with a facade that was almost concealed behind a vast array of charms and testimonials. Stepping through the double doors, Zhu Irzh found himself in a wide and well-appointed hallway.

"Good morning," said a voice. Zhu Irzh turned to see a young woman swathed in a coral robe. She smiled, displaying small, white teeth. Her eyes were a startling, but vapid, blue.

"Excuse me," Zhu Irzh said, not quite believing the evidence of his own eyes. "But aren't you human?"

The girl gave a vacant giggle, and did not reply. Then her face ironed itself out to perfect blankness once more, and she said as if by rote, "Do you have an appointment?"

"No, I'm sorry, I don't." Zhu Irzh reached for his badge.

"One moment. I will ask if the doctor can see you," the girl said. She glided around the edge of the desk and spoke rapidly into a gilded trumpet. Zhu Irzh studied her, narrow-eyed. The girl was definitely human, and a Westerner. She was even alive: he could smell her blood, her breath, hear the faint crack of her bones inside her skin. What she was doing here, however, remained a mystery.

"The doctor will see you now," the receptionist murmured, with a glazed smile. Zhu Irzh bowed in response, and stepped through the door.

The man inside looked up as Zhu Irzh came in. He, at least, was indigenous: an immensely stout person, whose crimson eyes were almost buried in the fleshy folds of his face. He displayed sharp teeth in a welcoming grin.

"I am Dr So. And you are a seneschal, yes? From the Vice Division? I have excellent relations with Supreme Seneschal Yhu, you know. We have a little poker session every Friday night."

"Poker?"

"A human game. From the West. Most stimulating."

Zhu Irzh tried not to show his dismay that Dr So knew his superior. Since he wasn't actually working for the Vice Division on this particular case, but was under the aegis of the First Lord of Banking, complications might ensue. Still, thought Zhu Irzh with a return to his usual insouciance, he'd cross that bridge when he came to it.

"Talking of humans," he said, "that's a charming receptionist you have working for you."

"You like her?" Dr So beamed. "Well, I'll let you into a little secret. She's not the only human I have working for me. She's really only one of my girls. If you are interested in getting to know any of them better, I'm sure we could come to some arrangement..."

"That would be delightful," Zhu Irzh said, somewhat insincerely. "Might I ask how they came to be in your employ?"

Dr So tapped the side of his nose. "Trade secret, I'm afraid. But you just let me know and I'll see what I can do. Now. What else can I help you with?"

"Well, it's like this," Zhu Irzh said. The pursuit of the medical practitioners on his cousin's list had given him some considerable time to come up with an appropriate cover story, and he was eager to try it out. Glancing towards the door, he said, "You do appreciate, I'm sure, that this is a matter of some delicacy, and I really would be most grateful if it went no further..."

"Of course," Dr So said, adopting an expression that was evidently meant to convey sympathy and interest, but which succeeded only in revealing the acquisitiveness beneath.

"There is a young lady, you understand," Zhu Irzh began with careful hesitancy, "of my acquaintance, who has something of a little problem."

"A common occurrence, alas."

"Indeed. I'm sure that a man of your experience and understanding will comprehend the often—restricted—lives that women of high breeding are compelled to endure, especially those of families attached to the Court. And I'm sure you understand also the temptations to which boredom can so often lead."

"I confront them every day."

"I knew you'd have a firm grip on the issues involved. In this case, the young lady has allowed herself to become—let's say, over-familiar—with a particular narcotic. One that is, unfortunately, in somewhat short supply."

Dr So's carefully manicured eyebrows crept up the lunar expanse of his countenance, like caterpillars. He said, "To what narcotic would you be referring?"

"Soma ore."

"I *see*. Yes, that is a problem. Ordinarily, one rarely sees cases of soma addiction—it's a drug that is far beyond even my own price range. But for someone attached to the Court—yes, I can see how she might have become exposed to it. And it doesn't take long to become addicted, they say."

"The young lady doesn't want to go through the regular supplier, for the very good reason that she purloined the initial sample from someone who had best remain nameless, and is worried about the consequences of that. However, happily for her, she is quite extravagantly wealthy and therefore well able to afford the actual narcotic—it's actually obtaining it that is proving so problematic. She tells me that the source lies within the Ministry of Epidemics, and I have it on good authority that you have contacts there. I need to get in there today—you know how hard it is to obtain an appointment with someone, but once through the door, I can achieve my goal with relatively little trouble. If you would be so kind as to put me in touch with one of those contacts, I would of course ensure that your help did not go unrecognized."

"That is perfectly understandable. Indeed, I would be willing—perhaps—to function as purveyor to the lady in question, if she so chose. But it will take time."

"That won't be necessary," Zhu Irzh said quickly. The object of the exercise was to get into the Ministry himself, after all. "She's really quite desperate. And due to her somewhat debilitated condition, I am the only one whom she trusts. Misguided, but you know what addicts are like…"

"Mmm. Well, I can certainly put you in touch with a couple of people. We would need to discuss the matter of recompense, of course."

"Perhaps you could jot down a few thoughts on that, and let me have them," Zhu Irzh suggested. His smile widening, Dr So scribbled a sum on a flimsy fragment of skin and passed it across the desk. Zhu Irzh was careful not to let his mouth hang open, and he had to remind himself that the First Lord of Banking was covering his expenses. Instead, he said, "That seems quite reasonable. I'll speak to the young lady today and arrange a payment. Through a suitably circuitous route, of course."

"I'll need a promissory note from you, first."

"Naturally," Zhu Irzh said.

He parted from Dr So with two names in his pocket and a certain apprehension as to what the First Lord of Banking would say when presented with the bill. *Still,* Zhu Irzh told himself, *if he wants to know what's going on, he'll have to shell out for it.* Information was, as everyone knew, the world's biggest money-spinner these days. He smiled at the receptionist as he left, but she was busy filing her nails and did not look up. It was only after he stepped through the door that Zhu Irzh realized she'd had nothing in her hands.

TWENTY-SIX

The temple of Kuan Yin was once more silent and still. Nothing stirred within as Chen, exorcist Lao and the ghost of Pearl Tang stepped across the threshold, followed by the gliding, elusive shape of the badger. It was no more than an hour until dawn. Lao was still complaining at having been roused from his bed at such an ungodly time, and Chen was unable to blame him. He had, however, been ruthless in his insistence that Lao abandon his slumbers and join them at the temple; a persistence which Chen now attributed to the several cups of strong espresso that he'd downed in an effort to remain awake. The coffee had merely served to provide a wide-eyed jitteriness; Chen felt like a puppet on a string, jerked in conflicting directions. He glanced up at the goddess, whose shadowy form still stood implacably at the far end of the room.

"What now?" Lao asked irritably.

"We'll need protection," Chen said. The last time he had set foot in the temple had been in the company of Zhu Irzh, and he still half-expected the demon to slide out of the darkness. Whatever might have befallen Inari, he was taking no more chances with the sad shade of Pearl Tang.

Grumbling, the exorcist set up candles and incense and delineated a protective circle. As he did so, Chen could sense the sentinel beasts of the Four Quarters as Lao awoke them to ritual presence: green dragon, white tiger, red bird and black tortoise. A small wind stirred within the temple, blowing a scatter of dust in from the silent courtyard. Beneath the rustling ceremonial banners that lined the walls, the badger whimpered.

"Sorry," Chen said. "Is this distressing you?"

"I am a creature of Hell. This celestial conjuring curdles my blood," the badger hissed. With a flicker of transformation, it changed, and then there was only an old iron teakettle settling back onto the reed mat.

"All right," Chen said, relieved. "Are we done?"

"Nearly," Lao murmured, scowling with concentration. He raised his hands for the final incantation and the protective circle shimmered up around them. From within it, as though through a heat haze, Chen could see the statue of Kuan Yin; cold, still, and green as glass polished by the sea. Bowing his head, he began to pray: not for himself, nor for Inari, but for the spirit of Pearl Tang, a sad life, made barren by privilege, and too soon ended. He did not glance up as he prayed, but he knew when the goddess turned his way. He heard Lao take a deep, indrawn breath, and then he raised his head.

Kuan Yin stood before him once more. This time, she did not look like a goddess: she was not radiant; she did not inspire awe. She was small, and quiet-faced, and middle-aged. She brought with her only a trace of salt like a sea breeze as she stepped over the protective bounds of the circle. Walking straight past Chen, she took Pearl Tang's nebulous hands.

"It is time to go where you belong," she said, and Chen saw Pearl's hands grip those of the goddess. This time, they did not fall through. Turning, Kuan Yin began to lead Pearl from the circle, but Chen whispered, "Wait." It seemed like the hardest word he had ever uttered. Kuan Yin looked at him, and now the goddess-aspect was back: Avalokiteshvara, the Buddha-field, surrounding her. Chen felt his knees begin to buckle.

"Wait?" the goddess echoed, in a voice that was horrifying in its calmness.

Chen said, "You know as well as I that this spirit has been rent from the web of life and cast into a purgatory not of her own making. But she is not the only one. I do not want to see a procession of Pearl Tangs rattling between here and Hell, snatched into a place where only undeserved suffering awaits them."

"What you may want, Chen Wei, is of no consequence."

"No, I know that. But do you agree that if I can prevent the exploitation of these spirits, the so-called ghost-trade, then that is what I must do?"

After a moment, which seemed eternally long to Chen, the goddess inclined her head. "What is to be done?"

"Pearl has information. She overheard a conversation at the very moment of her death, between her father and an unknown person, and I believe she still remembers it, even though she doesn't think she does. It is something that I believe to be of immense value to Hell—something that they have already gone to great lengths to retrieve. But I don't know how to reach it."

"Very well," said Kuan Yin, after a pause. "Then let us see what may be found."

Around them the temple began to melt and fade. Chen saw Lao's startled face mouthing mute words before snuffing out like a blown candle. Chen was standing in someone's bedroom.

"Where am I?" Chen asked, and then he knew. He had been here before. This was Pearl Tang's bedroom, in the now-vanished house. Behind and around him, Kuan Yin's voice said, "You are within what remains of Pearl's personality. When she sets foot upon the Celestial Shores, all this will be gone, but for now, all that is left of her consciousness is here. Search for what you need, but be swift. Dawn is coming, and I must send Pearl on her way."

It felt like being a burglar in someone else's head. It felt like a violation, and Chen hated himself as he hastily rummaged through drawers and ransacked closets. He did not even know what he was looking for, only that it was not there. He turned books from their shelves, glancing quickly at unrevealing titles: most were of the teenage romance variety, and betrayed nothing. He looked under the bed: nothing. The coffee he had so recently ingested was making him twitchy and uncoordinated, and some part of his mind reflected that this was strange, since he wasn't even in a real place at all. As he clambered to his feet, he heard the goddess say, "These are the last minutes, Chen. The sun is rising." Chen opened his mouth to protest but as he did so he saw a strand of light reflected from something in the far corner of the room. It was a pearl: round and glowing, set upon a crimson cushion. Lunging forward, Chen snatched it up as the bedroom in turn faded away, sucked into the opening fabric of the universe. Chen had a glimpse of a place that made him cry out: a golden sky above glittering, diamond-blossomed trees, and the fragment of shadow that was Pearl Tang running among them until it was lost in the light. He opened his eyes. He was kneeling, breathing hard, on the cold stone floor of the temple of Kuan Yin, whose statue stood mute and remote above him. His hand was empty, but the knowledge represented by the pearl struck home with sledgehammer force. He knew, now, what it was that Hell had gone to such great lengths to conceal and seek out. And he knew, too, how vital it was that he should find not only Inari, but also Zhu Irzh.

TWENTY-SEVEN

The trouble with Hell, Zhu Irzh reflected bitterly, was not so much the palpable miasma of evil (with which he was, after all, ingrained) but the bureaucracy. This was now the fifth hour he had spent at the Ministry of Epidemics, in the crowded queue for the Second Level Third Administrative Assistant's Appointment Maker. At least after the third hour he'd managed to procure a seat, but the room was packed to bursting point and smelt of sickness and sweat. If he'd known that this was the best Dr So could do in the matter of contacts, he wouldn't have bothered, though he had to admit that the doctor had at least provided him with the necessary documentation to get through the Ministry's impressive iron portals.

"Stop doing that!" the woman sitting beside him snapped. "It's getting on my nerves!"

Zhu Irzh gazed blankly at her. He hadn't been aware of doing anything at all.

"*That.*"

Her small, pursed mouth opened and a tongue flicked contemptuously in the direction of his tail, which was tapping impatiently against the iron surface of the floor.

"Sorry," said Zhu Irzh as insincerely as he could manage. With studied insolence, he curled his tail around his knees and glanced at the clock. It was getting late, and he'd promised to take one of his girlfriends to the opera. It had to be the razor-tongued Ren Ji, he thought with a sigh; it couldn't have been one of the others, the ones less likely to complain... The door of the appointment-maker's office opened and a frail figure shuffled forth. After a fifteen-minute wait, the lamp above the door glowed briefly, and the next in line went through. Zhu Irzh realized he was tapping his tail again. This was absurd. Time to take matters into his own hands, he thought.

"Excuse me," he said to the woman sitting beside him. "But do you happen to know where the lavatories might be?"

"Down the hall, on the left," the woman said ungraciously.

"Thanks. Would you mind keeping my place for me? I'll only be a moment."

"Certainly not. You'll have to join the back of the queue if you leave."

Grumbling convincingly, Zhu Irzh rose to his feet and pushed his way through the crowds to the door. Outside, he discovered that the queue extended down the hall, and was obliged to shove his way past a throng of muttering demonkind. This particular department of the Ministry was devoted to Hell's own citizens, not to the souls of those humans who had died from disease, and the queue represented just about every affliction that the Ministry was wont to test-drive on the locals. Zhu Irzh saw the ravages of tsetse fever; bone rot; open-lung, and the disgruntlement of people who could not rely on the mercies of death to relieve them from their suffering. Silently, he gave thanks to his Imperial Majesty that his own family position protected him from this kind of thing, not to mention the health insurance that consumed a large portion of his monthly salary, but you never knew when misfortune might strike. Suddenly aware of the tenuousness of his position, Zhu Irzh slipped through the door of the lavatories.

Inside, there were the usual stinking holes, and the floor was awash. Hissing with disapproval, Zhu Irzh twitched the hem of his coat out of reach and looked around him. One of the cubicles was occupied; he could hear the sound of prolonged retching. Another moment in here, Zhu Irzh decided, and he'd be coming down with one of those diseases so amply represented in the hallway. He stepped swiftly into a cubicle and closed the door behind him, then looked up.

Set into the low ceiling was, as he had anticipated, a ventilation grill. It was unlikely to serve much of a purpose insofar as actual ventilation was concerned, since it was clogged with dust and grease, but Zhu Irzh was not worried about that. It was narrow, but he thought he could probably get through it; it wasn't as though he was fat, after all. Reaching up, he hooked his talons in the wire of the grill and gave a sharp tug. Gripping the sides of the opening to the ventilation shaft, Zhu Irzh hoisted himself lithely upwards and pulled the grill shut behind him.

Inside, the shaft was wider than he had expected, and extended in both directions. Unfortunately, Zhu Irzh had very little idea of the layout of the Ministry, but he did know that, like all Hell's institutions, the highest levels were the most important. He therefore must find somewhere that led up. The shaft was too low for him to stand upright, but he could move faster in a crouch than on his hands and knees, and he was able to make reasonably rapid progress. He had been scuttling along for perhaps some fifteen minutes when he came upon yet another grill, set into the ceiling of the shaft. Not without difficulty, Zhu Irzh dismantled it, thereby dislodging a large rat that bolted into the shadows, its scaly body scraping against the metal floor. It left a faint trail of phosphorescence in its wake, and this proved helpful. Looking up, Zhu Irzh could see the tracks it had made in the upwards shaft, and although he was considerably larger than the rat, it was evident that there were rudimentary handholds in the walls of the shaft, provided by the grills which themselves led into other passages. Gritting his teeth, Zhu Irzh began to climb.

It was not easy going, and Zhu Irzh was relieved when the upwards shaft finally came to an end. Clinging to the sides of the shaft, he hooked the nearest grill with his tail and pulled, then levered himself into the passage. By now, dust had made its way down inside his collar and between the scales on his back, making his spine itch uncontrollably. There was a rip in the skirts of his coat, and his hair was full of cobwebs. Closing his eyes, Zhu Irzh directed a careful, precise, and hopefully untraceable curse in the direction of the First Lord of Banking. Then he froze. He could hear voices.

Very slowly, and as quietly as he could, Zhu Irzh inched forwards. The voices were muffled, but he could tell that one of them was female, and hissing in anger. Zhu Irzh hunched forwards until he was immediately above the source of the voices; here, too, a ventilation grill was set into the floor. Zhu Irzh peered through. He could not see the woman. He was looking down onto the top of a demon's head, and he could see that its owner's hair was combed carefully in long, black strands across a series of bald patches. The scalp revealed beneath was scabrous and flaking. Zhu Irzh once again thanked the fate that had seen him born into a family of scions of the Ministry of Vice. Plenty of interesting opportunities, and no hideously disfiguring diseases... He was unable to see the demon's face which, he reflected with a grin, was probably just as well. He squirmed round, trying to get a glimpse of the woman.

"You ought to be grateful," the demon was saying with some hauteur. "After all, have I not been magnanimous enough to forgive you, bring you back to the bosom of your home and family, protect you from the justifiable wrath of the *wu'ei*, who would otherwise cast you down into the Lower Realms for your disgraceful conduct. Well, haven't I?"

An inaudible murmur: possibly assent, possibly not.

"Come here," the demon commanded. "And stop muttering."

There was a shuffling sound as the woman made her way forwards, which was, Zhu Irzh realized, a result of the fact that her ankles were shackled. Her head was bowed: he could see the top of her glossy dark hair (no bald patches there, Zhu Irzh noted with approval). He could even smell her perfume: something subtle and spiced, a breath of sweetness in the rank air of the Ministry, and he inhaled it with gratitude. Then she looked up at the demon, and though her face was twisted with contempt, Zhu Irzh saw that she was beautiful. Pale soft skin, cheekbones like razorblades, eyes like wells of blood. She was wearing an extraordinary garment, which looked as though it had once been a dressing gown but which was now in tatters, revealing the curves of her body. The demon reached out a mottled hand and drew it along the underside of her breast, pinching the nipple with sudden force. Zhu Irzh, ambushed fleetingly by sexual fantasy, swallowed, and shifted position slightly against the floor of the shaft. He felt uncomfortably like a voyeur. Not that there was anything wrong with that, he reminded himself. The woman spat out a single glowing spark and the demon jerked his hand backwards. The tang of singed flesh rose upwards and Zhu Irzh's elegant eyebrows rose. She must be very angry indeed to do that, but given the circumstances, he couldn't blame her. He wondered who she might be: she was clearly someone of breeding, which made the references to the Lower Realms somewhat puzzling. What could she have done to merit such punishment, and such forgiveness? His voice furred with rage, the demon beneath said, "I don't have to tell you that you'll regret that."

"I don't care!"

Zhu Irzh winced. So beautiful, so brave, and so reckless... He entertained an idle fantasy of sliding down through the grill, knocking the girl's persecutor unconscious, and saving her from her own vile fate. In the fantasy, she fell to her knees in gratitude; winding her arms around his waist, her soft breasts pressing against his thighs, her mouth—Zhu Irzh blinked. This would not do. Whatever was happening in the room below, fascinating though it might be, was none of his business. Zhu Irzh tried to push the ever-present specter of sexual desire to the back of his mind and watched as the demon strode from the room, nursing his injured hand and leaving the woman to sink back onto the couch, her face defeated and weary. Surely, Zhu Irzh thought, all this could have nothing whatsoever to do with the matter on which he had come to the Ministry. Getting embroiled with this situation would cause nothing but woe, however beautiful the woman might be, however desirable... If he had any sense, he would move swiftly and quietly onwards. With that sensible thought well out of the way, Zhu Irzh pulled aside the grill and dropped into the room.

TWENTY-EIGHT

Lao stared at Chen in amazement. "Are you sure?" he said for the fourth time. Chen did not bother to speak; he merely nodded, wearily. "Well, that's bloody ambitious, I must say. Even for Hell. I told you letting that demonic vice cop hang around was bad news."

"I don't think it has anything to do with Zhu Irzh," Chen said, propelled reluctantly to the demon's defense. "He was as much in the dark as we were, remember, unless he's a spectacularly good liar." Somehow, recalling Zhu Irzh's limpid golden eyes, Chen did not think that this was the case. "It's the Ministry of Epidemics."

"What are you going to do about it?"

"I'm not sure what I can do. I could alert Heaven, via *that* one." Chen gestured towards the motionless figure of Kuan Yin. "In fact, I think I already have." He dimly remembered Kuan Yin's presence hovering at his shoulder in Pearl's spectral bedroom. "But Heaven plays by its own rules."

"A sort of Prime Directive," Lao mused. Catching Chen's puzzled glance, he said, "American television show. Science fiction. Oh, never mind."

"Heaven likes humans to do its dirty work for it, quite frankly. Anyway, as you are aware, I am not exactly in Kuan Yin's good books at the moment and I don't want to push my luck. Besides which, I think there's a good chance she actually knows about all this already. As I just said, Heaven plays by its own rules. I'll have to tell the medical services here, but there's always the problem of being believed. People never want to see what's under their noses, especially where Hell's concerned."

"The Minister of Health's an atheist," Lao remarked. Chen snorted.

"The Minister of Health's in pathological denial. We'll do what we can at this end."

"How do you start working on an antidote for a disease that doesn't even

127

exist yet?" Lao remarked.

"It'll exist soon enough," Chen replied grimly. He recalled the pearl: that gem of information snatched from the mind of a girl already dead, remembered the shock as he grasped its meaning. It came back to him now, that fragment of conversation between Pearl's father and the demon who had come to watch her die, echoing in Pearl's own whispering voice:

Your sacrifice won't be in vain. The Ministry of Epidemics is making a plague: one that will kill millions. They need blood. They need blood, and the souls of the innocent. Human blood and innocent souls, to make a drug that takes demons into Heaven.

And there the fragment of memory had ended. Chen stood up, feeling light headed with too little sleep and the shock of revelation.

"What now?" Lao asked.

"I'm going to call the precinct, tell Captain Sung what I think is going on. I'm also going to e-mail Zhu Irzh, if the bioweb's working." He took out his phone and began tapping characters onto the screen.

"The demon? That's a bit of a risk, isn't it? What if he's involved?"

"He's not working for the Ministry, I'm sure of that. Pearl seemed convinced that the Ministry of Epidemics is working independently from the rest of Hell—that's why they wanted this kept so quiet. And Zhu Irzh could be a useful contact, especially if we give him information." He watched, holding his breath, as the connection was finally sustained and the e-mail vanished into the ether between the worlds. "As far as Singapore Three is concerned, apart from yourself, there's one person here who can be trusted to notify the relevant authorities and get the city on full alert. And that's No Ro Shi."

"The demon-hunter? Actually, that's brilliant. He's well connected, highly motivated, and he doesn't give a shit about what anyone thinks of him."

"No Ro Shi can handle things much better than I can," Chen said, picking up his jacket. "And since I won't be here, he's the ideal replacement."

"Since you won't be here? Where are you going?" Lao asked, and then realization dawned. His face grew even longer with dismay. "Oh."

"Well," Chen said. "Where do you think?"

TWENTY-NINE

Inari watched hopelessly as Dao Yi strode angrily from the room, clutching his wounded hand. She could still taste the sparks of rage and fear between her teeth, but this time she swallowed them. She had done a stupid thing, hurting Dao Yi like that. She remembered his face, mottled and dappled with sores and flushed with fury, and winced. But if he hadn't touched her like that... she remembered Chen's gentle, considerate hands and the anger came flooding back. If it was a question between being Dao Yi's lowliest wife and getting summarily dispatched to the Lower Realms, the latter option seemed almost enticing. Perhaps she should take her chances with the *wu'ei* after all, now that the worst had happened and the Ministry had kidnapped her back to Hell... At this thought, there was a rattle from the direction of the ceiling and a shower of dust and grime. Inari jumped, as though the very idea had summoned up the *wu'ei*, but it was a demon like herself who dropped into the room.

Inari's first thought was to wonder why the demon was covered in filth. She had rarely seen anyone dirtier, and his coat was torn. Beneath the dust, however, his face was carved into elegant planes and his eyes were as golden as fire. He said, "Madam? It's plain that you're not where you wish to be."

"Too right," Inari quavered, not yet daring to hope.

"In that case," the demon said, "there is a way out, but I warn you, it isn't altogether pleasant."

"I can see that," Inari remarked, eyeing the demon's disheveled form. He glanced down in evident embarrassment.

"We'll need to free you from those shackles," he said. "What' your name, by the way?"

Inari thought quickly. She didn't want to reveal her true identity, in case this character remembered the old scandal and decided to use her as a pawn in further blackmail. She said hastily, "My name's Leilei."

"What a pretty name," the demon said, crouching down at her feet. The shackles fell away.

"Thank you," Inari sighed. "That didn't take long."

"No, I'm—I have some small skill at this sort of thing... Now. Let me help you up."

Before Inari could protest, he slid his arms around her waist and lifted her up towards the ceiling. She grasped the edge of the opening and hoisted herself through, feeling uncomfortably exposed in the rags of her dressing gown.

"Please don't look at me," she said, embarrassed.

"I wouldn't dream of it," the demon replied gallantly. She was sure he was lying, and she pulled herself up into the grimy shaft as quickly as she could. The demon swung up behind her.

"Now," he said. "We go this way. Try and be quiet."

Thinking of Dao Yi, and the magnification his fury would undergo when he found her gone, Inari did as she was told. It was not an easy clamber through the labyrinth of passageways, nor was it fragrant, and by the time they reached the base of the building and dropped cautiously through into the lavatory cubicle, Inari was as filthy as the demon himself. The dressing gown had also suffered further during the course of the climb; she was practically naked, she thought with angry shame. The demon glanced at her under the wan light of the lavatory, and Inari turned away, not wanting to see if his gaze remained upon her a little too long. Then he said, "I think you'd better take my coat. What's left of it, anyway." Removing the long length of grubby silk, he wrapped it around her, and Inari looked at him gratefully. "We'd better hurry," he said.

"Where are we going?"

"Don't worry. I know a place. Somewhere you'll be safe. Somewhere you can have a bath." He smiled down at her, and Inari smiled dutifully back, but inwardly, she could not help thinking: *It's always men. It's always men who rescue me, steal me, want to marry me... Why am I never in a position to help myself?* But then she remembered the man with the sword, the cold-eyed hunter, flying from the boat into the oily waters of the harbor, and of her tongue flicking fire into Dao Yi's groping hands, and of her initial refusal to marry him which was, after all, the primary cause of her standing here with some stranger in a stinking lavatory in the basement of the Ministry of Epidemics. *Not always men. I just need half a chance, that's all. And the first chance I get, I'll take it.* The demon was already halfway out the door, glancing warily around him, and with new determination in mind, Inari followed.

THIRTY

Predictably and reassuringly, No Ro Shi, the demon-hunter, believed every word that Chen said. He was immediately engaged with the task at hand, promising to get in touch with his vast range of contacts, and set the city on a war footing. Chen, sitting in the temple of Kuan Yin, was a little doubtful as to the success of this, but he directed No Ro Shi to his own desk (now carefully denuded of any reference to Inari) and gave him full use of the facilities. He had just finished running through the complex sequence of bioweb passwords when the voice of Captain Sung echoed over the phone. Evidently, he had been listening in.

"An engineered plague out of Hell, Chen. That's heavy duty stuff."

"I know. No Ro Shi's mobilizing the troops, so to speak. We'll need medical backing."

"It's not just a question of cleaning up after the fact, though, is it? What are we doing to make sure this doesn't happen at all?"

"I'm already on the case, sir."

"What does that mean?"

"Wait a moment," Chen said. He stepped through the door into the courtyard, away from the statue's accusing gaze. It wouldn't make any difference—the goddess had ears in the earth itself—but it seemed more polite, somehow. "I'm going to need a leave of absence."

"To do what?"

"Go to Hell, sir."

There was a short pregnant pause, then Sung said, "You nicked my line, Detective. All right. Leave of absence granted. Are you planning to take anyone with you?"

"No. I can't, anyway. That's not part of the deal between myself and the otherworlds. If I go, I go alone."

131

"All right. Can I ask what precautions you're taking?"

Chen had already given this matter some thought. He said, "I'll be adopting a basic disguise, as a laborer. Hell's full of them. I've got a cover story ready."

"So you'll be undercover? A *snake agent,* as the vice squad calls it?"

"That's right."

Sung considered this for a moment, then said, "Well, I wish you luck. But you should remember one thing. There have been a number of irregularities associated with this case, Chen. The disappearance of a prominent citizen, not to mention his house. The ghosts of girls going astray. Demons manifesting on the deck of your houseboat. Vice cops from Elsewhere. And now something that threatens everyone in the immediate vicinity of Singapore Three and presumably beyond, as well. We don't normally have this amount of activity, Chen, and I don't like it. I'll say here and now that there's no way you're going to be taken off this case, since no one else would touch it with a barge-pole. You have my full and total support, as long as I don't actually have to go any nearer to this supernatural shit than I can help, and as long as you sort it out. But if you don't, the city will be looking for a scapegoat. That scapegoat will be you, Chen."

"I rather assumed that would be the case." Chen tried not to sigh too loudly.

"Very well," Sung said, adding, "And be careful."

"I always am," murmured Chen, but he didn't sound too confident even to his own ears.

THIRTY-ONE

Inari had intended to make her escape from this charming, but suspect, stranger at the first possible opportunity, but that had been before the bath. They had made their way from the Ministry of Epidemics without incident. Inari, bundled up in the black silk coat with her face hidden, resembled just one more of the hordes of afflicted demonkind, and no one spared them a second glance.

By the time they stepped through the double iron doors of the Ministry, it was already close to dark. The band of sickly scarlet light that passed for sunset in Hell ringed the horizon like a migraine, and the storm clouds which continually raced across the skies were tinged with lightning. As they reached the bottom of the immense flight of steps that led down to the square in which the Ministry stood, Inari glanced back and saw a single electric crack of lightning illuminate the Ministry: an iron ziggurat, nine hundred and ninety-nine stories high, almost too vast to be encompassed by any eyes other than those of the *wu'ei* themselves. The blood-colored banners which flanked each corner of the ziggurat snapped in the rising wind, and Inari's hair was pulled free from the inadequate confines of the demon's coat and unfurled behind her. Far into the skies, at the very summit of the ziggurat, swirled lights the color of sickness, in eternal celebration of suffering.

"Come on," the demon said uneasily. "The further we're away from that place, the better."

"Where are we going?" Inari asked again, but he did not answer. Taking her firmly by the hand, he led her across the vast square and into the maze of streets. Soon they were out of the Old Quarter where all the Ministries lay. They hurried past shops selling poisons and lies and secrets: all the traditional wares of Hell, just as it had been for thousands of years, and Inari suppressed a pang. She had missed this world, in a way, and it hurt her to acknowledge that. At least she came from a place full of tradition, not like the mayfly civilizations of humankind... A rail crammed with dried scorpions rattled emptily as they passed, and someone threw slops out of a window. The demon cursed and dodged, pulling Inari off balance. She thought of making a run for it, but the hand that clasped her own was too strong. She wondered uneasily what he had in mind when they reached their destination. She thought she already knew.

They turned a corner and Inari realized with a sudden shock that she knew where she was. There in front of her was her brother Tso's Blood Emporium: its familiar gloomy facade hung with the black and red flags that advertised its wares. Menstrual fluid was on sale again, she noted absently, and the row of dusty marble jars that lined the window had not been touched since her last visit. The person who had taken over the shop after her brother Tso's disgrace—the scandal she herself had precipitated, Inari reminded herself unhappily—had kept the name, presumably for marketing reasons. She wondered what had happened to Tso: so conventional, so conservative, so devoted to respectability. She wondered, too, how he was managing with his reversed feet, and experienced a twinge of guilt so powerful that it made her gasp. The demon glanced at her.

"What's the matter?"

"Nothing. Out of breath, that's all."

"Not so far now," the demon said reassuringly. He led her into the maze of streets, towards the Garden District, and then into an alley that she did not recognize. "We'll go in the back way," the demon said. "Don't want to have to explain you just yet."

"Explain me? To whom?"

"I live in a boarding house. The woman who runs the place allows guests, but she charges a fortune, and after tonight, for various reasons, I might be a bit strapped for cash... Here we are."

He opened the latch of a gate and drew Inari through into a wild, neglected garden. At one time, however, this had been cared for and tended: in the last of the light Inari could see lilies nodding their dark heads over the gleam of water, and she smelt the bitter fragrance of night-roses.

"It's nice," she said.

"Well, I like it. And one can't be too fussy, after all."

He led her up the steps onto a rickety verandah, its black lacquer peeling from the surface of the wood, and fumbled for a key. Opening a pair of French windows, he motioned Inari inside.

"Through here."

Inari stepped through into a large, quiet room. The demon lit a lamp with a touch of his hand, and light rippled across a surprisingly tasteful array of furniture. Inari could not fail to notice that a large, curtained bed stood in the corner of the room. She sat demurely down on a worn couch beside a rather untidy array of lilies stuffed into a vase.

"You have a lot of books," she said.

"Unfortunately I don't get the chance to read much—too busy. Still, I like to think I'll catch up when I have the time…" The demon moved to the French windows and drew the curtains, first locking the latch securely. "Now," he said. "There is a bath through here, which you may use. I'll find you some clothes."

"I don't think your clothes would fit me," Inari said uncertainly. "You're taller than me."

The demon gave an oblique, somewhat smug, smile, thus confirming several of Inari's worst fears.

"I've got some ladies' garments. Things visitors have left here." He ushered her into a small bathroom adjoining the main room. "Hope the water's not playing up again."

The water was, however, both hot and clean, which was impressive for Hell. Inari wondered how much the demon paid for this place. She supposed she should take an interest in him.

"What's your name?" she called through the closed door.

"Zhu Irzh," came the muffled reply. It meant nothing to Inari. While the bath was running, she stripped off the rags, then sank gratefully into the seething boil of the water and closed her eyes. She came close to falling asleep, and it was only the thought that she ought to get out of here before her benefactor started suggesting recompense for his kindness in rescuing her that made her slide out of the bath. When the demon was bathing, she'd find the chance to slip away. A nightdress was sitting on the nearby chair: all air and black lace. Inari frowned. She hadn't heard anyone come in, but there was nothing else to wear, so Inari put the nightgown on, tied a towel around her waist for additional modesty and stepped cautiously back into the main room. Zhu Irzh was sitting on the couch reading the paper. He was wearing a long, silk dressing gown, and he was surprisingly clean. He smiled when she came in and said, "You looked so comfortable—I just slipped in with your nightdress, you see, and I didn't want to disturb you, so I went next door and borrowed my neighbor's shower. Are you feeling refreshed?"

"Thank you, yes," Inari said, inwardly cursing. It didn't help that the room was warm and fragrant, she was tired and frightened, and Zhu Irzh, now denuded of his layer of filth, was revealed to be extremely attractive. Something inside her wailed for Chen, for the badger, for her own familiar houseboat. For Earth. *You'll be back there soon*, Inari told herself firmly. *Stop fretting.*

"Come and sit here by me," Zhu Irzh said, patting the couch next to him. Inari came reluctantly across and sat down firmly on the opposite chair. The demon's smile widened. He gave a little nod. "All right," he said. "So tell me.

How did such a pretty thing as you come to be shackled and groped by that repulsive person in the upper echelons of the Ministry of Epidemics?"

Inari had a story ready, but she didn't know if it sounded remotely convincing. She launched into a hesitant explanation of how she was the sister of a Third Degree Administrative Assistant at the Ministry, how she came in now and then to help her brother, how the demon from whom Zhu Irzh had rescued her had taken a fancy to her and assaulted her, chaining her up when she refused to submit to his advances and—Inari paused for breath and stole a glance at Zhu Irzh. He was gazing at the floor, still with a slight smile. His startlingly long eyelashes gave him a disturbingly demure and feminine appearance, but then he looked up and the impression was abruptly dispelled in a flash of fiery gold.

"What a terrible story," he said lightly, leaving Inari in some doubt as to whether he was sympathizing or calling her a liar. "Still, all too common, I'm afraid." He sighed with apparent sincerity. "Never mind. You're safe now."

"Thank you for rescuing me," Inari whispered, and winced at the memory. She had said a very similar thing to Chen, but then it had been impelled by real gratitude, and real relief. She might be grateful to Zhu Irzh, but relieved? Not until she had a clearer idea of his motives. That clarification was not long in coming. Zhu Irzh said, "I'm so sorry. I've been a terrible host—I haven't even offered you tea. Would you like some?"

"Yes, please," Inari said. "Oolong, if you have it."

"Indeed. A gift from my grandmother. She was given a canister from the Imperial Court itself, on the occasion of her 500th birthday. I only save it for special occasions," said Zhu Irzh. His taloned hands rested lightly on her shoulders for a moment and she could feel their heat, radiating out from his palms. It made her shiver, and Zhu Irzh withdrew. Anxiously, Inari turned her head and saw him busying himself with the tea bowls. He was still smiling.

"There we are," he said, placing a black lacquered bowl, filled with tea of the same hue, on the table. "This'll make you feel better." And then, before Inari had time to react, he bent to swiftly and expertly kiss her. Somewhere beyond the sudden ringing in her head—an uneasy mixture of outrage, guilt, horror and desire—came the cynical thought that he'd obviously had plenty of practice. She pulled back, stumbling to her feet and upsetting the chair, and clapped her hand to her mouth like a schoolgirl. Zhu Irzh caught his lower lip between his teeth; he looked utterly charmed.

"I *can't*," she stuttered. Stepping across the fallen chair, Zhu Irzh took her firmly by the shoulders and looked down into her stricken face.

"Of course not," he said smoothly. "You've had some nasty experiences today; enough to unsettle the sternest soul. I don't know *what* I was thinking of." Bending his head, he kissed her chastely on the brow. "Now. Drink your tea and go to bed. I'll sleep on the couch—or down the hall, if you prefer.

I'm sure I can borrow my neighbor's couch."

"The hall," Inari managed to say. "If you don't mind—I mean, thank you, but—"

"It's quite all right," Zhu Irzh said soothingly. He gathered up a bundle of clothes and opened the door. "Sleep well, Leilei." It took her a moment to realize that this was her pretended name, and a moment more to realize that as he stepped through the door, Zhu Irzh's smile was once more wide.

THIRTY-TWO

"I've read about this," Lao murmured. "Never actually seen it done, though. How many times have you been through this now?"

"This will be the ninth," Chen said absently. He was crouching on the tiles of the temple floor, carefully arranging the sticks of red incense.

"That's more than I'd realized," Lao said with renewed respect.

"Yes, well, I've been at this game a long time," Chen told him. Silently, he added, *But never without Kuan Yin's blessing*. He decided not to share this thought with the police exorcist; Lao was more nervous than Chen had ever seen him. The long ends of his moustache seemed to twitch with unstable energy, and Chen could almost sense Lao's flickering *ch'i*. "Try to get centered," Chen said mildly, looking up. "You're throwing me off balance."

"Sorry." Lao sank back into a more relaxed stance and took a deep, steadying breath.

"That's better." It wasn't, but Chen didn't want Lao to become more distracted than he was already. In the normal field of operations, the exorcist was usually a fairly sanguine character, if irritable, but what they were doing now was a long way from normal. Briefly, Chen debated with himself whether to send Lao outside, but he needed the exorcist for the role that was usually occupied by the goddess. Chen was trying not to think too hard about the implications of this; he had enough to worry about.

"All right," he said, standing up and surveying the results of his preparations. "I think we're ready to roll." Lao gave a small, tense nod.

"You're sure?" Their eyes met briefly.

"No choice," Chen said.

"Chen—look after yourself, all right? Don't do anything too bloody stupid." The words *Unlike last time* hung unspoken in the air between them. "And bring her back safely, yes? Her *and* yourself."

Chen could not resist a wary glance at the statue of Kuan Yin, but the goddess was tranquil and unmoving. If there was a faint halo of disapproval around the serenity of her jade countenance, it was indiscernible from the products of his own guilty imagination.

"I'll be all right," Chen said, trying to sound sincere. "Don't worry. And keep an eye on No Ro Shi, whatever you do."

"Oh, don't you worry about that," Lao said, with something of a return to form. "I'm not letting that mad bastard out of my sight until doomsday. Or until you come back. Whichever's first. By the way—" he paused.

"What?"

"If that demon shows up—the vice cop."

"What about him?"

"What shall I tell him?"

Chen paused for thought.

"Tell him the truth. Tell him where I've gone. But don't tell him the whole reason why. Just let him know I'm going after whoever snatched Tang."

"And if he doesn't believe me?"

"Don't give him the luxury of choice. You'll just have to be especially convincing."

He reached out and gripped Lao's hand. "Lao—thanks."

"Let's get on with it," Lao said grimly, returning the grip for an instant. He stepped backwards, leaving Chen standing in the middle of the circle. "You're certain this will work?" he asked, picking up the laptop and settling it onto his bony knees.

"Yes, I'm certain. Pretty sure, anyway," Chen said, making a quick epistemological adjustment. "All you have to do is run the program."

"And you've done this before?"

"Well, no. Not exactly. Usually, the goddess herself recites the litany, but it's some nineteen pages of ancient Mandarin and, frankly, I haven't had the time to actually learn it myself, so it didn't seem right to ask you to do so. That's why I digitized it instead."

"Is that likely to make a difference?" Lao asked, alarmed.

"Well, it's true that there is a bit of a difference between the intonations of an actual deity from the Celestial Shores and a Sony-Hyundai voice synthesizer, but I'm hoping the effect will be the same," Chen said, more flippantly than he felt. "Right," he added, leaning down to touch a lighter to the incense sticks and stepping back as each one flared into fragrant smoke. "Off we go."

Through the incense haze he saw Lao's long fingers hovering over the keyboard of the laptop, and heard the first words of the litany that would send him down to the Night Harbor and on to Hell. He did not need to glance behind him to see that he had the goddess' full attention. He could feel her lambent eyes boring into the back of his head like a drill, and the full weight of her disapproval felt as though someone had thrown a bucket of icy water over him.

"Chen Wei!" The voice was a familiar one, and it echoed inside his head as if nothing lay between the twin walls of his skull. Chen concentrated on the uneven, artificial voice of the litany. "Chen, do you think I don't know what you are doing?" Uncanny, thought Chen, how the goddess' voice could sound so like that of his own mother in one of her more imperious moods, yet he could not find it surprising. He did not reply.

"If you are following her, Chen, the little demon whom you took to your bed, then all that you can ever be is one man. One man, without my protection, against the armies and legions of Hell. I am compassionate beyond measure, but even my compassion has limits."

In the matter of prejudice, Chen thought, *we are all the same. Goddess and demon, human and monster: none of us understand difference, but at least some of us make the effort to try.*

"Do you have the temerity to compare yourself to me?" the goddess asked incredulously, and this time Chen flinched. All Heaven's icy command was behind those words. *Yes, she is the compassionate and the merciful, but she is also a goddess, and woe betide anyone who forgets that.* But the litany was winding to its end. He could feel the heat rising, spiraling in the smoky air that filled the temple, burning through the soles of his shoes and snatching at the back of his throat. His head was beginning to ring like a bell, and a band akin to the iron grasp of a migraine seized his skull with crushing force.

"Chen Wei!" someone cried, but through the pain Chen could not tell whether it was the goddess or Lao, or some other, crying out his name from the depths of the abyss. Words echoed in his head: *if you gaze into the abyss, sooner or later you will find it looking back at you.* And then the temple was stripped away and he was standing in the great hallway that was the entrance to the Night Harbor, its iron doors at his back.

Even the air was different in this antechamber between the worlds. It crackled with anticipation, like the wind before a storm. Shadows chased across the hall, darting up into the metal lattice of the immense and distant ceiling. This portal of the Night Harbor reminded Chen of a Victorian railway station that he had once visited in London: there was something echoing and gloomy about it, with the edge of anticipation that one found in places where journeys were about to be made. From the corner of his eye Chen glimpsed a vast, milling crowd of people: both old and young, but all of them pale and weary. When he turned to gaze at them directly, however, he was unsurprised to see that there was no one there. The dark, indistinct form of a warrant officer was bringing a new ghost through the doors. At the far end of the hallway, seated behind an ornate desk, sat a receptionist filing her talons. Chen frowned, though he knew that administrative tasks were shared equally between the worlds and it was often true that demons were rather easier to deal with than the frequently hide-bound personnel from the Celestial Realms. Ignoring the insubstantial queue, Chen walked up to the desk. It was hard to get his balance: he found himself lurching as though he'd just stepped ashore, which to Chen raised interesting questions about the exact nature of gravity. When he reached the desk, he presented his credentials. The girl looked up. She was chewing something, Chen noted with distaste. Her gaze flickered incuriously across Chen, who said, "Police Department, Liaison Division. I'll be going to Hell."

He was expecting an argument over his authorization, but the girl merely shifted whatever it was she was chewing to the other side of her cheek and flicked up some records on a computer that looked as though it had been carved out of ebony. Her talons clicked across bone keys. She mumbled, "All right, then. Through there."

"It's all right if I go straight through?" Chen asked sharply, checking. The girl shrugged. She took a glutinous red lump out of her mouth, studied it for a moment, then replaced it. Taking this for assent, Chen went swiftly to the indicated door and pressed his scarred palm against its carved iron surface. There was a sudden warmth beneath his hand. He could feel a hundred pairs of envious eyes on his back as the door opened and he stepped cautiously through.

The Night Harbor was the greatest nexus between the worlds. It resembled such sites as Kuan Yin's temple and the Pellucid Island Opera House, but unlike these places, which remained firmly rooted in their own particular worlds, the Night Harbor constantly shifted and changed. It seemed to Chen to contain all possibilities at once, all destinations. Blossoms drifted by, fragile as snow, from the peach trees of Heaven's shores; turning to flakes of ice as Hell's configurations took precedence. Faces drifted by Chen: a young man whose mouth formed a gaping zero of horror; a girl in a Western wedding dress as white as the peach blossoms and ashes through which she was floating. Her dress was on fire, yet unconsumed. Pagodas reconstructed themselves against a sky that altered from moment to moment, and for a disorienting minute Chen found himself gazing up through water. His hand groped in his breast pocket and located the rosary, which anchored him a little. Chen knew that the embarkation queues were to be found in what passed for the south of the port area, as far as one could go from the entry doors before reaching the shores of the Sea of Night, but given the alchemical landscape in which he currently stood, finding a particular direction was not easy. Mountains streamed by; firecrackers thrown by a group of spectral children, their mouths open in silent, frozen laughter, snapped at his feet. Before his eyes they turned to dog spirits, the hounds of Hell, and he recognized the tottering buildings of Dog Village. There was an ululating howl as something smelled live meat.

Teeth snapped at Chen's arm and he turned, whipping the rosary across a long, dark muzzle. The spirit wailed, and fell back to flee on two spindly legs. Chen hunched his head into his shoulders, gripped his rosary and fled past the rickety houses with a snarl echoing in his ears.

Then the Dog Village was gone: the ground on which he walked was suddenly the whole of China and his head was in the clouds. *Concentrate*, thought Chen. *Concentrate.* He thought of Comrade No Ro Shi, the demon-hunter, attempting to make sense of these anarchic surroundings and smiled. Definitely not the party line; No Ro Shi would disapprove, deny, refuse to see. Perhaps No Ro Shi's way was the best after all; perhaps Chen should have taken a firmer stance in the matter of his own ideological convictions, but Chen could not resist the subtle appeal of shades of gray, which maybe made him the best person to navigate these shadowy shores after all. Maybe.

He could see something in the distance: a thin dark line like a crack in the world. It was not the first sight Chen had had of the Sea of Night, and he had crossed it in his travels between the worlds, in this life and in others, but it never failed to chill him. It was the great gulf, the line between Life and Death, and he could not help but be afraid. He came to the bridge across the abyss, and here Chen halted. He hated heights, and the bridge was no more than a few inches wide, as thin as a razor. Chen, panicking, thought: *I can't do it. I can't; I'll have to go back. You've done it before*, his rational self reminded him. But he could not imagine how. Inari's face swam before his mind's eye and then something striped and dark stepped in front of him. It was the badger. Dimly, Chen remembered a shape streaking into the circle at the moment of his departure from the temple. Black eyes gazed up at him.

"Follow me," the badger said without compassion. It placed a clawed foot on the bridge and stepped forwards. Fixing his gaze on the back of the badger's striped head, pointing like an arrow to safety and the other side, Chen took a deep breath and followed.

After what seemed like an eternity, they stepped safely onto the dock on the other side. The badger glanced back indifferently, as though it mattered little whether Chen had fallen silently into the abyss, but Chen could read much into that glance.

"Thank you," he sighed. He had rarely been more pleased to be on solid ground. He felt shaky and weak, as though death had come to claim him after all. The badger inclined its head in what might have been a bow.

As they drew nearer to the long quay, bypassing the scales that weighed the souls and the great mirror that would tell each one where its future lay, Chen could see the line of souls waiting patiently for the next boat across the Sea of Night. The quay itself was made of human teeth, the last payment made by the abandoned flesh, and it towered high above the transmuting ground of the port. A sharp, rickety tier of bone-steps led upwards. Chen took a deep breath of unnatural air and started climbing. The steps crunched beneath his feet. The badger glided alongside. Curious faces turned to watch their progress, until a swarm of spirits had gathered at the side of the quay. At last Chen stepped onto the quay itself and looked around him. There must have been a hundred spirits gathered there, still wearing the vestiges of their living selves. Most of them, Chen was glad to see, were quite old, a startling tribute to Singapore Three's rather less-than-adequate health-care system, but one or two small spirits flickered around his ankles like dogs and he saw again the girl in the burning wedding dress. Chen shivered, wondering what her story might be. There was also a sullen group of young men; the ritual scars on their forearms fading with the memory of the flesh but still sufficient to identify them as members of Singapore Three's various gangs. Even in death, it seemed, they kept to their tribes. Chen looked around him. There was no sign of the boat that traveled the Sea of Night. The spirits of the elderly people clustered around Chen, bewildered and vague, as if they had not yet realized they were no longer alive. He said, "I'm looking for the boat across the sea. Does anyone know when it leaves?" Wondering, pale eyes widened at the sound of Chen's voice, which seemed to echo out across the darkness beyond. Then the ghost of a middle-aged woman stepped forward; Chen could see the traces of an open wound carved down her smiling face. Her form was still clad in the red robes of a Buddhist nun. Her eyes narrowed as she saw him, with something that might momentarily have been envy.

"You're alive," she said, wonderingly.

"I know," Chen said, feeling guilty. "I'm with the police liaison department. I'm traveling to Hell."

"You're a brave man. Or a reckless one."

"I'm never sure which, myself. Do you know where the boat is?"

"It's on the other side of the dock. These folk are waiting for their final documents to be processed. Do you have proper papers?"

Chen nodded.

"Then come with me."

Chen accompanied her through the crowd. The nun walked slowly, limping. "You'll have to excuse me," she said over her shadowy shoulder. "Still not quite used to being dead yet. You forget, don't you?"

"How did it happen?" Chen asked diffidently. He had never quite ceased to feel that this was a somewhat insensitive question, but the dead seemed to take a grisly enthusiasm in talking about their means of demise.

"Kid in a stolen Daewoo Wanderer. Knocked me off my bike last night," the nun said. "It was very quick. I was a bit cross at first, then I thought, well, there's nothing I can do about it. It's not as if it's the first time, after all."

"We'll all end up here in the end," Chen said.

"We will indeed. Over and over again... At least I know where I'm going.

Half these poor souls haven't worked out what's happened to them yet, and not all of them are bound for the Celestial Shores…or Hell by choice, like yourself." She paused, nodding in the direction of a small, frail figure with its head bowed over its knees. "Like *that* poor soul."

The spirit looked up, and Chen saw with a jolt that it was the ghost of Mrs Tang. She gazed at him dully; there was no spark of recognition in her pale eyes.

"Wait a moment," Chen said. He sat down beside her, with the nun hovering solicitously nearby. As gently as he could, he said, "Mrs Tang? I'm so sorry we couldn't do more to help you. We tried to save you, you know, but I'm afraid there was nothing we could do."

"Oh," Mrs Tang said. A vague comprehension washed over her features. "It's you. And you're still alive… You living people all look the same to me, now—isn't that odd? But I do remember… yes. You tried to help, you and that tall man with the moustache." Her face twisted. "I was possessed, wasn't I? I don't like to remember."

"It's all right," Chen said hastily. "Don't think about it. It's over."

"It was my husband, of course," Mrs Tang said numbly. "At first I tried to pretend that it was nothing to do with him—Pearl's death, I mean. But I had my suspicions, and at last I decided to do something. I couldn't prove anything, and then I heard of you. So I went to see you. And he found out. He—did something. Called something up, to make me talk."

"Your husband's fallen foul of whoever he was in league with," Chen said. "Don't worry. He's already met his just desserts. But we still don't know who he was working with. Do you have any idea?" At his shoulder, the nun shifted, a little impatiently, but having found Mrs Tang, Chen was reluctant to relinquish his unexpected good luck.

"I don't know much," Mrs Tang said slowly. "I know he had some sort of arrangement with the Ministry of Wealth, but he didn't think they were doing enough for him. So he went to someone else instead."

"Do you know who?"

"Another Ministry, of Hell." The ghost of Mrs Tang shivered. "I don't know which one, exactly—there are lots, aren't there? I think it was one of the ones to do with disease."

"Mrs Tang," Chen said, trying not to look too exultant. "Would you be prepared to testify?"

"Against my husband?" Mrs Tang asked bitterly. "There's nothing I'd like better—he killed me, didn't he? He's the reason I'm sitting in the middle of this—this *nowhere*. But you have to understand, Detective—I know what he can do now. I'm sure he's got contacts in the otherworld—in Hell. I don't even know if they'll let me into Heaven. I've never really been religious, you see; I never used to believe in any of this stuff before I came to Singapore

Three and even then I thought it was just superstition."

Chen could believe this, thinking of chic Mrs Tang as she had been in life. Now, stripped of her designer clothes and her status and social position, she was nothing more than just another shade. It had often occurred to Chen how shattering it must be for someone who had devoted their whole life to material possessions to suddenly find themselves in a world where status depended on entirely more intangible matters. He glanced across at the nun, whose feet were planted squarely on the nebulous surface of the quay and who could not have looked so very different from her appearance in life. "And if I end up in Hell and I testify," Mrs Tang went on, "who knows what he might do?" Her hands wrung together in her lap. "I used to think there was nothing worse than death, and now—"

"Listen," Chen said. "Let's be practical. Your documents haven't been processed yet. We don't know where you're heading, and it may very well be that you'll get into Heaven after all. In that case, you'll have automatic immunity—the Celestial Realms look after their own. If you go—elsewhere, there may still be something we can do to protect you."

"Detective?" Mrs Tang said. "What *happens* now? I know what the religious people say, but what really happens when you die? I mean, after this? When will I be reincarnated? And what as?"

Chen sighed. "Mrs Tang, even I can't say for sure, and I've traveled between the worlds several times as a living person. No one is permitted to remember their voyage across the Sea of Night. All souls are sent back—reincarnated—after their time in Heaven or Hell. But we're not granted any real understanding of the mechanics of the process—the gods deem it best that we don't know, or if they tell us, then we forget. I'm sorry I can't be more helpful."

"It's all right," Mrs Tang sighed. Then her head snapped up. "Detective, my daughter! What's become of my daughter?" Her shadowy face twisted. "Pearl died because of what H'suen was doing, I'm sure of it. I think H'suen's new masters wanted a sacrifice. I think she was it."

"Don't worry," Chen said, and this time he was able to mean it. "She wasn't a sacrifice in the way you mean, though I'm afraid it's true enough that your husband killed her. She found out something of what he was doing, you see. But she's safe now. She's in Heaven, she was sent by Kuan Yin herself. I saw her go."

Mrs Tang's face crumpled and she clutched at Chen's hand. Then the distress flowed out of her face, leaving it smooth and pale. "Then I don't care where I go," she said. Chen glanced up. Someone was coming along the wharf, dressed in gray robes. Its face was smooth and inexpressive, with a bland smile, and it carried a bundle of documents. It was one of the wardens responsible for the passage of souls between the worlds: Chen had seen its kind before. As it neared the place where Chen was sitting, it said in a whispering voice, "Lily Tang? Here is your visa." It passed a slip of paper to her and glided on, with a half-curious glance at Chen. Mrs Tang's phantom hands were steady as she opened the slip of paper but one look at her face told Chen the bad news, belaying her earlier defiant words. He put a sympathetic hand on her shoulder and the nun came to sit by her side.

"Don't worry," the nun murmured. "Hell's not as bad as all that, and you may not even be there for very long. Before you know it, you'll be reborn in the world again and you won't remember a thing."

Chen did not think that Mrs Tang looked very convinced. He was about to add his own reassurances, but the smooth, gliding person was coming back.

"Embarkation is about to commence," the being said.

Mrs Tang turned to Chen and grasped his arm. Looking down, he saw that her spectral knuckles were white, but he felt nothing. "Detective? Will you stay by me, on the boat?"

"If I can," Chen said. He rose to follow the official. And after that everything became hazy: a succession of images, the red-lacquered bulk of the boat rocking above an ocean of darkness; his own feet gliding up a gangway and a spectral wind on his face. Later, through the mercifully hazy depths of fear, came the sudden vastness of galaxies, spawned in the hinterlands of the universe and spinning out stars like grain from a millwheel.

And then, much later still, a rasping hand grasped his arm. A voice hissed in his ear, "You do not have correct papers for disembarkation! You must leave now, and take your familiar with you!"

A dim memory of protest, hands tightening, a vertiginous tilt…Chen was falling. There was a banner snapping in an eternal wind, towers of iron and bone and pain, and a red and endless sky where no sun shone.

THIRTY-THREE

Inari sat bolt upright, shaking. She took a deep breath, inhaling the once familiar scent of Hell: old incense, and hatred, and blood, overlaid with the more fragrant odors of tea and the perfume of the night-lilies, which drifted in from the garden. She had been dreaming a dream in which Dao Yi had snatched her back to the underworld, and was mauling her with putrefying hands…It was a moment before she realized that this was memory, not dream; another moment still before the knowledge dawned upon her that it was not this recollection that had awakened her. There was something in the room.

Zhu Irzh, she thought. Carefully and quietly, she lay back down on the bed. Her hands, resting gently on the covers, flexed their long talons and she could feel the prickle of her incisors as they lengthened. Here in Hell, her own world, she was becoming more demonic by the minute, and she did not like it. She did not want to be this fierce, fearful thing longing for the taste of blood in her mouth, yet repulsed by her own nature and those around her. She wanted to be back on the houseboat, pottering about with the cooking, and the badger weaving in and out between her feet. Sunlight and salt, and fresh clear air...*remember who you have become, not who you once were...* But now she had to remember both. She could hear footsteps moving stealthily about the room. She turned over, sighing as she did so in the pretence of deep sleep, then rolled silently onto her back once more. There was a heavy rustle of silk as the curtains were pulled aside. Inari stirred, murmured, peered through half-closed eyes.

A little pair of hands protruded through the curtain. They were delicate hands, with long golden talons shaped into fashionable spirals, and even in the darkness Inari's night-eyes could see that the hands were as red as blood. Long fingers rippled and flexed in obscene anticipation and then, as if by magic, a length of black silk was conjured from the depths of a sleeve. The owner of the hands gave a small, breathy gasp, almost a giggle, and reached out with the garrote. Inari struck: rearing up from the bed and lashing out with a taloned hand. Silk curtains tore and something fell wetly to the bed: a long strip of decaying flesh attached to something bony, which sizzled into ash as soon as it touched the covers. Freeing herself from the bedclothes, Inari sprang to the floor. The figure wore an ornate ceremonial robe. Long hair cascaded down its back. Its eyes were huge and dark above the ruin of its jaw, and now Inari could see what it was that she had torn away: a strip of the creature's face and rotting jawbone. The creature's tongue lolled loosely from the back of its throat and it reached up a red hand and stuffed the tongue awkwardly back in. Then it came forwards in a crouching rush. Inari kicked out and hooked a foot behind its bony ankle, bringing it crashing to the floor. It struck out with a flailing arm and she grasped its wrist and twisted. The arm came out of its socket like a ripe plum falling from a tree. Gasping, Inari threw it to one side. She kicked the creature in the ribs and felt something cave rottenly inwards. The creature gave a whistling cry. Its ribcage began to expand outwards, each bone unpeeling itself from the sternum, dangling petals of flesh. The ribs arched back until they reached the floor, where they began to scrabble and thrash like the legs of some monstrous arachnid. Inari fled into the tiny kitchenette and dumped one of the cabinet drawers onto the floor. Seizing a long knife, she ran back into the main room in time to see that the creature had managed to turn itself right way up. It had now divested itself of all spare flesh except the legs, which remained entangled in the robe and trailed across the floor like long and empty bags. As Inari stumbled to a halt, its legs finally fell away, leaving the creature's spine free to arch upwards over its head. Its tongue, attached only by a thin and elastic strip of skin, finally fell off. The foremost ribs, now legs, clicked as the creature ran forwards. A sharp, dark thing like the thorn of a rose protruded from the end of the spine, glistening with venom. Inari dived over the couch just as it lashed forwards. The venomous spine shot through the back of the divan, where it stuck. Scrambling to her feet, Inari struck down with the knife, hacking frantically at bone and sinew until the spine was completely severed. The thing scuttled forwards, only to be knocked flying as the door surged open and Zhu Irzh leaped through, sword in hand.

"What the fuck?" he shouted, wide-eyed.

Loosened by the draught, the French windows had come open and now slammed to and fro in the rising wind from the garden. Glancing towards the verandah, Inari saw that the lock had been punched out, presumably as the thing had gained entrance into the room. She did not stay to find out what might happen to the spiny thing, nor to her erstwhile host. Instead, she sprinted out into the garden.

"Leilei!" Zhu Irzh cried, behind her. She heard the rattle of bones on the floor, but she did not stop. Thrusting the night-lilies aside, she bolted through the garden and scrambled over the fence into the alley. And then, clad in yet another dressing gown but with the knife clutched firmly in one hand, Inari ran until she could run no more.

THIRTY-FOUR

Zhu Irzh stared glumly at the ruin of what had once been his room and contemplated where to start clearing up. The divan was a wreck; the table had been split down the middle in the fight with the visitor, and two of his best tea bowls lay in fragments on the floor. Moreover, the carpet was now irredeemably stained with an inky pool of spinal fluid, which assiduous scrubbing had failed to remove. His landlady had been to see him first thing in the morning, about the noise. On seeing the remains of the creature, now hacked into fragments of cartilage and bone by the razor edge of Zhu Irzh's departmental sword, her face had taken on the expressive patina of ice. It had taken all the demon's charm and powers of persuasion, plus a month and a half's additional deposit, to induce her to let him to stay.

As for his guest... Zhu Irzh sighed. This was it. He had known it the minute he'd seen her. Previously, he had merely skirted the perimeters of love: tested the waters, so to speak, had a couple of practice runs in rehearsal for the real thing. And now it had dropped upon his unsuspecting psyche with all the force of a rhinoceros. Leilei's phantom face floated before his besotted imagination: the vast, dark-crimson eyes, the pale curve of her cheek, the night-velvet of her hair. She reminded him of the lilies in the garden beyond, but then, everything reminded him of Leilei now... With great reluctance, Zhu Irzh dragged his unwilling imagination away from thoughts of romance, and onto the immediate problems of the present.

The presence of the visitor had confirmed his already active suspicion that Leilei had been lying through her pretty teeth during her account of her reason for standing in shackles at the Ministry of Epidemics. Zhu Irzh didn't hold this against her; on the contrary, it only made her more intriguing. He preferred women with an imagination; it tended to extend into many areas. Moreover, he recognized the creature that now lay in stinking pieces at his feet: it was a hunter-tracker from the lower levels of Hell, a crab-demon which characteristically spent time scavenging in the graveyards of Laon Shu and Honan until it had gathered enough flesh to adequately disguise its skeletal form. Such creatures were rare, and expensive. Whoever had sent it after Leilei was not short of cash, and that meant that Leilei was rather more than a mere assistant's sister whom some apparatchik had happened to fancy. It also gave rise to curiosity about the demon who had shackled her in the first place: evidently he was someone sufficiently high up within the Ministry of Epidemics to be able to afford such expensive equipment as the crab-demon. Zhu Irzh could smell the distinctive odor of rising stakes, and the prospect of serious political intrigue both excited and dismayed him. Sinking to the remains of the couch, he debated the thorny question as to which aspects of recent events he should relay to the First Lord of Banking. He had the feeling that there was no optimum solution; he was likely to be castigated whatever he did, but at least there was the possibility that certain elements of his narrative would prove so useful to his employer that the rest would be forgiven. Zhu Irzh blinked at his own naiveté. He was definitely in love.

He was painstakingly constructing a suitable account of events when the phone shrilled. Hesitating for a moment, Zhu Irzh picked it up.

"Seneschal?" said a familiar voice, and Zhu Irzh frowned.

"Lord," he said, with careful neutrality.

"I have had a complaint about you. I will allow you, for the moment, the luxury of conjecturing the identity of the complainant."

Zhu Irzh took a deep breath. "Thank you, Lord, that is customarily gracious. I would surmise that any allegation might stem from the portals of the Ministry of Epidemics."

"How perspicacious of you," replied the First Lord of Banking, with more than usual acidity. "It is indeed from the Ministry, who might best be described as livid. Would you care to explain yourself?"

Hastily Zhu Irzh said, "I went to the Ministry as instructed. I was extremely careful. I made enquiries, and conducted an investigation. High in the levels of the Ministry, I discovered a potentially important witness who was under interrogation. In order to prevent her from disclosing what she knew to a hostile authority, I removed her from the premises and brought her here. Halfway through the night, however, someone dispatched a crab-demon after her, thereby corroborating my intuition that she is crucial to the investigation."

"Well, Seneschal," said the old dry voice at the other end of the phone. "You would seem to have acted with admirable speed, albeit with less than admirable discretion. And where is this crucial witness now?"

"Ah."

"Well?"

"She's not here, Lord. She was so disturbed by our nocturnal visitor that she fled from the house. I made an extensive search for her as soon as I got rid of the crab-demon, but she was nowhere to be found."

"Unfortunate," said the First Lord of Banking, without any inflection at all.

"Yes," said Zhu Irzh, wondering fleetingly if he should endeavor to provide some sort of justification for his actions. He decided against it. Hell was no place for excuses.

"And would you care to elaborate upon this critical secret that the witness was about to spill prior to your gallant rescue?"

"Not over the phone," Zhu Irzh said quickly. "One never knows who might be listening."

"Quite," the First Lord mused, and Zhu Irzh breathed an inaudible sigh of relief. "You'd better come here then, hadn't you? And tell me in person, as quickly as possible."

"I will indeed proceed as swiftly as I can to your august mansion—however, this is the third day that I haven't put in any appearance at work and frankly, Lord, I'm reluctant to anger my superiors. Normally, I am a most conscientious employee," Zhu Irzh said, buying time.

"Don't worry about that," the First Lord of Banking snapped. "I've spoken to Supreme Seneschal Yhu. He's granted you an indefinite leave of absence."

"That is most kind, most thoughtful, although I might perhaps draw your attention to one little detail—under current regulations, a leave of absence would entail that I am not entitled to be paid for the period in question."

"No, you're not."

"So, therefore..."

"You had better submit an invoice detailing your expenses to date to my under-secretary. We'll review it at the end of the month, with all other related claims."

"But it is now only the second day of Sho'ei, and by my calculation the month has another seventy days to run."

"Your calculation is quite correct, Zhu Irzh. I'm delighted to see that you are numerate. Perhaps if your leave of absence goes on for too long a period and you are fired, we might consider giving you a position here as an accountant," the First Lord of Banking said, chuckling at his little joke. "Goodbye for now, Seneschal. I'll see you very soon." With that, he rung off, leaving Zhu Irzh to contemplate the prospect of an eternity in an accounts department. The very thought made him sigh. Hell indeed.

THIRTY-FIVE

Something was sniffing at Chen's ankles. He rolled over blearily. There was a wetness beneath his hand, seeping through the fabric of his coat, and a familiar sour smell, which after a moment Chen recognized as the characteristic stench of Hell. He groaned and opened his eyes. No mistaking it; he was back. Storm clouds edged with red light like torn flesh raced overhead, and something sticky was dripping from the iron eaves beneath which he lay. Suddenly conscious of the movement at his feet, he hauled himself into a sitting position and groped for his rosary, but a leaden weight descended onto his chest, trapping his hand. A narrow visage, composed of monochrome stripes, peered into his own. Chen's gaze met dark eyes, with sparks in their depths.

"I did not think you would awake so soon," the badger said, with seeming unconcern. Its wet, black lips drew back from its teeth in a snarl and Chen saw that its long incisors were bloody. "There has been interest in you, from the little things, the vermin. I have kept them away."

"Thank you," said Chen feebly. He struggled to sit up. "Would you mind getting off my chest?" The badger rolled to the floor. A drop of something dark hissed to earth beside Chen's prone form.

"It's raining," Chen said, unnecessarily. He shook his head, trying to clear it. He felt as though someone had stuffed cotton wool behind his eyes. "We'd better get out of this. It's going to pour in a moment. Do you have any idea where we are?"

The badger shook its head. "I do not know this place." A second raindrop steamed to earth like molten lead, followed by another. Chen clambered to his feet, feeling stiffness in every limb, and looked about him. They were in some kind of back alleyway, a muddy track, congealed with refuse. Shacks lined each side of the alley. A door opened onto the track from one of these and from it Chen could hear sibilant voices. Then the door was kicked back, rattling on its hinges, and a pail of slops was hurled into the alley. Chen could smell something sharp and pungent, which smoked in the stormy air. He did not stay to investigate further. With the badger at his heels, he dodged among the piles of garbage and underneath the wider overhanging eaves. He was not a moment too soon. The rain began to come down in force, churning the muck of the alley to an oily soup and filling the gutters above them to overflowing. The alley began to steam in the humid air and Chen felt a stream of sweat begin to run down the back of his neck. He'd only been in Hell for ten minutes, and already he was aching, weary, and suffused in a bath of perspiration. Par for the course, he thought, resigned. Parts of Hell were really no worse than Singapore Three, a sobering reflection in itself, but it was the relentless combination of elements that Chen found so depressing. At his feet, the badger had caught the worst of the rain and now was a bedraggled heap of rats' tails. The water had brought out its shape, like a wet cat, and Chen could see the narrow body, the powerful shoulders and long claws, usually concealed behind the thick pelt of fur. But the badger exhibited no signs of distress: its opaque gaze remained on the rain, and it uttered no sound.

Eventually the rain began to ease off, and shortly after that, it stopped. Chen and the badger stepped cautiously out into the wet world. The shack with the open door was silent, and Chen avoided it, walking instead in the opposite direction. This brought him out into a maze of dark alleyways, dripping with the recent rain, but when he looked up he could see a much larger building behind the shacks: a place with a red-lacquered roof and gilded eaves. The lacquer was tarnished, encrusted with the greasy substance that seemed to permeate so much of Hell, and the gilt was flaking like eczema, but Chen recognized it nonetheless. It was the counterpart of the temple of Kuan Yin: the version that lay embedded like a rotting pearl in the scabrous landscape of Hell. On previous visits, he had always come here, direct as an express elevator to the underworld, and the fact that on this particular occasion Chen had landed summarily in the back alleyway did not escape him. Despite the warm humidity of the air, he felt suddenly cold.

"It is the temple," the badger said, rubbing it in. "And we are not there."

"No, we're not," Chen said. "And I think we'd better avoid going into it unless we absolutely have to." No point in testing the limits of the goddess' tolerance, assuming he hadn't already done so.

"Where are we to go then?"

"If that's the temple, then I know where we are," Chen said with a flicker of relief. "Just let me get my bearings." He frowned with concentration, remembering. This part of Hell, this city, was after all the counterpart of Singapore Three, and the landscapes of the two places overlapped to a considerable, though not to an inevitable, degree. Chen had never been given to understand whether Hell lay alongside the everyday world, mapping its boundaries and distinctions with faithful regularity, or whether its representation was more complex. Certainly there were differences between the aspects of Hell: the afterlife of the Christian peoples seemed very far removed from this particular underworld, for example. Yet Chen suspected that Hell lay somehow contained in the group soul of a people, delineating its pathways in accordance with their dormant beliefs. If he entered Hell from one of the portals of Beijing, he knew that he would find an analog to that ancient city... But these speculations were simply distracting, an attempt by his weary mind to make sense of spiritual violation. Chen marshaled his thoughts.

To the northwest of the temple lay the residential Garden District of Hell and the Opera House. To the southwest he would find the immense towers and ziggurats of Hell's Ministries. To the east lay the mansions of the underworld's elite, and in the centre of the city, like a great decaying heart, sat the Imperial Court itself: the hub of the wheel of Hell around which all else must spin in weary obeisance. But to the south was the commercial quarter and the docks; where souls disembarked from the boat that sailed the Sea of Night, and where all the dubious trades and practices for which Hell was so justly infamous were carried out. It was in this region that the correlate of Zhen Shu Island was to be found; it was here that the brothel lay into which the sad shade of Pearl Tang had been sold. And it was here, in the gloomy confines of Zhameng Square, that the most famous Blood Emporium in all Hell was located: the shop called Tso's, which Chen's brother-in-law had once owned.

"Come on," Chen said briskly to the badger. "Time to make a move."

"Where are we going?" asked the badger, in its slow, earthy voice.

"We're going to Tso's."

THIRTY-SIX

By late afternoon, or what passed for it beneath the eternal skies of Hell, Inari had made her way into the hills. The storms that circled the city so endlessly had succeeded in drenching her twice, but Inari had stopped caring. She plodded wearily on, climbing the narrow tracks that led through groves of bone-tree and spinewort, and threaded through rocks so laden with iron that they were red and rusty to the touch. Zhu Irzh's fine silk dressing gown was nothing more than a limp rag; sartorially, she was no better off than she had been at the Ministry, and the brief respite of comfort and cleanliness at Zhu Irzh's small apartment might have been nothing more than a dream. Unwillingly, Inari remembered the demon's warm mouth against her own, and then she thought of Chen. A wave of weakness glided through her, and she leaned back against a nearby rock and closed her eyes. It was only now that she was beginning to realize, with dull horror, that she could never go back to Earth. She had caused her husband so much trouble, so much grief, and it just wasn't fair to cause more. He had jeopardized his position and his life for her and she could not ask him to do it again. She would stay here where she belonged, in Hell, she thought drearily, but as she gazed out over the darkening towers of the city towards the limitless southern horizon, in the direction of the Sea of Night at which not even a demon might look for long, she could not repress a shiver. The rain was circling back; carried by the great mass of clouds through which lightning ripped. Inari sighed with admiration at the spectacle, but it was beginning to be born upon her that, storm lover though she might be, she had never been exposed to the elements for such a long time and here in the hills it was cold. Drawing the remains of the dressing gown more tightly about her quivering frame, Inari rose grimly to her feet and started walking.

It was not long before the rain hit once more. At first, it was almost refreshing: warm, heavy drops saturating her hair and keeping out the chill, but then the rain grew harder and harder, until it was coming down like a wave of the sea and she could barely see her hand in front of her. Inari stumbled and slipped on the muddy ground: falling once and cutting her palms on the sharp, metallic stones that littered the track. Gasping, she scrambled upright, only to see something taking shape in the mud by her feet. It rose up from the track itself like the blind, questing head of a clam. It was a dark, mud-stained red and it took a moment for Inari to realize that it was forming out of her own blood, generating something in the hideously fertile earth of Hell. A tiny, narrow mouth opened to display needle teeth. Slipping, Inari scrambled backwards and the thing struck out. Teeth grazed her ankles, leaving a twinge of poison, and the scattered drops of blood began to grow and seek in turn. Inari backed away, but her foot caught in a razor-sharp coil of wireweed and she fell heavily to the earth. The growing things were hunting her, their blind heads snaking out in search of her warmth and the blood that had given them birth. They devoured one another as their twisting bodies met, until there were only four: curling five or six feet through the rain. Inari cried out as they crept closer, and struggled to free her ankle from the entrapping wireweed, but it tightened as she pulled and the blood-births were almost at her feet... Then she was seized by the arms and dragged backwards. Something bright and sharp cleaved down to cut the wireweed away. Her left arm was abruptly released. A bolt of heat hissed past her ear and the blood-births sizzled to ash, quickly dispersed by the rain. Wrenching herself free, Inari turned.

A woman was standing by her shoulder. She held a long, curved knife in one hand. The other palm was upraised and Inari could see that it was marked with an intricate spiral scar, still smoking in the dying rain. She wore robes of gray and red, like the rocks from which she had come. Her head was shaved in the manner of a Buddhist nun, but her scalp and face were delineated by a further labyrinth of scars. She turned to gaze calmly at Inari, who saw with distant amazement that her eyes matched her robes. One eye was as serene and gray as the South China Sea at twilight, but the other was a fierce and fiery crimson, like old wine.

"Who are you?" Inari whispered, feeling inexplicably small and shy.

"I am called Fan. But I answer to other names," the woman said. Her voice was very calm. She reached out a hand. "You should come out of the rain. Rain makes things grow and change, even in Hell, but growth isn't always good... There's a place of shelter not far from here." Without waiting for Inari to reply, she turned and began making her way up the slope.

"Wait—" Inari started to say, but the scarred woman was already vanishing among the rocks. In the rainy half-light, her bi-colored robes made her almost invisible against the rocks and Inari was suddenly afraid of losing her. She took a deep breath and stumbled in the woman's wake, only to find when she came through the narrow chasm between the stones that Fan was nowhere to be seen.

"Where are you?" Inari called, noting with dismay that she sounded suspiciously close to panic. But the woman's calm voice answered, "I am here."

Inari looked down to meet Fan's strange eyes. It was as though the woman had disappeared beneath the earth; she seemed to be peering out from a kind of burrow. Inari, uncomfortably reminded of spiders, crouched down, then hesitated. She found herself instinctively trusting this curious person, and in Hell, that was a very bad move.

"Come down," Fan said. "It's quite safe." She reached out a hand and Inari took it. The woman's scarred palm felt sandpaper-rough in her own, but it was a solid, somehow reassuring grip. "I'll help you," the woman added. Gently, she guided Inari through the narrow opening in the rock until Inari was standing beside her on dry earth. There was a curious, musty smell, as though this were an animal's lair. The woman smiled at Inari's dubious expression. "Not so fresh, is it? It wears off after a while."

"It's not too bad," Inari said, afraid of being tactless. In fact, now she came to think of it, the odor reminded her of the badger: dark and furred and earthy. It was a reminder of what she had lost, and Inari turned her face abruptly away. "Where does this go to?" she asked. "And what are you doing here?" *Indeed*, she thought, *what are you?* But it was not a question that one asked lightly, here in Hell.

"I live here," Fan replied simply.

"Why?"

"Because it is necessary. You asked me where this leads to. I'll show you."

She stepped into the shadows beyond the slit of the entrance, and once more Inari followed, treading gingerly over the rough ground. Her night eyes enabled her to see with a reasonable degree of clarity, but she could make out little of the passage through which they walked. It had been carved out of the same iron-bearing rocks of the surface, but here they were dark and polished to the consistency of obsidian. Faces sprang out of their mirrored surface: Inari jumped at her own reflection, smiled at her own foolishness, then realized that the face had not been her own after all, but a visage that twisted and turned with its head to one side, looking at her before fading into nothingness. She could hear the sound of whispering, but it ceased whenever she turned to see where the noise might be coming from. None of this seemed to bother Fan, who strode calmly ahead through the darkness with a cat's measured, silent tread. At last they came out into a wider space.

Gazing up in wonder, Inari saw that it resembled a bowl carved out of the rock. A domed, ribbed ceiling stretched above her head, and the floor was cut from the same stone. Along one curve of this round room were set two immense holes in the wall, with a triangular doorway between, but there was only blackness beyond. She could see her own perplexed figure staring back at her, upside down in both directions. Fan glided around the room, igniting glittering lamps which threw refracted light into a thousand prisms.

"Sit down," she told Inari, over her shoulder. Inari found a rush mat of the kind used by peasants, and settled herself. It lacked the comfort of Zhu Irzh's apartment, and Inari was by no means sure that this woman could be trusted any more than Zhu Irzh himself, but it was a relief just to sit down. She watched as Fan measured water from an earthenware jug and handed her a small stone cup.

"Drink this. It has herbs in it; they'll warm you up. And don't worry; there's nothing that will harm you in it."

Inari was not sure whether she believed her, but she drank the water anyway, and sighed as warmth spread through her.

"Now," the scarred woman said. "Tell me. What is the daughter of the Shi Maon family, runaway to Earth and wife of a man, doing here on the storm-driven hillsides above Zeng Zha?"

"You know who I am?"

"Oh yes. *I* know who you are, Inari. The question is, do *you?*"

Inari stared at her. She was about to ask what the woman meant by such a query, but instead she heard herself saying, "I don't know."

THIRTY-SEVEN

The First Lord of Banking was keeping Zhu Irzh waiting, and this was not a good sign. Zhu Irzh had now been cooling his heels in the lushly appointed antechamber for more than an hour. It was like the Ministry of Epidemics all over again. Zhu Irzh studied his long, trimmed talons, and sighed. He knew very well that this was a message, the unmistakable odor of displeasure, and he did not have to look very far to find its source. However, it seemed his luck had held, even if he had temporarily misplaced the love of his life. Immediately prior to coming here, he'd checked in at his department to smooth things over with his superiors and there he had found the e-mail from Chen: sent some time before and carefully encoded. Zhu Irzh leaned back in his chair for a moment and closed his eyes. Surely this would please the First Lord; it was the very answer they'd been looking for. Consumed with the need to impart this information, Zhu Irzh fidgeted.

"How long did you say he'd be?" he asked the secretary, a pinched person with a face like an old sour plum and thinning hair arranged in precarious strands across his pointed scalp. The secretary's mouth disappeared inwards, as though his tongue had turned into a lemon.

"I've told you already. The First Lord has a guest—an *important* guest—and is not to be disturbed. He will see you when he is ready."

"Who's the guest?" Zhu Irzh asked, more out of a perverse desire to irritate the secretary than from any real need for information. The secretary was shocked.

"I would not presume to expect such an august personage to make himself known to me. I suggest you follow my example."

Zhu Irzh bowed his head.

"I'll do my best," he remarked with irony. The secretary opened his mouth to reply but before he could utter a suitable retort the door of the First

Lord's office slid open and someone stepped through. Zhu Irzh was unable to suppress a hollow twinge of dismay in the pit of his stomach. He did not recognize the person who stood before him, but it was pretty obvious where the demon had come from. The demon's face was blotched and mottled, and it dragged down one side, revealing an uneven array of teeth. A wizened hand was tucked inside the left sleeve. The demon carried with him an overpowering smell of decay. He was dressed in a glossy robe of dark and polished skin; not a Westerner's hide, but one of the African races. To Zhu Irzh's mind, this meant that the demon was not of the highest echelons of the Ministry of Epidemics, but he was certainly high enough. A quick glance revealed that the demon's feet were reversed: someone of moderate wealth and power, then—perhaps an Under-Minister or Deputy. The demon's contorted smile froze when he saw Zhu Irzh. He rocked backwards on his back-to-front feet, and then he pursed his lips with difficulty and spat. The globule of spittle landed some way from Zhu Irzh's feet, but immediately began inching forwards like a slug. Fastidiously, Zhu Irzh stepped back, and the demon's smile grew mirthlessly wide.

"You," the demon said in a thick, mucus-filled voice. "You are to be *dealt with.*" Without another word he stalked past Zhu Irzh, in the mincing gait characteristic of the podially reversed, and was gone through the door. Hissing with disapproval, the secretary rushed forwards with a little brush and gathered the creeping spittle from the fine red carpet, just as the First Lord of Banking appeared in the hallway.

"Who was that?" asked Zhu Irzh, forgetting titles and etiquette. For once, the First Lord did not appear to notice this lapse and it was only later that Zhu Irzh realized the depths of unease that this betrayed.

The First Lord said, "That was a person named Ki Ti. I don't need to tell you where he came from." Sniffing, he extracted a heavily perfumed handkerchief from the depths of one sleeve and held it to his face. "I know it's a mark of identity and commitment, but I do wish the Ministry of Epidemics would do something about the manner in which their personnel present themselves. A really quite repulsive smell—worse than that aftershave everyone seems to wear nowadays. I know we abide in Hell but one has to have *some* standards... Anyway. Come in."

Zhu Irzh followed him through the door and into the office. The First Lord of Banking snapped imperious fingers and the secretary scuttled after them.

"Windows!" Even the stuffy air of the world beyond was preferable to the odor in the office. "Now. We'll come to my visitor in a minute, but first things first. This woman whom you so gallantly rescued. You said she had a secret. What was it?"

"Lord, I think I know what the Ministry of Epidemics has been up to,"

Zhu Irzh said, skillfully avoiding the issue of exactly who had imparted this information. He intended to say nothing of the e-mail from Chen. Let First Lord think it was the girl; it would save all sorts of problems. The First Lord of Banking swung round, his face a sudden paradigm of greed. "Oh? Tell me."

"They're making a plague. Not just the usual sort of plague, but one which will affect perhaps millions of humans. They want human blood and innocent souls, to manufacture a drug."

"A drug? What kind of drug?"

"I don't know."

"But I think I do. There have been rumors of a new drug, Zhu Irzh—a drug that will let demons into a place where we have been eternally forbidden to go—into Heaven itself. Interesting," the First Lord mused, ignoring Zhu Irzh's surprise. "It seems, Seneschal, that you have been rather more efficient than I'd previously expected. And this woman was certain that this is what the Ministry is doing?"

"Yes, quite certain," Zhu Irzh lied. He felt it necessary to add a little veri-similitudinous doubt to add weight to his case. "Of course, she might have been wrong."

"She might have been... and yet the Ministry is very keen to keep *something* quiet," the First Lord of Banking mused. He tapped the edge of his ornate fan against his teeth. "Tell me, Zhu Irzh, what do you know about humans? How might this disease be spread?"

Zhu Irzh thought for a moment.

"Sexual contact? The Ministry has had some real successes with those recently. Also poverty, and overpopulation. Crowded conditions allow diseases to spread."

"Perhaps. These methods, though—they're old-fashioned, Zhu Irzh, and that's what's wrong with them. This is the constant criticism from the Imperial Court—we simply have to move with the times. Look at my Ministry, for example. There's nothing old-fashioned about Wealth. We're well up to date on the new technology, economic theories, manipulation of the earthly organizations with whom we've taken care to establish excellent relations—like the World Bank and the WTO. And that's why the Ministry of Wealth has continued to move up in the world, whilst War and Epidemics and such are struggling to consolidate their power base. Take War, for example. They had an ideal strategy with the rise of nuclear power, and did they capitalize on it?" The first Lord of Banking swung round to face Zhu Irzh. Dutifully, the latter replied, "No, they didn't."

"Absolutely right! They squandered the perfect opportunity to engage the world in mass destruction. No wonder the Imperial Court's cut their funding. And look at them now—relegated to dealing with petty tribal conflicts in Europe, of all places, not to mention the former Soviet Union. And Epidemics is the same. A limited success with that smart STD of theirs—what was it? Can't remember the name—"

"AIDS?" Zhu Irzh supplied helpfully.

"That's the one. And that was only due to a short-term contractual agreement with the Ministry of Lust. Now that contract's ended, what happens? Humanity finds a cure. Whereas the really virulent viruses—Ebola, Marburg—have never been properly supported. They haven't been *nurtured*, Zhu Irzh, and I call that an inexcusable waste of resources."

"Lord, may I ask a question?" Zhu Irzh ventured.

"I suppose so."

"What's the relationship between Epidemics and your Ministry?"

The First Lord of Banking sighed.

"It's never been easy, Seneschal. You see, we're in the business of making money. Pure and simple. But diseases are not a lucrative business, if you look at them from the perspective of their field of operations. Where they *are* lucrative is in the matter of the drugs that are used to treat them. That's why most of our work in that area is dedicated to the pharmaceutical companies."

"So," Zhu Irzh said, frowning. "You're actually in the business of helping humanity—of finding cures for the diseases that—literally—plague them?"

"I know we've often been accused of gratuitous altruism by those who know no better," the First Lord of Banking said, rather stiffly. "But one has to understand the nature of these operations. By keeping the price of treatment drugs artificially high, and making sure that only those who can afford it have the opportunity of a cure, we're actually supporting the work that the Ministry of Epidemics does. I mean, look at Africa and our liaison with the Underworld there. If it hadn't been for us, human doctors would have been able to treat the entire population against a whole range of diseases, and Epidemics wouldn't have enjoyed one of its very few success stories. I've tried time and time again to explain this to the Minister of Epidemics, but he doesn't seem to understand it—typical B-stream civil servant, even if he does pretend to be an aristocrat."

"I see," Zhu Irzh said slowly. "So would you say, Lord, that there's a certain amount of historical resentment between Wealth and Epidemics?"

"To put it mildly."

"And you mentioned to me that when you met the Minister of Epidemics at the opera he seemed to think that you were taking some interest in his affairs."

"Clearly so. Indeed, Seneschal, he was right. We were—we just didn't know it at that point."

"So if the Ministry is planning to wage some enormous campaign against humanity in order to consolidate its own position and win renewed favor with the Imperial Court, what are the chances that it might be planning to take Wealth down with it?" Zhu Irzh thought uneasily of his rescue of Leilei from the depths of the Ministry of Epidemics, and wondered what would happen if the latter organization connected him with the First Lord of Banking. As seemed obvious, now that someone from the Ministry had seen him cooling his heels in the First Lord's front office, and the crab-demon had tracked Leilei to his own home. He glanced up at his employer. The First Lord's eyes were as cold as glass in winter.

"That seems entirely likely," the First Lord said. He gave a bleak smile. "You are correct in the supposition that has displayed itself so transparently upon your features, Zhu Irzh. No, you have not helped. However, given that your actions have resulted in a piece of information that, if acted upon correctly, might save all our skins, I am inclined to overlook your youthful enthusiasm."

"Thank you, Lord. Most generous."

"I know. Have you found any trace of the young woman?"

"No."

"Has she outlived her usefulness?"

"On the contrary, Lord," Zhu Irzh said quickly. "I suspect she holds a vast store of information that can only be to our benefit. However, I was planning to question her further when I was interrupted by the crab-demon."

"I see. Well, if she's that useful, you'd better find her then. But first," the First Lord of Banking said with a ghastly smile, "I have an additional task for you."

THIRTY-EIGHT

Tso's Blood Emporium had not changed, Chen thought. The row of huge, sinister jars remained in the window, still covered with a patina of thousand-year-old dust. The banners that hung from the balustrade still swayed restlessly in the winds of Hell and the air smelled of iron, of meat, of the sour sweetness of death. Chen remembered the stench that used to emanate from the ventilation grates during distillation days, and grimaced. Shortly after his last visit here, he had brought Inari out into the bright, fresh air of his own world, and he had hoped never to set eyes on Tso's Blood Emporium ever again. The badger sidled up against his legs.

"Now do you know where we are?" Chen murmured. The badger twisted its head in the animal approximation of a nod.

"This is Lord Tso's property."

"Not any longer. I understand he's been demoted to a more menial position," Chen said grimly. The badger's eyes were opaque and blank, and he realized that it was in a sense incapable of acknowledging such an upsetting fact. The badger-teakettle was a retainer, after all, one of the familiar spirits which had attended Inari's family ever since the birth of their First Ancestor; their woes were its own. "Anyway," Chen continued. "Tso might still be useful, nonetheless."

He stepped out from beneath the shelter of a balcony, only to leap back again as someone came around the corner into the square. Chen and the badger-teakettle had managed to weave their way through the alleys without meeting anyone; it appeared that their luck had now ended. Warily, Chen watched as the demon—an elderly woman with the clawed feet of a hen and a sharp, beaky face—made her slow, grumbling way across the square. She carried a bag, tightly clasped in both hands, which squirmed and wriggled: Chen did not like to contemplate what might be in it. At last the old demon disappeared into a basement entrance, and was gone.

"Come on," Chen said to the badger. "Quickly!"

They slipped through the shadows cast by the tall buildings of the square, keeping close to the walls, and after a few fraught minutes they found themselves standing directly in front of the Blood Emporium.

"There's a back way in," Chen mused. "We'll have to be careful. Tso's unlikely to be the only one around."

"How do you know he'll be there?" the badger asked. "It is early."

"That's why I expect him to be there. The normal distillation process takes place overnight, and it's the task of the minions to oversee it. It's a job that tends to get landed on the lowliest of the low and I don't suppose Tso's in terribly high favor, since he was the one who helped Inari escape from Hell." Chen smiled. "When Tso was running the Emporium, as I recall, he rarely rose before midday, but he's not running it any longer... Well. We'll see."

With the badger at his heels, Chen crept around the corner of the building and found a pair of wide double doors. A metal ramp led up to them, and its surface was scuffed and scratched.

"This is where they bring in the blood-barrels, I remember... I don't want to go in here. Let's try further on."

At the back of the building was a small, pinched doorway. The door itself was ajar, and Chen could hear voices coming from within. This seemed promising, and he cautiously put his ear to the crack of the door and listened.

"—was perfectly in place last night!" a voice protested. Chen smiled. The voice was thin and self-pitying, conscious of great and constant injustices perpetrated upon its owner. Tso may have fallen from favor, but it didn't seem to have made any difference to the way he spoke. He'd always sounded like that, no matter what the circumstances. And yet, Chen reflected, Tso wasn't really a bad sort, as demons go. Self-pitying he might have been, and he was certainly an inveterate sycophant, but at least he had found from somewhere the courage to help his sister escape from a marriage which she had no wish to make.

"—all over the floor now! Look at it! Half a pint, quite wasted. There's a leak in one of the seals, only a moron could fail to see that. Now do something about it." Chen did not recognize this voice. It was pompous and ill-natured, with a thick note of decadence beneath: typical of the aristocracy of Hell. Or anywhere, if it came to that.

"But—" That was Tso. There was a sudden soft, brutal sound, as of a gloved fist meeting the back of someone's head, and then a faint cry. Chen grimaced. It sounded as though Tso was having a hard time. He drew back into the shadows as mincing footsteps retreated into the distance. When he was quite sure that they had gone, he slunk to the doorway and glanced in.

His brother-in-law was kneeling on the floor, muttering and clutching the back of his head with one grimy hand. The other hand was busily occupied in scraping a rusty red substance from the flagstones with a pallet knife, and depositing the resultant residue into a jar. Chen looked around, craning his neck to get a better view. He could see no one else in sight. Very softly, he called, "Tso!"

There was no response from the figure on the floor. Chen called again. "Tso! Over here!"

This time Tso looked up. He glanced wildly about him for a moment, then saw Chen peering in at him through the open doorway. Chen gave a little wave. Tso's mouth dropped open into a perfect O of astonishment. His small, red eyes darted in all directions, like red-hot marbles. He made anxious flapping motions with both hands, dropping the pallet knife. Taking the hint, Chen stepped back from the doorway. After a moment, the door creaked and Tso stood teetering on the step.

"What are *you* doing here? I thought never to see you again. Don't you know how dangerous it is for you to be here?"

"I know," Chen said. "I didn't have a choice. Look, Tso, I need to talk to you. It's urgent."

"But I don't want to talk to *you*," Tso said petulantly. "You've caused me enough trouble. Go away."

There was movement from the shadows and the badger's elongated mono-chrome figure glided forth. It bowed its head in obeisance as soon as it set eyes on Tso.

"What's that creature doing with you?"

"That's one of the things we need to discuss," Chen said, meeting Tso's red gaze. The demon drooped. "More woe, I suppose. I finish my shift this evening, not before then. It's nearly three now. I'll see you later. But not here."

"Where, then?"

"There's a place not too far away. I sometimes go there, they have private rooms, spell-guarded. It's the only place we can talk without the risk of being overheard. I'll take you there when I come out, but no one must see you."

"What shall we do then? Stay here?"

"No! Someone might smell you. You'd better wait in the dray," Tso said. Hurriedly, he took them around the corner to the back of the Emporium. A cart stood in the uncertain light, packed with barrels. Something stood patiently in the shafts and Chen recognized the heavy haunches and sinuous, twitching tail of a *ch'i lin;* one of Hell's most common beasts of burden. It turned as Chen hoisted himself up among the barrels, and he glimpsed a hot eye and a row of needle-teeth beneath the thick spiral horn protruding from its forehead. It grinned at him for a moment with malign intelligence, and then its long tongue flickered out to impale one of the myriad buzzing flies.

"Stay here where it can't smell you," Tso instructed. He picked up the protesting badger and heaved it into the dray on top of Chen, then tottered backwards.

"Are you all right?" Chen asked with some concern. "You don't seem very steady on your feet."

"And whose fault is that?" Tso hissed. Turning, he hobbled back in the direction of the entrance, and Chen saw then that the taloned toes of his brother-in-law's feet, instead of pointing backwards in the ancient and regal manner of respectable demons, were directed in a more human direction. Chen looked down at the badger in his lap and met an unfathomably dark gaze.

"Worse than I had thought," said the badger-teakettle softly, and Chen could only agree.

THIRTY-NINE

Inari had now been in Fan's strange home for over a day, and she still knew nothing about her hostess. The scarred woman seemed to spend most of her time in solitary contemplation; either within the polished hollows of her underground cavern, or outside on a narrow ledge of rock that overlooked nothing but a gorge filled with bonewort and stones. Inari knew the values of meditation, so she did not interrupt Fan during these periods. However, when the woman returned to prepare food for their evening meal, Inari ventured a question.

"How long have you been here?" she asked tentatively.

Fan smiled.

"For a long time, I think. But I'm really not sure. It's hard to measure time here, isn't it? Or perhaps you don't find that."

Something about the manner in which she said this gave Inari the impression that Fan was not a native of Hell, but it was hard to tell whether this was the case. The scarred woman did not smell human, and with her red and gray eyes she did not look like one, either, but neither did she have the characteristic presence of demonkind. She was most unlikely a celestial entity; what would a goddess be doing in Hell? Inari had never heard of such a thing; the Celestial authorities did not work that way, being fastidious about where they spent their time.

"I don't know," Inari said, in reply to Fan's question. "I've lived most of my life in Hell, so it doesn't seem so strange."

"And yet you chose to leave," Fan said quietly. She turned to face Inari. It was unsettling to be confronted with those eyes, the one so fierce, the other as tranquil as a cloud.

"I said it did not seem strange. I did not say I liked it."

"Demons do not generally choose to leave their world, not for long. You must love that human of yours very much to have given up everything for him. Or perhaps the fact of it is that Hell gave *you* up? It is difficult to know the truth about you, Inari. I hear many conflicting stories."

"You seem very interested in me," Inari said nervously.

"I find you interesting, that is why."

"Listen," Inari said. She stepped close to Fan and laid a hand on her sleeve. The woman's arm felt warm, as though she was radiating an unnatural degree of heat. Fan looked down at Inari's hand with a slight smile, as though she had never expected to see such a thing.

"Yes?" she said.

"Fan," Inari said timidly. "Can you help me? I have to get a message to my husband. I have something important to tell him."

"What is it?" Fan asked mildly.

"I—I'd rather not say, if you don't mind."

Fan looked up. She was still smiling, and her strange gaze seemed suddenly to encompass Inari's own: red and gray like the skies of Hell, whirling her up and up into a vortex that encompassed all the worlds in one. And then Inari was floating down, pulled by the duality of the woman's eyes; a leaf blown down the walls of the worlds. She heard her own voice saying far away, "Because I'm leaving him. I'm not going back to the world of the humans. I'm staying here." And inside her there was a quick, sharp tug of utter anguish that brought her hand to her mouth like a broken doll. Fan steadied her, and the woman's fingers felt like bands of iron. It was then that Inari realized dimly that Fan was far stronger than she was, even though she was a demon and the scarred woman was—well, what? She stared dumbly into Fan's face and heard the woman say, "It's all right, Inari. Something has changed, that is all. Sit down and I'll get you some medicine." She helped Inari settle against the wall, and folded her hands in her lap. *I am nothing but a puppet,* Inari thought, *my strings are cut.* Numbly, she looked down at her own hands: noting the long fingers, the gilded talons. The varnish was wearing away now, chipped by flights and battle, and she could see the thick ivory surface of her nails beneath. *That is me,* she thought, *I will be worn down until there is nothing left but bone; not the pretty doll of my mother's house, nor the ornamental human wife on the houseboat... I cannot walk on the earth of Earth; my feet burn as though they are bound. I carve vegetables into pretty shapes; I smile at my husband and go to the market in the morning. I am bound by my culture as surely as any wife of ancient China and yet I am a demon, a supernatural thing, a creature to terrify and fear. And if I stay in Hell, where will I go?*

"You can stay here for the time being," Fan said in her quiet voice, as though answering the question that Inari had not asked aloud. "Until we work out what path we are going to take." Inari looked up. The scarred woman was holding a bowl, filled with bitter herbal tea, and her face was devoid of expression. She reminded Inari suddenly of the badger-teakettle: swift to help, curiously loyal, yet keeping its own mysterious counsel. Inari had never received any impression of affection from the badger, and never expected to. That was not what it did; that was not what it was. It moved in its own strange path like a moon around the world that was herself, and she had the same sense from Fan. Except that this time, Fan was the world, and Inari the moon: passing into its dark phase, hidden, eclipsed.

"We?" Inari whispered.

"You and I together, yes. There is a task I must accomplish."

"So you'll help me?" Inari asked, disbelieving, and Fan nodded, sadly and with faint surprise, as though it was the last thing that she had intended to do.

FORTY

Mindful of the possibility of further visitors, Zhu Irzh opened the door of his room with his sword drawn, but at first sight everything was as he had left it. He glanced quickly around the room, then strode across and flung open the door of the bathroom. Nothing. This seemed less than enterprising on the part of the enemy, Zhu Irzh thought. He crossed to where a pan filled with water sat on a small iron hob and absently lit the flame beneath with a touch of his hand, intending to make some tea. The fire flared up with a blue spark, and Zhu Irzh frowned. That wasn't right: the flame was burning far more fiercely than it should, and if he left it like that the pan would be scorched... He lifted the pan off the hob and promptly dropped it. The handle was red hot; too hot even for a demon's touch. The pan rolled under the sofa and Zhu Irzh, through a haze of pain, could hear the scuttling of little clawed feet. Hissing, he dropped to his knees and flicked under the sofa with his tail. The sharp spine of the tail grazed something and there was a hoarse cry. With his rosary wrapped tightly around the knuckles of his uninjured hand, Zhu Irzh peered cautiously beneath the sofa. A trail of dark blood led into the shadows. Zhu Irzh hauled the sofa aside and saw an immense, mottled salamander. It gazed at him from malevolent jade eyes for a moment, then said softly, "You'll regret that, demon. Oh, you will." Then it disappeared behind the skirting board, squeezing itself fluidly through a crack. As it disappeared, Zhu Irzh saw that one of its back legs was bleeding, and the droplets of blood that remained behind soon sizzled into ash. Zhu Irzh cursed. No way to run a trace, then. His hand was stinging, as though someone had lashed it with a whip. Glancing down, he saw with dismay that the palm was already beginning to swell. The flesh had become puffed and sore, and oozed minute drops of blood. The handle of the "pan" must have been the salamander's poisonous tail. A bolt of pain shot up Zhu Irzh's arm like bitter lightning. This was serious.

172

He needed medical attention. Of all the times to run foul of the Ministry of Epidemics... But he could be reasonably sure that they had been the ones who had sent the salamander in the first place. Grimacing in pain, Zhu Irzh tried to remember whether there was any other institution that dealt with health, but as far as he knew the local doctors and apothecaries were indentured to the Ministry itself. It was highly debatable whether he'd find anyone to treat him, and if he didn't—well. Death to a demon was different from the death of a soul, but it was still nasty and lasted a long time, and Zhu Irzh had no wish to experience the various delights of any of Hell's lower levels for the next few centuries. No use dithering about here, anyway. Wrapping his hand in a piece of cloth, Zhu Irzh hastened out into the city.

It was still early evening, and the main streets were crowded with people going home from their day's work. Zhu Irzh encountered two tall, spined warriors of the Ministry of War, their eyes as black and shiny as polished marbles. He passed a woman from the Ministry of Lust exuding a complexity of pheromones into the steamy air around her as she swayed along on tiny, bound feet. Her hair drifted on the wind like seaweed; her face wore a painted dark smile. Despite the growing pain in his hand, Zhu Irzh was unable to resist a second look. He thrust his way through a group of minor civil servants clad in the gray robes of some dull functionary's office, twittering and whispering like crickets as they relayed boring office gossip to one another, and then past a diverse collection of whores from the Pleasure Quarter: denizens of some demon lounge out for a night on the town. Compared to the executive from the Ministry of Lust, they seemed tired and brittle; their limbs arranged in a series of mannered poses as they moved. Their leather and skin garments creaked as they walked, and they smelled musty. Zhu Irzh made a mental note never to patronize whatever establishment they might come from.

The pain in his hand was growing increasingly intense and Zhu Irzh winced. If he didn't find an apothecary soon... He glanced upwards and saw all manner of signs: makers of razor kites, purveyors of bones, manufacturers of knives, but no one who offered simple healing. Sometimes Hell really did live up to human expectations. The crowds were beginning to annoy him, and in his debilitated state he did not want to take the chance of having his pocket picked, or of being furtively wounded by any of the covert hit-and-run knifers or acid-throwers who tended to congregate in crowded places, so he turned off into a side street. There was more chance of finding an apothecary here, anyway, away from the crowds. He hastened along the shabby streets filled with steam from the restaurant vents and the pungent smell of rotten vegetation, and turned a corner to see, with an overwhelming combination of relief and apprehension, the red neon sign of an apothecary.

Zhu Irzh hammered on the door with his good hand, and after a moment, it opened. A wizened face peered out, above a quivering rat's tail moustache.

"What do you want? I'm closed."

"I can pay. I need help," Zhu Irzh told him.

"Have you got health insurance?"

"Of course I've got insurance. What are your charges?"

"Depends what's wrong with you," the apothecary said, small, yellow eyes gleaming in the growing twilight. Sighing in exasperation, Zhu Irzh stuck out his injured hand.

"Poison. A salamander."

"An elemental, eh? Such injuries, while not rare, are not easy to treat. Or cheap."

"Can you help me or not? I told you I could pay."

"No. I don't have the equipment."

"Imperial Majesty! It's blood poisoning. How difficult can it be?"

"It is not merely a question of infection. It is the matter of magic where elementals are concerned, and I cannot help. You need an alchemist, not a mere apothecary."

"Where can I find an alchemist then?"

"The Guild of Alchemists is a subdivision of the Ministry of Epidemics and is not allowed to advertise. I suggest you make enquiries of them." He began to close the door, but Zhu Irzh wedged his tail in it.

"No," Zhu Irzh said firmly. "That's not good enough." Fishing in his jacket pocket, he took out his badge and stuck it in the face of the apothecary. "Get me the name of an alchemist—now. An independent operator, not someone with Epidemics. You know as well as I do that such people exist. And if you don't give me a name, I'll have you closed down."

Grumbling and muttering, the apothecary trundled to the back of the shop. He fished in a cabinet and took out a laminated business card, which he handed grudgingly to Zhu Irzh.

"Here you are."

"This doesn't mention anything about alchemy. It says this character's a trader."

"I suggest you read it more thoroughly. See there, on the very last line? *Pharmaceuticals*. That's the one."

"Very well," Zhu Irzh murmured. He didn't seem to have much of a choice, and the alchemist did not live very far away: somewhere in the backstreets of the Pleasure Quarter. He tucked the business card in his pocket and turned on his heel to go.

"What about my payment?" the apothecary cried.

"What payment? You haven't done anything."

"I gave you the name, didn't I?"

"Think yourself lucky I didn't have you arrested," Zhu Irzh snapped. The apothecary's curses followed him up the street: he could feel the faint prick as each one burst against his skin, like a shower of needles, but they were not especially effective and soon they had faded away. Far more worrisome was his arm, which now throbbed with monotonous regularity; pushing up his sleeve, he saw a thin dark line running up the swollen flesh, almost as far as the elbow. If he didn't hurry, he thought with dismay, it would be the lower levels for sure.

FORTY-ONE

Chen and the badger huddled behind the barrels on the dray, trying desperately to keep out of sight. They had spent the afternoon waiting, and were now both uncomfortable and hungry. Tso had told them that his shift would end early in the evening, but it was already well after twilight and the draymaster had begun to secure the tailgate, ready to take the dray on its nightly rounds. The stench of blood beneath the closed tarpaulin of the dray was overpowering, and it made Chen's head pound with rhythmic nausea. He closed his eyes and leaned cautiously back against the wall of the dray, his fingers resting in the thick, soft fur of the badger's back. The badger was trembling, and Chen was not quite sure why. The creature did not usually seem to feel fear. Perhaps it, too, was affected by the heavy, sour odor of the blood. Chen opened his eyes as the sound of voices filtered in.

"Last minute check. Master's orders." That was Tso. Chen took a deep breath of relief.

"I've already fastened up the tailgate; it's too late now."

"But master was insistent!" Tso's voice rose to a mosquito whine, almost as unbearable as the stink of the blood. There was the sound of footsteps, and then the tailgate once more rattled down. Tso's face gazed up at them like a stray moon.

"One... two... three barrels... All seems to be in order. Sorry to trouble you," he said loudly, extending a clawed hand to help Chen down. Chen and the badger clambered as quietly as they could from the back of the dray and Tso slammed the tailgate up and locked it. Chen dodged behind a nearby stack of barrels as the dray rumbled out of the courtyard, the lashing tail of the *ch'i lin* sending a swirl of dust into the evening air.

"Where were you?" Chen hissed.

"I had things to do. I was as quick as I could. Now let's get out of here,"

Tso said, and set off in his stumbling gait towards a small door in the back wall of the courtyard. Stepping through, Chen found himself in a narrow alleyway, which led out onto one of the main thoroughfares.

"Where's this place you're taking us?" he asked.

"It's in the Pleasure Quarter."

"And you're sure we can't just talk here?"

"No!" Tso said, glancing nervously around him. "My master has set all manner of spies and traps—he's paranoid about employees siphoning off the blood. The place isn't very far, but we'll have to keep to the back streets. Here," Tso added. "Take this." He handed Chen a floppy and ancient hat, heavily stained by some unmentionable substance.

"It's the foreman's," Tso said, by way of explanation. "He left it in the office. It'll hide your face. Pity we can't do anything about your smell."

After a few hours in the dray, Chen felt as though he'd stink of blood for the rest of his life, but Tso evidently thought differently. Chen supposed that it was rather like Europeans, who always seemed to feel that they were per-fumed like the very rose but who to his discerning senses often had that odd milky odor... He stuffed the foreman's hat unceremoniously upon his head and pulled it down over his face. Tso was already heading down the street, followed closely by the badger-teakettle. Chen followed.

The Pleasure Quarter had changed since Chen's previous visit. He recog-nized none of the warren of streets through which Tso was hastening, but this did not surprise him. The Pleasure Quarter was defined by its capacity for transformation. Streets altered position overnight, shops disappeared as if swallowed by some vast maw, and brothels rose to take their place. Inari had once told Chen that the Pleasure Quarter was in fact far larger than it appeared: buildings folded back upon themselves and were bigger inside than out. Along with the Imperial Palace itself, the Pleasure Quarter was one of the oldest regions of this part of Hell, as befit the vices which it entertained. Chen supposed that Seneschal Zhu Irzh, as an employee of the city's Vice Division, must be exceedingly familiar with this bit of the city. Tomorrow, depending on what Tso was able to tell them, he would try to contact the demon. It was not reassuring to have as his only allies—unless one counted the badger-teakettle—a disgruntled brother-in-law and a highly unreliable member of Hell's police force, but Chen supposed that without the favor of Kuan Yin he must take friends where he found them. Impeccability was a necessity that he no longer felt able to entertain.

Someone was plucking at his sleeve. Chen turned and saw half a young woman. Her face was plump and pleasantly smiling, her teeth were lacquered red and intricately carved, but she was completely hollow, like a melon rind scooped out from the back. He was uncomfortably reminded of Pearl Tang. She bowed, and Chen could see straight into the meaty hole of her skull.

"Would you like to take tea with me?" she asked prettily, like a wind-up doll. Chen smiled.

"Not just now," he told her. She bowed again, jerkily, and glided away. Tso was waiting impatiently beneath an awning.

"Don't talk to people! Do you want to attract attention?"

"It would create more of a fuss if I ignored them," Chen said mildly. "Are we nearly there?"

"Not far now," Tso muttered. They were standing in a little square: one of the many courtyards of the Pleasure Quarter. From an uninformed perspective, the scene before them could almost be an attractive one: lots of bright colors, smiling faces, ornamental clothes. It wasn't until one looked more closely—very closely in certain cases—that one began to see the decay, the mutilation, the rotten lace and stained velvet. This, Chen supposed, was the problem with Hell: it was all facade, and even that was shoddy. Tso stepped down a side street, lurching to the side as his reversed feet came into contact with one of the many potholes that rendered the sidewalk so unstable. Chen turned to follow, but found himself suddenly in the middle of a crowd of creatures.

They were elemental dancers. He'd seen their kind once before, performing beneath Inari's balcony at the command of her then-fiancé Dao Yi. They were not indigenous to this part of Hell, and he knew that they were very old, perhaps dating to the animistic days before Buddhism. They were animal spirits: Chen recognized a deer, staring up at him with great dark eyes above a mouth filled with most undeerlike fanged teeth. Its spiral horns twisted in mesmerizing rhythms. A clawed hand slipped into his own and held it with casual intimacy, but the green lizard gaze that stared so unblinkingly at him was as cold as river ice. Dark feathers brushed his face; hair as soft and thick as fur slid against his cheek. They were turning him around, murmuring in inhuman voices, and the heavy perfume of the narcotics from a local café was making his head spin, drawing him down, deeper and deeper... Something nipped affectionately at his throat and then sharper teeth snapped at his ankle. The intense pain brought him abruptly back to reality. He cried out, whirling in a t'ai ch'i dance of his own that sent the animal spirits flying from him. Laughter echoed and they turned and ran in a pack: tails twirling, graceful hands waving in mocking placation. From an upstairs window, someone echoed the laughter: Chen glanced up to see a woman with her hand to her face, stifling her mirth. A purplish tongue lolled out between her fingers. Chen's ankle felt as though he'd stepped into a napalm bath. He looked down to see the badger staring grimly up at him.

"You should be more careful," the badger said. There was again blood on its long, pale incisors, and it licked them, once, with a relish that Chen found unnerving. He nodded.

"I know. Thank you."

"Follow me," the badger said, and disappeared into the torchlight shadows beyond the little courtyard. Limping, Chen followed, and saw that a metal door was set into the wall. His brother-in-law was waiting behind it.

"Where have you been?" Tso hissed. "I thought I'd lost you."

"I'm sorry. I got distracted."

Tso swore through his teeth and pointed towards a staircase.

"Go up there. It's third on the left. And don't get into any more trouble. I have to pay someone for the room."

Stifled giggles came from somewhere in the depths of the building as Chen ascended the stairs, and he remembered the face with the spilling tongue, gazing down from the balcony. Presumably this was a demon lounge of some kind, but it seemed to be devoid of the usual panoply of prostitutes. A surreptitious glance into one of the rooms off the landing caused Chen to revise this hypothesis: the room was filled with demons, each lying on a narrow pallet. The air was thick with a narcotic haze and the floor was littered with ornate metal syringes: some habits passed between Earth and Hell with alarming ease. Chen found the third door and stepped cautiously over the threshold.

The room was mercifully empty. It contained only a couch and a small iron cabinet with many drawers, set against the wall. The black velvet of the couch was stained and mottled; Chen sat down rather gingerly. He did not know what Tso got up to in here, and he had no intention of asking. A man's private business was no concern of his, and besides, it was almost certainly repulsive. He wondered whether he'd ever get the reek of blood out of his clothes, and his ankle stung painfully. After a few minutes, Tso hastened nervously into the room and shut the door behind him. He carried four sticks of crimson incense, which he lit. The little room was soon filled with an acrid cloud of smoke, which Tso directed with a taloned hand until it wrapped around the walls like a smoke ring, connecting with the spells that guarded the room.

"Sound precautions," Chen said approvingly.

"You can't be too careful. I've already had more than enough trouble over all this... No one can hear us now." He collapsed on the couch next to Chen. "So what's been going on?"

As concisely as possible, Chen apprised his brother-in-law of recent events. When he had finished, Tso stared at him in horror.

"My sister? Inari? Back in Hell?" He sounded surprised, but there was something overdone about it, and Chen could not suppress a sudden intuition that this was a fact Tso already knew very well. He'd always been a terrible liar: one of the few characteristics he shared with his sister.

"You don't seem exactly pleased," he said, hoping to draw Tso out.

"Of course I'm not pleased! Don't you know what helping Inari has cost me? My job, my status, my salary, my good relations with my family... Not to mention my feet."

"I'm truly sorry," Chen said, and meant it. "But you knew what defying Dao Yi might lead to. And in a way, I saved you a lot of problems by taking Inari away from Hell."

"I know, I know. And you're right. If she'd stayed, who knows what Dao Yi might have done to her? He was furious about the whole scandal—he sued for false engagement, remember? But I thought he was only concerned about the money, and we paid that back with interest once the case had gone through court."

"I think Dao Yi felt that your family had made a fool out of him," Chen said.

"Oh, almost certainly," Tso replied bitterly. "Once she'd gone, I thought all the fuss would die down but Dao Yi never really stopped persecuting us. It's worn mother to a rag. They're like that in Epidemics—vindictive. They've got long memories, like dormant germs. Just when you think you're cured, they reinfect you. And, of course, there's the *wu'ei*."

Even the name made Chen shiver. "Have you seen them?" Chen whispered. "Have they come to you?"

Despite the wall of smoke, Tso glanced anxiously around him before answering. "They came once. They came in the night—I don't remember much. They took my secrets from me—they learned for themselves how I'd helped Inari. They were limited in their powers because we hadn't directly disobeyed the law, we'd only helped another person to do so."

"To travel between the worlds, without license from the Imperial Court?"

"Yes. But what they did was bad enough. They left my father's mind a wreck; he couldn't stand the questioning. As for me, it was the *wu'ei* who reversed my feet, as punishment. O Ji—my boss—suggested it. As a warning. They crippled me, with the promise of more to come. I can do nothing for Inari, Chen. I do not dare. The *wu'ei* will be searching for her now, and if they find her..." He stared down at his back-to-front feet and said no more. Chen sighed. He knew his brother-in-law and there was no point in pressing him further. He said, "All right. I understand what you've been through, Tso, and I'm grateful you've given me this much. I won't trouble you further."

"No. That isn't enough. You have to leave Hell. Forget my sister and go back where you came from. If the *wu'ei* find you here, they'll come after me and my family. Inari's made her own bed of nails and she'll have to lie on it."

"She never intended to return to Hell! Someone took her!"

"Who?" Tso asked nervously. Again, Chen got the impression that Tso already knew.

"I don't know. But everything that's been happening seems to lead back to the Ministry of Epidemics. If I'm looking to anyone as a culprit, I'm looking at them."

"Always Dao Yi," said Tso, and spat a fiery spark of contempt. It sizzled as it hit the carpet, leaving a small, smoking hole.

"I'm sorry, Tso, but I won't leave Hell without your sister, even if I have to pay a visit to the Ministry myself. I'll be as discreet as I can."

Tso opened his mouth as if to protest, but then he said, "Very well, then. You must do what you have to do, I suppose. But I cannot help you."

Agreement was the last thing that Chen expected. He glanced at Tso. His brother-in-law's round face was as closed as if a shutter had fallen across it.

"I understand," Chen said quietly. "If you withdraw the wards on this room, I'll be on my way. I won't trouble you again."

"Where will you go?"

"I have—other contacts," Chen said. "I have a place in mind."

Tso nodded. He raised a hand, and the wall of smoke dispersed. Chen crossed to the door, feeling the prick of spells against his skin as he stepped through the dissipating barrier. He left Tso sitting on the couch and, followed by the badger, made his way down the stairs.

As they came out into the courtyard, the badger said, "You cannot trust Master Tso." It spoke abruptly, as though the words had been wrung out of it, and Chen was heartened by this display of reluctant loyalty.

"I know," he said. "That's why we have to get as far away from here as possible. Tso won't waste any time."

"Why did you not lie to him? Tell him that you would leave Hell, forget Inari?"

"Because he'd know it was a lie. Tso understands me well enough. Besides, the more lies I tell, the more trouble I'll have with Kuan Yin later." He sighed. Caught between goddesses and demons...what was that Western saying? Something about a rock and a hard place? Or was it a devil and the deep sea? The truth of both statements was brought abruptly home to Chen as he stepped out of the entrance to the courtyard.

The animal spirits had come back. They stood in a patient semicircle. They were quite still and their eyes were bright. At his feet, the badger gave a long, low growl. Chen glanced behind him. There was no obvious way out of the courtyard, unless he bolted into the maze of downstairs rooms. The thought of being trapped in that narcotic maze was not appealing, but going back was better than going forwards. The spirits, moving as one, took a step towards him. Chen slipped his hand into his jacket pocket and found with a sudden sick dismay that his rosary was no longer there. As if sensing his disquiet, the animal spirits surged through the gateway and Chen turned and ran, nearly falling over the badger in his haste. He was heading for the staircase, but as he neared it a door slammed shut and he heard the snap of a bolt. He wondered fleetingly if that might have been Tso's doing, but there was no time for speculation. Accompanied by the badger, Chen fled along the covered verandah towards the far end of the courtyard. A spirit loomed up before him with the faceted eyes and quivering wings of a dragonfly, but its mouth was soft and human and wet. Desperately, Chen shoved it aside: it felt brittle, and yet somehow disconcertingly solid. As it fell, it began to hum. The humming filled the air, and the tendrils of the black vine that covered the verandah started to coil around Chen, caressing his face and entwining painfully in his hair. At the end of the verandah was a small, closed door: if he could only reach it—but a leafy frond of vine reached out and snagged his injured ankle, bringing him down. Chen rolled as he fell, freeing his leg, but even as he began to crawl towards the door more tendrils were creeping about him and their grip was strong. He could feel the long body of the badger beneath him, struggling. Looking frantically over his shoulder, he saw a mosaic of eyes above him: green and golden and meat-red. The badger lashed out with a clawed paw but this time the spirits simply rippled, as though made of water. Still moving as one, still moving with grace, they bent their heads and the tip of a cold spectral tongue flickered over his skin.

Then the small door at the end of the verandah burst open and something whistled over Chen's head. A lizard spirit was catapulted, hissing, into the leaves of the vine. The dragonfly sailed up as if pulled by a string, a long spine whip cracking against its carapace. The tendrils of the vine shriveled back and Chen was free. A hard hand caught him by the wrist and pulled him unceremoniously upright. Staggering back against the wall, he found himself looking into the wild, molten eyes of Seneschal Zhu Irzh.

INTERLUDE
Earth

Sergeant Ma had spent the morning painstakingly filing traffic violations. It was a boring job, but Ma did not have a problem with being bored. *Boring* meant familiar, comfortable and safe. It did not mean golden-eyed demons with sharp and dangerous smiles, or the flittering ghosts of murdered teenagers. It did not mean kidnapped houses whirled up into the darkness between the worlds. It did not mean the utterly pedestrian, yet somehow deeply sinister, presence of Detective Inspector Chen—now who knew where on who knew what supernatural errand. As a lowly sergeant, Ma had largely been left out of the urgent series of talks that had taken place between the captain, Chen, the lugubrious exorcist Lao and the madman from Beijing. This suited Ma very well. He could continue to potter about the office doing routine (but necessary) tasks and pretend that the nightmare world that perpetually hovered just beyond his dreams had never even existed. In a moment, Ma thought, he might even go and get another cup of tea.

It was therefore with a sinking sense of dismay that he glanced up to see No Ro Shi, the demon-hunter, looming over him. The man seemed to carry with him a constant aura of night; he was even worse than Chen. No Ro Shi's eyes were the dead black of old stone, and his face was as pale as a cadaver's. No Ro Shi said, "Sergeant Ma? The captain asked me to have a word with you. Says you've worked on a case with Detective Chen."

"Only because there wasn't anyone else," Ma said, fear easily overriding pride.

No Ro Shi gave a swift grimace that passed duty for a smile.

"You are commendably modest, Sergeant, a quality that is all too rare in these self-aggrandizing times. Hubris is a certain path to Hell, you know." He glanced swiftly over his shoulder. "However, the captain tells me that you acquitted yourself moderately well on previous occasions, and even Chen spoke highly of you once or twice when recounting his report of your adventures. The captain thinks you might be the ideal man for the job."

"Oh? What job?" Ma asked, with a sinking heart.

"Chen thinks something serious is about to happen. Something cooked up by Hell that could affect all this sorry world. It may even have started already and that's what you and I are going to find out. I'd take the departmental exorcist, but the captain wants Lao for a case of exorcism in the Business District."

"I—I don't think—"

"Good man," said No Ro Shi. He clapped Ma on the shoulder and even through Ma's regulation shirt his hand felt icy cold. "Get your jacket. And your gun."

The demon-hunter said nothing more on their way to the car, which Ma found ominous. No Ro Shi had said nothing about where they were going, nor why. That was the problem with these supernatural types, Ma lamented; they never told you everything, so you were left to wonder, and panic. Even Chen was better than this. In fact, Ma admitted to himself, Chen was actually a pretty decent bloke, behind all the spectral stuff. He wondered how Chen had got into this sort of thing in the first place: How *did* you get recruited by the gods? Did you dedicate yourself? Take a vow? Was it some kind of penance? And that last thought made him wonder what Chen might have done to pay so heavy a price.

"I'll drive," No Ro Shi said, unlocking the car door. "Get in. And keep your window up."

Nervously, Ma complied. He did not like the thought of being at such close quarters with No Ro Shi. He squeezed himself tightly into his seat, trying to keep as far away from the man as possible without actually causing offence. He glanced at No Ro Shi, but the demon-hunter didn't seem to have noticed and Ma felt a little reassured.

No Ro Shi swung right off Shaopeng Street, into the series of congested underpasses that ran beneath the city. Driving down here always made Ma nervous: the lower they went, the closer to Hell he felt he was getting. He knew the relationship between the worlds was not nearly as simple as up and down, but he couldn't shake off the feeling of unease. It was the same on Singapore Three's rather unreliable metro. Moreover, the traffic in the underpasses was usually dreadful, especially at rush hour, and Ma had never grown used to driving in such claustrophobic conditions. Out in the countryside of Da Lo, where Ma had grown up, the roads were dusty and narrow, and the few vehicles moved at an uncomfortable bumping crawl. No Ro Shi paid no attention to the traffic. He shot between two lumbering buses, overtook a Mercedes on the inside and came out of the other end of the underpass onto the Ghenreng arterial like a cork out of a bottle. A few minutes later, Ma opened his eyes to discover that they were already halfway along the coast road that curved out from Singapore Three's long shore to lead up into the mountains.

"Where are we going?" Ma ventured to ask.

No Ro Shi took one hand off the wheel to gesture vaguely in the direction of the container port, which shimmered in the afternoon haze. Ma could see the dim shadow of the typhoon shelter beyond, and then the immense expanse of the sea. They hurtled into yet another tunnel, angled into the hillside and framed with mirrors to placate any negative *ch'i*. No Ro Shi took a bend at speed, still one-handed. Ma's eyes screwed shut once more.

"We're going out to Danlien."

"Danlien? But there's nothing there—it's just warehouses, isn't it?"

"A lot of the container cargo is stored there, but recently they've been converting spare warehouses into something else. *Gherao* dormitories."

"*Gherao* dormitories?" Ma echoed. He had not really followed the communications revolution very closely, preferring to take the attitude that if the bioweb worked, it worked, and if it didn't, it didn't. As far as Ma knew, the old electronic system was good enough, and he didn't really understand why human beings had to be used as nexi points. But people seemed to think it was a good thing—employment had soared since the *gherao* system had been introduced, and the Chinese government had even been fleetingly popular as a result. Besides, the newspapers said, the *gherao* system was ideal for poor youngsters who lacked skills and qualifications: a year or two in the dormitory, acting as nexi nodes for the bioweb, and they'd earn enough money to set up their own small businesses. In India, so Ma had read, girls were earning their own dowries through the system, and easing the burden placed on their families. It wasn't supposed to do the nexi any harm, either—scientists had done tests, and proved it. Ma trusted scientists: he wanted to believe in reason, and logic, and all the things that were antithetical to Hell. But he couldn't see what a bioweb dorm had to do with the current case, and he didn't want to look even more of an idiot by asking No Ro Shi further questions. Instead, he gazed out at the passing view and wondered uneasily what might be happening to Chen.

PART FOUR

FORTY-TWO
Hell

Shrieking and chittering, the animal spirits swarmed up the side of the building and vanished sullenly into the hanging mass of the vine. Beneath the verandah, Chen gaped at Zhu Irzh as though he'd never seen him before. The demon's hot golden gaze seemed to burn even more brightly, fierce as fever, and the skin of his face was tight and damp. He was holding one hand close to his body, cradling it protectively.

"Zhu Irzh?" Chen said. "Are you all right?"

The demon spoke quickly, the words running together.

"No. No, I'm not. I had a most unwelcome visitor, a salamander creature—I touched its tail and it poisoned me. I was on my way to an alchemist's when I saw it again, or something like it, that lizard thing, it was sliding under that gate, so I followed it to order it to tell me who'd sent it, and I found you. What are *you* doing here, Chen?" he added, as if in afterthought.

"I came after our mutual friend," Chen said, with a warning glance upwards. "Did you get my e-mail?"

"Yes. I took it to the—the proper authorities, I didn't tell them where it came from."

"Which authorities? Did they believe you?" Chen asked, taking the demon by his uninjured arm and steering him through the gate. The demon's arm was radiantly hot beneath his hand, as though he was holding his palm above a stove. Zhu Irzh nodded.

"My employer. And yes. Yes, he did." He stumbled as they stepped through the gate and leaned back against the wall.

"Where's the alchemist?" Chen asked urgently. The demon was obviously not in a very good way.

"That's the fucking problem, I don't know," Zhu Irzh said wildly. "I went to some apothecary, some quack, and he refused to treat me. I'm damn

189

sure the thing that attacked me was sent by Epidemics, and all the doctors here are under license to them. The whole medical profession has probably been ordered to give me the runaround until I fall down dead and end up Imperial Majesty knows where in some horrible lower level for the next few hundred years."

"That's not going to happen," Chen told him.

Zhu Irzh snorted. "So you say. I don't know how long I've got. Not long, probably."

Looking at him, and allowing for the usual hyperbole of the supernatural, Chen was inclined to agree. The demon's hand was so swollen that his talons protruded from his fingertips like pins from a pincushion, and the flesh was shiny and cracked.

"Look," Chen said, taking a deep breath as he made his decision. The goddess wouldn't approve, but then Kuan Yin hadn't approved of anything he'd done in the last year, so what else was new? He'd just have to square it with her on some yet-to-be-determined day of reckoning, along with everything else. One thing was certain, however: Kuan Yin wouldn't like it. Healing demons was definitely not within his job remit. He glanced quickly around him. Twilight was falling fast, and the glowing red lamps of Hell were casting bloody shadows around them. Squalid buildings lined the street, and across the way Chen glimpsed the neon sign of a demon lounge.

"Have you got any money?" he asked Zhu Irzh.

"Some," the demon replied.

"Go over there and hire us a room."

Even in his anguished state, Zhu Irzh's mouth twitched in a smile.

"Detective Chen. I'd no idea you thought of me like that."

"I *don't* think of—oh, never mind. Make sure you get a room facing the street, on the ground floor. Tell them you're on your own; show them your badge if you have to. Then open the window."

Zhu Irzh stared at him for a moment, then apparently decided that trust might be an appropriate emotion. "All right," he said. Wincing with pain, he ran across the street and hammered on the door of the demon lounge with his good hand. The door opened. Chen saw the demon speaking to someone within, then reaching awkwardly into his pocket and extracting a handful of notes. He vanished inside. A few minutes later, a window just above the street flew open.

Chen sprinted over the road and, followed by the badger, hauled himself across the sill. The room was a standard one, bare except for a wide couch and soft rugs. For Hell, it was almost salubrious.

"Now," Chen said, rolling up his sleeves. "Sit down."

Obediently, the demon did so. Chen crouched beside him and lightly touched the injured hand, which Zhu Irzh snatched hastily away.

"Okay, okay," Chen said soothingly, as if to a wounded animal. "All right. I know it hurts. I'm going to have to cut your sleeve off, I'm afraid."

"You seem literally hell-bent on ruining my entire wardrobe," Zhu Irzh said bitterly.

Chen smiled. "Vanity's a sin, you know. Not that it matters here... I'll do this quickly. I warn you, it's going to hurt."

Taking a small, folding pair of crane scissors from the pocket of his jacket, he slit Zhu Irzh's sleeve as far as the elbow. The demon made no sound, but he grew as still and stiff as stone.

"I wouldn't worry about being brave," Chen murmured. "It's a bit late for *face* now."

"It's not a matter of honor," Zhu Irzh said through gritted teeth. "Someone might come in if I start screaming the place down."

As gently as he could, Chen examined the injured hand. Despite the swelling, and the darkness of the demon's skin, he could tell where the spines had gone in. A series of little holes marched in regular array across Zhu Irzh's palm.

"Have you done this before?" the demon asked nervously. "Whatever it is you're going to do, that is?"

Chen nodded.

"Yes. Once or twice, and not under similar circumstances, but I have done it." *And with the goddess' protection and favor, both times,* he thought. He drew a flat packet of acupuncture needles from his pocket and opened it.

"I think perhaps I ought to tell you," the demon said rather weakly, "that I don't like needles very much."

"Don't look, then," Chen said. There were five holes in the demon's palm. Chen took five slender needles out of the case and laid them carefully across the top of the box. The kit contained a minute autoclave, and he didn't want to run the risk of the needles touching anything that might contaminate them. "You won't feel a thing," he told Zhu Irzh encouragingly. The demon sniffed in disbelief. Taking Zhu Irzh's arm, Chen placed it across his own knee, then took the longest of the needles and inserted it into the first hole in Zhu Irzh's hand. The demon's swollen fingers curled slightly, but he made no sound. Taking the rest of the needles, Chen placed them in the holes, working fast and murmuring the shortest and most potent of the Healing Mantras as he did so. Once all the needles stood quivering in Zhu Irzh's wounded hand, Chen took a box of spirit-matches from his pocket and lit one. Breathing across the demon's hand, he lit his own human breath so that the needles were ringed in fire. Then he resumed the mantra: holding Zhu Irzh's wrist lightly between his fingers and concentrating ferociously on healing. Not having the rosary was a blow, and he was painfully conscious of the goddess' absence, but as he came to the end of the fifteenth recitation of the mantra he was suddenly aware of a minute stirring at the edges of the universe: a note plucked in the eternal strings of the Tao. It did not have the familiar warm presence of Kuan Yin's favor; it was nothing more than a quirk of interest on the part of the Tao itself, but the needles flamed up into five thin columns of golden fire and fell away, consumed to ash. There was nothing left except Zhu Irzh's smooth, long-fingered hand, patterned by five tiny holes which, as Chen watched in fascination, closed like flowers in the cold, leaving only the smallest frost-scars in their wake. Zhu Irzh opened his eyes and stared down at his healed hand.

"Thank you, Detective Inspector. I think you've just saved my life. In a manner of speaking."

"As you saved mine," Chen said, with a smile. "Are you keeping track? Because I've lost count."

Graciously, the demon inclined his head. His hand curled around Chen's wrist for a moment, and then he rose and crossed to the window. "Well," he said. "Time to pay a visit to the Ministry."

FORTY-THREE

Fan was standing on the edge of the precipice, gazing out across Hell. She had been there for some time now, and Inari was by no means sure what the scarred woman was seeking. Perhaps it was some kind of meditative practice, but Fan seemed dangerously exposed on the lip of the rock. The perpetual wind caused her robes to stream out behind her like a banner of fire and ash, and her hands were upraised as if to catch the wind. Far below, all the way to the dark horizon, the lights of the port city of Hell guttered and burned.

Fan had told Inari to stay behind in the cave, but Inari had grown tired of being cooped up, and tired, too, of being told what to do, so she had crawled up the narrow passage into the last of the light, and now struggled against the wind to where Fan was standing. She did not want to startle the woman and make her fall, though it seemed to Inari that nothing very much would alarm Fan. She stepped onto the rocky ledge and called, "Fan? It's me. Inari."

The scarred woman did not turn her head. She called back, "Inari? It is coming." It was as well that Inari had a demon's hearing, for the words were snatched and swallowed by the wind.

"What?" Inari asked, bewildered. "What's coming?"

Fan lowered her hand in the direction of Hell and spoke a single word. An arc of smoking flame shot from the palm of her hand, rending the windy air. As Inari came to stand beside her, something fluttered out of the wild darkness and came to rest on the tip of the flame. Fan began to draw the flame back into the palm of her hand, like someone reeling in a fishing line, murmuring as she did so in a swift, urgent mantra. Soon, the fire was gone, and a soot-black thing crouched in the centre of Fan's scarred hand.

It was small, and covered in oily dark feathers. It had no eyes. Its toothed beak gaped for air, and the talons of its four feet settled around Fan's fingers with the grip of a vice.

"My messenger," Fan said. "Now, quickly, back inside. Creatures such as this attract attention so far from the city, and they don't ride the storm alone." She cast a swift, wary glance up into the racing sky. "I told you to stay inside."

"I'm sorry," Inari said. "I—"

"It doesn't matter. We have to get below ground." Firmly, Fan grasped Inari's arm and led her back along the lip of rock towards the entrance of the cave. The messenger clung shrieking to her shoulder, talons splayed, and Inari could see thin, red bars of blood creeping out from beneath Fan's robe.

"It's hurting you," she said in dismay

But Fan only echoed, "It doesn't matter." She shoved Inari towards the entrance. Inari had to bend her head to duck under the rock. As she did so, she looked up and what she saw nearly made her fall down the stone steps.

Something was passing overhead. It was immense. Its body was too vast to be seen properly, but she caught a glimpse of a coiling, rolling back. Spines drew down lightning from the upper skies, illuminating the span of its scales. Its thick lips were drawn back in a permanent snarl, concealed by the clouds of its breath, and a single crimson eye like a sun swiveled in the direction of the ground.

"Get in," Fan hissed, and kicked at Inari's fingers. The edge of her boot only grazed Inari's hand, but it was enough to make Inari lose her paralyzed grip and stumble. She fell heavily to the stone floor on her hands and knees, and was joined a moment later by Fan and the messenger.

"That was one of the *wu'ei*," Inari heard herself say. Her shaking arms gave out at that point and she collapsed onto her face. The floor felt cool against her skin, and reassuringly solid. Fan's hand reached out to grip her shoulder.

"Get up," the scarred woman said gently. "Do not forget what you have just seen, Inari. It is you whom the *wu'ei* are looking for. This is why I told you to stay below. You'll be safe here, underground beneath the dome of the old devil's skull, but outside it is a different story. Now rise, and let us see what my messenger has to say."

FORTY-FOUR

Zhu Irzh seemed to have recovered his exuberance along with a return to health. They had now been making their way through the Pleasure Quarter for some twenty minutes, and despite Chen's protestations, Zhu Irzh still wouldn't stop talking. Since the demon was clearly too streetwise to use names, the conversation was not only one-sided but cryptic in the extreme.

"—remarkable how they thought they could pull a stunt like this without anyone *noticing*," he said over his shoulder, as they passed a stall selling deep-fried knucklebones. "After all, it's hardly as though they don't have enemies. Such conceit! And such carelessness, too—the only reason that the relationship between the worlds has survived as long as it has is because of mutual self-interest and support."

"You mean your people set up deals with powerful humans and bleed the rest dry," Chen remarked at the demon's retreating back.

"Well, precisely! What other arrangement did you have in mind? The whole justification for having such a bureaucratic system in the first place is so that balance is maintained, and so that one institution doesn't benefit at the expense of all others. Imagine the chaos that would ensue on Earth and in Hell if the Ministry of War were perpetually triumphant! Humans would be decimated and half of Hell would be out of a job." Zhu Irzh ducked under an awning of sinews and waited for Chen and the badger to catch up.

"How's your hand?" Chen asked, to stem the flow of socio-economic analysis. The demon waved it negligently at him.

"Fine now, thank you. I really am most obliged, Detective Inspector."

"Good. Where did you say we were headed?"

"First, to my employer. As I explained to you, the notion of further investigating our friends at the You Know Where is an excellent one, but having been assaulted by an entity masquerading as my own saucepan in my own front room, I am somewhat loathe to do so without reinforcements of some kind. Hence we are going to visit my employer."

"By which you mean the Vice Division?"

"Actually, ah, no." Zhu Irzh's face betrayed some slight unease. "Although Vice is, indeed, my *principal* employer, I've recently been co-opted by someone else. I'd rather not name names now, if you don't mind. One never knows who might be listening."

He led Chen down a further warren of side streets. They had left the Pleasure Quarter behind, now, and were making their way through the shadowy, unlit streets of one of the residential quarters of Hell. This region seemed to Chen to be aiming at a certain degree of bourgeois respectability: each small house bore a neat, black lawn, like an undertaker's apron, and he could see a familiar corpse-light neon flicker within.

"You have television here?" he whispered to Zhu Irzh. Somehow, this was an aspect of Hell that had passed him by. The demon merely grinned.

"Who do you think invented it? Some of your finest technological advances emanate from the laboratories of Hell, after all. Not all of them have been granted their export licenses yet, if what I understand from my cousin in Customs and Excise is correct, but once the paperwork's been sorted out I'm sure you'll find your world makes a few further technical strides... Through here."

Chen followed him through a small, dark park. Dim lights glistened in the shadows, and there was a faint, unpleasant sound of whispering. A soft, sucking noise drew Chen's attention, but Zhu Irzh drew him away.

"That's what the Vice Division likes to see," he murmured. "Young people out enjoying themselves... Another couple of blocks and we'll be there."

Turning the corner, Chen saw that they were now standing in a wide square, lined on one side by spiked iron railings. A pair of tall and imposing gates led onto the square itself; surprisingly, these were open. Zhu Irzh frowned.

"Unusual."

"Is this where your employer lives?"

Absently, the demon nodded. "Yes, but his security's generally pretty good—they only let me in because I've got a pass."

"We'd better take a look," Chen murmured. He followed Zhu Irzh's cautious, sideways path towards the gates. They were flanked by a small guardhouse, presumably the place where security normally stood, but it was empty. The headless body of a winged, doglike creature still clung to the peaked roof of the guardhouse. The badger-teakettle gave a long, low growl.

"What do you think that was?" Chen asked.

"*Ro'ei*," replied Zhu Irzh, staring up at the corpse. "Like a security camera. Someone's made sure it can't see much anymore... Follow me."

He angled around the gates, careful not to touch the glistening iron, and

Chen followed his example. They were now standing at the top of a short drive, paved with a white, smooth substance that Chen at first thought to be stone. Then he realized.

"Bone paving," he said aloud.

Zhu Irzh nodded. "My employer's not short of cash. You should see the inside of the house." He gestured towards the mansion that stood at the end of the driveway, and Chen's eyebrows rose. The curling, lacquered roofs and gilded gargoyles were impressive enough, and so was the immense colonnade which ran the length of the facade, but it was the height of the building that Chen found so remarkable. It must have been at least nine stories high: the size of a small office block, and every inch encrusted with ornate decoration. Typical of Hell, thought Chen: overdone and ostentatious and overwhelming, designed to cow an already beaten populace.

"Wow," he said. The demon grinned sympathetically.

"It is a bit excessive, isn't it?"

"Who does it belong to?"

"My employer is the First Lord of Banking. Head of the Ministry of Wealth. He—" Zhu Irzh broke off and grabbed Chen by the arm, dragging him backwards into the spiny bushes. The gates were opening. Crouching uncomfortably in the shrubbery with the badger at his feet, Chen stared, aghast, at what was coming through.

The creature was covered in thick, black scales. Eyes like stars glittered beneath heavy brow ridges and its clawed feet grated against the bone surface of the driveway. It was at once more horse than dragon, and more dragon than horse, depending on the angle from which you viewed it. A surprisingly anomalous array of ebony plumes nodded above its elongated head; its bridle was encrusted with silver. It was drawing a carriage: a huge, round construction that seemed on continual verge of toppling over. As this ensemble rushed past towards the house, Chen glimpsed a pale, pinched face peering out from behind the veils that concealed the carriage window, and there was the unmistakable reek of decay.

"The Ministry of Epidemics?" Chen whispered.

"I think so. Certainly smells like it."

"Why are they here?" They were crushed so closely together in the midst of the bushes that Chen felt, rather than saw, Zhu Irzh shake his head.

"I've no idea. Someone from the Ministry paid my employer a visit a day or so ago: they're keeping a close eye on each other."

"And you said your employer is the First Lord of Banking? I've never had any dealings with him."

"My family has ancient associations with the Ministry of Wealth. In fact, it was a bit of a scandal when I decided to go into Vice—my dad thought it was too respectable—but we patched it up. I don't know why they've come—" Chen nudged him sharply in the ribs. Others were coming through the gates: a battalion of the troops of Hell. They marched in the traditional rows of three abreast: they carried pikes, and their swords were swung over their shoulders. They moved with the spiky lurch of insects, though their feet were invisible beneath the long leather armor. Chen could see their faces only dimly: desiccated human brows and noses above loose, toothed jaws. Zhu Irzh's grip tightened on his arm as they passed, but Chen had already seen it. Each warrior bore a badge upon his arm: a sun, in eclipse. The sign of the High Imperial Court of Hell.

Zhu Irzh clasped Chen by both arms and hauled him backwards through the shrubbery until they were standing on the lawn. Mouthing, "Come with me," the demon ran in the direction of a nearby pergola, keeping to the shadows. Chen followed. He could still hear the sound of the coach as it thundered up the drive, and as he joined the demon beneath an arbor shrouded with the heavy scent of blood-roses he saw the coach sweep around the side of the house and come to such an abrupt halt that splinters of bone sprayed out beneath its wheels. Lights were going on inside the mansion, until the vast structure was lit up like the Pellucid Island Opera House. A moment later, a figure appeared on the balcony. Chen saw that it was wrapped in what looked like a bulky dressing gown, and from its curious gait he determined that its feet were reversed. This person was one of the honored ones of Hell, then. As he watched, the figure shimmered, as if seen behind a haze of heat: a protective spell had been cast.

"Is that the First Lord?" he whispered to Zhu Irzh.

"I think so." Zhu Irzh poked him in the back. "Look."

Someone was getting ponderously out of the coach. This person wore stiff, pale robes, and moved with a heavy, rolling stride. The dragon-horse snorted restlessly as he passed. The odor of disease momentarily overcame the drenching scent of the blood-roses.

"I think that's the Minister of Epidemics," Zhu Irzh murmured.

"This is serious then. Demons of that status don't normally leave their own institutions. They don't have to."

"Unlike their minions," Zhu Irzh remarked bitterly.

"Sshh! He's saying something."

The Minister's voice drifted across the gardens like a plague cloud.

"I am here on the authority of his Imperial Majesty! You are to surrender this property and all its works to the Ministry of Epidemics, my own organization, without ado. Failure to comply will result in the immediate forced appropriation of your assets."

"This is monstrous!" the First Lord of Banking cried from behind the haze of his spell. "I protest in the strongest possible terms."

"So you are refusing to comply with my authority?"

"I most certainly am!"

The Minister of Epidemics motioned to the Imperial warriors, who now surrounded the house.

"Bind it!"

The warriors who stood closest to the balcony raised thin, spidery hands. A tangle of wet, black silk shot forth and clung to the lacquered underside of the balcony. The First Lord of Banking hissed like a viper, and stepped from within the protective spell. A bolt of light shot from his hand, severing the sticky silk with explosive force. Fragments of charred cobweb rained down upon the garden. The First Lord of Banking seized a metal staff from a shadowy associate and sent it spinning through the air. It howled as it flew towards the Minister of Epidemics, who hastily erected a protective spell of his own. Deflected, the staff whirled away and struck the Minister's coach with a resounding report. The coach fell neatly into two halves. The dragon-horse reared and bolted, dragging the wreckage of the coach behind it as it fled through the gardens, leaping the ponds and bridges with ease. The Minister raised a gloved hand and sent a meteoric bolt of light into the nearest pond. The flailing golden bodies of carp were catapulted into the air as if dynamited, and the entire garden began to smell pervasively of fish.

"My carp!" the First Lord of Banking cried, enraged. "Do you know how much those *cost?*"

"Doubtless more than your miserable life!" replied the Minister. "I'll see you in the menstrual pits for this!"

As if on cue, the Imperial warriors raised their hands, and silk shot from their palms to form an immense web that hovered over the mansion for a moment before settling down upon the roof. Chen heard the First Lord of Banking give a single, muffled cry before the black threads began to weave a swift and complex cradle around the building. The Minister raised a hand. There was a dark bolt of lightning, the signature of a reversed spell, and the figure of the First Lord toppled wailing from the balcony to land in the seething waters of the pond below. Soon, the mansion of the First Lord of Banking resembled a huge insect: trapped in the mesh of a vast web and ready to be sucked dry. The Minister of Epidemics gave a soft snort of laughter, and wiped his wet mouth. He snapped his fingers in the direction of the Imperial Guards, four of whom trotted forwards and picked him up. Borne on their bony shoulders, the Minister of Epidemics was carried swiftly back down the drive, leaving the silent cocoon of the mansion behind him.

FORTY-FIVE

Fan's messenger spoke an ancient dialect called Gei-lo-fang, with which Inari was barely familiar. She listened carefully, trying to understand, as the messenger slurred and whispered into the scarred woman's ear, but she only caught a few words that she recognized. "Danger" was one of them, and "grave" another. Inari found this less than reassuring, and she did not like the closed, watchful expression on Fan's face. She could not help remembering the *wu'ei*, drifting vast as clouds above the city, seeking her own small self, and she wished with a wave of immense longing that she was back on the houseboat, worrying about nothing more than whether her feet would burn if she went to the market.

"Inari," Fan said, and her face revealed nothing. "It seems we may not have to send a message to Earth after all. My messenger tells me that a human has come from that world, here to Hell. A man, not young, not old, who once had the favor of the goddess Kuan Yin. Your husband."

Inari felt herself struck by two conflicting sensations: terror, and relief. She whispered, "Chen Wei is here? When?"

"Not long ago. He has been here for no more than a day. My messenger has made enquiries. Your husband visited your brother, and then he was attacked."

Inari stared at her, appalled, and Fan went on: "I'm sorry. That was tactless. He isn't dead, Inari, or even badly hurt. He was set upon by a band of spirit-dancers, but someone saved him."

"Who?"

"My messenger does not know. It says that he was saved by one of your kind, by a demon, but it is not clear who or why." Inari noted that slip: *your kind*. So Fan was not a demon herself. What was she then?

"Where is he now?"

"My messenger does not know. Inari," Fan said, and the warning note in her voice was unmistakably clear. "You told me that you would leave Chen, and stay here in your own world, no matter what the price, so as not to bring him to further danger. Do you still mean what you said?"

Inari looked at her. The scarred woman's face was as calm as a summer sea, but the depths of her strange eyes were fathomless. Inari felt suddenly as though the world itself hung on her answer. She thought of the houseboat, and the little life that had been her own for no more than a year: the breeze from the sea, the light that fell over the towers of the city in the morning, just before dawn. A complex, changeable, varied world unlike the perpetual storms and winds of Hell. A world where a person could be different, not bound by conventions as ancient and desiccated as old bones. Then she thought of Chen himself: all the images and memories that she had pushed away ever since she had returned to Hell. How he woke up slowly, was meticulous when preparing tea, was silent at the right times. How he never criticized her cooking, even when it was charred to a crisp and he was late getting home. He never made a fuss over things that didn't matter. How things seemed inexplicably to strike him as funny—a comment on the radio, a bird diving awkwardly into the sea—and he'd sit silently shaking. In all the old stories of romance that Inari had devoured as a young girl, "funny" never seemed to come into it. Love was always dark, and serious, and mysteriously tragic: it was never ordinary. But her love for Chen was ordinary, Inari reflected now, and that was why it was special, and why she couldn't put him through all this anguish all over again. He must go back without her, and find someone human, someone with whom he could live a normal life.

"I haven't changed my mind," she said, in a voice that was no louder than the wind through the hollows of the cave. "I'll stay here in Hell, and I'll give myself up to the *wu'ei* if I have to." She paused, glancing up into Fan's unreadable face. "But I want to tell him myself. He mustn't risk himself here. I have to find him. I have to send him home."

Somehow, Inari was expecting argument, but Fan only bowed her head. She grew as still as stone, so unmoving that the little blind messenger grew alarmed and plucked at her shoulder with restless claws.

"Fan?" Inari said, and the scarred women looked up at last. Her face was filled with weariness, and there were tears in both eyes, the red and the gray. "What is it?" Inari asked, bewildered, but Fan only murmured, "It is nothing... Inari, if we are to find your husband, we have to go back to the city but we cannot return down the path by which you came. We have to find a way which the *wu'ei* will not readily discover."

"I don't know of such a path. The only road I know is the one I took."

Unexpectedly, this made Fan smile and Inari was abruptly reminded of Chen. The scarred woman said gently, "I know. But I think I remember a way:

an old path, little used. It leads into the city from these hills."

"Won't it still be dangerous?" Inari asked, thinking of the coils of the *wu'ei* in the stormy air above her head.

"Yes, dangerous, but not the danger you're thinking of. This path leads underground, Inari, deeper and deeper yet. And it passes through the lower levels of Hell."

FORTY-SIX

The shrubbery of the First Lord's midnight garden had given Chen a rash. The skin of his hands had broken out in a series of painful welts, and he felt hot and sick. Zhu Irzh, though sympathetic, was of little help.

"I really am sorry," the demon said apologetically. "I'm afraid I lack your healing skills—I've never had much call for them, to be honest. Perhaps it will go away."

Chen sighed. "Probably. Still, at least I'm still alive. I think."

After the debacle at the mansion, they had made their way swiftly to the nearest sanctuary, which took the unlikely form of a teahouse run by a small, dour demon in an apron. Judging from the rest of the sparse clientele, this was an establishment that asked few questions. Zhu Irzh procured a booth at the back, away from the windows and facing the door, and ordered a pot of gunpowder green tea.

"This is most unfortunate," he murmured. The tip of his tail tapped unhappily against the iron floor like a ticking clock. "I hadn't bargained on having my patron's very abode trussed up like a holiday chicken... certainly not with my patron inside it."

"Just like Tang's. Kidnapping buildings seems to be a trademark of the Ministry of Epidemics," Chen said, taking a swallow of hot tea. Its bitterness reminded him that he hadn't eaten for more than a day, but it was always risky to consume food in Hell. Thoughts of Inari ricocheted through his tired mind. He hadn't realized he'd spoken her name aloud until he glanced up and saw the demon staring at him.

"You're thinking of your wife," Zhu Irzh said.

"You know her name?"

The demon nodded. "You must be aware that you made a great many enemies when you stole her from Hell."

"You heard about that," Chen said, with a kind of gloomy satisfaction. He had rarely met anyone who hadn't, at least in the lands of the dead.

"You must admit, it was something of a *cause celebre*," Zhu Irzh remarked. "I must say, I greatly admired your audacity. For a human to steal a scion of the Shi Maon from the very bosom of the family home—quite a feat." He shook his sleek head in brief awe. "I wondered where you knew Tso the blood-dealer from. Her brother, of course. I hope she doesn't share his looks."

"For the record, she'd already fled from the family home by then, and I didn't steal her, she came of her own accord."

"Even worse. I'm surprised they didn't send someone to bring her back once the fuss had died down."

"They tried. At least, her parents did. The rest of the family disowned her. Her father sent her brother after her, but we—well, we managed to talk Tso out of it. No, the only reason why I'm not strung by my heels on a hook in Hell right now is because the Celestial authorities—under whose protection I currently reside, as you know—" he added, with a pointed look in Zhu Irzh's direction "—called in a number of favors." *And then withdrew their patronage.*

"You know, of course, that there's a price on your head. Yet you'd still risk your immortal soul in performance of your duties, or for love," the demon said, curiously. "Your wife must be a remarkable woman. Is she beautiful? I've never seen her."

"Yes," Chen whispered.

"You're a strange man, Chen Wei. There is an adage about bravery and foolishness being part of the same package. It is a description that you would appear to fit."

"That remains to be seen," Chen said bleakly. For the first time he allowed himself to consider the dreadful possibility that Inari really was lost to him, that he might never see her again. It was as though an abyss had opened up beneath his feet. The demon sighed.

"Love's never easy, is it?"

Something about the way he said it made Chen look at him more closely. Zhu Irzh's handsome face was drawn, and he looked more unsure of himself than Chen had ever seen him.

"It sounds as though you've been having problems of your own," he said. Zhu Irzh rubbed a taloned hand across his brow.

"Yes, you might say that. Demon meets girl, demon loses girl... that sort of thing."

"Was she human?" Chen prompted gently. From the particular Gweilin word used by Zhu Irzh, it wasn't clear whether the lady in question was mortal or fiend.

"No, she was a demon," Zhu Irzh said. "And guess where I found her? In the Ministry of Epidemics."

"What?" Chen said, blankly. On the seat beside him, the badger's ears twitched.

"She was shackled. Some official had decided she was going to join his harem, but she didn't seem to fancy that, so I rescued her."

"That seems uncharacteristically chivalrous for a member of the Vice Division. Or did you have ulterior motives?"

Zhu Irzh grinned. "I always have ulterior motives, Chen. It just depends what I do with them... On this occasion, however, I was the soul of gentility. I took the lady home, gave her a bath, and I even lent her my bed. Without me in it, which is uncharacteristic, I must admit."

"So where is she?"

"We had a visitor in the middle of the night. Something from the lower levels, a crab-demon, almost certainly sent by the Ministry. My beautiful guest chose to flee through the garden and I haven't seen her since. I intended to look for her, but things intervened." He grimaced, flexing the fingers of his healed hand.

"And—just out of interest—what was her name?" Chen asked cautiously. Possibilities tugged at the corners of his mind like the ripples of the Tao.

"Leilei," the demon said.

"I see."

"She could have been lying, of course. People do, when they're not sure of their circumstances."

"They do indeed," Chen said thoughtfully. He drained his tea and poured some more into the bowl for the badger. "So. What do we do now?"

Zhu Irzh caught his lip beneath a glittering fang. "No idea. I think going back to my place is out; it's probably been gift-wrapped by now. There are almost certainly assassins on my trail, and we know there are assassins on yours. My department has probably disowned me. Your brother-in-law seems to have shopped you to your enemies, and all in all, the Ministry of Epidemics is out for our blood. What do you think we should do?"

"If the Ministry's looking for us," Chen said, taking care to catch the demon's gaze, "then I think we should go to the Ministry."

Zhu Irzh smiled. "And when we get there?"

"Then," Chen said, "we will conduct an investigation."

INTERLUDE
Earth

No Ro Shi parked the car some distance from the *gherao* dormitory, behind a high razor-wire fence that would, Ma estimated, render it invisible from the *gherao*. This, combined with No Ro Shi's maniacal Beijing-trained driving, made Ma even more nervous than he was already, and the grim set of the demon-hunter's countenance did not lessen his unease.

"What happens now?" Ma ventured. No Ro Shi turned to look at him and Ma was appalled at the bleakness in his eyes. It made the demon-hunter's previously dour demeanor seem almost jolly.

"This is where it begins, Sergeant," No Ro Shi said softly. "Welcome to the end of the world." With that, he slid out of the car and began walking quickly along the fence, without waiting to see if Ma was behind him. *Ten out of ten for style*, Ma thought with uncharacteristic irony, *but several minus points for team work*. Or, indeed, explaining things. He got out of the car, making sure that the doors were locked, and followed the demon-hunter.

At the end of the fence, No Ro Shi stopped and crouched down on the ground. Taking a thick pallet of incense from his pocket, he scratched a small hole in the dry, dusty earth and inserted the pallet into it. Then he passed his hand over the half-buried incense and murmured a word that made Ma's head ring. The incense began to glow, and the demon-hunter stood up, dusting his hands.

"That should hold us," he muttered. After his brief period working with Chen, Ma knew better than to ask what he meant. No Ro Shi turned to him.

"Sergeant? I want you to stay here, keep an eye out for anything untoward. I'm going to take a look at the dorm. Call me at once if *that*—" he pointed to the incense "—changes color, or if you see anything."

Ma nodded, in some bewilderment. "All right."

"Good," said the demon-hunter, and loped swiftly in the direction of the dorm. Ma tried to watch him go, but No Ro Shi was suddenly difficult to see: there was only a long shadow, perhaps a gull's, moving fast across the dust and the scrub. That was a neat trick, Ma thought, scared and impressed. He craned his neck around the fence, trying to see where the demon-hunter had gone, but no one was in sight. Ma looked out across the port, which lay basking in the late afternoon light, thinking how peaceful it all seemed. The only sign of activity were the long necks of the warehouse cranes moving at the far end of the wharf, loading cargo from a ship with a Macau flag. A gull sailed high overhead and cried out, making Ma jump. He sighed and squatted down by the fence. He glanced at the incense, but it still had the same cold glow, almost lost in the afternoon light. Idly, Ma watched the cloud shadows drift over the sea, dappling the water so that it was first dark, then mirror-bright. Sunlight sparked from the chain links of the fence, gleamed off distant warehouse roofs, flashed from a window on the far headland. The light dazzled Ma: it seemed to spin and turn, locking him into a world where suddenly nothing was substantial anymore, there was only sunlight and shadow, unweaving the world itself until there was nothing left…

The shriek came from high above his head: as cold and malign as the cry of a bird. Something flashed through the falling light, a blade made of darkness that cast the world around him into nightmare midnight and beneath it, something fell squealing. Ma rocked painfully back against the razor-wire fence but a hand caught him and hauled him to his feet. He gaped down at the thing that lay twitching at his feet, its mantis features dissolving into acrid light.

"You were lucky, Ma," No Ro Shi said harshly, sheathing the black blade. "It nearly had you."

Ma stared at him, trying to process an overload of information. "I didn't see anything," he said, aware of how feeble it sounded.

"I noticed. If it's any comfort, Sergeant, the *zu'a* have crept up on better men than you."

"*Zu'a?*"

"Sun-demons, Sergeant. Someone must be controlling it; they're woven from light. Temporary creatures, but dangerous." He poked the mound of dust in which the incense was buried with the toe of his boot: the little light was ashy dead. "Now. I've been taking a look at the dorm. Something's horribly wrong." He put a hand on Ma's arm. "Come with me."

Ma still felt weak and shaky, but he could not disobey: the demon-hunter's voice pulled him up like a puppeteer jerking the strings. Together, they ran across the wasteland to the dorm. The gates of the razor-wire fence that protected the property were closed and bolted, and so were the heavy double doors.

"Most of the building's underground," No Ro Shi said, glancing behind him. "We have to find a way to get in."

"Don't these places usually have a security team on base?" Ma asked.

The demon-hunter nodded. "Yes, they do."

"So where are they?" Ma asked uneasily. No Ro Shi did not reply. Instead, he reached out and touched a gloved hand to something red and wet adhering to the razor wire. Ma looked away.

"How are we going to get in then?" Ma asked, suddenly hating the way his voice sounded so high and nervous. Perhaps that wasn't the plan. Perhaps they could just call for reinforcements and he could watch from behind the police car while a SWAT team kicked in the doors. Ma, while lamenting his own cowardice, did not feel that he was in a position to substantially address it; better just to go with the flow. Looking at No Ro Shi's iron countenance, however, he realized that calling for reinforcements would not be an option.

"Stand back, Sergeant," No Ro Shi instructed him. Ma was only too happy to comply. He shuffled back a few paces, careful to keep tabs on what might be happening behind them. He watched with a sinking feeling of familiarity as No Ro Shi raised his sword, held in both hands by the blade so that a trickle of blood ran down the sleeves of his armored coat, and began to chant. He flicked the blade upwards, and Ma winced as a sharp burst of light stabbed his eyes. Then the sword was falling, skewering sunlight as it fell, and No Ro Shi caught it by the hilt and sliced through the locks of the door as though they were soft as bean curd.

"After me!" he shouted, kicking in the door. Ma swallowed a lump of fear, drew his gun, and plunged after the demon-hunter before he had time to think better of it. Whatever he did in front of this character was going to make him look like an idiot, he thought, so he might as well obey orders. The metal doors were blasted back on their hinges as No Ro Shi charged through, pursued by the panting Ma.

Next minute, Ma found himself in a reception area containing a desk and a number of chairs. The carpet was of good quality, and the smooth pale walls were lined with upbeat portraits of smiling workers. At the far end, an artful photograph of a nexus floating in her tank formed a dramatic introduction to the open-plan stairwell. Ma studied the nexus' face: she had been airbrushed to perfection, and she looked as though her dreams were happy ones.

"Downstairs," No Ro Shi ordered, after a quick and thorough search of the reception area. "That's where the dorms are."

Ma followed him down a steep staircase that terminated in a doorway. The heavy metal door was wide open, revealing its complex locking mechanism. It led into a kind of airlock, ending at a second door. This, too, was open. There was the rasp of metal against silk as the demon-hunter drew his sword, wrapped a rosary around his free hand, and motioned to Ma to be quiet. Then he stepped through the door. Ma's own fingers were white around the grip of the gun as he steeled himself for whatever might lie inside.

Inside, the dormitory was anticlimactically silent and still. The coils of the bioweb apparatus hung in serpentine arrays from the ceiling, filling the upper half of the room, and spiraling back towards the regeneration units at the far end of the room. Viral liquids seethed within. The bodies of the nexi bobbed in their tanks like weed caught on the tide, and everything was so peaceful that it was a moment before Ma noticed the smell: a too-pungent, antiseptic odor, concealing decay. He crossed to the nearest tank and peered in curiously. In all the infomercials he'd seen, the nexi had appeared to be sweetly asleep, hands crossed modestly on their breasts, eyes shut, smiling as they dreamed within a delicate cradle of fine filaments. He did not recall seeing the thick tubes that penetrated the nexus' mouth and anus, nor the bruising crawl of wires beneath her skin. And the eyes of this nexus were open, gazing sightlessly into nothing. The liquid in which she was floating resembled a thick, murky soup. No Ro Shi's hand caught him by the shoulder, jerking him backwards.

"She's dead," the demon-hunter whispered. "Like the rest of them."

"Dead?" Ma echoed in dismay. To his horror, No Ro Shi drew his sword and severed the ridged locks that secured the tank. The side of the tank swung slowly down with a hiss of hydraulic hinges, and the fluid within drained away into the service tubes. The nexus, still connected to her tubing, lay limply on the floor of the tank, and now Ma could see that her pallor was not due to the filtered light of the tank. No Ro Shi reached out with a gloved hand and detached the tube from her mouth, leaving it distended in a gape of horror.

"Bloodless," he said, probing the sides of the girl's mouth. "She's been drained."

"Who by? And why?"

No Ro Shi tapped impatient fingers against the sides of the tank.

"By the powers of Hell. As to why, we need look no further than the Ministry of Epidemics. A plague, Chen said. A plague is coming, and I believe that this is one of the places where it starts."

"A plague?" Ma had sudden visions of himself being consumed by disease. "You've brought me into a *plague* zone?"

"Don't worry," No Ro said, with a lipless grin. "You and I are protected, at least for the next hour or so. I have a patron deity, you see, who negotiates to keep us safe. But he won't be able to do that forever. Now that I've confirmed my suspicions, we need to take samples and get out of here." He took a slender black case from inside his coat and opened it. A number of small instruments lay within. Ma, peering nervously over the demon-hunter's shoulder, noted that there seemed to be a preponderance of scalpels, and something that resembled an apple corer.

"Take a look around the rest of the building," No Ro Shi instructed, selecting a scalpel. "I'll get started here."

"Hang on," Ma said. "That thing that attacked me— the thing made of light. You said it was being controlled by someone. What if—" He glanced nervously around him.

"It's around," the demon-hunter said abruptly. "I can smell it. A demon of some kind, but it's keeping out of the way. The things that invoke sun-demons aren't themselves strong, but they are clever. Just watch your back. And I expect you to watch mine, too."

"All right," Ma said unhappily. Then he added: "If this actually is the beginning of a plague—I mean, shouldn't we get one of the special units in?"

No Ro Shi did not reply for a moment. He was occupied with detaching a small fragment of skin from the dead girl's throat. Then he said, "Sergeant, this is a conundrum with which I frequently find myself dealing. Too much attention drawn to the wrong thing, and one finds oneself—blocked. Mysterious obstacles are placed in one's path by one's superiors, and the more critical an incident seems to be, the more quickly those obstacles appear. You'd be surprised at the number of times I get taken off a case, just as some crucial breakthrough's about to happen." He sounded bitter, and Ma couldn't blame him. "Singapore Three's different from Beijing. Your captain's a relatively enlightened man, I think. He supports Chen instead of undermining him, but Chen tends not to deal with major incidents—no disrespect to the honorable Detective, but his work's pretty routine. The things I deal with are different, and there are a great many people who have made it their job to ensure that I fail more often than I succeed. I'm sure you understand the nature of politics today, Sergeant. Hell's never very far away, as I'm sure you've learned. Now, get on with your job. We haven't got all day."

He bent his head once more to his macabre task, leaving Ma to trail reluctantly back towards the stairs. As he did so, he noticed to his dismay that there was a slimy trail along the floor: a faint iridescence as though a large snail had oozed across it. It led through the doors and into the reception area.

No sound came from the reception area itself. Ma followed the trail into a nearby corridor and discovered a series of small rooms, obviously offices. All were deserted. In the second office, two cups of half-drunk coffee stood on a table. They were still tepid. Leaving them where they stood, Ma peered into the third office. Nothing. The drawer of a filing cabinet was open, and Ma leafed through a thick stack of what appeared to be medical records, but they weren't very revealing. A rattling noise from the corner made him jump, but it was only a batch of paper tumbling out of the shredder. Ma doubted that demons would need to use recycling technology but, like the coffee cups, it raised the question of how long this place had been abandoned. The back of his neck prickled cold. Turning, he went back out into the corridor and headed towards the final office, where the slimy trail terminated. He encountered the smell before he stepped through the door. It was overpoweringly strong: the smell of blood.

Very cautiously, his gun drawn, Ma put an eye to the crack in the door. The office was awash. There was no attempt at subtlety—no arcane symbols daubed across the walls, no sanguinary warnings inscribed in ancient scripts—just blood. It looked as though someone had simply hurled a tank of red paint into the room. Holding his breath, the gun extended before him, Ma plunged through the doorway. There wasn't even a body. He'd been half-expecting to find the imaginatively butchered corpse of some nurse or technician spread-eagled against the wall, but there was nothing to show where the blood originated. Ma made a cursory search, but there was so much of the stuff that he couldn't even determine the angle it had come from. It painted the doorframe, covered the walls and had made the carpet squishy. Gagging, Ma backed out and ran stickily down the corridor, thoughts of plague running rife through his beleaguered brain.

All No Ro Shi said was, "I expected something like that. Right. I've finished the sampling, we might as well go. Once we're out of here I'll call your captain and get the dorm sealed. Don't mention this to anyone else. The less fuss the better."

PART FIVE

FORTY-SEVEN
Hell

Inari and Fan had now been traveling for almost three hours, and Inari was hopelessly disoriented. She had tried to keep track of the labyrinth of passageways, but the twists and turns were too intricate to keep in mind: it was as though they were moving through a vast honeycomb of bone. Indeed, Inari thought, the walls of the passages more closely resembled bone than stone. They were pale as ivory, smooth and cool. She remembered what Fan had said: *you'll be safe here, beneath the old devil's skull.* Yet whenever she tried to ask the scarred woman what she had meant, Inari's throat constricted and her mouth grew dry as dust so that the words would not come. Fan turned. Her face was luminous in the darkness, as though she shone with her own light. She murmured, "Inari? It won't be long now before we reach the transition point. We need to prepare ourselves."

"Transition point? What's that?" Inari asked.

"Where the worlds cross."

Inari blinked. "I thought we were still in Hell. Do you mean we're going to be on Earth?"

Fan shook her head. "No. Inari, this is a route through the levels of Hell. The geography of Hell is complex, and even I don't understand it fully—it travels back upon itself, like intricately folded cloth. We're going to go a stage further down; perhaps even deeper than that."

"Do we have to?" Inari, used as she was to Hell itself, had never visited the lower levels; indeed, her family had always considered it a rather disreputable thing to do, grubbing about beneath the layers of the world like worms. Fan gave a faint smile, as if she knew what was going through Inari's mind.

"I'm afraid we have no choice. We've attracted the attention of the *wu'ei*, remember? They'll be looking for you, and there are few better ways of covering your tracks than by traveling in the worlds beneath." She turned and

215

began walking swiftly along the narrow, sloping path.

"Don't they have jurisdiction in the lower levels?" Inari asked, following. She heard Fan's soft laugh.

"They have some. They'd like to think they have a great deal, but the truth is, Inari, only the Imperial Emperor himself has any sway over what happens in the lower reaches. The denizens of those parts go their own way; they are perverse, inconsequential, intransigent. Elemental forms, very old, and slow to change. You'll see."

Inari opened her mouth to ask another question, but they had reached a slender split in the rock, as perfect and regular as the curve of a crescent moon.

"There," Fan said with evident satisfaction. "Here is where we make the transition." She glanced round. "When we pass through, you may notice a change in me. And in yourself. As in all movement, something is lost and something gained... Take my hand." She reached behind her, and after a moment's hesitation Inari gripped her rough fingers. Fan stepped forwards, drawing Inari with her, and now Inari could see that the arch in the rock was nothing more than an illusion: a crack in the dark air itself. Inari's fingers curled more tightly around Fan's, and they stepped through. But even though she had moved, Inari could not repress the sudden sensation that she had remained still, that the world itself had shifted around her, as though she were the hub of an immense wheel. Inari's vision dimmed and swayed; she staggered, and Fan's iron hand pulled her upright.

"Do you see?"

Inari blinked. For a brief, disorienting moment, it seemed that she gazed out across a vast expanse: a great plain of crimson rock, above which hung three ashen moons as fragile and wan as soap bubbles. Two immense cities jostled out across the plain, composed of spires of red rock that reached up into the heavens; she could see the smoky fires burning in the streets, and hear voices on the wind. It looked like a scene from one of those science-fiction movies that Chen was so inexplicably fond of watching; it looked nothing like the worlds she knew. As she tried to make sense of it, however, it disintegrated, and there was nothing more than a cool, gray twilight.

"The cities of the plain," Fan said into her ear. "Very old—so old that some philosophers say that the world is gradually configuring itself to meet their image, and what we see is nothing more than a glimpse of the far future. But others say that this is not so, and there are no triple moons, no plain; only a writhing chaos onto which we project our own images." Her hand tightened around Inari's as she shrugged. "But it doesn't make a great deal of difference in the end, if you ask me. It still has to be dealt with."

"We're going across?" Inari faltered. The glimpse she had seen was somehow terrifying, something that not even a demon should be permitted to see.

"No," Fan murmured. "We're going *in*."

FORTY-EIGHT

Above Chen's head rose the enormous iron spire of the Ministry of War: a spike some nine thousand feet high that reared towards the heavens from a tripod base, as though some mad giant had been let loose on the Eiffel Tower and told to make a few improvements. Around the foot of the Ministry extended an obsidian wall surmounted with writhing live razor wire that thrashed and squirmed in perpetual blind motion, seeking prey. From the base of the wall ran a long flight of shallow steps, leading down to the main administrative square, and a pair of gigantic metal lion-dogs on plinths. Chen, Zhu Irzh, and the badger-teakettle were crouching at the base of one of these plinths, contemplating the ziggurat bulk of the Ministry of Epidemics across the square.

"How are we going to get in?" the demon enquired rhetorically. They were at the time of day which, in Hell, passed as dawn. A chilly, gray light suffused the buildings of the administrative district, and the wind had changed direction, though Chen noted that his shadow still streamed out behind him any which way, as if incapable of making up its mind where to fall. He had long since given up trying to work out where the light was coming from, but the inconstancy of his shadow continued to set him on edge. He stared across to the Ministry of Epidemics. Shadows seemed to wreathe it like a miasma of plague. In its distant upper stories, lights were burning red. The great iron doors that led onto the main square were firmly closed.

"You say it has no back entrances?" Chen murmured.

"None whatsoever. I checked. The drainage system is also apparently complicated, since the city officials clearly don't want the Ministry infecting the rest of the population via that particular route—believe it or not, sanitary controls here are quite strict." Zhu Irzh caught sight of Chen's skeptical look, and protested further. "They really are! So we can't get in via the sewers. On

218 蛇警探 Liz Williams

that previous occasion, as I told you, I simply strolled through the doors with the rest of the patients, and strolled right out again with Leilei." His face took on a momentarily pensive cast. "But that was before the Ministry started dispatching assassins after me. I've no doubt that my person carries some telltale sign that will set alarms clanging all over the place if I so much as set foot in the forecourt. And Imperial Majesty only knows how they'd react to *you*."

"No, obviously we can't go in via orthodox means: that's out of the question. Do you know of any means of disguise? Could we pass ourselves off as sick?"

Zhu Irzh looked at him dubiously.

"You're obviously human, that's the problem. And don't take this the wrong way, Detective, but you smell like one, too. All that fresh blood and meat and bone—" He broke off hastily at the look in Chen's eye. "They'd sniff you out, is what I'm saying."

"What about magic?"

"All government departments tend to have detectors for magical disguises, that's the trouble. There's too much internecine warfare between agencies; everyone's paranoid."

"Could we get in through one of the upper-level windows?" Chen mused, instantly discarding his own suggestion. "No, I don't suppose we could."

"Not a chance," the demon agreed flatly. He stared across to the sheer, gleaming side of the Ministry ziggurat. "Fifty feet of wall before you get anywhere near a window. I doubt if even a glue-footed gecko could make its way up that on a hot day."

"And no chance of you getting in anywhere?" Chen asked the badger, frivolously. The badger raised a clawed hind foot and scratched its ear with vigor, not deigning to reply. Beside them, Zhu Irzh became suddenly tense. His fingers reached for Chen's arm, drew him abruptly back into the shadows below the plinth.

"What?"

"Look," the demon hissed.

"I don't see anything."

"There—crossing the far edge of the square," Zhu Irzh whispered urgently into his ear. Chen peered obediently in the direction indicated, but his weaker human eyes could still see nothing. Then a beam of Hell-light fell through the breaking clouds. Chen could not refrain from a gasp of astonishment. The thing that was now crossing the square was more than familiar. Recently, he had spent several hours cooped up in the back of it, and even as he watched, the pungent odor of blood seemed to drift across the square. It was the delivery dray of Tso's Blood Emporium, drawn by the sinuous, lumbering *ch'i lin*. It trundled across the flagstones and turned the corner so that it was lost to sight around the back of the Ministry.

"Quick," the demon snapped. "Follow me."

Before Chen could stop him, Zhu Irzh was running across the square. Cursing, Chen followed, the badger at his heels. The iron spire of the Ministry of War seemed to swing around, aimed directly at his retreating back. From the corner of his eye, he glimpsed the ornate and roseate portals of the Ministry of Lust, with red pagoda towers carved in a sequence of disconcertingly genital images. Anyone who happened to glance from any one of those towers, from Lust, Epidemics or War, could hardly fail to notice the three fleeing figures: the square was immense, and exposed.

Chen desperately thrust all thoughts of their vulnerability to the innermost pit of his mind. Ahead, he saw that Zhu Irzh, with youth, longer legs, and a demon's speed, had reached the far side of the square and was sprinting around the side of the Ministry. His chest heaving, Chen followed, and shivered as he passed within the purview of the Ministry. It was almost as though the building itself were conscious: a vast, malign bulk that could at any moment turn and crush him. Zhu Irzh was standing with his back flat against the wall of the steps that led up to the Ministry; as Chen panted to a halt, he reached out a warning hand and drew Chen to his side.

"See what they're doing?" he whispered. Cautiously, Chen peered past the demon. The dray had been parked at an angle to the flank of the building, so that they were temporarily, and mercifully, concealed from view. The *ch'i lin* stood blinkered in its shafts, impatiently clawing at the ground. Behind the dray, Chen could see two pairs of feet: one inverted, and one not. The non-inverted feet wore a stylish pair of curled slippers: not quite Tso's style, Chen thought, but it was hard to tell. The thunderous noise of barrels being unloaded from the dray ricocheted across the early-morning silence of the square.

"What are they doing?" Zhu Irzh asked, in an undertone.

"At a guess, unloading the morning's consignment of blood," Chen murmured.

"That's what the dray's carrying, is it? How do you know?"

"Because the company that the dray comes from used to belong to my brother-in-law," Chen told him. The demon's elegant eyebrows rose.

"Tso's? Yes, I remember you telling me. But Tso's blood isn't cheap—as far as I know, the Ministry tends to use low-grade blood for experimentation." He paused. "Perhaps they're having a party."

"That I doubt. However, they almost certainly *will* be having a party if we don't get in there and stop them from creating their cursed plague."

The demon gave him an uneasy glance. "So what do you suggest?"

Chen nodded towards the dray. "Hiding in one of the barrels."

"You're joking." Zhu Irzh peered anxiously into Chen's face, and discerned truth. "Oh," he murmured. "You're not."

"I'm afraid it may require the ultimate sacrifice of yet more of your garments," Chen added. "But it is for a good cause."

"I suppose so," Zhu Irzh muttered, and gave an involuntary shiver.

"I thought demons liked blood?" Chen said.

"It's the same kind of thing as humans liking chocolate. Most do, but some don't and anyway, too much of it makes you sick. It doesn't agree with me. It gives me migraines."

"Keep your mouth closed then," Chen instructed unsympathetically, and headed stealthily in the direction of the dray.

As they had stood and watched, the morning light had crept further along the square. Glancing over his shoulder, Chen could see the metal spire of the Ministry of War catching the light, and sending fragmented refractions from the *ch'i* mirrors placed along its upper struts into the turbulent skies of Hell. The Ministry of Epidemics, however, stood in a black block of shadow, and Chen could no longer see the pinnacle of the ziggurat, which was wreathed in cloud. Followed closely by Zhu Irzh, and with the badger prowling at his heels, he sidled around the wall and waited. The two pairs of feet were, in their respective fashions, facing the back of the dray. The front stood unguarded, except for the restless presence of the *ch'i lin*. Chen heard a grunt of effort; the tailgate of the dray rattled as yet another barrel was unloaded, and the feet shuffled towards a gaping dark space in the ground. Clearly, this was some kind of cellar, into which the barrels were being unloaded.

Something plucked at Chen's ankle. He looked down to meet the lambent gaze of the badger.

"This is something I can do," the badger murmured, so low that the words were almost lost in the rumbling of the barrels. "I will distract them. You go. There." Its narrow head swung in the direction of the hole in the ground.

Into Chen's ear, Zhu Irzh murmured, "It's better than a barrel. Believe me."

Chen was inclined to agree, and in any case, there was little time for debate.

"All right," he said, and gave the badger's sleek side a nudge with his foot. "You go."

With Chen and the demon behind, the badger slunk around the side of the dray. Chen peered through a slit, and saw one short, squat demon and one tall, thin one. The latter's carefully coiffed hair was dangling about his face, which was an unbecoming shade of puce. He was saying bitterly, "—miserable little bastard's probably sleeping off a hangover somewhere. Disappeared, indeed! I don't believe a word of it." With an evident effort, he slung the barrel into the hole with the aid of his companion, and wiped a sticky brow.

The squat demon mumbled, "I told you, Lord. I haven't seen him since yesterday morning. I even rang Tso's house, but his landlady said she hadn't seen him either."

"House? Ha! Tso clings to squalor like a beetle to shit; he lives in some repulsive room in a squalid guest house on the Liu Ho Road. They wouldn't notice if he rotted right under their noses."

Zhu Irzh nudged Chen. "Looks like your relative's gone missing," he whispered. Chen nodded.

"—would be *now*, of course, that my so-called staff decides to run out on me," lamented the tall, thin demon. "I am simply not used to this manner of degrading physical labor. I—" But at that point the badger shot out from beneath the wheels of the dray and bit him sharply in one back turned ankle. The tall demon emitted a spectacular hoot and whirled to face the dray. The squat demon struck out at the badger and missed. The tall person teetered on the edge of the hole, leaning at a bizarrely steep angle above the gaping space before abruptly righting himself. The badger wove smartly around his ankles, with a further nip for good measure, and raced away down the side of the Ministry. Uttering shrill cries of wrath, the demons turned in pursuit, trailing sparks of fury behind them.

"Now," Chen said, but Zhu Irzh needed no encouragement. He ducked behind the tailgate of the dray and slid down the hole like an eel. Chen heard a faint, startled cry from below, a thud, and then silence. Swiftly, he lowered himself down through the hole only to find himself standing on a narrow, rickety scaffold. Zhu Irzh loomed beside him in the darkness, and at his feet lay a stocky, still form. From the pits beneath came the overpowering odor of stale blood.

"There's no one else down here," Zhu Irzh said. He pointed towards the far end of the platform where a spout protruded over the edge. "That's where the blood goes."

Chen prodded the unconscious demon with his foot and rolled it over. Rather to his surprise, the demon was female: a stout form with a long, black tongue that now lolled between slack lips. Her face had the squashed, sat-upon look of a prize Pekinese.

"Lower caste," Zhu Irzh murmured. "Maybe even lower level." Before Chen could stop him, he inserted the toe of his boot beneath the demon's prone form and shoved her over the edge. She disappeared into the darkness without a sound; moments later, there came a distant thump.

"Zhu Irzh," Chen said, pained. The demon looked round, surprised.

"What? No need to be squeamish, Detective Inspector. She can't die, can she, not really?"

"That's not the point," Chen murmured. "Neither can you, but you still didn't want to end up in the lower levels." However, he did not feel it appropriate to begin lecturing Zhu Irzh on moral conduct at this particular juncture.

"Those two will be back in a minute. I suggest we start exploring."

Zhu Irzh swung himself over the edge of the platform and hung there for a moment like a large, black dragonfly, eyes glittering in the faint glow of light from above. Then he was gone, sliding with agility down the fragile mesh of poles. Chen, sighing, followed. He had no great head for heights, and he'd never been especially good at climbing. He put one hand after another, methodically searching for footholds, descending further and further until at last Zhu Irzh put out a steadying hand and Chen found himself standing on solid ground.

"You know," the demon murmured into his ear, "I'll be really hacked off if we find out this delivery has nothing to do with Epidemics after all and we're in the Ministry of War's cellar."

Chen grinned into the darkness. "In that case, better hope it's the Ministry of Lust."

"Mmm," the demon remarked rather languidly. "It's been much too long since I paid them a visit—ah well."

"Don't worry," Chen whispered, thinking grimly of Tso and the blood-dray. "This concerns Epidemics, no mistake about that... Do you have any idea where this leads to, in relation to the street?"

The demon wheeled around, gazing into the darkness. "We came down more or less directly, so if we can find a passage leading there—" he pointed "—we should actually have a reasonable chance of ending up in the Ministry's basement."

"All right. Let's get going then."

"What about your furry friend?" Zhu Irzh asked.

Chen frowned. "The badger will have to look after itself, I'm afraid. It knows where we've gone, anyway." Stepping past Zhu Irzh, he began to make his way through the dark cellar.

The place in which they stood seemed enormous, and there was little light; only a faint gray gleam from above. Chen was obliged to rely on Zhu Irzh's superior eyesight rather more than he liked, but it couldn't be helped. Occasionally, they stopped and listened, but there was no sound from the shadows. The demon came to an abrupt halt.

"What is it?" Chen whispered.

"There's a door."

A muffled rattling ensued, presumably as Zhu Irzh tried the latch.

"Is it locked?"

"Seems to be... I don't want to take any chances, not with this Ministry... Stand back."

Obediently, Chen slipped back against the wall. There was a sudden glow. Zhu Irzh's face manifested briefly in the darkness, lit from below by a gleam of rosy fire; it made him look more demoniacal than Chen had ever seen him. The glow was emanating from the demon's own rosary, which he wore in an insouciant loop around his wrist.

"Now..." Zhu Irzh murmured. "If I can just remember..." He drew a sharp talon across the palm of his hand, marking a character in blood. Intriguing, thought Chen, noting the parallels in technique. Zhu Irzh held up his palm to face the doorway and there was a kind of flash of sound; a synesthetic disturbance that made Chen reflexively blink. In that split second, the demon had leaped backwards, covering his face with his sleeve. A cloud of myriad motes, like sparkling dust, swirled forth from the open doorway and rose upwards in a swarm. But the fleeting, protective spell by which Zhu Irzh had opened the door continued to hold. One by one, the little lights faded and died, to drift like the ghosts of moths down towards the floor.

"Disease," murmured Zhu Irzh, in response to Chen's unspoken question. "Don't know which."

"There are bound to be other traps," Chen said. "Best go carefully."

He heard the demon sigh. "That means I go first, then. Otherwise you'll be stumbling about like a bat in a bottle. Have you ever considered laser surgery?"

Chen laughed. "I'd need pretty powerful eye surgery to enjoy eyesight like yours. Very well, then. Lead on."

The doorway led into a sequence of other passages. Chen tried hard to keep his sense of direction, but it was soon lost, and he was once more compelled to rely upon Zhu Irzh's surer instinct. If only he had a working compass... but direction was maliciously unstable in Hell. At least the disease-impregnated doorway seemed to indicate that they'd broken into the right Ministry, but it was entirely feasible that the door had been trapped in some other way, probably with an alarm. He thought uneasily of the Blood Emporium employees: What would they do, when they returned from chasing, and hopefully not catching, the badger-teakettle? Would they finish unloading the dray? Presumably. What would they do when they found their female helper missing? Probably they would investigate... it all made Chen wonder exactly how much time he and Zhu Irzh had before some kind of security alert was sounded. Hell was a notoriously incompetent and chaotic place, and this was to their advantage, but the Ministry of Epidemics had already demonstrated the capacity to act swiftly and effectively when the need arose, and Chen was certain that the stakes were sufficiently desperate for the Ministry to take maximum measures. One only had to think of the gift-wrapped mansion of the First Lord of Banking to be certain of that. He wondered what had happened to Tang.

Even as these thoughts were revolving around Chen's mind, there came the sound of tramping feet from an area off to the left. Zhu Irzh grasped his arm and hauled him back against the wall. Holding his breath, and hoping that he didn't stink too betrayingly of humanity, Chen listened as what sounded like an entire battalion pounded past the top of the passage. He recalled the sight of the Imperial troops with a sinking heart. Cautiously, Zhu Irzh moved forward. Chen touched his arm.

"What about ventilation shafts?" he murmured.

"It's a possibility. But I only got away with it before because they weren't expecting anyone to be crawling around in one. Now that they're on the lookout, it would occur even to some low-level bureaucrat that the shafts might be a good place to check." He paused. "Although I'm not sure we really have a choice."

"The shafts would be too easy to flush out—with gas, with disease. I think we may have to take our chances down here in the tunnels."

Warily, they moved on. They saw no more patrols for a while, though the sound of movement came from the surrounding passages. Eventually they came out into a narrow hallway, at the end of which was an antiquated lift. Illumination came from dim, pale lamps in the form of gargoyles. Chen and the demon looked at one another.

"We can't risk it," Chen said. "Better find the stairs."

Zhu Irzh nodded.

"Agreed. Pity, though. My feet are beginning to hurt."

The sound of footsteps behind them was suddenly loud. A voice was crying out orders in the thin, stifled dialect of the Imperial Court, which Chen had difficulty understanding. He glanced around. There was nowhere to hide. The demon sprang forwards and pounded the buttons of the lift. After a heart stopping pause, the door slid open, and Chen and Zhu Irzh stumbled inside. A hasty glance at the panel confirmed that the lift would carry them to the twenty-third level. Zhu Irzh slammed the top button and the lift shot upwards. The demon turned to Chen and whispered, "What if they flood the shaft? You're the healer. Do you have any protections against disease?"

Chen shook his head.

"Not enough. But why should they? They don't know it's us, do they? There's no evidence of any surveillance equipment in here." Not for the first time, he called down a sardonic blessing upon the divisiveness, lack of co-operation, and internecine bickering that had caused Hell's modernization program to grind to a halt, leaving its technologies at the level of the twentieth-century Soviet bloc, apart from the odd high-tech lab. Not unlike China, really. Comparisons were always invidious. The lift rumbled upwards, each button faintly smoldered as they passed the relevant floor. Once, the lift lurched to a brief stop, and Chen flattened himself against the wall, bracing himself for confrontation, but the mechanism merely gave a dismal creak and the lift trundled on. Finally, after what seemed like an eternity, the lift ground to a halt and the doors opened.

FORTY-NINE

When he saw the person who was standing before him, Tso wondered despairingly why he'd ever considered himself to be a person of consequence. A pair of reversed feet was nothing compared to such splendor, such elevation. Admittedly, the eminent person did appear to be in an advanced state of decay, but that did nothing to lessen the aura of the Imperial Presence that hung about him in a palpable miasma. The thought *if you could bottle that* crossed Tso's mind, and was instantly quelled by the more conservative part of his personality as being irredeemably irreverent. The personage's clothes were impressive enough: a thick mantle of human hair, as soft and blond as corn silk, hung over a cloak of pink and living flesh. Tso could have counted every tiny capillary and vein that meandered across the cloak, like rivers across the surface of a map.

"Do you know who I am?" the personage asked, in a voice that made the air ring. Tso's own voice, in comparison, was barely audible even to his own ears. "Eminence, I—please don't hold this unworthy person's ignorance against him, but—"

"So the answer's no, then?"

Tso could only nod, once, and feebly. The personage spat at his feet, a gesture somewhat at odds with the magnificence of his garments and bearing. The globule of spittle frothed and writhed, boiling away to produce something that resembled a sticky black seedpod. Tso stared. The seedpod cracked in two, and a long thing like a two-tailed scorpion scuttled out and ran up Tso's leg. Tso yelled and struggled, but it was no use. The guards held his arms in a firm grip, and he was forced to stand helpless as the scorpion-thing snaked inside his collar and coiled itself tightly around his throat. He could feel the delicate prick of its double stings, just below his jugular.

"You really don't have any idea why you've been brought here to the Ministry of Epidemics, do you?" the personage asked with contempt. Painfully aware of the sting at his throat, Tso burst into a voluble and impassioned plea.

"With the utmost respect, Lord, I do not. Have I not provided vital aid and succor to the Ministry of Epidemics? Has it not been my company who has supplied your august institution with the required amount of fresh, top-quality human blood, the very fluid of life of several hundred young girls—at *very* short notice, I should point out, and at maximum expense and difficulty, given that they were alive at the time? Have I not placed into your hands my own accursed brother-in-law, the protégé of Kuan Yin herself, thus thwarting an attempt by the human authorities to bring ruin upon the Ministry's most worthy and intricate plans? Haven't I—"

"All this," said the personage in a voice like a plangent bell, "has been for nothing more than your perceived personal advantage, and is regarded as nothing more than barely sufficient recompense, after the grave affront your family has delivered to the Imperial Court. Did not your own sister, doubtless with your connivance, seek to deceive a good and worthy public servant, who wished only to make her his bride and cherish her for eternity?"

"I had nothing to do with it!" Tso cried. "She—"

But the personage intoned relentlessly on. "And did not that sister, also with your complicit approval, run off to marry a human when your sad scheme was discovered—that self-same protégé of the goddess? Are you aware of the policies of the Imperial Court regarding miscegenation and consorting with Immortals of the heavenly persuasion? If you had kept better guard over your womenfolk, Master Tso, you would not find yourself in the sorry position that you do now. Did you seriously expect to find yourself rewarded for turning your brother-in-law, the contemptible Chen Wei, over to us—a task in which, I might add, you significantly failed to do, given that he's still at large."

But Tso had nothing to say. The personage grinned a dreadful, vulpine grin, and added, "However, it may be that even such a worthless person as yourself is not wholly useless. After all, you share some defiling degree of human blood with your shameful sister, and that makes you a possible candidate for certain of the Ministry's experimental purposes. We shall see if you might be of use after all." He picked up a small, delicate bell from the desktop and rang it. At the far end of the room, a door was flung open, as though someone had been waiting eagerly for their summons. And when Tso saw what stepped through that door, it was as though the blood in his veins, both human and demon, was nothing more than icy water.

FIFTY

Zhu Irzh and Chen shrank back against the sides of the lift, but there was only another empty hallway. This one, however, was considerably more lavishly appointed than the one below. Thick, sulfur-colored drapes masked the walls, and a plush carpet reminiscent of moss covered the floor. Abandoning the lift, Chen and the demon stepped carefully into the hallway.

"Where now?" the demon asked.

"No idea. Let's try that way." Chen indicated one of the long corridors that led from the hallway. The demon padded alongside, occasionally stopping to peer at the closed doors that led off from the hallway. The air smelled musty, with a curiously antiseptic undertone, and beneath that, the unmistakable odor of sickness. It reminded Chen of an old-fashioned and gloomy hotel, crossed with a hospital and a mortuary. Shortly, they came out into a reception area, paved with peeling lacquered tiles. A clerk sat at the desk, writing moodily in a ledger and occasionally coaxing a single strand of hair back across a mottled bald scalp. Zhu Irzh and Chen sidled back behind the curtains.

"What now?" Chen murmured. "Should we go back?"

The demon gnawed thoughtfully on his lip with a gilded incisor. "Might be more people elsewhere. I'll deal with him."

Chen reached out a warning hand but Zhu Irzh was already strolling across the tiles to the desk. The clerk looked up indifferently. Chen held his breath, but the clerk's expression did not change.

"Good morning," the demon remarked politely. "I wonder if you could possibly tell me the location of a Dr Jhang—he's, ah, treating a lady friend of mine for a rather *intimate* complaint and I need to have a word with him."

"How did you get in?" the clerk asked suspiciously. "I thought they'd closed the main doors today. Have you been waiting all night?"

Zhu Irzh gave his most engagingly predatory smile and murmured, "Connections." A wad of Hell money appeared in his hand as if conjured out of thin air. The clerk's red rheumy eyes widened momentarily. "Would you mind just stepping round here a moment?" Zhu Irzh murmured. With his gaze fixed on the hypnotic wedge of money in Zhu Irzh's hand, the clerk did so.

"Is it real?" he mumbled cautiously. Chen once more inappropriately invoked the blessings of Heaven upon a realm where casual workers were so poorly paid, if at all.

"Real?" purred Zhu Irzh. "Straight from the hands of a priest himself—you can smell the incense on it." He dangled the wad of cash temptingly beneath the clerk's pug nose, and as the clerk obligingly bent his head, Zhu Irzh's free hand chopped him smartly below the ear. He fell without a sound. Chen emerged from the curtains.

"Neat," he murmured. Zhu Irzh beamed smugly and put the money back in his pocket. Then he dragged the unconscious clerk behind the curtains and bound him with the length of tasseled rope that secured them to the wall.

"Now," he remarked whimsically, looking towards the row of double doors that led from the reception area. "Which to choose?"

"At least we can see," Chen said. He went swiftly to the nearest door and peered through the dusty glass pane. He felt himself grow very still, and cold.

"What is it?" Zhu Irzh asked impatiently.

"See for yourself." Chen could feel the pulse of nausea beginning in the pit of his stomach. He turned away from the door, leaving the demon with an unrestricted view. It was hardly likely that Zhu Irzh would be so affected, and indeed, the demon merely remarked with interest, "Looks like some kind of laboratory. People being tested. Shall we take a look inside?"

"Do there seem to be any medical personnel around?" The words came close to sticking in Chen's throat, like the glue of grief.

"Can't see anyone," Zhu Irzh remarked. "Might as well, eh?" He gave the door a gentle push and it swung open.

Inside, the air was stuffy and rank, clotted with the smell of suffering. Light filtered in through grubby, slitted windows at the far end of the room, or emanated from a flickering neon tube high above Chen's head. The walls were painted that biliously institutional green common to both Earth and Hell, stained with an ominous rust. The test subjects, if such they were, lay on stacked racks arranged in two long aisles down each side of the room. Chen made a hasty estimate of some nine people to every rack: most of them were women, and very young. But as he stepped reluctantly closer, he saw that they were barely alive; indeed, they seemed hardly present at all. Their small forms were shadowy and indistinct: their pale faces peered up through a miasma of vague air. Tentatively, Chen placed his hand on the shoulder of one of the girls and it passed straight through, although there was a curious sensation of presence, as though the air itself was warm and wet like a humid day. Zhu Irzh's puzzled expression suggested that the demon had noticed the same thing.

"The ghosts of the innocent," he murmured. "A plague to garner innocent souls, and human blood: that's what the Ministry needs to make their drug."

"These ghosts are *between*," Zhu Irzh said, wonderingly. Chen frowned.

"Between Earth and Hell? That's not possible."

The demon shook his sleek head.

"I fear that you're wrong, Detective Inspector. It is not impossible, only extremely rare."

"That's what gods do," Chen whispered. The demon smiled.

"These young ladies are hardly deities. They are humans, that is all, and most unfortunate. Deep magic can summon the flesh halfway, while the mind and the soul wander freely but impotently across the void. It isn't a magic to which anyone I know has access, but then, I'm not an Imperial institution."

"Not all governmental bodies in Hell have this kind of power, though," Chen said. "Just as well, otherwise we'd see all manner of chaos."

"Quite so. They don't. That's why the more inventive among us are forced to seek out the demon lounges: movement between the worlds seems to fascinate us all. As I say, it's deep magic, and as such, you need a high level of authorization and competence in order to apply it. It seems that the Ministry of Epidemics has been so fortunate as to garner such august dispensation," Zhu Irzh replied dryly.

"The capacity to deploy deep magic; Imperial troops moving against the Ministry of Wealth; rumors of a plague aimed at all mankind…This is even worse than I thought. This whole situation is a glove that the hand of the Emperor would seem to fit well."

Zhu Irzh nodded, uneasily. "So it would seem. The Ministry must be very sure of themselves this time. The Imperial Court doesn't usually involve itself so deeply in departmental affairs—upsets the balance, as you know. The Celestial powers demand redress and that can tie up even the Imperial Court in the knots of an eternity of paperwork. Let's see what's through the doors at the end of this room."

The doorway led to a further chamber, in which the racks lay empty. Zhu Irzh picked up a syringe, which dangled from a greasy plastic pipe that led into a mesh of webbing high in the recesses of the wall.

"Looks like they're preparing for more inmates," he said. Chen nodded grimly.

"Doesn't seem to be much of interest at the moment, but this is obviously a part of the new operation." His eyes narrowed; he was thinking aloud. "This lab, the new plague, the Blood Emporium… they're all connected. A drug, to be made from human blood. But what would such a drug do?" His gaze met Zhu Irzh's hot golden eyes.

The demon said, "The First Lord told me that it was a drug that would take people to Paradise. Whatever that means."

Voices were coming from the first lab. Zhu Irzh and Chen dived behind one of the racks, and listened for a tense moment before the doors swung open and a group of people stepped through. Between the bars of the rack, Chen could see a heavily built person, dressed in the most ornate clothes: a blond-collared cloak of flesh that fell in heaving ripples to the floor. Chen could only see part of his face, but it was puffy and mottled with disease. An ulcerated laceration marred one distended cheek. He was accompanied by a smaller demon wearing a grubby white lab coat, and a rotting demon with a cold, patrician face whom Chen recognized with a sudden lurch of the heart as Inari's erstwhile fiancé, the repugnant Dao Yi. These three, however, were also accompanied by someone else, and at the sight of this third person, Chen felt himself grow still. Beside him, even Zhu Irzh swallowed a sharp, indrawn breath.

The fourth member of the party was tall, some seven feet in height, and gaunt. The talons of one hand had been permitted to grow into intricate coils, signifying his elevated status. His skin was a bright, raw red, the musculature clearly visible, as though he had been flayed. His lipless mouth was set in a permanent grin, and Chen got the alarming impression that this was no mere trick of ravaged feature, but that the demon was genuinely and perpetually amused. His eyes were slanted and black and dead, and his face was crowned with an upsweep of something that more closely resembled tentacles than hair, gathered together in a loose, writhing braid. He wore the crimson, gray and black robes of an Imperial Alchemist, and a ceremonial machete hung from his sash. Zhu Irzh nudged Chen sharply in the ribs, and mouthed, "We've got to get out of here."

Chen nodded in silent, but fervent, agreement. He glanced around, but the only possible exit remained the door by which they had entered. There were no windows, and both floor and ceiling were a seamless expanse of tiling. Dao Yi, Inari's former fiancé, made a small, fastidious gesture and said, "Gentlemen! I have great pleasure in welcoming you to this, our third *gherao* ward, which is in the process of being made ready for the next intake of spirits. I'm happy to say that it's been completed on schedule, and on budget."

"Gratifying," the personage in the flesh cloak murmured, in a thick voice like syrup. The small demon in the lab coat nodded anxiously, as if eager to provide reassurance. The alchemist simply gazed around him with mad, black eyes. "And you're quite sure that the program is proceeding according to plan?"

"Quite sure, Minister, yes," Dao Yi said, nervously. Chen took more careful note of the demon in the cloak of flesh: this, then, was the Minister of Epidemics himself, dimly recognizable from the figure seen in the First Lord of Banking's ravaged garden. "We've been most fortunate to procure the services of Tso's Blood Emporium, one of the most reliable old firms in the city, to process the human blood." This remark was clearly made for the benefit of the alchemist, who took no notice whatsoever, but continued to stare around him with his lipless grin. Evidently disconcerted, Dao Yi's mouth compressed into a thin line.

The Minister said acidly, "Reliable? I was under the distinct impression that Master Tso—who in any case no longer runs the Emporium—had been detained. I understood there to be bad feeling between his family and yourself."

"This is indeed the case," Dao Yi said hastily. "However, Tso has been of minimal value in providing us with some important information regarding the human protégé of one of the Celestials, and will moreover go to serve His Excellency the Alchemist in some potentially useful capacity."

"Pleased to hear it," the Minister grumbled. "And how is the blood being collected from source?"

"Our people have been targeting the dormitories of the so-called bioweb, a new form of technology sold to humankind by Hell. Our technicians have had some hand in the research and development. The bioweb provides an ideal context from which to obtain both blood and innocent souls: the components of the web are female and generally young. They are also confined within tanks, and therefore quite passive and unable to put up a struggle. Our agents go in, siphon the blood to a collection point—usually one of the free rooms in the establishment—open a portal and transfer the blood to Hell. It's pumped straight to Tso's, where they have the equipment to treat it. The souls of the girls are then harvested and placed in the liminal state you see here so as not to attract the attention of Heaven."

"A convenient piece of technology, this bioweb," the Minister said to the alchemist, who was paying no attention whatsoever.

"We were, you see, able to make some very favorable deals with the human in charge of the corporation, and he was happy to assist us with the necessary details; security personnel and medical staff are removed shortly before the harvesting, without a fuss, and—"

The alchemist's head came up like a hunting dog's. Chen could see the ravaged nose sniff savagely at the air, as though the alchemist had scented a truffle. The alchemist said in a sibilant voice, "Why, there is a human here!"

Dao Yi's mouth fell open in shock, and even the Minister looked startled. The alchemist took a great bounding stride behind the racks and came face to face with Chen.

"Run!" Chen shouted, shoving Zhu Irzh aside.

"No! You can't fight—"

"Just *go!*" Chen roared. For once, the demon did as he was told, thrusting both Dao Yi and the Minister out of the way and bolting back through the doors, which slammed behind him. Chen was left to face the alchemist. He fell into a fighting stance, realizing as he did so that it was probably doomed, and struck at the alchemist's fire-colored face. The alchemist twisted aside with reptilian speed and gripped Chen by the throat in one taloned hand. He hauled Chen easily off his feet; choking, Chen stared down into the nightmare visage.

"Well, well, well," the alchemist said in evident delight. "Did I not tell you over tea this morning, Minister? The balance of the universe is changing. The very path of the Tao itself is being cajoled aside to favor Hell. Our time is coming, wouldn't you say?" The hideous mouth opened in a soundless zero of exultation; the taloned hand tightened, and for Chen, the world was abruptly no more.

FIFTY-ONE

The worst thing about the lower levels was not the thin, high voice that sang incessantly through the streets like the whine of a vast mosquito, nor the jets of acrid flame that shot at random from between the stones, but the dust-laden wind which blew in from the distant barrens. Dust stained Inari's skin and seeped beneath her clothes, matting her hair and blocking her nose. She couldn't stop sneezing: it was worse than the hay fever to which she'd been prone on Earth. Neither the wind nor the dust seemed to greatly affect Fan, whose red and gray robes appeared as fresh as though she'd recently retrieved them from the laundry. She cast Inari an occasional sympathetic glance, but when Inari begged to sit down for a moment and wipe the dust from her eyes, Fan said no.

"We have to keep moving. For all we know, the *wu'ei* might be close behind."

"I thought you said their power was limited in the lower levels?" Inari protested, and Fan gave a small, grim smile.

"If you are *wu'ei*, even limited power is enough. We can't take the risk," she said over her shoulder, and hastened on. Inari glanced at her, curiously. Throughout this whole strange affair, Fan had given no real hint as to why she was helping Inari, even though the very mention of the *wu'ei* was usually sufficient to send the denizens of Hell scuttling for cover. She wound her robe more tightly around her face, and hurried on.

Just as the cities of Hell mirrored the world above, so did the lower levels reflect Hell itself. Yet the reflection was an imperfect one: sketchy and crude, and uncaringly unfinished. The buildings, made of a coarse red or black stone, were crumbling and often unroofed. Streets ended in nothing but a barren wasteland, sometimes with only half a house trailing away into loose stone and dusty earth, where nothing grew. Here there were none of the dark flowers of the uppermost level, nor the shady, insect-haunted trees, only stone and a thick lichen that grew like a scab over exposed surfaces. The inhabitants of the ramshackle houses were small and squat, with squashed faces; their eyes were like filmy coals, and they had long, sharp teeth. They wore rags and tatters; Inari saw an infant with an unnaturally old gaze sitting in the dust, half-covered in a rat-skin cloak. It leered at her as she passed, and smacked its lips. The traces of Inari's human blood seemed to flinch in her veins.

"I do not like these people," she said with a shudder, as they turned the corner and came out into a decaying square surrounded by metal poles, on which chunks of flesh were drying in the raw wind.

"Don't you?" Fan said, with seeming amusement. She nodded towards a metal shield hanging on a nearby wall. "Take a look, as we go by."

Inari did so, and gasped as she caught the distorted reflection of her own face. It was longer and narrower: more like the muzzle of an animal, with a low forehead and thrust-out jaw lined with pointed teeth. Inari flicked an experimental tongue across her own incisors, and sure enough, they were longer, and her tongue seemed to have grown, thickly filling her mouth.

"I told you," Fan said softly. "This place may change you."

Inari turned a panicky glance towards her guide.

"But you're no different," she said.

Fan smiled. "I change very little," she said. "Wherever I am."

"Why not?" Inari asked, but the scarred woman only turned and began walking swiftly through the maze of alleyways. Inari glanced down at her own hands and saw that they, too, had altered: the fingers were almost twice as long as before, and even as she stared, aghast, her talons began to grow into gnarled shapes, so that the remaining polish cracked and split. Fan was staring at her with a trace of impatience.

"Inari, come *on...*"

Inari swallowed her fear and hurried after the scarred woman. They made their way over piles of broken brick, through ruined courtyards where eyes like glitters of broken glass gazed from the shadows. The high, eerie keening seemed to swirl in eddies of air, becoming amplified by the hollow homes. Fan glided beneath gutters pouring rivulets of dust, and skirted exposed cellars filled with the ghosts of bones. The dust filled Inari's eyes once more and she stopped to wipe them: when she could see again, Fan had gone.

"Fan?" Inari called. There was no reply. She hastened around the corner, but the street ahead was quite empty. "Fan?" she cried again, but nothing answered, only the unceasing wailing voice and the echoes on the wind. Inari stood and listened, feeling cold fear run clammily down her twisting spine, and now the wailing voice seemed louder. She could detect words within it: it spoke in Gweilin.

"Save... save..."

She could not tell whether it was male or female, or even whether it was the same voice she had been hearing since they entered the lower levels. And if it was Fan... Inari glanced around, trying to decide where the voice was coming from. She followed it down the street, and she could smell something now, something thick and rank.

The building at the end of the street was a collapsed palace: its facade crumbled until none of the once-ornate carvings remained. A balcony extended down one half of the property, then broke abruptly away. The voice drifted through the ruined stones: *Save... save...* Tentatively, Inari stepped through into the hallway, but there was nothing there, only a few dusty tapestries. She made her way out into a courtyard, but it was utterly dead. Even the air was heavy and still.

"Fan?" Inari whispered. *Save... save...* It was coming from somewhere just beyond the courtyard. Pushing aside a dry mass of something that at first Inari took to be creeper, but which on closer inspection seemed more akin to hair, she found herself in what had once been a formal garden. Yet nothing was growing here, only clumps of the thick, yellow lichen, and petrified clusters that might once have been shrubbery. A decaying bridge crossed a dark pond, and it was from here that the voice was emanating.

With trepidation, Inari went over to the bridge and looked down. The pond was filled with dark, clotting blood, and she could see something moving in the liquid shadows. A mouth like a bag broke the surface and spoke. "*Save me...*"

It was not Fan. It was undoubtedly something dangerous and unpleasant, but just then it sank deeper into the blood and its last plea was nothing more than a string of thick bubbles. Without stopping to think, overtaken by pity, Inari knelt by the side of the pond and plunged her misshapen hand in. It was immediately gripped so tightly that she was almost pulled in. The reek of the pond filled the air, choking her lungs. Inari hauled and tugged and pulled, and slowly, by degrees, something began to come up out of the pond.

Its hair was matted with blood. Its face was indiscernible beneath the fluid, and it was weighed down by its heavy robes. It took a long, rasping breath and spat redly over the cracked paving stones. Then it raised itself up on its hands and stared at her with cold crimson eyes.

"Who are you?" Inari asked.

The dripping figure replied, with as much dignity as it could muster, "I am the First Lord of Banking."

Inari gaped at him. "But you're—you're the head of the Ministry of Wealth. What are you doing here?"

"It is a long and sorry tale," the First Lord of Banking said bitterly, spitting gobbets of blood. "I have been sorely wronged, by one of my so-called governmental colleagues, no less—by the Minister of Epidemics. He took my house, he wrapped it up—"

"He *wrapped* it?"

"—flinging me from my own balcony into my own pond as he did so. Then everything went dark, and I found myself here. In *that*." He pointed a trembling forefinger at the pond. "Menstrual blood. Cast over generations by adulteresses and abortionists. And I could not get out."

"Then how is it that I was able to help you?" Inari asked, puzzled, and a calm voice said from over her shoulder, "Because you felt pity, and not for yourself. A rare thing, in any level of Hell, and therefore powerful."

Inari turned. Fan was standing behind her, scarred hands folded neatly into the sleeves of her robe. "I am sorry, Inari. I was moving too quickly. I lost sight of you."

"I *know* you," the First Lord of Banking said to Inari, wiping blood from his eyes. He then squinted at the scarred woman and frowned. "Who are you?"

"I am Fan."

"The name means nothing."

"No matter. I think you should come with us, but not in your present condition." She bowed in the direction of the First Lord of Banking, and immediately the blood drained out of his robes and hair, trickling swiftly towards the pond, where it was immediately reabsorbed. The First Lord of Banking stared wide-eyed. "How did you do that?"

"Come," said Fan. "We are losing time."

Inari saw that she was right. Already it was growing darker. Thunderclouds clapped and snarled overhead, and a thick substance began to fall. At first, for a bewildered moment, Inari thought it was real rain, but then she realized the truth: the clouds were raining a bloody dust, which left smears and stains on her skin and clothes. The First Lord of Banking gave a sigh of utmost irritation. With wonder, Inari saw that Fan remained untouched, but the scarred woman was staring up into the broiling skies.

"Inari," she whispered.

Inari looked up and saw with a bolt of horror that the skies were splitting. An immense crack was opening between the clouds: for a moment, she glimpsed what might have been stars and a rainy moon, but then it was gone, obscured by the vast presence of what was coming through.

It might have been a demon. It might have been a dragon with a human face and a great crimson eye, but it was simply too large to see properly. It was covered in dark scales that were themselves the size of clouds. It was one of the *wu'ei*.

"Imperial Majesty!" the First Lord of Banking breathed.

"Inari!" Fan shouted. "Run!"

But Inari could not move. The *wu'ei* filled the skies, gliding overhead, and far, far in the distance of the heavens she saw it turn and look back. Iron fingers clasped her arm as Fan caught hold of her. The woman's mismatched eyes were huge and black, yet somehow she did not look afraid.

"Come, Inari," she said, and her voice rumbled around the echoing ruins like the thunder itself. The power of her voice unlocked Inari's frozen joints and she ran, gripping Fan's hand tightly in her own. The First Lord of Banking was close behind, holding the skirts of his robe up from his flying feet. They bolted through the dying streets, which even now were crumbling around them. A block of masonry fell from a roof, smashing into fragments a few feet from Inari's head. Splinters of wood struck her flesh as a doorframe exploded silently into nothingness, but her skin had become horny and hard, and she barely noticed. Above, the dragon-form of the *wu'ei* coiled and its hot breath overtook the wind, scorching the dust. Fan dodged through a courtyard, dived around a crater in the road, and leaped over the splintered edge of a verandah. They came out into an immense square: clearly the correlate of the administrative centre of Hell-above. Ahead, Inari could see the iron ziggurat of the Ministry of Epidemics, but here in this lower level the metal was rusted away to reveal the building's huge skeleton, and the upper stories were twisted into a fractured mass of girders. On the other side of the square, the Ministry of Lust was no more than a rotting mass of flesh.

"Run!" commanded Fan. "And don't look back!"

Still clutching Inari's hand, she sprinted across the square. Stumbling and staggering as her toenails grew and curled, Inari tried to keep her gaze fixed on the ruin of the Ministry ahead, but she could not help glancing up. The *wu'ei* was disappearing into the heavens, and for an elated moment Inari thought that it was going away, but then she realized that it was coiling upwards to strike. Her legs seemed to be growing shorter, the knees cracking as they bent awkwardly backwards. She caught her foot on an uprooted paving stone and fell flat, but Fan and the First Lord of Banking dragged her up.

"We're nearly there…"

A great shadow fell across the square as the *wu'ei* dived. A blast of heat preceded it, as though someone had opened the door of a vast furnace. As it struck, Inari, the First Lord of Banking and Fan sprang up the uneven steps of the Ministry and through the wreckage of the iron doors. Inari collapsed, her distorted chest heaving, on the threshold of the Ministry of Epidemics, and over the sill she saw the *wu'ei* dive headfirst into the ground. Flagstones hurtled through the air, striking the Ministry with a sound like a hundred beaten gongs, and a wall of red dust billowed through the desolate vaults of the hallway. The gleaming mass of coils thundered down through the air, and Inari saw the end of a barbed tail, the length of an express train, flick behind them. Then the *wu'ei* was gone, leaving a tornado of dust in its wake and a gaping crater where the square had been. Fan gave a chilly smile.

"Where did it go?" Inari gasped. Her tongue lolled out between her lips as she spoke; it was suddenly difficult to keep it inside her mouth. She caught a glimpse of herself in the dusty surface of a once-bright wall panel and saw something squat and monstrous. Fan said, "It's plunging down through the levels. It could not stop itself in time."

"When—" Inari had to gesture; it was too hard to talk. "—when—up?"

"Not for a while," Fan said. "And now we have to find your husband"—but that suggestion really made Inari panic.

"Not—" she pointed a claw at her own mutated face "—not—this."

"Don't worry," Fan said, still smiling. "People change back once they ascend the levels. Usually. Come on. We have to find a way up."

FIFTY-TWO

When Chen began to come round, it seemed that the world was spinning about him. Things also appeared to be upside down, a fact that Chen initially attributed to being half-throttled and banged on the head, but which he swiftly realized to be no more than empirical fact. It was not the room that was revolving—slowly, like a spider in the breeze—but himself, and since he was also suspended by the heels, this accounted for the otherwise baffling inversion. The unlovely figure of his brother-in-law was dangling several feet away, and Chen could see that Tso's ankles were securely bound by a chain attached to a hook in the ceiling. Flasks, alembics, and other chemical apparatus lined the walls and the acrid smell of ammonia filled the air, making Chen's eyes sting and water. Chen permitted himself the luxury of a pang of *Schadenfreude* on behalf of his brother-in-law who was, despite his treachery and deceit, now no better off than himself. Then he devoted all his energies to working out a way to get down.

Twisting and spinning, he managed to get a look at a nearby table, where scalpels and other instruments lay temptingly displayed. Among them, Chen saw with a leap of the heart, was his lost rosary. Tso must have picked his pockets at some point—probably when they were getting into the dray—and stolen his main means of defense. Its beads were stony cold, seemingly dead, but if he could just reach it... Tso was hanging nearer to the table.

"Tso!" he hissed. "Wake up." Tso mumbled something unintelligible. "What? Come on, Tso. Wake *up*."

The demon's bloodshot eyes snapped open, caught sight of Chen's furious face, and abruptly closed again. Tso emitted a thin whistle of distress. As he twisted on his chain, Chen could see a long, angry welt through the thinning hair of the demon's scalp. He could also hear someone moving around outside, muttering to themselves. Something about the crazed eagerness

239

of the tone of voice suggested that the alchemist was outside the door. As Chen listened, footsteps retreated down the passage and Chen breathed a momentary sigh of relief.

"Tso, I know you've probably had a bang on the head, but I'm quite well aware you're still conscious. We have to find a way of getting down."

"No use," the demon whined. "There's no way out of here."

"Nonsense," Chen said briskly.

By dint of much cajoling and pleading, he finally induced Tso to make a grab for the rosary. Tso did so, catching the string of beads on the end of his long, barbed tongue and flicking it towards its owner, but though Chen lunged for it, he missed. The rosary wound itself tightly around the ornamental carved pineapple adorning a nearby desk and hung there, just out of reach. The footsteps were coming back. Frantically, Chen began to swing on the end of the chain: faster and faster, like an immense pendulum. His erratic path knocked his shoulder against a precarious rack of alembics: some of these fell, sending glass and an acidic fluid spilling across the floor. From a cracked flask there was the sudden, cough-medicine odor of ether and this gave Chen an idea. Swinging against the desk, Chen opened his mouth and caught the rosary between his teeth. As soon as the beads registered the presence of their owner, they began to burn and glow. Chen could feel the heat radiating out from them; he was careful not to let them touch his tongue. The door was opening. Grimacing wildly, Chen swung backwards and forwards, flicking the rosary out towards the cracked flask. The alchemist stepped through the door, clasping his ceremonial machete. Seeing Chen, his terrible smile widened. Light glinted from the rippling surface of the machete. Chen, swinging, let the rosary go. It wrapped itself around the cracked flask. Chen swung back, muttering warding spells for all he was worth.

As soon as the red-hot beads touched the flask of ether a great flower of fire ignited, running along the shelf and blossoming up towards the doorway. The blast brought down half the ceiling, Chen and Tso with it. Fire licked Chen's hair and the hem of the alchemist's robes and the alchemist went up like a torch: the chemicals which stained his robes burning now ultramarine, now amber. The alchemist fell against the door with a wordless cry, beating at his blazing robes. Half-blinded by heat and flame, muffling his scorched head with his sleeve, Chen saw that the brittle shells which guarded the mandarin talons of the alchemist's left hand had also caught fire, and were burning like so many incandescent candles. The last glimpse Chen had was of the blazing alchemist staggering out into the hallway and falling to the floor in a welter of flames.

Inside the laboratory, a tongue of flame licked one of the alembics that stood on the opposite shelf. It exploded like fireworks, sending sparks showering into the room.

"Bloody marvelous!" Tso cried. "You've doomed us both!"

Chen had to admit that his brother-in-law had a point. After all, he could die here and probably end up in exactly the same place—an interesting metaphysical question—whereas Tso would be consigned to one of the lower levels. However, to someone as concerned with status as Tso, this was probably worse than death. The fire on the floor, caught in the backlash of the warding spell, guttered and died.

And then a long, black coat, greatly the worse for wear, swirled through the drifting smoke and Chen saw Zhu Irzh's intrigued face peering down at him. Struggling to rise, he found to his shame that his legs were shaking. The demon hauled him upright. Zhu Irzh's eyes were wide.

"I don't know, Detective Inspector. I leave you alone for no more than an hour and you manage to get captured, torch a laboratory and dispatch an Imperial alchemist with a blast of flame. What did you have in mind for an encore?"

Chen tried to speak, but the acrid fumes had rendered his voice no more than a hoarse whisper. He gestured towards Tso, still entangled in the chains. Tso's anguished, angry eyes were watering profusely from the effects of the fumes.

"Who's that?" Zhu Irzh asked sharply. "Your brother-in-law, at a guess."

"That's right," Chen croaked.

"What do you want to do with him?"

Chen considered this. There was a strong case to be made for leaving Tso exactly where he was: firmly secured and out of mischief. There was also an argument for dispatching him to one of the lower levels, but Chen did not feel that he could cope with even the limited death of a demon on his already weighted list of sins. It took no more than a moment to make his decision.

"Leave him where he is," he said hoarsely.

"No!" Tso protested. "You can't leave me! Get me out of here!"

Zhu Irzh grinned. "No chance," he said.

"Chen Wei! As the brother of your wife, I appeal to you! I—"

"Sorry," Chen said. "As far as I'm concerned, any obligation I had to you vanished when you sold me out to the Ministry."

"I had no choice! My status—my feet, I—"

Zhu Irzh snorted. "Come on, Chen. Let's leave him to it."

"Wait a moment," Chen said. He snatched up a skein of cloth from a nearby shelf and, ignoring Tso's cries, gagged him with it. Zhu Irzh, who was already halfway through the door, nodded in approval. Followed by Tso's muffled shrieks, they picked their way through the ashes into the corridor. To Chen's mingled alarm and relief, there was no longer any sign of the alchemist: only a black, greasy stain along the walls and floor.

"Where do you think he's gone?" he asked uneasily.

Zhu Irzh shrugged. "The lower levels, probably. Don't worry about him. He's out of the picture."

Chen wasn't so sure. He lingered for a moment, sifting through the ashes while the demon waited impatiently by his side, and found what he was looking for. His rosary was, encouragingly, untouched by the blaze: the beads bright and untarnished. Hoping that it was a sign that his luck was turning, Chen wound it around his wrist and followed the demon down the corridor.

"What happened to you?" he asked, as they hastened on. Zhu Irzh actually seemed to have some idea as to where he was going, which was more than Chen did.

"I fled," the demon said, somewhat embarrassed. "I hid in a closet in that first lab. I heard them leaving, and when I thought the coast was clear I followed them—the Minister, the alchemist and the guards. They had you all trussed up. That sour-faced prick Dao Yi was all for putting an end to you there and then but the Minister insisted that you be kept alive, and the alchemist agreed. The Minister said you'd have information, suggested they torture it out of you when you came round, but the alchemist overruled him—said he had something else in mind, something more important than information. The Minister obviously didn't like it, but he didn't put up much of an argument—which in itself is weird. People of that sort of status usually don't take no for an answer."

"I think the alchemist's running this particular show," Chen said.

Zhu Irzh glanced back without breaking his stride, and nodded. "I agree. And that means the Imperial Court."

The thought of a direct confrontation with the Emperor of Hell was enough to send icy rivers of apprehension down Chen's already bruised spine, but there was little he could do about it now. He'd been implicated from the moment Mrs Tang put the sad photo of her dead child on his desk, perhaps before. There was nothing to be gained by regrets.

They came out into the junction of two hallways and Zhu Irzh paused in indecision.

"Where are we going, by the way?" Chen asked.

"I'm looking for the Records Office. We've seen the labs, we know what the Ministry's up to, but we need proof to take to the Ministry of War."

"Why War?" Chen asked, but he thought he already knew.

The demon said, "The Imperial Court rules us all. You know that, and there's not a great deal anyone can do about it. If they're implicated in this plan, then they've come down on the side of the Ministry of Epidemics, and there's unlikely to be any form of direct redress. However, the Imperial Court isn't united."

"That's an understatement," Chen said, thinking of the numerous antipathetic factions that racked the Imperial Court with intrigue.

"Maybe. But the most powerful Ministry in Hell is War, and if they suspect that Epidemics is trying to steal a march on them, they've got enough influence with their own factions at Court to seriously embarrass the Ministry. Maybe even stop them. That's what I'm counting on, but I need proof."

"Do you have any idea where that proof might be found?" Chen asked. The demon seemed very sure of where he was heading, and not for the first time, Chen felt a flicker of unease. The events of the previous few days had lulled him into a relationship with Zhu Irzh that, if not precisely trusting, was not so far removed from it, and this was a luxury that had to stop. It was certainly well within the bounds of possibility that Zhu Irzh was luring him into a trap; after all, he only had the demon's word for the attempted assassination-by-saucepan, and Hell was noted for the cruelty and ingeniousness of its games. Even if Zhu Irzh was not in league with the Ministry itself, he was nonetheless a citizen of Hell; a subject of the Imperial Court and it was improbable in the extreme that he would seriously balk at any scheme designed to discomfort mankind.

Unaware of Chen's misgivings, the demon was saying, "Because when I overheard the alchemist and the Minister talking, the Minister mentioned schematics. The alchemist asked where they were, and the Minister told him that the relevant data was in the Hall of Records. There was a floor plan in the entrance hall to the labs, I took note of it."

"So you know where we're going?"

"More or less. I think so, anyway."

"And have you devoted any thought as to how we're going to get out of here?"

"No," Zhu Irzh remarked with sublime insouciance. "I thought we'd cross that bridge when we came to it."

INTERLUDE
Earth

Sergeant Ma first began to notice the changes when they swung back up through the Ghenreng tunnel and onto the coast road. The narrow strip of lights that normally illuminated the tunnel was dead, plunging the highway into shadows. With a hiss of irritation, No Ro Shi switched the headlights on. Glancing up, Ma saw that the fans of the air-conditioning units that dotted the ceiling of the tunnel at regular intervals were no longer turning, and indeed, the air that was being funneled inside the car was heavy with fumes. As they came to the end of the tunnel, they hit a traffic jam.

"Get on the radio," No Ro Shi ordered. "See how bad the holdup is—I'm not sitting here for the rest of the afternoon."

Ma did so, and found that the usual channel was nothing more than a hiss of static.

"It's not working," he said.

The demon-hunter glared at him. "Why not?"

"I don't know."

"Well, then, find out! Try some of the other frequencies."

At last, Ma managed to contact the precinct and speak to the operator, but her voice was wavering and distorted, audible only at brief intervals. She seemed to be trying to explain something, but it was impossible to tell what she was talking about and after five minutes or so, Ma gave up.

"Well?" No Ro Shi said.

"It's no use. I can't hear a thing."

No Ro Shi muttered something that Ma didn't catch, then added, "At this rate, we'll be back at the precinct round about November. I'm not putting up with this." He slammed his hand down on the horn so hard that the mechanism jammed, producing a single unwavering howl. No Ro Shi gave a wolfish grin.

"Know what they call that in Beijing, Sergeant? Sixth gear." He snapped into reverse, backing up so fast that the driver of the car behind hammered his own horn, then did a brutally swift U-turn. Moments later they were speeding back through the tunnel, on the wrong side of the road.

"Where are we going?" wailed Ma. No Ro Shi, swerving to avoid a speeding truck, did not reply. Hurtling out of the tunnel, he dodged back onto the right side of the road and speeded towards the Lao Shih turnoff. They passed a Merc on its side in the ditch, and further on a truck upside down on the hard shoulder; its cargo of watermelons lying split and squashed all over the road. No Ro Shi's foot came down hard on the accelerator and they shot through a junction. Ma squeezed his eyes tightly shut, but was unable to avoid hearing the sudden squeal of tires.

"No lights, that's the problem," the demon-hunter barked in his ear. "Traffic signals aren't working."

"Why not?" Ma asked, baffled. No Ro Shi grimaced.

"Because the bioweb's finally crashed once and for all, that's why."

Ma thought back to the rows of sad, waterlogged figures in the *gherao* dormitory and was silent. No Ro Shi took the car onto the upper coast road: a narrow, winding one-lane track that the new highway had replaced. The road dipped and bent, revealing alarmingly sudden vistas of sea, and Ma gripped the sides of his seat until his knuckles hurt. They swerved down through the northern suburbs and came out onto the upper reaches of Shaopeng Street. None of the lights were working. At the Hsi junction, two trams had collided and derailed; they lay on their sides in the road, surrounded by crackling, jumping electric cables. Beneath the mass of twisted metal, Ma glimpsed a hand: outstretched as if in supplication.

"Ambulance services are still working," No Ro Shi said with grim satisfaction, looking down the length of Shaopeng to where blue lights were flickering ominously. "That's good."

As they entered the banking district at the south end of Shaopeng, they saw that the streets were filled with people, milling aimlessly about in front of their offices. Most of them, Ma noted, were office workers, dressed in shawl-collared suits and neat white shirts; they seemed bewildered, like school-children released early from class. Alarms were sounding from all sides, and the automatic double-doors which led into the Shanghai and Macau Bank were sliding maniacally back and forth. The air was full of smoke: drifting in the currents and eddies generated by the buildings on either side of Shaopeng, and when he opened the window, Ma was alarmed to note the acrid smell of fire. A container tanker, spilling some viscous chemical from its side, was jackknifed across the road. With a curse, No Ro Shi slammed the car to a halt and leaped out.

"Can't get past. We'll have to go on foot. Can you call the precinct?"

Panting after him, Ma tried, but with no result. Both his radio and his mobile were dead.

"Communications are down," he called after the retreating figure of No Ro Shi. The demon-hunter did not turn.

"Where are we going?" he shouted, his breath raw in his throat. "To the precinct?"

No Ro Shi said something that Ma did not hear. Hands plucked at Ma's sleeve; voices assailed him:

"Officer, my friend's trapped in her cubicle—the door won't open—"

"—got to help him—I can't feel a pulse—"

"—why aren't the police answering any calls? Don't you realize—"

"Wait!" Ma called desperately after the demon-hunter. "We have a situation here, and—"

Someone was coming out of the foyer of the Shanghai and Macau Bank: a man in khaki trousers and a shirt that was heavily sweat-stained beneath his armpits. He was staggering, and as Ma turned, a gush of blood poured from his nose. His eyes rolled back in his head; he fell, and lay still. Ma shouldered his way to the fallen man and bent over him, absently noting as he did so the technician's badge on the man's shirt, now half-obscured by blood. He was about to check the man's pulse when a hand on his shoulder spun him around. He looked up into the cold black gaze of No Ro Shi.

"Touch him," the demon-hunter hissed, "and you're dead as well. Come with me."

Ma tried to protest, but it was suddenly as though that black gaze filled the whole of the world. His vision swam, and his head felt as though someone was stuffing cotton wool into his ears. The command echoed in his head like the beat of a drum. *Come with me.* Then No Ro Shi turned and was running.

As though pulled by a string, Ma clambered to his feet and pounded along in pursuit of the demon-hunter, fending off the general public as best he could. No Ro Shi veered off down an alleyway that Ma recognized as the scene of a dozen illicit gambling dens: good thing it was daylight, he thought. A man in a soft velvet hat with a sallow face gaped in amazement as Ma rushed by, elbowing him out of the way. Ma's chest burned and he could hear himself wheezing; vaguely, he wondered why he could not seem to do other than follow the demon-hunter—but the notion slid from his mind like greasy water and he ran on. Another alley, a twist, a turn, and the light of the port lay glassy and bright over the rooftops. Ahead lay the temple of Kuan Yin.

PART SIX

FIFTY-THREE
Hell

"Here it is," Zhu Irzh said with satisfaction. They had paused before an immense pair of metal-paneled doors, bearing the legend RECORDS OFFICE on a small, bronze plaque.

"Careful," Chen said as Zhu Irzh made to open the door. "You don't know what's in there."

The demon waved a hand and replied, "Don't worry about it. I know these departments. The only people who'll be in here are a few clerks."

Cautiously, he opened the door, and came face to face with the lipless, fire-blackened visage of the Imperial alchemist. Behind the alchemist—silent except for the rhythmic clicking of their jaws, and entirely filling the vast vault of the Records Office—were row after row of Imperial troops.

Immediately, Zhu Irzh moved to slam the door shut, but it was torn out of his hands by the alchemist's scorched claw. The alchemist uttered a shriek of fury and triumph and swung the black blade of the machete downwards. Zhu Irzh ducked; the blade buried itself in the metal door. The alchemist roared again, wrenching the blade free with a squeal of tortured metal that made Chen's teeth sing in his head. The front row of troops gave a great bound, springing forwards on curiously jointed heels. Zhu Irzh kicked upward, catching the alchemist on the wrist. The last loosely attached shards of flesh and bone came apart and the alchemist's hand, still grasping the machete, clattered to the floor. The alchemist wailed aloud: a thin, eerie sound like a screaming frog. He raised his good hand in command: fire shot from it, once more singeing Chen's hair and setting alight the skirts of the demon's much-maligned coat. Chen lifted his rosary, stilled his breath in his pounding chest and began to chant. Zhu Irzh snatched off the coat, balled up the flaming bundle and hurled it into the alchemist's face. Then he drew his sword, slicing across the alchemist's midriff. The alchemist folded over the sword like a broken puppet, only to snap up again moments later. He opened his mouth wide and a gout of flame shot from it, still stinking of chemicals from the laboratory. In the split second before he dived to the floor, Chen realized how the alchemist had survived the fire: he had simply swallowed it. The protective chant diverted the blast of flame, which roared upwards and torched the drapes of the hall. Chen rolled beneath the blast of heat; came up on his feet on the opposite side of the hallway. Zhu Irzh was still slashing at the alchemist; the fire had missed him. The Imperial troops took another leap and this time their efforts landed them in the blazing hallway. Chen found himself facing two huge warriors; the time had come for flight.

"Zhu Irzh!" Chen shouted, evading the slash of an axe blade. "Leave it! Run!" He turned to bolt down the corridor and this time found himself facing the Minister of Epidemics. The Minister's face was distorted and purple with rage. Any thoughts that the Minister might still want them alive were dispelled in the next instant.

"Kill them both!" the Minister roared. "Kill them now!"

But at that point the fire abruptly hissed out. A great cold wind blew through the hallway, scattering the Imperial troops like so many ninepins, and Chen's breath was sucked out of him as violently as if he had been shoved through an airlock. Someone struck him, knocking him against the wall, and Chen recognized Zhu Irzh's gaping face. The doors of the Records Office slammed shut, trapping the Imperial troops behind them. The alchemist collapsed like a bag of bloody bones, and Chen could breathe again.

And three people were sprawling in the wreckage of the hallway.

FIFTY-FOUR

Ma had vaguely expected the temple of Kuan Yin to be quiet, a haven from the mounting chaos in the city beyond, but the courtyard was full of people. They clamored prayers as they besieged the elderly priest; some were frantically reading their fortunes as they tried to make sense of what was happening to them. No Ro Shi shouldered them aside, and ignoring the priest's protestations, made his way through the temple doors.

Ma had been to the temple once before, to pay his respects to the goddess, and it was just as he remembered it. The jade statue of Kuan Yin stood serenely at one end of the long room; fresh flowers covered the altar. No Ro Shi strode towards the statue without breaking his stride.

"What are we doing here?" Ma asked.

"Things are happening much faster than I reckoned, Ma. The plague's already loose. There's nothing we can do to stop it in this world, we'll have to go to Hell."

"What?" Ma quavered, not believing what he'd just heard.

"Chen will need our help," the demon-hunter said, gathering an armful of incense sticks. "We don't have time to go through the Night Harbor. Come and stand over here."

"No way," Ma said.

The demon-hunter turned and his gaze was once more dark and compelling. "Do as you're told, Ma. You might not be a lot of use, but I want someone at my back."

FIFTY-FIVE

"Inari!" cried Chen.

"Leilei!" sighed Zhu Irzh in the same instant. Inari was gazing down at her hands, her mouth wide, and then her face crumpled with palpable relief. Scrambling to her feet, she took a tottering step forwards and fell into Chen's arms.

"That's your *wife?*" Zhu Irzh asked in dismay.

It was then that Chen's suspicions were confirmed. Over Inari's quivering shoulder, he said, "Yes, she is. Zhu Irzh, I'm sorry. I didn't realize—how could I?"

"Just my luck," the demon muttered.

The First Lord of Banking stepped forwards. "Where is he?" he hissed at Zhu Irzh.

The demon stared at him, blankly. "Where's who?"

"The Minister of Epidemics, who else? I suppose you've been mooning over some strumpet while I, *I,* have been suffering in dire extremity in the depths of Hell." His face was suffused with rage.

Hastily, Chen detached his quivering wife and bowed, saying quickly, "Eminence. We were both witness to the woeful destruction wreaked upon your house by unscrupulous persons. Seneschal Zhu Irzh has been working tirelessly ever since to seek those responsible and bring them to justice."

"Very well," the First Lord of Banking said, somewhat mollified. "Then where are these self-same culprits?"

Chen pointed at the wreckage of the alchemist.

"Well, there's one. Slain by Seneschal Zhu, unless I am greatly mistaken. The Imperial troops appear to be confined behind these doors. I don't know what happened to the Minister of Epidemics."

"I know," someone said in a still, quiet voice, stepping forwards. Chen felt

252

his knees turn inexplicably to water.

"You do not know me," the scarred woman said, pre-empting him. "I am Fan. And I know where the Minister of Epidemics has gone."

"Where, then?"

"To seek sanctuary."

"Sanctuary?" the First Lord of Banking asked, brow furrowed.

"This game has become too public. It has attracted the attention of Heaven, of the world above, and of the Lords of Hell, such as yourself, and I am sure you would be the first to agree that the Ministry of Epidemics has overstepped the mark."

The First Lord of Banking snorted. "That's one way of putting it. I do not expect inter-departmental backstabbing to be taken to such extremes. But if the Ministry has the backing of the Imperial Court, what can one do?"

"The Lords of Hell can do little. But Hell alone does not have a say in what happens in the world. The endeavors of the Ministry of Epidemics have attracted Heaven's attention, too. And that is where the Minister has gone."

"To Heaven?" Zhu Irzh asked, amazed. Fan smiled.

"Not quite. To the nearest incarnation of it, to seek asylum from the wrath of his Imperial Majesty. To the temple of Kuan Yin. And that is where we must go, too."

"All very well," the First Lord of Banking said. "But first we've got to get out of the Ministry." He glanced uneasily at the Records Office, where a persistent banging had replaced ominous silence. The troops were trying to get out.

Fan nodded. "Then let's go."

They hastened through the hallways and passages of the Ministry of Epidemics, and as they went, Chen saw that changes were taking place. The drapes had become moldered, and stank of damp. Some of these had fallen away from the walls, revealing scabrous patches upon the bilious green plasterwork. The gaps between carpet and wall had begun to ooze a thick, slimy fluid which seeped into the carpets and made them sticky, causing both Inari and the First Lord to slip. Behind them, the banging was growing louder, reaching a rhythmic intensity that suggested the release of the Imperial troops was imminent.

"What's happening?" Zhu Irzh asked, puzzled, but it was Chen who first realized what was taking place.

"It's the Ministry," he said. "I think it's sick."

Zhu Irzh stared at him blankly.

"Sick?" Inari echoed doubtfully.

Chen nodded. "For once, that's a good sign. In a way."

The First Lord frowned. "I don't see how."

Patiently, Chen explained. "The Minister of Epidemics has fled; the Imperial Court has withdrawn its favor due to the Minister's bungling. Without the

254 蛇警探 Liz Williams

Minister to oversee it, and with the destruction of the Imperial alchemist, the building itself has become infected with its own bio-organisms. It's breaking down."

"That could be possible, you know," the First Lord admitted, glancing back. "The building itself may seem to be made of metal and stone, but it's impregnated with the essences of all the plagued spirits who have ever passed through its portals."

"That's a lot of spirits," Zhu Irzh murmured, after a pause.

"Indeed."

A thunderous bang came from the direction of the Records Office, and the pounding of many inhuman feet. By now, Chen was almost dragging Inari along, and even Zhu Irzh's breath was coming fast and ragged. They turned a corner into an immense antechamber, with a neat placard at one end that indicated a flight of stairs.

"Over there!" Chen panted, pointing. They bolted for the stairs, but the doors were locked.

With a glance at one another, Chen and Zhu Irzh kicked them in. The party tumbled down into a shadowy stairwell, which opened out onto a space so vast that at first Chen had a hard time taking it in. He could see all the way up to the uppermost stories of the Ministry, and all the way down. The stairwell ran around a great column of dark air; it was a very long way to the bottom. Holding fast to Inari's hand, and followed by his companions, Chen started the descent.

It became immediately evident that the stairs were not designed for human feet, nor even for their analog. Some steps were exceedingly wide, some very narrow, as though the architect had tried to please everyone via the dubious method of insane and haphazard compromise. They had gone no more than two flights when the doors by which they had entered were blown back on their hinges. One of the doors came loose and hurtled past the startled party, only to drift as softly as a leaf down into the depths of the stairwell. Above, the Imperial troops were coming through. Their talons grated on the stone; they emitted a high, sibilant whispering. Chen and the others speeded up, half-falling down the uneven stairs in their haste, but the Imperial troops moved too quickly, bounding down the steps like dogs. In the next moment, the troops were nearly upon them, so close that Chen could see their crimson throats between their long, sharp mandibles. Desperately, Chen prepared to fight. Zhu Irzh followed his lead, drawing the sword with a hiss. The Imperial troop leader bounded through, and past them. The first line of troops followed, flowing around Chen and Zhu Irzh, and down the stairwell. As the rest of the battalion of Imperial soldiers scrambled after them, Chen and the others were left standing, open-mouthed, in disbelief.

"I thought they were after us," Inari said; and the First Lord of Banking replied, "Which makes me wonder what they're running from." As one, they all glanced up toward the shattered doors, but Chen felt it long before he saw it. It was like sickness, like the first clammy onset of plague. It was absolute wrongness. Chen grasped Inari around the waist and hoisted her up.

"What are you doing?" she cried.

"No time!" Chen shouted. "Follow me!" Then he threw himself and Inari over the banisters and into the void of the stairwell.

They fell so far and so fast that for a moment, Chen blacked out. He came round in a panic to see Inari's face pressed into his shoulder, her eyes squeezed shut and her face screwed as tight as an unfurled lotus bud. Over the top of her head, he saw Fan floating downwards. Her arms were crossed upon her breast; her robes were wrapped tightly around her and she was spinning slowly, like a giant top. There was no sign of either Zhu Irzh or the First Lord of Banking, but then Chen was spun around and he saw them falling far below. The two demons had joined hands, and they rode the air like birds: Zhu Irzh's shirt and the First Lord's robes swirling around them in dark wings. There was a soundless, percussive blast from high above. Bits of banister, shards of wood and stone and metal, and a tangled mass of something that had once been alive surrounded them. Chen's face was gashed by a piece of flying glass and the blood flew out in droplets. Seeing the blood, Inari tried to speak but velocity ripped the words out of her mouth. Chen was trying not to think about what would happen when they hit the bottom, which, if the patch of solid darkness below was anything to go by, was not far away.

There came another soundless explosion and a rent half a mile wide was ripped in the walls of the Ministry. Chen saw a patch of stormy daylight ahead, and then he and Inari were flying, not down but outwards, carried through the rip in the Ministry like specks of dust on a whirlwind. Chen had a sudden view of Hell unfolding below, as they were cast out over the port area. He wondered, through the roaring in his ears, if he were screaming. Ahead, the immense darkness of the sea was coming up fast. Inari was clutching him so tightly he was beginning to choke, and then they were once more plunging down.

Chen did not have time to think about dying. They hit the sea like diving gulls, but instead of unconsciousness or the sudden burst of water into their lungs, all was suddenly calm. It was then that Chen realized that the Sea of Night was as literal as its name implied: made not of water, but of darkness. Inari released her grip and they floated apart, hand in hand, drifting on a cool current of night. A very long way below—or perhaps the word had no meaning here—Chen could see something that looked like a great watery star, hovering in the depths. A glittering skein of lights spiraled up from the deep: Chen had no idea what it might be, but it was so beautiful that he could only stare in wonder. Catching sight of Inari, he saw that same dreaming sense reflected in her face. His vision was growing dim, and a warmth was expanding in his chest; they could just stay here, he thought dimly, and sail all the way back to the world itself... Inari tugged urgently at his hand. He glanced at her, and saw that the dreaminess in her face had been replaced by panic. She cried, "Chen Wei! We're drowning!"

Her voice sounded quite clear, but very far away. Chen smiled benignly.

"Don't be silly. We're floating in air, not water," he thought he heard himself say.

"I don't care! We're still drowning! We have to get out!"—and without waiting for an answer, Inari kicked up strongly, taking Chen with her. Blood pounded in his head, and his chest felt tight. He did not want to go back up to the surface, back into Hell; he wanted to stay here, in this drifting, dreaming, under-air world, and he tried to pull away from Inari's hand. But her long talons cut cruelly into his flesh, bringing with the pain a measure of sanity. He struck upwards, matching her strokes, and after what seemed like a spinning eternity they shot out into the fumes of Hell.

It was still light. The surface below them was glassy and serene, and Chen saw that they were not far from a jetty, on which a number of figures were standing.

"There!" Inari cried. They swam towards shore, and as they neared the jetty they saw that someone was leaning down to help them up: Zhu Irzh, with the First Lord of Banking at his shoulder.

"Thought you'd gone," Zhu Irzh said, wide-eyed. He began to wring out the perfectly dry hem of his shirt. "Feels odd," he added, in response to Chen's raised eyebrows. He was, Chen could not help noting, careful not to look at Inari at all.

"Where's the scarred woman?" Chen said. The First Lord gave a boneless shrug.

"No idea. Somewhere out there, perhaps." They gazed soberly out across the heaving surface of night.

"No use looking," Zhu Irzh remarked pragmatically. Inari's face was troubled.

"She was good to me," she whispered.

The First Lord said grimly, "Never mind her. Look at *that*."

Chen turned. They were standing across from the port area of Hell, with an unimpeded view over to the main administrative square, which he and Zhu Irzh had crossed so little time ago. Where the Ministry of Epidemics had stood was a twisted framework, covered by a dark, crawling mass. A humming, buzzing note was distantly audible, and the smell of decay fought for pre-eminence with the usual odors of Hell.

"The Imperial Court must have been really pissed off," Zhu Irzh said, with some awe.

"What is that?" Chen murmured, and the demon said simply, "Flies. They've turned it into a hive."

"One of the Seventh Seasonal Curses," the First Lord amplified. "Usually applied to individuals, however, not governmental departments. I would echo the Seneschal's succinct comments."

"Fan said that the Minister had fled to the temple of Kuan Yin," Chen said. "Let's go." Reaching out a hand to Inari, he strode down the wharf, followed by the others.

FIFTY-SIX

Since the temple lay in an analogous position to the ones in the worlds above, Chen and the demons were obliged to traverse the port area of Hell in order to reach it. For once, Chen was grateful to be in the company of so many of Hell-kind. The city was in chaos. Most of the dingy shops and emporiums were closed, and as they passed the doorway to a nearby demon lounge, the shutters went down with a bang, closing off the establishment from the street beyond. Small groups of demons clustered everywhere, casting unsettled glances in the direction of the former Ministry of Epidemics, the rank, diseased odor of which permeated the city like a urine-soaked sponge. Chen was wondering how the demise of the Ministry would affect his own world: Would the incidence of plagues and viruses decrease until the Ministry—or whatever might be left of its personnel—crawled back into Imperial favor? Would suffering be reapportioned so that war, say, would suddenly break out? A higher incidence of lust might be no bad thing, but Heaven wouldn't like that. As if he had read Chen's mind, Zhu Irzh remarked, "It's only temporary, you realize. The Ministry will have to rebuild. It's too valuable an asset."

"Tell me," Chen said, directing the question towards the First Lord of Banking. "Has this sort of thing happened before?"

The First Lord nodded. "Several times, throughout the long history of our eminent region. The Ministry of Civil Strife copped it last time—a matter of the Maoist revolution. That wasn't supposed to be quite so successful, I understand."

"It brought its own woes. I'm surprised there doesn't seem to be a Ministry designated for oppression."

"I believe it's a subdivision of War," the First Lord said absently, gazing around at the empty street. "And talking of government departments, where did all those Imperial troops go?"

Zhu Irzh shrugged. "Out to sea with the rest of us."

"The Imperial Court wouldn't have put all its demons in one basket," said Chen. "I think we should go more carefully."

Mindful of this, the little group ducked down an alleyway and Zhu Irzh led them through a familiarly confusing warren of streets. After some time, during which they met no one save ordinary citizens, the red roofs of the temple rose above its surrounding wall.

"Looks pretty quiet," said Zhu Irzh.

"I don't find that reassuring." Motioning the rest to silence, Chen crept around the wall to the main gate and peered cautiously through a crack in the door.

"Can you see anything?"

"No, it all looks quiet enough." Warily, he touched the lock, gave the door a slight push, and stepped back to where the others were standing in the shelter of a dark grove of spine-trees. The door swung open. Nothing happened.

"I hope you won't take this for rank cowardice," the First Lord of Banking said with unaccustomed diffidence, "and I am mindful of my own loss of *face*, but I would prefer not to enter the domain of one of the Immortals."

Chen smiled. "You don't get on with gods, then?" *But I'm not sure I do either, anymore,* he thought.

The First Lord said, "They are in a sense my counterparts, but frankly, I find their presence gives me a headache."

"I suspect it's mutual," Chen said. To his surprise, the First Lord gave a rather thin smile in return. It was then that memory returned to Chen.

"You said you don't get on with gods," he said. "Would you know one if you met one?"

"Of course I'd know," the First Lord said, bridling. "Do you take me for an idiot? Why do you ask?"

"I have a reason," Chen said, thinking back to the Records Office and of Fan standing serenely amid incipient chaos. "I'd rather not elaborate just yet, though."

"Up to you," the First Lord said, not without suspicion. Chen turned to Zhu Irzh.

"What about you?"

The demon shrugged. "I've been in there before, in your world." He shivered, once, and a shadow crossed his face.

"Are you all right?" Chen asked, concerned. Zhu Irzh nodded.

"Yes. Just remembered something, that's all. I'm coming with you."

"So am I," said Inari with conviction. "I'm not staying out here with *him.*"

"I believe, madam," the First Lord said with some hauteur, "that I could offer adequate protection against most eventualities. Even in these uncertain times."

"I don't doubt it," Chen said. "Very well, then. You keep watch here, we'll go inside. But Inari's coming with me."

Together, they stepped through the gates and made their way across the temple courtyard, which was silent and still, heavy with incense. The door of the temple itself stood open. Chen looked through. No one was there. Zhu Irzh, Inari and Chen stepped inside.

The statue of the goddess stood upon the altar, and though the interior of the temple seemed meaner and shoddier than its counterpart on Earth, the statue was unchanged: flawless, green and cold. Zhu Irzh glanced around.

"That woman said the Minister was here. Seems she was wrong."

Chen was about to reply when his ears were assailed with the scrape of metal upon metal. The doors were closing. Zhu Irzh ran forward, but he was too late. The doors abruptly clanged shut. Zhu Irzh pulled at the huge bronze handle which served to open them, but nothing happened. The doors were tightly closed, and as Zhu Irzh and Chen tugged at them, they heard the bolt strike home. Chen looked wildly around. The temple had no windows, and only the single set of doors. They were trapped.

"I can hear something," Inari said fearfully. Chen listened. He heard a snapping, crackling sound, just beyond hearing, but still familiar. Then he realized. It was the sound of fire. Zhu Irzh brought up his sword and stabbed frantically at the wall, releasing a shower of musty plaster. A crack of daylight appeared between thick, impenetrable beams; peering through, Chen saw the motionless figure of the Minister of Epidemics, leaning on a smoldering brand of incense the size of a quarterstaff and smiling with buttery satisfaction. Beside him stood the chilly, mutilated form of Inari's former fiancé Dao Yi.

"The bastards are trying to burn us out," Zhu Irzh shouted. He turned on Chen. "Can't you do anything?"

"What makes you think I could do something?" snapped Chen.

"She's *your* goddess. It's *Her* temple. Can't you send up a quick prayer or something?"

"I told you. I'm not her favorite person right now." Smoke was beginning to creep beneath the door, making him cough. The ancient straw matting that covered the floor would go up like a torch, and there was nothing they could use to force their way out.

"We'll have to break the door down," Zhu Irzh shouted, eyes streaming.

"You're joking! With what?"—and then, with an icy shock of realization, Chen knew what they could use. Crying, "Zhu Irzh! Give me a hand!" he ran to the statue.

This time, it was Zhu Irzh who lingered. "Hold on," he said. "You can't use Her image as a battering ram. I mean—she's a *goddess*." It was then that

Chen's last shred of loyalty to the deity who had demanded, albeit merited, so much finally snapped.

"Zhu Irzh," he rasped. "I don't give a fuck."

Zhu Irzh's elegant eyebrows shot up, but he said no more and assisted Chen in hauling the statue down from the altar. Indeed, Chen thought, it was just as well that Zhu Irzh did not have further objections because the statue, a life-size piece of jade, was extraordinarily heavy and the demon's more-than-human strength was a considerable asset. With Zhu Irzh at the head and Chen at the feet, they paused at the foot of the now-empty altar. Smoky sweat rolled down Chen's face like tears. The smoke was thickening; Inari was no more than a wraith.

"One," said Chen, gritting his teeth and praying that nothing would rupture before they reached the door. "Two! Three!"

Stumbling and cursing, they ran the statue at the door, managing to strike it directly on the lock, which shattered. The door split down the middle and flew open. Chen and Zhu Irzh dropped the statue, which shattered. Sword and rosary drawn, followed by a choking Inari, they staggered out into the courtyard. Neither the Minister nor Dao Yi were anywhere to be seen. There was a roar from behind as the temple roof gave way, sending a shower of glittering sparks up into the air. The cloud of sparks grew and grew, until they formed a curtain of fire, and through the curtain fell No Ro Shi, the demon-hunter, accompanied by Sergeant Ma.

Chen turned, but then he saw a mottled, reversed foot disappearing behind one of the great iron incense holders. With a cry of pure rage he bolted after it, seized it by the scruff of the neck and dragged it, spitting and snapping, out into the courtyard. It was Dao Yi.

"You!" roared Chen. "And now you're going to answer to me!"

Across the courtyard, from the corner of his eye, he saw the First Lord of Banking dragging the Minister back through the gate. The First Lord's long tail was wrapped tightly around the Minister's plump throat, and the First Lord's face was incandescent with fury. Chen shook Dao Yi like a rat.

"Chen," Zhu Irzh said from somewhere behind him.

"Not now!"

"I think you'd better take a look, actually."

"I said, not now!" But then a voice that was much, much more than human spoke:

"Chen," it said, like the voice of the sea. "Put him down."

Chen turned. The fragments of the shattered statue were flowing out into a pool and then together, extinguishing the flames as they rose until an immense column of liquid jade towered over the courtyard. Slowly, it began to coalesce, reforming into the familiar figure of the goddess Kuan Yin, the Compassionate and Merciful, She Who Hears the Cries of the World.

Released by the First Lord of Banking, the Minister of Epidemics fell to his unwieldy knees, Dao Yi by his side.

"Sanctuary!" he implored. "Sanctuary for your unworthy servant, under Statute 12 of the 1472 Theological Reform Act!"

The goddess looked down at the Minister with arctic eyes.

"You burned down my temple. You assaulted my servants. You attempted to engineer mass destruction upon innocents, and now you demand sanctuary. You've got some nerve."

"Maybe," Dao Yi said, and his gaze was suddenly no longer that of a supplicant, but as fixed and cold as the eyes of the goddess herself. His hand darted towards the breast of his robe and then it was holding a dagger: black and iron and ancient, trembling with power. He threw. The dagger shot like a lance towards Kuan Yin's breast. But Chen was already leaping forward, with reflexes he didn't know he possessed, to snatch the speeding dagger from the air. From the corner of his eye, Chen saw a striped and sinuous form bolt from the temple gate and hurl itself at Dao Yi, knocking him backwards. The dagger struck Chen's palm; in the moment before the blinding pain hit, he saw its point emerge from the back of his hand. Zhu Irzh lunged for the badger, but he was too late: its long teeth met in Dao Yi's throat and Inari's former fiancé crumbled into a mess of curdled flesh. Snatching the badger up, Inari buried her face in its bloody fur. The air blurred and changed; someone stepped out of it as if through a door. The Minister was still on his knees, staring up at the scarred woman who stood above him.

"You!" the Minister said in utter shock.

Fan nodded wearily. "Who else?"

"Who are you?" Chen asked, bewildered. Kuan Yin stepped forward and looked for a moment into Fan's mismatched eyes, then she nodded.

"The Goddess of Plague. Xian H'si, also called Fan. She who walks the war zones, She who listens to the call of blood."

"Why aren't you helping him then?" Zhu Irzh demanded, pointing to the Minister of Epidemics. Through a haze of pain, Chen heard the scarred woman say, "It is true that I generate the sorrows of the world, disease and death. But you must understand that such things are necessary, that I have the mandate of Heaven. The Ministry of Epidemics, which works ultimately beneath my jurisdiction, does valuable work. Plagues limit populations, generate movement and social change. Disease is necessary for human destiny to move forward."

Chen frowned. "Are you sure about that?"

"Hush." Kuan Yin reprimanded him.

"But it seems my servants sought my overthrow, tried to curry favor with the Imperial Court. This planned plague, which I learned of only recently, would have been too great, its effects too widespread. It would have led to imbalance, and I took it upon myself to correct it. And now my servant must pay, for acting without my consent, for seeking imbalance."

Before anyone could say another word, she reached out, plucked the dagger from Chen's hand, and cut the Minister's throat. He dropped without a sound, thick, black blood seeping into the dust and ashes.

Standing above the Minister's form, Fan looked up into the middle distance. Something was coming. Chen could hear it humming and buzzing, and then he saw it, falling like an arrow out of the upper skies. It was a vast cloud of flies, which swarmed over the Minister's body, filling his mouth and eyes. Then, slowly, tottering from side to side, the mass of flies took off, carrying the Minister with them. Chen took careful notice of their flight through the stormy air, and saw that they were heading north, towards the Imperial Court.

"And now," said the Goddess of Plague, folding her hands into the sleeves of her robe and bowing in the direction of Kuan Yin, "I must return to my Ministry. We will meet again."

"I don't doubt *that*," the goddess said, with a thin smile. The hem of Fan's robes swirled the bloody ash into a sudden brief whirlwind, and she was gone.

"Now," the goddess said. She crossed her hands on her breast and bowed low. As she did so, Chen felt a disorienting, vertiginous shift, as though he were bowing over the very edge of an abyss. The pain in his hand ebbed away like a tide. He blinked. The world changed around him, and when he could see again, he was standing on soft grass, with a sky like illuminated dark glass above his head, filled with stars. Peach trees were growing all around, bearing heavy globes of fruit—or were they worlds?—yet at the same time thick with blossoms. Inari, Zhu Irzh and the First Lord stood some distance away, motionless as though frozen, but the demon-hunter No Ro Shi and Sergeant Ma were gazing around in wonder.

Chen turned to the goddess. Her face was as cold and still as glass.

"Chen Wei. Do you think you have acted with impeccability throughout this affair?"

"Lady, I—"

"Perhaps I should remind you. You consistently disobeyed My instructions. You came to Hell in search of your demon wife. You healed a demon from his sickness, aided and abetted others. You have lied, and stolen. Last but not least, you used My sacred image as a battering ram. Does that sound like impeccable conduct to you?"

"Frankly, no," Chen said, standing his ground.

"Chen Wei, I will give you a choice. I will permit you to come under my aegis once more. But in order to do so, you must renounce your wife. I see from her thoughts that she was prepared to renounce you for your own protection—let us see if you can do better than a demon. Renounce her familiar also. Deliver these beings—" here she indicated Zhu Irzh and the First Lord of Banking "—to the Courts of Heaven and the Jade Emperor. And then you will be under my protection once more."

The merest whisper of a thought crossed Chen's mind: *They are demons, after all. They are beings of evil, whatever qualities they might possess, and I devoted my life to combating evil.* But it wasn't that simple, it never was, and Chen knew it. He looked up and met No Ro Shi's steely gaze. The demon-hunter was watching him closely. *There stands one who would never understand shades of gray.* He turned back to the goddess, and simply shook his head.

Astonishingly, there was no immediate outburst of divine wrath. Instead, Kuan Yin said, "Chen. Walk with me a moment."

Chen fell in beside her as she stepped delicately beneath the peach blossoms. She seemed suddenly smaller, not quite as tall as he. She walked until they were out of hearing and sight of the others and then she turned to face him so that he was looking directly down into her depthless, inhuman eyes.

"Well?" Chen asked quietly. "What is my punishment to be this time?"

"There is no punishment," the goddess said, almost sadly. "Children grow up, after all, and never so fast as when they are pushed from the nest."

It took Chen a moment to grasp what she meant. Wonderingly, he said, "Then all that—the withdrawal of your protection when I married Inari, your anger, all that was an *excuse?*"

"You were relying on me too much, Chen. It's natural, with deities and mortals. You had a hard task to do, you could do it better without my safety net. You took risks, made your own decisions. Do you really think that I, compassionate as I am, merciful as I am, would turn aside my faithful follower on some arrogant caprice because you wouldn't do what I told you? You are a man, Chen, not a slave."

"Are you telling me you thought I was getting soft?" Chen asked, momentarily outraged, and the goddess laughed. The sound of her laughter brought the peach blossoms showering down from the trees, again and again, so that soon she was engulfed in a cloud of petals, like snow.

"Speak to me," her fading voice said, as the petals swirled up. "You won't be entirely on your own. I'll still be listening." The cloud of peach blossoms engulfed him with sweetness, filling his senses, and causing light to dazzle and sparkle before his eyes until it faded, and he was standing in the courtyard before the smoldering remains of Kuan Yin's temple, with Inari by his side and the towers of Shaopeng gleaming in the late afternoon sun. Outside the temple, a voice drifted in from a radio in someone's apartment:

"Authorities report that the recent virus outbreak has now been brought under control. The Net Corps have issued a joint statement, saying that the bioweb has now been temporarily closed down, pending investigation. The causes of the recent near-disaster are held to be—" but then a window rattled down and the sound was abruptly cut off. Chen turned and saw that Sergeant Ma and the demon-hunter were standing nearby, blinking.

"Glad you made it back," Chen said. No Ro Shi, his face creased in bemusement, stalked off without a word. Ma just nodded, staring at Inari with wide eyes. But of Zhu Irzh and the First Lord of Banking, there was no sign at all.

EPILOGUE
Three Weeks Later

It had been a peaceful enough day at the precinct—a haunting in Hsu Tan, reports of a ghost sighting in the north of the province—but Chen was nonetheless pleased to get home at a reasonable hour, after a couple of beers with Sergeant Ma. He wandered along the dock, absently kicking small stones into the glittering water, and gazing out to the golden place where the sun was setting over the South China Sea. Across the water, the houseboat rocked in the gentle breeze, the waves sending shimmering reflections along its flank. He could see Inari pottering about in the kitchen, the badger-teakettle scratching itself on deck.

As he reached the end of the dock, however, the world rang. The golden sea turned dark. When his head cleared, Chen saw that someone was standing before him. The figure wore a long, silk coat, and a sword was slung over his shoulder.

"Seneschal Zhu Irzh," Chen said, shading his eyes against the sudden glare of the light. The demon bowed.

"Detective Inspector Chen. Good to see you again."

"I'm glad you seem to have escaped Heaven in one piece," Chen said, and meant it. The demon grinned. "Heaven, yes. Pretty place, I thought. Bit insipid."

"You may have a point. So what are you doing here?"

The demon scuffed the toe of one boot in the dust; he appeared mildly embarrassed.

"The thing is... Hell's settled down a bit since the recent unpleasantness. They're rebuilding the Ministry of Epidemics. The First Lord of Banking gave me a very favorable report, but my department felt that, what with the Imperial Court being involved and everything, that they really didn't want me around for a bit. Political embarrassment and all that. So they've sent me here. On assignment."

"I see," Chen said, momentarily lost for words.

"They cleared it with your department. I'm to stay for three months. There was," the demon cleared his throat, "some talk of my acting as your partner."

"Where are you going to live? Have they sorted out your accommodations?" If he concentrated on the practicalities and ignored the future for once, it made things easier. Zhu Irzh nodded.

"I'm in a boarding house off Shaopeng Street. There are all manner of people in there. I like it. I've just come from there." Looking carefully at a point past Chen's shoulder, he added with studied indifference: "By the way, the Ministry of Wealth has unwrapped the First Lord's house. I went to see him a few days ago, met his family. He has a daughter, very charming girl, who seems to have taken something of a liking to me... Anyway, what I'm trying to say is that there are possibilities."

"I see," Chen said, smiling. "Well, I'm glad." And rather to his surprise, he found that he was pleased, too, that Zhu Irzh would be around for a while. They worked well together, and it would be nice to have a colleague who didn't regard him with manifest suspicion—though it was true that Sergeant Ma's awe seemed to have diminished considerably since his own excursion between the worlds. Zhu Irzh interrupted his thoughts.

"Thank you, Chen," he said. "I hoped you might be."

"Since you're here, you might as well come and say hello to Inari. Have you eaten?"

The demon brightened. "Not yet."

"Well, then, come to dinner."

Chen stepped from the dock onto one of the pontoons, and with the demon following, he made his way home, across the gilded, dappled water.

An excerpt from the new Detective Inspector Chen novel:

THE DEMON AND THE CITY

Prologue

The Chinese inhabitants of Singapore Three say that August is an unlucky month. They say that it is called the month of the dead, for it is always during the endless burning days that the dead return, looking for the living, drawn by blood and breath. They tell their children: *You do not know how it was when we lived in the suburbs of Beijing and Guangzhou, or the willow villages of Szechuan, in the ancient cities where people understand how to keep the dead at bay. But in this great new city of Singapore Three, where the entrances to the Hell are closer and the veils between them are fractured, we no longer live in a place when a story is only a story, told to frighten a child in the darkness. Nor do you remember when the demons and the hungry ghosts were only dreaming shadows in an ordinary life, until we left the old cities and came to the new, and found that during certain months and certain times, when the eternal Wheel of Life and Death grates on its spokes, the world changes.*

At such times, one can only prepare for the possibility of death as best one can.

Deveth Sardai, stepping from a downtown tram, was not thinking of death. She was, instead, wondering how to extricate herself from the latest disastrous relationship. The policy of ignoring the girl was clearly not working: Sardai had not phoned her since the previous Monday, but a litany of messages, of increasing desperation, had been left on her answerphone.

Sardai smiled thinly as she walked down to the retailers' market, to wander, anonymous, beneath the girdered roofs of the warehouse shelter. The market was crowded with people on their way home from the production lines of Haitan. In fruitsellers' quarter Sardai nearly tripped on the vegetables that spilled out over the floor, squashed into mush across the dank concrete. She kicked aside a burst cucumber, turned the corner and found herself out of the fruitsellers' street and into the meat market. The *butcherei,* mostly women, glanced at her incuriously as she passed. The mild-eyed heads of the black cattle, swinging on their racks, held more expression. Sardai stepped queasily between the remnants which littered the floor; the concrete was washed with a faint pink gloss. Nothing was wasted, Sardai knew. The cattle were reared in the derelict lots between the apartment buildings of Bharulay and Saro Town; genes acquired on the black market and manipulated to produce Indian cows, of a sort. The *butcherei* slaughtered them illegally, bleeding them dry in hidden locations among the back streets in a literal moveable feast. The traders brought the bodies here before sunrise. The horns and hooves would be the first to go, sold off to the herbalists to be ground into powder and marketed as fraudulent aphrodisiacs.

At the end of butchers' street, a shrunken, cheerful woman was washing out a cloth in a bloodstained bucket. She beamed up at Sardai, who had paused.

"What you want?"

"I'm looking for the remedy market," Sardai said. It seemed to have moved since her last visit; they rearranged the market frequently, to baffle the inspectors. No one was fooled, except the hapless customers.

"Oh, sure." The woman wrung out the cloth a last time and heaved herself to her feet. "I'll show you."

She walked with Sardai to the end of the meat market. Beyond, in front of the pilings that raised the market from the water, the butchered cattle lay in heaps of unidentifiable flesh. From the corner of her eye, Sardai saw a lean dark, shape slink behind the piles.

"There!" the woman said, pointing. At the end of the meat racks, a helpful yellow line led along the warehouse floor. Obediently, Sardai followed it and came round to the familiar red-canopied corridor, the scarlet awnings incongruous beneath the rusted ironwork roof of the remedy market. The stalls were fringed with amulets: the almond-eyed shepherd god; My Lady simpering in a violet mantle with a sheaf of corn in her tiny arms; the little fox-faced demon of the mines. They shimmered before Sardai's gaze. Maybe she should buy her girlfriend a present, make it clear that it was a parting gift. She didn't dislike the girl, after all, it was just that once the first rush of intoxicated desire had passed, Sardai had started to feel suffocated. It was the same old story; it had happened before, it would happen again. Sardai gave a mental shrug. That was just the way she was. She did not intend to give way to guilt. She did not believe in it, and it solved nothing. Almost involuntarily, however, her hand reached out and unhooked the icon of a girl, an inch long, with the crescent moon on her brow. It was the sort of thing you hung in the kitchen window, or saw swinging on the dashboard of taxis. Sardai asked, "How much is this one? Can I have her?"

A swift hand, its owner unseen, wrapped the icon in red tissue paper to keep her safe on her journey, and Sardai dropped the little package into her bag. Our Lady of Storms, the woman from the sea, reposed amidst Sardai's pens, card wallet, keys and the rest of the junk in her bag. Her girlfriend would like the little icon since she lit candles to the goddess at festival time. Sardai herself followed a different path. Thinking of this, she smiled again. All magic is art, she thought, and she considered herself to be an artist in the truest sense of the word: one who is not afraid, one who dares to gamble for great stakes. She walked on to the herbalist's. Dried carcasses of snakes rustled in their pannier with the semblance of life. Someone was having a little joke, but Sardai wasn't going to gratify them by being startled. She leaned over the dry, writhing bodies and purchased a pinch of bitter mint and then a tiny bag of lobelia, imported from the West. The herbs were horribly expensive, but Sardai didn't care. They were useful, if one practiced a particular kind of art.

Her purchases completed, Sardai wandered to the end of remedy street and came out opposite the yawning exit. Beyond, the slick waters of the harbor were apricot in the falling light. It was time to go home. Sardai walked along the slippery platform that led from the market entrance and out into the southern end of Siling Street, a meandering labyrinth of iron shelters and cookhouses. The smell of frying meat and peppers filled the evening air. Chickens were rotating on a spit in the nominal gutter, where a shadowy man was blowing a fire into life. Sardai walked quickly; it was growing dark. She slipped into her usual routine, imagining herself ten feet tall and looking down on the people she passed, with her square shoulders back and her hand on the mace canister. Guns were banned; they were common enough on the black market but the penalty for shooting your assailant was death, anyway, so why bother? Sardai was always careful; there were very few nice parts of town.

At the end of the street a humpbacked bridge led over a narrow arm of the main canal, a winding stretch of water called the Taitai: the little wrist. Sardai crossed into a wilderness of apartment blocks separated by vacant lots where sparrow vine covered the fallen masonry. Something was always being built up or torn down. The exception was the Waste, the stretch of land which crossed Jhenrai southeast to northwest, a ragged scar created when an old mine had caved in and taken the apartment homes with it. The fires still burned, fueled by some persistent gas seepage beneath the soil. People lived on the Waste: the rootless, the insane. Sardai avoided it in daylight and at night took detours out of its way, but she was well past the Waste by now and nearly home to the row of old rickety houses in the eastern part of the quarter.

Turning back, she saw a last strip of pale green sky over the harbor. The tower of the Paugeng Corporation snaked up in absurd modernist spirals above the docks; the red bird logo catching the dead sun and glowing against the rearing wall. That was a weird setup, Sardai thought, with grim amusement. She had known the Paugeng heiress, mad Jhai Tserai, from their debutante days. And now, they had an even stronger connection. Smiling, she turned back and continued walking.

Something came fast out of the shelter of the darkness. Sardai had a brief glimpse of a lean shape moving too quickly to see, and then it was gone. She'd seen something in the retail market, her bewildered mind told her, sneaking among the bones, but that had been a dog, a little thing. This was a person. She swung the mace canister out of her pocket, looked about her warily. She could see nothing. She backed off, starting to run down Mherei Street, but it was right behind her, alongside her. She could see it out of the corner of her eye, pacing beside her, silent. She stopped, nearly stumbling, and turned but there was nothing there. Her breath whimpered in her throat. There was a great wave of soundless motion behind her, the smell of the sea, hot salt washed over her, roaring in her ears, bearing her down into the well of the apricot sky. She saw the crescent moon swing round, and then she was out into the gentle shallows, leaving it all behind.

Neatly, quickly, she was dragged into the silence behind the dark streets. No one had seen, animal-sense said, no one was watching.

One

"Do we know who she is?" Seneschal Zhu Irzh asked, idly flicking the ash from his opium cigarette. The body sprawled at his feet, outlined by a faint nimbus glow. The girl had not long been dead, though there was no trace of her dismayed spirit in the immediate neighborhood and surprisingly little blood, given the state she was in.

Sergeant Ma eyed him askance and said, "No, not yet. Forensics is trying to get a positive ID on her now. And you shouldn't be smoking those. They're bad for your health."

"My dear sergeant, in case it had escaped your attention, I *am* already dead. In a manner of speaking, of course, seeing that I am a demon." Ma merely grunted. Zhu Irzh smiled to himself. Ma's attitude towards him was a combination of the disapproving and the protective, which was a long way from the sergeant's earlier attitude of insensate fear. Zhu Irzh had only been attached to the Singapore Three police department for a few months, but had already managed to provoke strong reactions in his colleagues, both positive and negative, yin and yang. Zhu Irzh liked to think that it was the hallmark of a masterful personality, but Detective Inspector Chen, his immediate superior, witheringly attributed the phenomenon to Zhu Irzh's otherworldly origins.

Zhu Irzh reflected on this as he stood over the mutilated remains of what had, after some initial investigation, proved to be a young woman.

He found himself frowning. He missed Chen, and the Detective Inspector had only been gone for a week. If anyone deserved a holiday, Zhu Irzh thought, it was Chen, but still, Singapore Three's temporary loss was Hawaii's impermanent gain. He hoped, not without a trace of bitterness, that Chen and his wife were having a nice time. Meanwhile, he was still stuck here in the city, dealing with humans who had been foolish enough to get themselves mangled by unknown persons.

"If forensics doesn't turn anything up, we could go to the Night Harbor, couldn't we? Interview the victim directly," Ma remarked.

"I suppose so. Though I don't fancy shoving my way through that throng on a Saturday night trying to work out which spirit is minus her face. Or other bits. And I'm still having problems with my visa." Zhu Irzh gave a martyred sigh. Initially, he had been excited about his reassignment from Hell's Vice Division; the result of a political embroilment which only now was beginning to subside. The human world was novel enough to be interesting at first, but now it slightly depressed him. The colors seemed so insipid, the air so bland. It wasn't as bad as Heaven, which he'd visited only fleetingly, but it was getting close. The food was like the sort of thing you fed to cats: it smelled all right, but it didn't taste of anything. Besides, he'd had little to properly occupy him since he got here: a few routine gang killings, and a long and indescribably tedious investigation into the Feng Shui Practitioners' Guild, resulting in several boring visits to renegade dowsers. Zhu Irzh had done his best to get out of this last task, but had been thwarted by Chen. The latter seemed to be enjoying the novelty of having an underling, and had disturbingly little compunction in handing the most banal tasks over to Zhu Irzh. If one was of a flamboyant personality, the demon felt, one might as well make the most of it. He had not been allowed near the work of the Vice Division, where his experience lay. It was nothing but a waste. An earlier, oft repeated conversation, replayed itself in his mind.

"Your experience," Chen had said firmly, "has been in the *promotion* of vice, not its suppression. You surely can't seriously think they'll let you anywhere near drugs or prostitution, not given that Hell's vice squad is responsible for most of it?"

The demon had bridled. "I'm not unremittingly evil—and me saying that just goes to show that I'm not a typical demon. I have feelings, too. I have a conscience. I helped you save the world, didn't I?"

Chen, though conceding that there was a measure of truth in this, had remained resolute. "I don't think you're unremittingly evil," he said. "I just think you're…slightly dodgy." Zhu Irzh had pretended to be annoyed, but admitted to himself that Chen might have a point. Vice was pretty much a consuming interest with him, and why not? It was fun, after all. It was a *vocation*.

However, human women tended to give Zhu Irzh a wide berth, thus negating another of the demon's consuming interests. This was perhaps understandable, but also cause for some lament. Back home in Hell, he had barely been able to turn round without falling over one or another girlfriend; here, it was a different story. And it was *cold:* even in this summer that humans described as sweltering. Morosely, Zhu Irzh poked the limp corpse with the toe of his boot, revealing the shattered pelvis and ribcage. Ma gazed at him in reproach.

"Don't do that. It's disturbing the crime scene. Forensics won't like it."

"Oh, don't worry," Zhu Irzh said. "She's probably swanning around the Night Harbor as we speak, awaiting her departure to the peach orchards of Heaven and unutterably grateful to be temporarily relieved of the shackles of her mortal flesh."

"Suppose she's destined for Hell?"

"I hope you're not implying that this unfortunate young lady deserved to die?" Zhu Irzh remarked satirically, adding under his breath, "And if she did, then lucky her."

"It's always a shock," Ma said defensively. "I don't suppose she thought that this would be the day of her death, poor girl."

Zhu Irzh laughed. "Few people ever do."

Two

Dowser Paravang Roche, kneeling before the statue of the goddess Senditreya, was not thinking of death—at least, not of his own. Senditreya's temple was dark, shrouded in shadow and wreaths of incense. A complex sequence of patterns was outlined in silver on the floor, showing the energy lines which lay beneath the city; the energy wells of *ch'i* and *sha*. Among the hazy coils of smoke sat the statue, holding out her divining rods and her compass, and smiling down at her supplicants.

Bitch, thought Paravang Roche. He had an ambivalent relationship with his deity. He looked sourly up at the statue; studying the gilded loops of hair, the three bands tied around each wrist to signify the founding member of the dowsers' guild, elevated into goddess-hood seven hundred and twenty years ago.

To the left of Paravang, a man swayed forward on his mat, moaning and muttering. Paravang regarded him with distaste. Surely it wasn't necessary to make so much noise about one's worship. His neighbor rattled a hollow canister and shook out the yarrow sticks. Hastily arranging them into a pattern on the woven mats, he stared for a moment and then began to chuckle.

Well, good for you, Paravang thought sourly. *I'm glad someone is having good fortune, because I'm not.* He glared at his hilarious companion, who caught the enraged look on Paravang's face and subsided. Paravang arranged himself into a more decorous position and stared up at Senditreya. Sometimes he thought she winked at him. Sometimes he was right.

Underneath the carpet, and the stone floor, and the earth itself, Paravang could feel the energy line of the Great Meridian, running to the confluence of energy, the lake of *ch'i* which lays beneath Senditreya's temple. With such *ch'i*, how could there fail to be good fortune? Paravang asked himself. One would have thought that some of it, at least, might have rubbed off on a poor *feng shui* dowser. Paravang's lips pursed in resentment. He had worked hard all his life to win first this coveted place here in the temple, and then his contract with Paugeng Mining, and now it was all going to be taken away.

Above him, Senditreya's cow-eyed gaze blurred and faded, to be replaced by another face: the color of a shadow, golden-eyed. It was the face of a demon, named Seneschal Zhu Irzh. It was the face of his most recent enemy, and to Paravang's feverish gaze it seemed quite real, as though the demon himself were standing before him. As, indeed, Zhu Irzh had been, a week ago today.

Paravang had opened the door to find him standing on the step, a most unwelcome visitor. The scene replayed itself through Paravang's mind, as it had done so many times over the past few days.

蛇警探

"Who are you?" Paravang had quavered. "What do you want?" He'd always taken care to limit his dealings with Hell, but it seemed he hadn't been careful enough.

"I'm here about an irregularity in your *feng shui* dowsing license," the demon said. "My name's Seneschal Zhu Irzh. Want to see my badge?" At this point he had produced a piece of paper which, to Paravang's horrified gaze, had proclaimed him to be not only a citizen of Hell, but also a member of Singapore Three's police department. To Paravang's mind, this was a truly nightmarish combination. "Mind if I come in?" the demon asked, and without waiting for a reply, had brushed past Paravang into the narrow apartment and taken a seat on the sofa. It had all gone downhill from there.

It seemed that Paravang had actually forfeited his dowsing license some time before, the result of a small matter of unpaid taxes and undelivered bribes. Unlicensed, he was therefore practicing *feng shui* illegally, and must apply for a new license as well as pay the requisite fine to the authorities.

"Never mind," Zhu Irzh had remarked cheerfully. "I'm sure you'll get it all straightened out. Shouldn't take more than a few months." With this less than reassuring remark, he had left Paravang Roche to grind his teeth with helpless fury and hurl curses at the demon's unresponsive back. He had contacted the authorities, hoping that this might merely be some malignant joke on the part of Hell, only to find that Zhu Irzh was a fully paid-up member of the police department, assisting a Detective Inspector Chen, and completely entitled to act as he had done. Given the city's formidably ponderous bureaucracy, it would indeed take months for Paravang to retrieve his license, and a correspondingly huge drop in revenue.

蛇警探

Why do you despise me, Goddess? Paravang thought now, helplessly. The endless perfidy of the divine never ceased to amaze him. You gave your all, you turned up four times a year for the festivals and twice every week for your devotions; spent your hard-earned capital on presents and offerings; wasted nine minutes morning, noon and night in the requisite prayers, and for what? Only to be scorned. Rising abruptly, Paravang threw a handful of rice at the feet of his capricious deity and walked out into the evening dusk.

Three

The city was baking in the morning heat, and Robin Yuan was late for work. The downtown tram rattled by her, dangling like a child's toy from its pylons, as she turned the corner of the block. She started to run, but it was too late. The downtown slowed for the next stop, saw no one waiting and picked up speed, vanishing around the curve of Shaopeng Street as Robin reached the platform. She swore. An ochre-clad nun swung around to stare at her reprovingly.

Screw you, Robin thought. *I'm late.* She was already sweating in the morning heat. Here at the junction of Shaopeng and Jhara, the restaurant backs emitted clouds of fragrant steam: *ghambang* and chowder for breakfast today. Robin had eaten prawn crackers, left over from the night before, stiff and cold in their greasy folds of paper. She watched the high-collared, shawl-suited men and women vanishing into the dark interior of the Pellucid Island Hotel and envied them.

The hot rails sang and the next downtown hurtled out of the Jhara embankment tunnel. *It's not going to stop! Too many people!* Robin thought, panicking, but the tram slowed to a halt and she squashed herself inside; leaning back from the bulging doorway and forward again as the doors closed. The downtown took off, lurching. The woman beside her directed a venomous glance at Robin.

"Can't you move?" she snapped. "I can't stand up properly."

"I don't think I can," Robin said. This was true; there was no room at all in the carriage and Robin couldn't reach the strap. It wouldn't matter if the downtown suddenly had to stop: she was too tightly constrained to fall.

"But I'm standing on my toes!" her neighbor wailed.

Grumbling faintly, the carriage rearranged itself in some minute fashion. Robin's neighbor lost height, sighing in relief. Robin stifled a yawn. Trying to keep her balance on the swaying, roaring tram, she wondered whether Deveth would call today. She had wondered the same thing for the last week, her spirits rising every morning, then sinking towards midnight as the day grew old, and still Dev did not call or come by. *Where are you, Deveth Sardai? Was I just your bit of rough trade?* If she'd had the nerve, Robin reflected, she would have called Deveth's parents, but the thought of contacting the aristocratic Sardais and interrogating them as to the whereabouts of their daughter made Robin's mouth go dry. She was fairly sure that this was one relationship which Dev would have taken care to keep quiet.

The downtown ground to a halt at Phikhat Square, spilling its cargo onto the crowded street. Wearing dark blue, ochre and gold, the money-workers made for the temples and Robin was able to sit down at last. She collapsed onto a slatted bench and watched the tops of the city whirl by in the steaming air. There were seven more stops to Semmerang and the laboratories. At last the downtown rang in triumph for the final stop, ready now to turn around and go back. Robin got out, her rubber-soled slippers padding on the platform, and headed for Paugeng Corporation and another day at work.

Inside the labs surrounding the Paugeng tower, there was a stirring atmosphere of activity and anticipation. People gathered in little knots, chattering. Robin was not part of the elite team, the chosen core, but the excitement infected her like a contagion as she hastened through the double doors of Y Lab. She passed her flustered colleagues and went straight through to the lift, heading for the basements. There, in the warren of rooms and corridors, the experiment was waiting for her, sitting up in his cot, arms around his knees, blinking blue eyes.

"How did you sleep?" Robin asked, a little anxious. "I'm sorry I'm so late."

The experiment smiled at her, vaguely. "It doesn't matter. I slept well, thank you. I dreamed."

Robin and her experiment had a number of choices about the playing of their particular game. So often it could take the form of doctor and patient, like the games you play in childhood, with the *frisson* of the forbidden. Sometimes, Robin was well aware, it could degenerate into torturer and tortured, if the controller had insufficient authority elsewhere. People take power where they can get it. Without really thinking about it, Robin knew exactly to which of her colleagues this description applied, but she did not find that axis seductive. She sympathized too much with her experiment, though she was well aware that she was not supposed to think of him as a person. He had no name, only a number. Robin, in a brief flouting of regulations, had asked him what he was called, but the experiment had only smiled and uttered a long string of syllables in a language like water. Robin, after some effort, had managed to break them down into something vaguely recognizable, and now she called him Mhara, but only under her breath, or in the privacy of her own head.

The experiment seemed too gentle to be demonkind, which made Robin's job even more difficult. But if he was a demon, then experimenting on him was necessary, wasn't it? Last year, the denizens of Hell had almost succeeded in vanquishing the city with a terrible engineered plague, and after that a number of research programs had been started up to combat the menace via scientific means. Paugeng had been given an enormous grant and the city's blessing; shortly after this, the experiment had appeared.

Robin had asked Mhara which level of Hell he came from, of course, but he had merely given her a vague smile. Robin was desperate to find out more, but the experiment was classified and she was unwilling to risk her good job by asking awkward questions. Yet despite their situation, Robin still got the feeling that Mhara trusted her, and at a time when she had little enough satisfaction, this was a source of comfort. He *needs* me, she thought now, vaguely aware of the abyss that was opening beneath her feet. Now, Mhara sat up straighter, and Robin plumped the pillows.

"Could I get up today?" he asked.

"I'm sorry," Robin said again. "Not today. One more day, and then we'll see how you're doing."

Mhara said nothing. Robin hated herself. She looked at the downcast experiment and the blue gaze turned to her as he smiled. They were marvelous eyes, and the contrast with his pale face and crow-blue hair was strikingly attractive. He looked nothing like the demons she had seen in the research files.

"It's not your fault, Robin. I know that."

It didn't make Robin feel any better. Stifling guilt, she went through the various tasks of her day in peace, until late afternoon when there was a sudden hubbub in the lift landing.

"Excuse me," Robin said. "I've got to go. I'll be back in a moment."

The experiment nodded. Robin went out and found her employer striding down the corridor. Jhai Tserai, wreathed in an amethyst silk sari, was surrounded by an adoring crowd, the young turks of Y Lab. Tserai's trademark cascade of dark hair was drawn back from the elegant curves of her face. She appeared delighted to see Robin standing drably in the office doorway.

"Robin!" She kissed Robin's cheek. "What a week, eh?" She gave Robin that eye-to-eye look which meant: *We've really been through it, haven't we? But we're still one hell of a team.*

She really isn't much taller than me, Robin thought, and yet somehow Jhai always seemed to be looking down on her. Robin deeply distrusted Jhai's attempts at friendliness, but when bathed in Jhai's famous charm, she couldn't help but respond. How did Jhai always manage to catch you off your guard? Robin wondered. She supposed it was some kind of charisma, but whatever it was, Jhai had it in spades. The subtle, provocative smell of Jhai's perfume followed her into the lab.

The morning medication had taken effect. Mhara was sleeping, lying curled on his side and breathing peacefully. He always slept neatly, like a cat: no drooling or snoring.

Jhai peered at the winking lights on the monitor. "Seems fine to me. Good work, Robin. It's never easy." She gave Robin a dark, concerned glance.

"He's so—accepting," Robin said guiltily.

Jhai reached down and turned the experiment's shoulder gently. The blue eyes were a dark well, open yet dreaming. The oval face was shadowed beneath a fall of hair.

"Where do we go from here?" Robin asked. Her boss shook her head.

"We just keep going until we figure out whatever neurological configuration it is that gives him his predictive abilities." Catching sight of Robin's unhappy expression, she added, "We need him, Robin. He can glimpse the future and we need to make sure that we're one step ahead of Hell."

Regular scientists were horrified by Jhai, Robin reflected. She was unmethodical, subjective, running on half-expressed intuitions, heretical and unrepentant. But because she was running the show she could work any way she pleased, and in the past the results had been impressive. Her disciple technicians trusted her, even when she outraged them. She rode the dragon and they ran along behind, imploring hands outstretched, pleading for her to slow down. She rewarded people who enjoyed being outraged: Robin was not one of them. Jhai, so forceful and vivid a presence in the dingy little lab, made her uneasy.

The experiment stirred and whimpered. Robin started fiddling with the hookups on the monitor. Another few minutes and then she would go home, and maybe Deveth would have rung. Better yet, perhaps she would find Deveth waiting on the step, her arms full of groceries, smiling up at Robin. *Dream on*, Robin thought. She glanced up to find that Jhai was staring at her, the gaze full of that assumed concern.

"Are you okay, Robin? You look a little tired."

"I'm fine," Robin lied.

"Good. Well, let me know if anything happens."

Robin nodded, willing Jhai to leave, and at last, after a final data inspection, Jhai did so. Robin turned back to the bed. The experiment was awake. The blue eyes burned into her own.

"Mhara? What's wrong?"

"The world," the experiment said, almost conversationally, "is going to end. Very soon."

"What?" Robin faltered. The experiment's gaze blurred; his voice murmured in the vaults of her skull.

"I can see everything," the experiment whispered. "Everything that will happen: blood and darkness and fire, demons devouring the city, ghosts running hungry through the streets. The end of *everything*."—and suddenly Robin could see it too, a vision of apocalypse conferred without grace. A tower crumbled and fell, crashing down into the street. The ground split and splintered under her feet and above her, the sky, too, cracked like a fractured eggshell. Robin's vision receded into a tunnel of night. She reeled back, her hand painfully striking the metal edge of the couch, and the lab was as before.

"What's going to cause the end of the world?" The question was no more than a thought, but the answer hissed in her head.

Jhai Tserai...

Robin blinked, and the vision was suddenly gone. The experiment sank back against the pillows.

"Mhara?" Robin whispered. She sat down heavily on the edge of the bed and gripped his shoulders. "Mhara? *What was that?* What did we see?" but he was already back in the tranquilized trance that passed for sleep.

Her mind racing, Robin tidied up the desk in the lab, made a final check of the monitor and settled the experiment down for the night, attaching the linkmote that would alert her if anything went wrong. She smoothed the dark hair over the experiment's brow. He smiled vaguely in his sleep. He looked so innocent, but the memories of what she had glimpsed were still vivid as nightmare.

"Goodnight," Robin whispered. She locked the door and took the lift up to the atrium. She walked through it in a daze, automatically checking her employee card at the door, barely hearing the doorman's farewell. Above her, the tower hummed with life; Paugeng worked round the clock. Robin stared numbly up at it as though she had never seen it before, and finally got herself sufficiently together to head for the tram. There was some hitch in the Shaopeng service, announced on the departure board, and the downtown was late, eventually arriving after seven. Robin's journey passed swiftly, lost in a haze of speculation.

She had been instructed to report anything Mhara said, directly to Jhai, but she did not want to anger her employer, and informing Jhai that she was apparently the cause of wholesale destruction seemed a good way to go about this. Robin herself was not even sure that she believed in Mhara's predictive abilities, but Jhai believed, and that was the important thing. Robin tossed questions to and fro in her head until she was too tired to think.

By the time she got home, the sky had darkened to rose. Deveth was not waiting on the doorstep. Robin tried to stifle the hope as she stepped into the hallway, but found to her own disgust that she was holding her breath. No one was waiting for her. *I told you so,* Robin said to herself. She climbed the interminable flight of stairs and opened the front door.

The apartment was minute: a box, a coffin. Inside the box, the heat was unbearable. Robin threw open the windows and a suffocating smell of garbage entered. The only choice was to stifle or gag. Robin compromised, shutting the little window in the bedroom and turning on the kitchen fan, which after a minute started to limp around its central spoke. A single step took her back into the main room. She took off her overall tunic and bundled it into a ball so that the Paugeng logo was no longer visible, then stuffed it under the pillow of her futon. The last thing she wanted to think about was work, and if she glimpsed it out of the corner of her eye, the logo looked like a bloodstain. If she looked crumpled next morning, then so be it. She turned on the television, hoping for the news, but no sooner had she sat down than there was a bang at the door. Robin bounced up and flung it open.

"Deveth—" she began, but there was only the empty air. Robin looked down. A small, resentful face was turned upwards in reproach.

"I got your noodles," it said sourly. "And your pak choi."

"Good!" Robin said. She had forgotten that she had hired next-door's child to bring her a takeout. She forced money, evidently not as much as the child was expecting, into its grimy hand.

"Is that all?" it said.

"That's all you get," Robin told it, and shut the door.

She carried the oily paper packet back to the television, eating absently with one hand. On the viewer, Malaysian screen idol Inditraya Samay held up a rosy pomegranate and moved her winsome head to one side. *Revolting,* Robin thought. What had happened to the news? She reached for the remote and Samay's pretty pout was ruthlessly intercepted. A long shot of bodies on stretchers was more promising: the news on Channel 8. Robin settled down grimly to watch. Tremors in Sengeng had collapsed a road, compressing its four parallel lanes into a grisly sandwich. The cause—either a grumbling fault line or excessive open-cast mining in Sengeng Paray—depended on political affiliation. No mention was made of the Feng Shui Practitioners' Guild who had, it seemed, failed to predict the disaster. One of the senior dowsers was featured, loudly protesting their blamelessness.

Finishing her noodles, Robin took the greasy packet out to the kitchen. It was a mess. Normally, an old lady named Mrs Pa came in to do the cleaning, but poor Mrs Pa had been sick over the last few days, and the general chaos natural to Robin's apartment had mounted. A tower of takeout packets spilled over the sink and a stack of dirty plates sat precariously on the little work surface. Robin could barely see the floor of the main room for the clothes that were scattered over it. She piled them in a heap on the floor of the cupboard, then furiously attacked the kitchen, piling the rubbish into a bag and sealing it shut with a snap. She stacked the plates in the sink and hauled the garbage bag out through the small rectangle of the kitchen hatch onto the fire escape, which rose up from the side alley like an ironwork plant from its composting bed.

It was still hot, a humid, reeking heat. The neighboring buildings were squat shadows against the taller buildings of Shaopeng, and the sky was a deep, clear crimson, unusual for the polluted port. As Robin stepped out onto the fire escape, the evening heat wrapped around her like polythene: a moist embrace of carbon dioxide, drains and the oily reek of the river. Another, more organic, odor insinuated itself into the air. Looking down from the top of the fire escape, Robin saw that the black garbage bags had accumulated at the bottom until they burst, spilling a mélange of rotten vegetables around the iron feet of the staircase. Through this bath of odors wound a thread of incense from the apartment below, a spicy breath out of the squalor.

A rattling, scuffling sound arrested Robin's attention halfway down the fire escape. She stopped and peered into the dim alleyway. The sound was purposeful, determined, and came from the bottom of the fire escape. She leaned over the railing, and saw that the black back of the uppermost garbage bag was heaving. From her position at the fourth floor, and directly above, it resembled a seal; it rolled and wallowed in the filth that littered the alleyway. The bag spat tins, and a sheaf of old papers. Two floors down, a door was flung open and the voice of the occupant roared, "What's all that fucking racket? Get out of there! Bloody dogs!"

The animal backed out of its larder and bolted down the alley. Robin caught a glimpse of an ungainly gait and a fat, spotted spine; it did indeed look like a dog of some sort, but much larger. She descended the fire escape and picked her way warily through the litter. The animal was nowhere to be seen. Robin dumped her bag and pushed the rest of the mess around with her foot, until it lay in a heap. Let the collectors sort it out. By morning, half of it would be gone, sneaked away to sell to the recyclers. There was a pungent, animal smell around the alley, unfamiliar, but redolent of earth and meat. Uneasily, Robin climbed back up the rickety escape and shut the kitchen hatch. She spent the evening in front of the television, pondering her problem of Mhara's horrible prophecy until her head pounded.

Deveth did not call.

Four

Until this week, Zhu Irzh had been residing in a somewhat seedy boarding-house in Lower Murray Street, but Chen's trip to Hawaii had brought an unexpected offer.

"You can look after the houseboat for me, if you like," Chen had said, glancing amiably upwards at the demon standing by his desk. "We'll be gone for three weeks; I'd like someone to water the plants and look after the badger."

"You're not taking the badger with you?"

"No, it might cause problems taking him on the plane even in his inanimate form and, anyway, he says he's happy to stay at home. I don't suppose he'll be much trouble. He'll probably be in teakettle mode most of the time. So. What shall I do, drop off the keys on our way to the airport?"

Thus, in the space of a morning, Zhu Irzh had acquired a new home and a familiar. He was becoming almost domesticated, he thought. He had always wanted to live on a boat, that traditional last resort of the poor. It was a long way from that pagoda fortress of his home in Hell, the balconies and verandahs of the Irzh clan, but Zhu Irzh didn't miss the luxury all that much. At least he didn't have to put up with his mother, and that was worth a bit of poverty.

The boat was moored some distance from the waterfront which, a short distance later, led round to Ghenret harbor. Chen had moved the boat closer to shore before a recent typhoon, and it was now reached via a few short hops over a series of pontoons. It looked out over the polluted waters of the Shendei, which, despite their filth, was why Zhu Irzh liked it. He supposed that Chen felt the same way. He could sit on the windowsill in the evening and watch the freighters plough across the harbor, until the swift night fell out of the sky and they became only moving lights.

It was a long way down the wharf. Zhu Irzh passed one of his neighbors on the way; an elderly lady who seemed faintly familiar, though all these people looked alike to him. She did not seem to see him, which was probably just as well. It would have been easier in ways if he had been equally invisible to his human colleagues, but the police station was covered with revealing spells, just in case something nasty decided to slip in and wreak havoc, and so Zhu Irzh stood out like a sore thumb once inside the walls of the precinct. The spells made him sneeze, to add insult to injury. Zhu Irzh tended to unnerve those folk who could actually see him, though the people who lived around the harbor seemed a fair old mix themselves. Sometimes fights broke out on the wharf; mostly, it was quiet. The whole community, with the exception of Zhu Irzh and a few other reclusive souls, decamped to the bars down the road during the evenings and lived out their dramas in more congenial surroundings.

Zhu Irzh unlocked the door and shut it behind him. The room was stuffy, so he opened the windows and let in a faint breath of air from the sea. At one end of the cubicle was a tiny shower, which generally worked. He stripped and stood, resigned, under the trickle of water. At least it was cold. Stepping from under the shower, he rummaged for fresh clothes, glancing at himself in the reflected mirror door of the closet as he did so. The reflection smiled back at him, turning and posing. Zhu Irzh frowned. He didn't feel much like the glittering image in the mirror. Any longer, and he might—terrible thought—start losing his looks. The human world was taking it out of him, depleting his energies. He needed a diversion. He needed a *girlfriend*.

Williams joins A.A. Attanasio and China Miéville as one of the best contemporary practitioners of a kind of imaginative literature that fuses the intellect of SF with the heart of fantasy. — Paul Di Filippo, *Scifi.com*

Liz Williams

THE DEMON AND THE CITY

A DETECTIVE INSPECTOR CHEN NOVEL

The Demon and the City
ISBN-10: 1-59780-045-7
ISBN-13: 978-1-59780-045-7
Trade Hardcover; $24.95

Night Shade Books Is an Independent Publisher of Quality SF, Fantasy and Horror

ISBN-10: 1-59780-057-0
Trade Paper; $14.95

From Elizabeth Bear, 2005 John W. Campbell Best New Writer Award winner and author of the critically acclaimed and wildly popular Jenny Casey Trilogy: Hammered, Scardown, and Worldwired comes The Chains that You Refuse, a collection of dazzling short fiction featuring twenty-one genre-bending stories and one poem, including the exhilarating and previously uncollected Jenny Casey origin story "Gone to Flowers."

Whether you are already a fan of Elizabeth Bear or not, The Chains that You Refuse demonstrates, beyond a doubt, why David Brin called Elizabeth Bear "a talent to watch."

ISBN-10: 1-59780-057-0
Trade Paper; $14.95

Hugo and Nebula Award-nominee Kage Baker, creator of The Company series, and the fantasy novel *Anvil of the World*, delivers a spectacular collection that includes stores set in both universes, as well as several stand alone pieces of fiction that demonstrate why she is one of the most talked-about writers in the sf/fantasy genre.

While the settings and characters from Mother Aegypt will leave you breathless, it is Baker's accessible, yet oddly whimsical style that will keep you turning pages and coming back for more.

Find these Night Shade titles and many others online at http://www.nightshadebooks.com or wherever books are sold.

Night Shade Books Is an Independent Publisher of Quality SF, Fantasy and Horror

ISBN-10: 1-597800-02-3
Hardcover; $25.95

Dissolution Summer: the soon-to-be-former UK was desperate. The world was in the grip of a fearsome economic depression. The anti-globalization movement threatened stability throughout Europe, supported by rioting youth, bitterly disaffected voters, and encroaching environmental doom.

The Home Secretary decided to recruit a Countercultural Think Tank: pop stars would make the government look too cool to be overthrown. It was just another publicity stunt for the rockers, until the shooting began. Will the accidental revolutionaries, Ax, Fiorinda and Sage find a way to stay alive while the UK disintegrates under their feet? Will rock & roll's revolutionary promise finally deliver, or will ethnic, social and religious violence drown hippie idealism in rivers of blood? Either way, the world will never be the same.

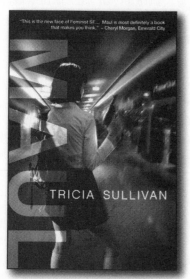

ISBN-10: 1-59780-037-6
Trade Paper; $14.95

Sheri S. Tepper meets Neal Stephenson (and kicks his ass!) in this feminist-cyberpunk thriller by Arthur C. Clarke Award-winning author Tricia Sullivan.

In a mall, a gang of teenage girls is caught in a maelstrom of violence and shopping. But it's not only their own lives they will have to fight for—It's that of a man trapped in another world, with very different enemies; a man they haven't met, but who could change the future of the human race.

"Two stories unfold in parallel in this fast and furious blend of gender issues and balls-out action. Maul is a thoroughly enjoyable, well-written novel that stares hard down the barrel of sexual politics and happily sticks its finger in the muzzle." – *infinity plus*

Find these Night Shade titles and many others online at
http://www.nightshadebooks.com
or wherever books are sold.

Liz Williams has been a science fiction fan since the age of ten, but started writing seriously about seven years ago. Since then she has had Seven novels published. Her background is in History and Philosophy of Science: having earned degrees in Philosophy and Artificial Intelligence at the Universities of Manchester and Sussex, she then completed a doctorate at Cambridge, graduating in 1993.

A variety of part-time jobs – including a now-infamous stint on Brighton's pier as a tarot reader – preceded full-time work as administrator for an education program in Kazakhstan. This program was not entirely successful and resulted in a partial collapse of the then-Kazakhstani cabinet. Following this, Liz worked for an educational consultancy in the region and relocated to Kazakhstan in 1996. The following years were spent traveling back and forth between the region and the UK. Subsequently, she spent a year running an IT program at Brighton Women's Centre, and became a full-time writer in 2002.

She currently lives in Glastonbury, England, where she is co-proprietor of a witchcraft shop and is working on her next novel.

Find Liz Williams online at her Livejournal:
http://mevennen.livejournal.com
or at her Night Shade Message Board:
http://www.nightshadebooks.com/discus